Cristofori's Dream

a novel by

ROBERT ITALIA

This is a work of fiction. Names, characters, places, and incidents are the product of the author's imagination or are used fictitiously, and any resemblance to actual persons, living or dead, business establishments, events, or locales is entirely coincidental.

All rights reserved

Copyright © 2015 by Robert Italia

www.Robert-Italia.com

Cover design by Tango Communications

ISBN-10: 1507648715

ISBN-13: 978-1507648711

Printed in the United States of America

A NOTE ABOUT THE TITLE: *CRISTOFORI'S DREAM*

Contemporary piano and New Age music fans certainly recognize this title. It is the signature album and song of Grammy-nominated pianist David Lanz—a tribute to the inventor of the piano, Bartolomeo Cristofori. Originally released in 1988, *Cristofori's Dream* topped Billboard's New Age chart for twenty-seven weeks and eventually went platinum. Twenty-five years later, this celebrated album has been re-released as *Cristofori's Dream . . . Re-envisioned.*

Though this novel has no affiliation with Mr. Lanz, his album and song of the same name, or its subject, the music did inspire the writing. The title merely reflects this novel's main theme, which is why it was chosen.

For more about David Lanz and his inspirational music, please visit his website: www.davidlanz.com

COVER CREDIT

The Nightmare, Henry Fuseli (1741–1845).

This work of art depicted in part on the cover is in the public domain in the United States, and those countries with a copyright term of life of the author plus 100 years or less. This file has been identified as being free of known restrictions under copyright law, including all related and neighboring rights. The image and reproduction thereof are in the public domain worldwide. The reproduction is part of a collection of reproductions compiled by The Yorck Project. The compilation copyright is held by Zenodot Verlagsgesellschaft mbH and licensed under the GNU Free Documentation License.

TEXT CREDIT

Scripture texts in this work are taken from the New American Bible, revised edition © 2010, 1991, 1986, 1970 Confraternity of Christian Doctrine, Washington, D.C. and are used by permission of the copyright owner. All Rights Reserved. No part of the New American Bible may be reproduced in any form without permission in writing from the copyright owner.

United States Conference of Catholic Bishops

For my angel, Karen

Contents

PROLOGUE   The Monster   1

✦

PART ONE: COPING
ONE   The Demon Horde   1
TWO   Dinner with the Angel   10
THREE   Staring into Heaven   21
FOUR   Judgment Day   32
FIVE   The Fallen   42
SIX   Banished   50

✦

PART TWO: THE HOLY SEASON OF MAGIC
SEVEN   Resurrecting the Tree   61
EIGHT   The Wish List   75
NINE   Treatment   85
TEN   The Church   92
ELEVEN   The Gift   97
TWELVE   Shadows from the Past   103
THIRTEEN   The Grand Experiment   109

✦

PART THREE: THE DREAM WORLD
FOURTEEN   The Dream Village   124
FIFTEEN   The Artist's Studio   134
SIXTEEN   At the Vanity   142
SEVENTEEN   A Dream Come True   158
EIGHTEEN   The Manor   161
NINETEEN   The Sleigh Ride   167
TWENTY   To Dream within a Dream   171
TWENTY-ONE   The Bridge   175
TWENTY-TWO   The Game   181
TWENTY-THREE   The Grove   185

TWENTY-FOUR   The Orbs   193
TWENTY-FIVE   The Morning Light   200
TWENTY-SIX   The Old Cottage   205
TWENTY-SEVEN   At the Ruins   213

✦

PART FOUR: BACK TO REALITY

TWENTY-EIGHT   Meeting of the Minds   223
TWENTY-NINE   Waiting   235
THIRTY   The Letters   239

✦

PART FIVE: THE QUEST

THIRTY-ONE   The Escape   246
THIRTY-TWO   The Old Mill   251
THIRTY-THREE   Natale per Sempre   261
THIRTY-FOUR   The Study   288
THIRTY-FIVE   The Observatory   297
THIRTY-SIX   Assessment   303
THIRTY-SEVEN   In the Kitchen   310
THIRTY-EIGHT   At the Window   315
THIRTY-NINE   Caterina's Dreams   321
FORTY   The Plunder   326
FORTY-ONE   The Storm   331
FORTY-TWO   The Machine   341
FORTY-THREE   The Paintings   350
FORTY-FOUR   The Chamber of Light   355
FORTY-FIVE   Pandæmonium   365
FORTY-SIX   Epiphany   374
FORTY-SEVEN   The Old Ghost   382

✦

PART SIX: MIRACLES

FORTY-EIGHT   The Awakening   392
FORTY-NINE   The Night Before Christmas   399
FIFTY   Between Two Worlds   408
FIFTY-ONE   Cristofori's Dream   410

PROLOGUE

The Monster

"Chris, Chris, wake up, wake *up!* The Monster...it's coming."

The little girl's strained whispers crashed through his head like a clap of thunder that scattered the dreamscape and left only blackness.

The Monster? Here? Wait, where exactly am I?

His eyes flew open, and as the wind began to rise, Chris saw his sister's dark and ghoulish figure standing in her nightgown next to his bed, and backlit by an eerie light. Her breaths were rapid and shallow. It was Janey—poor, sad Janey, longing for their mother, fearing a storm, and seeking comfort and protection. *Right?* He blinked hard, sparking a flash. The thunder crashed again. A storm or *the* Storm? This was getting crazy.

Feeling gutted but fully aware of what happened earlier in the day, Chris sat up and wiped the drool from the corner of his mouth. Then he glanced about. Stark walls, barren floor...his familiar prison firmly in place. Yet something strange *was* happening. His clothes were drenched in sweat, and his skin tingled from the strong charge in the air. Along the periphery, shadow figures—never seen before, their origins unknown—stood shoulder-to-shoulder and shifted nervously, as if they wanted to flee. The red light on his clock radio glared at him and seemed to record his fear. And the voices inside it mumbled their steady alarm...and his name. "Janey?" he said, grasping for some sanity. His lips felt hard to move. When she didn't answer, Chris squinted, fine-tuned his hearing, and detected other troubling telltale sights and sounds.

Please don't leave us, not with him, his voice cried from beyond.

I'm sorry, his mother said. *I don't know why this is happening.*

At the window, the glittering but deadly white butterfly, tapping the glass as it fluttered, trying to get in. Behind it, radiant snowflakes as big as feathers drifted down in the warm raging air. Far beyond, the pulsing spires of the Bethlehem Star, shining just above a pointy treetop, looking for that safe place to send the Child, and finding them instead. Its gaze lit the room with the ghostly light.

The stage was set, props in place. And then the Story took hold...

The grandfather clock in the foyer struck midnight. Its clanging echoed up through the loft. Janey's face froze in a pale mask of fright, and her shallow breaths ceased. Then she shrank and hovered with golden translucent wings. In her tiny hands, cupped so precisely, she held the glowing Purple Orb. Suddenly, as if it knew, some *thing* pounded slowly but with deadly intent up the foyer's wooden stairs, a chain dragging behind, raking the treads.

Be strong, and take care of your sister.
But Mom, you know who he is. He'll kill us.

With the winds still howling, the footsteps reached the landing, stopped for a moment, then continued their loud and steady climb. Like a drumbeat, but with a sledgehammer. Iron pounding wood. A bad dream, a false alarm? Whatever it was...was heading their way. Chris blinked hard again, inciting a crackling flash. The pounding refused to yield. Still hovering, Janey seemed accepting of—no, oblivious to the madness. Just playing her role so loyally. And though, in this form, she possessed a great strength, Janey stared at him with round black eyes and whispered in a small voice: "Don't let it get me."

Don't worry, I'll be watching over you.
Will you? Will you, really?

There had been signs before, this year of Sandra's demise: a flash here, a rumble there—and intrusions that he brushed aside—hinting at something frighteningly beautiful, just beyond this world, that they all had created to escape him. But this? Playing like a movie toward an unknown end? And then Chris saw it, like each of the paintings, so painfully obvious and factual. This nightmare was his fault. He had abandoned his post and let her down again, leaving the *White Rose* unguarded, if only for just a bit. And while he had slept, thinking only of himself, bad thoughts and dreams written in the Book that controlled the Dark Power of the Other World seeped in like a fog and quietly altered parts of reality, just as he designed it to do. Now they were in it, and he could not reverse the horror that was surely coming for them.

Chris sprang from the bed and rushed to the door to slam it shut. Then he darted to the closet and threw open the folding louvered doors. "Hurry!"

Promise me you'll take care of her. Promise me you won't give up our secrets. He mustn't find them—not ever.

Janey flew beneath the hanging wardrobe and curled up in the corner, trying to make herself as small as possible, and protect the Orb. This nightmare might be unending if she lost that precious thing. Chris stepped inside the closet and closed the doors as best he could. But in his haste, he left a small opening. No time for precision, they had to be still. He huddled there with her in the slotted light and hoped that the Monster would pass by.

Don't forget to use the Book. It will save you.

But Mom, I want you to save us.

The heavy footsteps arrived at the bedroom door. Chris and Janey held their breath. They dared not make a sound, even in the tumult. Maybe, just maybe, the thing from that Other World would turn away and disappear into the Boiling Black Cloud from where it came. How he wished she *hadn't* given him the Book, that he hadn't written the Story. Then maybe they'd be safe.

Quickly, now. I need to hear it.

I promise, Mom, I promise.

At that instant, Chris heard the sound he feared the most: the bedroom doorknob rattling with a fury. The Monster's intent was truly clear. It was looking for them, to do her harm, and obtain the sacred Orb. They would have to endure the horror this night—by themselves, now that the Sorceress had abandoned them. And God, shining His light on them, for His amusement, refusing again to answer their prayers, so He could watch them suffer.

I'll see you one day in the Village, yes? In the Village.

Don't do this to us. Please don't.

Janey let out a yelp—smothered by Chris' firm hand. "Shhh!" he said. Though their outer defense might crumble, they remained safe in the closet, as long as they kept silent. The Monster was powerful but its mind was addled by hate and greed. If it saw that the bedroom was empty, it might turn away.

Oh my God. Oh my God. I can see it!

See what? Mom? Mom!

The rattling continued, more furious than before, as the creature groaned at a device it could not understand or defeat. Then unexpectedly, the rattling stopped. What now?

Forgive me. It is time.

No!

The bedroom door exploded inward.

In the roaring wind, Chris heard the chain dragging on the bedroom floor, the cloven hand sliding across the wall just behind him. He clutched Janey tighter and shut his eyes once more. But then as he listened to the thunder, his lids rose like a theater curtain. He just had to see.

With all those tufts of fur and curling horns, the Monster and its shadow drifted past the closet, a woolly Medusa, eclipsing the slats of light. The cloven hooves pounded the floor, iron on wood. The cloven hand slid down the door. *Clack, clack, clack.* Drafts exhaled from flaring nostrils like steam from a locomotive, and filled the closet with its foul but familiar breath. Chris pressed one side of Janey's head against his chest and covered her exposed ear with his hand. He did not want the frightful sounds to enter her mind, to be captured there like floating orbs that could haunt her forever. But though they had been in a similar situation once before, he could not stop her from trembling.

The Monster jammed the bed against the wall and stopped, as if to ponder. Chris' eyes widened. *That's what it wants?* Yes, yes, now he could see: What a stupid place to hide anything!

But Chris had to frown as the shadow of the Monster's rising arm flickered through the louvers. The chain rattled, ready to strike. But at what? *Them?*

The bedside lamp exploded from a furious blow. Shards of glass peppered the closet doors. The Monster bellowed so loud in its bull-like way—deep from the dark chambers of its massive chest—that Chris could hardly hear Janey's shriek.

Chris wrapped her in his arms as the assault began. He could feel her writhing, attempting to flee, as she had tried years ago. If Janey escaped, she'd fly into the thrashings. And that was something, playing *his* sacred part, he would never allow. Furniture splintered, glass shattered—everything lashed with the chain. The Monster groaned with the howling wind, trying to alter the hated reality in its own way, to wipe it clean and expose the treasures, just as the Sorceress had warned. The whole house seemed to quake, ready to collapse. For a moment, Chris felt as if the tornado had found them, and was tearing up their lives once more.

But then, just like *that* awful storm, the thrashings ceased, the fury spent. All he could hear in the eerie calm was the sound of the Monster...weeping. Tears of acid and self-pity, its suffering never-ending. At least that part was working out well.

Chris sighed, and rocked Janey in his arms. He had saved her again, like he was supposed to do, and their secrets remained safe. "It's okay, it's over, it's over." The worst of it, anyway. But she could not stop crying or shaking, for which he felt a sickening guilt. Now, all he wanted to do was disappear, back into the beautiful part of his dream, into the World of the Paintings, where he once thought he had full control. But he had to wait for the final act to play out, and continue to hold her. Only then could they emerge.

All at once, more pounding—on the foyer's front door. Then the frantic tolling of the foyer bells, as loud as the booming thunder. Chris heard a man shouting, but he could not identify the voice. Had Katie heard the roars? Would she rush over to investigate? My God, what would she think? Those were Sandra's worries echoing in his mind, but he couldn't help himself. He was just as much a part of her as he was of his father.

The Monster, still weeping, threw the chain against a wall, then, transforming once more, drifted away with the Boiling Black Cloud...down the hall...down the stairs...and back into the study. The pounding and the shouting and the ringing stopped when the front door latch snapped open, sparking one final flash that cleared his mind and the freaky air. The Story, already abridged for this episode, had come to an abrupt end.

"Victor," the man's voice boomed above the thunderclap, "I was out in back, and heard some awful noises. What's going on?" A pause, and then: "My word, Victor, what happened to your hand?"

"She's dead," Victor said with a slur. "It's *your* fault she's dead!"

"Yes, yes," the man said in a hurry, without remorse or sympathy. "Where are they, Victor?"

"Damn house, damn kids. I don't want this. It's my money. She stole it from me. And then she gave it to them."

"Victor—the children."

"They're hiding something, I know they are! Damn house, damn kids. Now what am I supposed to do?"

"No, you love your children. Say it, Victor, *say it!*"

"I love my damn kids."

"Tell me where they are. Did you hurt them?" Another pause, then a shout: "Chris? *Janey?*"

Someone started running up the stairs.

Now certain who the man was, Chris pushed open the closet doors, stood up, and held out his right hand to his sobbing sister. Her human stature had been restored, and the Orb had vanished. She still seemed unaware. "Come on, Janey, the Monster's gone." So this is how it worked. He'd have to keep that from her as well.

Janey reached out to Chris and they stepped from the closet. The ceiling light flicked on and sent ripples of anger across his skin. Chris turned briefly from the glare, his eyes narrowing. A lanky, middle-aged man in a tan windbreaker one size too small entered the room with a flourish—then froze like a statue. Their reluctant neighbor, Doctor Samuel. An astrolabe no bigger than a pocket watch dangled from a delicate gold chain around his long neck. They had seen the doctor earlier in the day, under similarly dreadful circumstances. But now his presence brought little comfort. He seemed out of place in all of the rubble. After all, this was part of their existence he was never meant to see.

Dr. Samuel raised his wild brows, and his tired eyes brightened. "What in the world?"

Chris pulled Janey to his side. She clung to him for protection and support. He was glad she still saw him that way, after this. Then he scanned the bedroom. He could not accept this final act of madness on a day that had already become incomprehensible. The nightstand was a jumble of stained wood, the headboard splintered. Only an experienced eye would recognize the rake marks from that awful chain. And his clock radio, somehow unscathed and beneath it all, the red light still peering. The dresser lay on its face, its cardboard backing punched with holes. The curtain rod on the window hung diagonally across the opening, and a breeze ruffled the valance. Worst of all were the bloody prints that streaked every wall. Should have known this would happen, that the Power he helped create would turn against them. The signs were there, after the funeral. But like the intrusions, Chris chose to ignore them. Now he had been reminded, the warning delivered. The Monster *was* gone, but it would be back, seeking the treasures—and an outcome it should not contemplate.

Dr. Samuel lowered his stunned gaze on them. "Are you two all right?"

This was his chance to tell Dr. Samuel everything, and show him the Book. But the doctor had terrible powers of his own. If the awful truth did get out, if he knew what was truly happening in these Chambers of Doom, Dr. Samuel would rip them apart, just like the Monster wanted to do. Nothing in this world, or any other, could be worse. And as with every other problem he faced, Chris would tackle this one on his own, without anyone questioning his judgment, or wondering if he were insane. "Yeah, we're fine, just great," Chris said at last, as a matter of routine, as if nothing happened, as if nothing ever happened, just as Sandra often did. They had to stay together and endure, and never *ever* give up their secrets. But already, he twitched in uncommon defiance of that long-standing tradition.

The doctor kept staring. Then his wild brows dropped into a frown, and the light in his eyes intensified.

Chris turned away and bowed his head. He knew what the doctor was thinking. Suddenly, Chris saw it: *Libro Omnia*, The Book of Everything, unearthed from the land of those revered Alpine woods and mountains, and steeped in the scary legends that were part of the Story, and his being—now protruding from beneath his lumpy, cockeyed mattress. *Bauerneinband*, full vellum, with gilded spine and borders. He snatched this treasure with his left hand and clutched it to his chest, making certain that the doctor could not see its blind-stamped cover, its controlling power over all others now undeniable. With her final words, the Sorceress had bestowed that power. That was so obvious, too. Anyone would get it—even Janey, if he ever told her what he knew. Yet even now, with the rules becoming clearer, Chris could not understand fully how the bad part of their holy fantasy had slipped into this reality, becoming real, and so deadly. As the Grand Experiment was teaching him, he'd have to accept the horror as fact just like everything else that was wrong. Because it did happen. He saw it, he heard it, and he felt it. And no one could convince him otherwise, not that he'd give anyone the chance. Why bother trying to explain things? They wouldn't understand. Especially Dr. Samuel, who doubted everything, and wasn't so easily fooled.

"Chris, watch Janey," Dr. Samuel said, as if Chris had to be told. "I'll be right back." The doctor rushed out the door.

Looking to cause more trouble, no doubt, and send in his agents. He'd have to find a way to fool them, too. "C'mon, Janey," Chris said, "just you and me. Just you and me." The Pact, as he had promised only a few nights ago.

Chris led his whimpering sister into the hall. They would hide in her bedroom tonight, behind a locked door, and try to mend their wounds with words. But none would be spoken. It was their escape from this world that he had to carefully plan. And it really had to work. But use the Book for that purpose, as the Sorceress had begged him to do? And leave beautiful Catherine behind? *Katie Cat Kate*, so close and so perfect in every way, who he couldn't live without. Where would that dark path lead? An idea, born from that twitching defiance, blossomed in his mind—an amazing idea, really, though he doubted Katie would go along with it, considering what had to be done. Somehow, he had to *make* her understand, because he would not go without her. Even to him it seemed so impossible, and frightening. Janey would agree with that, once she found out. Already their lives were tumbling in a new direction, toward an uncertain future.

After all, it *was* just them.

The Book.

And the Monster.

PART ONE

Coping

Chapter One

The Demon Horde

Because of last spring's totally misunderstood Church Incident (*and that's all it was, really,* he once wrote), Christopher Russo had to stand silently in line with the other freshman football wannabes in the dank bowels of Holy Cross High School, wait for his turn with "Clueless" Coach Joe Przybyszewski at the equipment counter, just ahead, and endure the humiliation about to burst from that otherwise jolly face. The portly coach, in his traditional black workout garb, was mulling over the wannabe roster with pen in hand like a judge about to sign a commitment order. Chris stood rigidly in his powder-blue shirt and baggy, deep-blue trousers. He didn't dare step across or even touch the black line taped to the concrete floor until he was told to do so, fearing his reaction to the howls from the Demon Horde, its hated members scattered among the blue-clad wannabes behind him, watching his every move, and hell-bent on total domination. Confronting them was never good for him *or* them. Certainly not here, in the volatile dankness, with Coach Joe present, and certainly not now, with the Book's controlling power still available, which remained a permanent but unseen part of reality, like gravity and the air, flowing everywhere, and through everything.

Which Chris could still use to change everything...

...if he really wanted to.

"Next, please," the coach said like a polite grizzly, his tiny eyes focused on the roster.

The ridiculous greeting ritual, complete with its own strange language, started up again as Chris reluctantly approached.

"Ah, Cristofori Russolini, my little *bambini,*" the coach bellowed, for all the world to hear, "how's your *mamma mia?* You're lookin' a little thin. Aren't you gettin' e-nuffa *pasta fazuli?* Or isn't she makin' that for you-*uh* no more-*ay?*"

"Hey, coach, *'That's Amore'!*" someone sang. A new twist of the knife. The others in line erupted in laughter.

Then, as if the entire scene had been rehearsed, which wouldn't have surprised Chris all that much, the coach checked something off the roster, strolled down an aisle between the metal racks, and began to sing like a baritone: "*When the Moon hits your thigh like a big piece of pie...*"

With his face burning, Chris arrived at the counter, bowed his head, and carefully closed his eyes. Their cruel words, though expected, still felt like daggers. He didn't wannabe a football wannabe. He wanted to disappear. But he resisted, because he just had to. Part of his new strategy to survive in this reality, before another escape attempt occurred, with all its inevitable dramas, and unintended consequences. "She's dead," Chris muttered at last, to remind himself, and them—and to shut them up. He could only take so much. But, oh, how he hated to say it—that, and singing.

Coach Joe snapped his broad head around, and his shallow brow crinkled. The laughter continued. "Par-*doni?*" the coach said.

You want more? "I said she's dead!"

Coach Joe's eyes widened, and he reeled from the force of the statement. The equipment room fell silent, except for a few snickers that lingered like those sobering last drops from the storm. They were embarrassed—good. He had returned the favor, and restored order in a normal-human way. But they still didn't care, and that still bothered him.

The coach returned to the counter and set down a wire basket full of pads topped off with a spotless purple helmet. "Hey, I'm sorry, son, I didn't know. When did that happen?"

His mind went blank, which was a rare occurrence. Chris never committed the date to memory. Never wanted to, so he kept it foggy, like lots of things. "Two years ago, I guess."

"From what?"

"Cancer." That word, and others, once written respectfully in the Book of Everything as a proper noun to signify its power over all, was now used for the power it held over all of his detractors. It did not betray the Legacy that he so desperately fought. How little they knew of her, or him, or anything that mattered. He intended to keep it that way, for the sake of his larger plans.

Coach Joe ran his fat hand across his dark flattop, then fumbled with the pads. "You know, if you'd talk more, I might find out about these things." He slid the basket toward Chris. "Here ya go, son. Give 'em Hell out there."

"Yeah...good word." Already on the List and in the Story, each an important part of the Book that controlled the intruding Dark Power. Hell was his life on the practice field...and in school, and... He put a clamp on his negative thoughts, just as his mother, fearing the Legacy, begged him to do while she lay dying—when the Way to Pandæmonium opened wide a few nights later, and its Dark Power overwhelmed him. He, and she, despised self-pity. That was straight out of Victor's playbook. Chris wanted and needed more self-control of his emotions, of everything in this upside-down world. That was his idea of happiness, and why he had banished the Book. He vowed to keep fighting those negative impulses, no matter how reserved those efforts made him look.

Chris grabbed the basket and whirled around. But he refused to make eye contact with any of the Horde, certain that they were still watching, trying to decipher his thoughts. If he looked at them any longer... He headed down the dimly lit concrete tunnel to the locker room, with *its* disturbing shadows, the sickening smell of chlorine and sweat building with each unwilling step.

Despite the razzing and the danger the coach's odd words fostered, Chris didn't feel much ill will toward the man. He couldn't. Not even the "Gee, that's too bad—let's play football" attitude bothered him all that much (since he was friendless, Chris got a lot of that after she died). Unlike the wannabes and the Horde, Coach Joe was new to the scene, and the crucial facts. The truth was, Chris was no more Italian than the many jars of grocery store red sauce in their home pantry. Sure, Chris' father was born to Sicilian immigrants (who brought with them a secret). But Sandra's parents were Austrian (they brought the treasures and the legends, and secrets of their own). So that made him "Austalian," Janey liked to say. Austalians were a uniquely talented and colorful breed (with things *they* needed to hide). Still, from day one of football practice when he first bellowed roll call, Coach Joe seized upon Chris' distinctive last name of Russo. "Russo" quickly became "Russolini" (*After Mussolini? I'll have to ask someday*) and "Chris" became "Cristofori." The correct translation was Cristoforo. But somehow—as Chris found out by chance one day while reading the "C" book of his antiquated encyclopedia collection for the umpteenth time—Coach Joe got the translation mixed up with the inventor of the piano, Bartolomeo Cristofori. Maybe the coach thought most Italian words ended with an "i." Or maybe he wanted to draw attention away from his impossibly-difficult-to-spell last name. Whatever the reason, because of his own flawed knowledge of the language, Chris accepted Coach Joe's peculiar brand of playful but mangled Italian as authentic, which Chris duly noted often in his diary. (*Anything written in the Book becomes official—another good reason to hide it.*) So all kidding aside, Chris considered Coach Joe an ally. He was one of a few at joyless and appropriately girl-less Holy Cross High School who wanted Chris to make the freshman starting team.

If only the coach knew how vitally important it was.

And, most damning of all, why.

This whole salvation-through-sports thing was Victor's decree. Unforgiving Victor the Monster (aka his worthless father), pacing at home, alone with the Keeper of the Sacred Orb (aka the still-believing

3

Janey), dreaming of the riches she commanded and the respect that he didn't—and demanding daily reports of Chris' expected progress. Chris was in no position to cross him. The escape plan (and because of the Monster, they still desperately needed one), worked upon so diligently for an entire year, was now in tatters and they were stuck as Chris built and tested a new plot—all because of the Twelfth Night, and the annoying Epiphany setback with Katie, so unexpected, but safely hidden, which nevertheless showed him the folly of his former childish ways. The New World, *Forever Christmas*, The World That Soon Would Be. Such a beautifully wicked place, always crackling in his mind. And he desperately wanted it to be true, until he realized that he could not control its horrors. In the end, the Grand Experiment, though shuttered as a dangerous disaster, had shown him a new and healthy way to understand things, which would even make Dr. Samuel proud. Despite the continued intrusions, that New World was more like a haze, lacking any real mass, permanence, or benefit, other than to hide in for a time. (*Fake, phony, just a lie.*) His insecurity blanket, no doubt. He needed real results, involving real things from this reality where they *were* stuck, that wouldn't place Janey in harm's way. And yet, he had to be careful. The brilliant Way to that fake and phony World—and its violent trigger—was always open and still accessible, with the willful blink of an eye. And though he had managed to construct an effective method to keep it all under control, the Book and its Story remained powerful things that could ensnare him, and make him a lie as well.

 Chris arrived in the locker room and started down an aisle crowded with wannabes suiting up. One by one, they stared back at him, sizing *him* up. Suddenly, someone behind Chris blew a whistle. His scalp bunched like a kicked-up rug. "Ten minutes to calisthenics," Coach Pete Wozniak shouted from his office doorway. "Let's go, kiddies. Your mommy's not here to dress you."

 Coach "Woz" had sounded the alarm. Bodies scattered. Metal locker doors everywhere were yanked opened or slammed shut. The sounds boxed his ears.

 Chris rushed to his locker, dialed the three-number combination that opened the door to his torment, and undressed. He hated getting into trouble. He had the Legacy to thank for that. The football pants were first, then the shoulder pads and practice jersey—all the instruments of his enslavement. Finally, he checked to make sure that the unholy copy of his playbook, its photocopied hand-drawn diagrams already photocopied to memory, rested on the top shelf with his spikes. (*Lose that book, lose your life.*) Like the book that powered their hokey religion and hid the truth and caused so much trouble, the playbook set the path to another insanity.

 "Hey, dago," a voice called out.

Chris looked to his left and saw Tom Fitzgerald standing at the end of the aisle. As the anointed starting quarterback of the freshman team, "Fitz," though hardly original with his name-calling, had the power to draw Chris' attention whenever he appeared. Not that Chris admired Fitz. (*No way!*) It was a survival instinct, first deployed when they attended middle school together. Like the other members of the beloved and mindless Demon Horde, Fitz showed signs that he, unlike Chris, was morphing into something he didn't deserve: manhood—patchy but shaven beard on a pimply face, pronounced brow, a tinge of deepness in his voice. Overall, he was taller and more muscular than Chris, who felt like a cowering boy in his presence.

"Better get your spikes on, wop," Fitz said. "You know what happens if you're late."

Out of the corner of his right eye, and separate from the shadow figures (their origins still unknown), Chris saw a colorful someone reaching into his locker. A large, freckly hand snatched his spikes. Chris turned right and saw the redheaded Jim Koch—rangy but powerful—running away as he laughed with Chris' spikes in hand.

"Now that's *amore*," Fitz said. "See ya on the practice field, Cristofori."

Chris took up the chase. When he slid to a stop at the end of the aisle, Chris saw Koch disappear around the far corner of the lockers. Chris pursued him and soon reached the frosted glass door marked Pool that was slowly closing. Without breaking stride, Chris turned his left shoulder into the door and pushed with his forearm into the heated arena. A ripple on the pool's surface radiated outward from two slowly sinking and distorted black objects. Koch stood at the opposite end of the pool. He laughed again, and then slipped through another frosted glass doorway. *Steady...steady.*

But time was running out. Wading into the pool was out of the question. The spikes were in deep water. Chris returned to the locker room and searched for someone—anyone—who could help. But the locker room was empty.

Racing back to the pool area, Chris spotted a lifesaving extension pole partially buried beneath a tangle of ropes, buoys, and nets. It took him much too long to retrieve his spikes, grab his helmet, and reach the berm-lined practice field in time. By then, all the wannabes, aligned in neat rows, went about their exercise routines as Coach Wozniak and Coach Joe looked on.

With clipboard in hand, Coach Woz blew his whistle, stopping all activity. Chris was front and center beneath a white-hot spotlight. Hell had different forms, too.

"Name?" Woz said, eyes locked on the clipboard.

"Russo," Chris said, though he knew Woz was aware of this fact.

Woz's stoic expression remained unchanged. He stared over the top of his glasses at Chris, but the whites of his eyes seemed to be on fire. Wozniak was not an athletic-looking man. Much older than Coach Joe, Woz had rounded shoulders, skinny arms and legs, knobby knees, and his pencil-thin neck was no match for his oversized head that begged battering. But Woz commanded their respect, even drew fear, because he could shatter everyone's impossible sports dreams with a quick thumbs down. "Russo, what?" he said.

Chris sighed. How he loathed these power games. Only Dr. Samuel deserved the respect. "Russo, sir," Chris said finally. He heard snickering, like the stuff from his clock radio, which ended the moment Woz looked about. The coach gazed down at Chris' wet shoes and nodded repeatedly without emotion. Then he stared at Chris. "You want to tell me how that happened, kid?"

Chris glanced at Fitz, at Koch, at all members of the Horde—a collection of guys who had grown much faster than the likes of Chris, and who never hesitated to use their superior physiques to their advantage. Chris still had a special place in his heart, in his Book, and in the Story, for them. *Åsgårdsreien!* It was always tempting to shout it, and tear this world apart. He could see their eyes sinking into their skulls, their flesh rotting. Chris carefully closed his lids and breathed deeply to silence the booming echo and reset the image before the Dark Power took hold and swept them all away into its fog of deception. At least it wasn't The Holy Season of Magic, when the Story could run wild and control him for weeks on end, like last year. Still allowed, with its countdown and rules etched in stone, that time was coming, and everyone remained especially vulnerable. It'd be here before they knew it, or suspected a thing.

But for now, their horrible grins were almost impossible to endure. Somehow, without using the Power, the Demon Horde needed to be stopped. Of course, Chris wanted to tell everything he knew about Woz's chosen ones: how they conspired, bullied, lied, and cheated their way through sports, school—even life—all the while gaining complete admiration from coaches, teachers, students, and parents for their ability to push a goofy ball one hundred yards down a stupid football field. *It's about teamwork and achieving a goal, kid.* Yeah, yeah, yeah—he got all that. Because he was good at them, Chris actually liked sports. But, just like Victor, Fitz and the Horde had their own special take on sportsmanship, which severely altered the appeal. *Tell all? I'd be glad to. Are you ready, coach? Are you ready?*

"Well, kid?" Woz said.

Chris saw in Woz's dark eyes that this was yet another test—to see if he was willing to run with the loser herd and not cause trouble. Victor insisted on this. "They...they fell in the pool, sir."

Woz frowned. "What were you doing in the pool area?"

"Looking for my shoes, sir."

More laughter, more glaring, more silence. Then Woz looked at Chris. "You want to make this team, you gotta show up on time."

"Yes, sir."

One final stare, just to see if Chris dared to speak his mind. "Okay, kid, take a lap."

Chris' eyes widened. A lap? That was his reward for going along?

"Is there a problem, kid?"

"No, sir."

"Then get going."

To keep the peace and the world real, Chris turned away, strapped on his required helmet, and headed west over the berm, then south along tree-lined Pine Street, which took him past the hated apple grove, where the Horde often met at lunchtime to steal a snack and hatch their plots against him. A few hooded, robe-clad Franciscan brothers worked in the grove, trimming branches and picking fruit, the unwitting accomplices to the insidious evil that had seized the entire complex, including the apples, which Chris dared not eat. The brothers, housed on the complex, often stopped Chris in the halls to remind him of their counseling services for those "in need." But it was much too late for that. Sure helped explain why he was running a lap.

A lap was no ordinary punishment. A lap was often reserved for the most belligerent, the most despised of the freshman tryouts—worthless know-nothing "unfocused kids" like Chris, with "attitude problems." A lap meant missing more than an hour of practice at his tailback position. Without Chris' presence, the competition would get more playing time—more time for the coach to admire other talent, and forget Chris'.

Still, Chris knew he was the fastest guy on the team, which up to now had saved him from being cut, and condemned forever to that blazing subterranean palace he had once condemned others. Chris had always been a fast and elusive runner. He had developed his skills playing tag on the asphalt playground during the glory days at St. Boniface Middle School. The object? Run from one end of the playground to the other without getting dinged. If you did, you'd be forced to join Fitz's own vile horde that roamed the lot in search of prey. (Fitz, too, had honed his skills at St. Boniface.) After a while, most of the eighth grade class fell victim to these predators. But the fastest and most resourceful stayed alive to the very end of recess—guys like himself, Larry Witosz, and Matt Cavanaugh, the undisputed king of their elite group. Matt organized them and devised strategies to defeat Fitzgerald and his followers, sometimes arranging a wager, which grew each time he goaded Fitz into accepting the challenge. Matt would often sacrifice himself at the very end, so Chris could win the game, and the cash. But those days were gone. The king was deposed, exiled to his own private and lonely Hell—some out-of-state military school—leaving Fitz and the Demon Horde to cast their evil spell over the Holy Cross freshman class. Without their leader, Chris and Larry became lost souls and disgraced outcasts. But Chris knew well that this unfortunate outcome was not solely Fitzgerald's doing. Far from it.

The lap seemed to go on forever as Chris pounded his way in the grass along the streets that lined the complex. His legs felt heavy, and his lungs burned as he listened to the sounds of his labored breaths and the late summer wind howling through his helmet's ear holes. At least the light protected him. (*Maybe that's what Mom saw the night she died.*) It wasn't the memory of Victor's threats, forever hanging over him, that kept Chris going, not at this moment. Visions of that night, and Janey's voice, spurred him on. *Don't let it get me.* Letting her down was the greatest sin of all—that, and breaking the Pact. He had to become a football star.

Chris arrived at the church on the northwest corner of the complex. Then he turned south along Pine Street where he finally reached the parking lot entrance. Time to face them again.

Clomp, clomp, clomp.

Chris stopped and gazed northward, his line of sight searching the empty street as he listened intently through his heavy breaths. A postal truck crossed the intersection. A bicyclist streaked past the church.

Clomp, clomp, clomp.

Intrusions, drawing near—in the daylight, no less! All his fault. He shouldn't have thought about it. But where were they? Sounds always preceded appearances as these things slipped through the *White Rose's* blinding gap. Were they really on their way? As that horrible night had showed him, Chris had to keep his guard up—and them at bay—while he appeased and thought and plotted.

Chris kept his eyes peeled northward and his emotions in check. But when nothing unworldly appeared, he raced to the practice field where Woz and Coach Joe, at the fifty-yard line, watched the first team execute their designed plays. Still gasping from his long run, Chris—after one last glance toward the parking lot—removed his helmet and stood beside Woz. The exhaustion was unlike anything Chris had experienced. He was great at sprints, not marathons. His stomach was in a knot, his vision blurred and spotted, and his head pounded with every furious heartbeat. But he refused to let Woz know he was in such misery. Many outcasts never made it back from a lap. Either they returned along the same path on which they left, only to be banished from the team, or they returned their equipment and went home. Chris wasn't allowed to give the coach what they both wanted.

Woz glanced at Chris, and then fixed his gaze on the first team. Fitz took the snap and handed it off to Jim Wenzel. "The Weasel" tried to hit the hole, but it closed too quickly. So he bounced to the left end where Koch had John "Dirty" Dahlberg tied up in an expert block. Koch pushed Dahlberg toward the sideline. That created a huge gap between Koch and the left tackle. Instead of cutting up the gap, Wenzel followed Koch. Dahlberg spun away from Koch, wrapped the Weasel up in a bear hug, and slammed him to the ground. The Weasel shot-put the ball at Dahlberg's face, but Dirty slapped it away. He loomed over his victim, ready to pounce. All the while, Woz looked on emotionless, the whistle dangling from his neck. Chris could tell that Woz was pleased. He was building "character."

    Still in his black shorts and T-shirt, and unprepared for the reality of the Dahlberg and Woz they all knew too well, Coach Joe charged in like a grizzly as he retrieved his whistle from his fanny pack. A rapid series of whistle blows finally quelled the anger. Dahlberg began to walk away—and stepped on the Weasel's pinky finger. Fitz rushed over and shoved Dahlberg. But Dahlberg stood his ground and smiled, as if hoping for a fight. Fitz refused to take the bait. Not even Fitz wanted to mess with the guy.

    "All right, all right," Coach Joe said, "that's enough. Fitzgerald, get back in the huddle. Dahlberg, you do that again and I'll kick your butt all the way to the locker room."

    "What?" Dahlberg said, arms wide. "What'd I do?" Not even he wanted to mess with Coach Joe.

    "You've been warned," Coach Joe said. Then he turned to the Weasel. "You okay, son?"

    Sitting up, Wenzel nodded. He tried to shake the pain from his hand. Wenzel was much bulkier than Chris. He spent a lot of time in the weight room. Chris didn't. This wasn't supposed to be a job. When he got free time, he preferred to spend it in other ways—even gazing at the stars and beckoning a real angel, when he was allowed.

    "You shoulda turned it up field," Coach Joe said to the Weasel. "Kick in that extra gear."

    "Yes, sir," Wenzel said. He returned to the huddle, tail between his legs. They all knew that gear didn't exist, not in the Weasel.

    Coach Joe looked at Woz, then at Chris, then back at Woz, as if to say: *That's what Chris would have done.* "How about giving Russo the ball? Wenzel's still hurting."

    "He'll be fine," Woz said. But he refused to look at Chris.

    Chris stood idle next to Woz for the remainder of practice, thinking of the pacing Monster, not far away. The coach didn't speak another word to him.

Chapter Two

Dinner with the Angel

    Chris sat in the oppressive heat and suffocating silence at the glass dining table, Victor at one end, in his wrinkled golf shirt, his back turned in spite to the bank of untreated casement windows that offered a full and sun-drenched view of Dr. Samuel's rolling estate. (*How he hates that view.*) Chris and Janey sat on opposing sides of the table as Chris hopelessly waited for the tension to lift while listening to cheap flatware scraping chipped porcelain, and moist mouths chewing hastily prepared food. The sounds irritated and sickened him. But he had no desire to smother those noises by starting a conversation. That would get Victor involved—the last thing Chris wanted. Slipping away from the potential danger was always the first option. Chris was good at that, on and off the football field, with or without the Power. And so he kept his head down and began this real escape attempt in a most dramatic way: he carefully rested his fork on his plate. Then, not daring to wipe the beads of sweat on his brow, Chris waited patiently for Victor's reaction while staring at the table. The table. Another real and humiliating hand-me-down. So too were the mismatched wooden chairs on which they sat. And the mismatched forks and knives—very real, too. Most of their house was furnished this way, furniture from relatives who Victor had long since alienated with his moods and outbursts and drinking. But from the outside, didn't the two-story, brick-facade Chambers of Doom look grand?

    It was the second home in which they lived. A storm tore up their first house years ago. Instead of rebuilding, Victor took the insurance money and used it as part of a down payment on a four-bedroom house in a pretentious and appropriately treeless neighborhood (*with jerks like him who hate children*) that his independent sales position could not afford. (*Never really figured out what he does for a living. These days, he calls himself a "manufacturer's rep." Keeps lots of small generators, gears, and roller chains in boxes in the house and garage. But his phone hardly ever rings. So he has lots of free time for "sports," and is gone often. That's okay with me. But he's still a loser. I know what he wants to do with his life, and to us. And I know what to do with him, if I really have to. That, too, is written.*) Victor stuck himself here, thinking it would make him happier. But the move only made things worse. In Victor's world, pleasure always came before work. Chris had long since noted in the Book that the storm marked the beginning of Victor's slow demise, and—because Victor needed his scapegoats, and money—helped put them in the constant peril Chris and Janey now found themselves.

But tonight, they would feast—on a concoction of ground beef, chopped onions, and kidney beans, blended together with tomato soup and served on a plop of mashed potatoes. "German chili," Victor called it, mockingly. Janey called it "mish-mash," and she loved it. It was Sandra's recipe. Chris liked to resurrect it now and then, when he needed to keep things calm. It seemed to bring all of them a small amount of comfort.

So now, as he did every evening his father decided to come home for dinner (*mostly to check up on me*), Chris tried to gauge Victor's mood. He slowly lifted his head and looked for cracks in Victor's moody face that could foretell the kind of night they would have. Silence was never a good omen. But silence also brought the current escape opportunity. While Victor stared at his plate, far off with his floozies or in the Kingdom of Darkness, Chris hoped to avoid discussing today's events on the practice field. That would only create conflict, and raise the defenses.

"This is really yummy," Janey said as she picked at her dinner, "but I think there might be too much salt. The soup already has plenty. You should check the ingredients. And maybe next time, you could put in less onions—too onion-ey."

"Onion-ey, huh?" Chris said, his line of sight drifting toward his sister. "Great word, Janey." Janey. The Keeper of the Sacred Orb. Sandra's little angel, born on Christmas Day, who must have a better life. Despite the heat, she wore tattered jeans and a frayed pink sweater. Yet seemed cool and in control, even when she wasn't. And not a drop of perspiration on her fair skin. How he wished he could be like that. He decided to run with her innocuous topic. All he had to do was deposit a coin, then sit back and let her go, like the twirling music box angel that she was. He loved that about his sister. Way too happy, even in their fun-filled world, Janey made up for his social inabilities, and kept away unwanted scrutiny. "And the potatoes?"

"Well, now that you mentioned it, they are a little lumpy. I don't think you cooked them long enough. Don't use the hand-masher next time, use the ricer. It'll break up the lumps better. And add more butter and some cream, and—"

"What happened at school today?" Victor said, pulling the plug, his hooded eyes aimed at Chris.

Chris withered under the glare. Instinctively, he glanced at Janey—this time for salvation, as he once did to Sandra. His mother was alive, in Janey. Anyone who knew Sandra could instantly see her in Janey's youthful face: the small nose and ears, hazel eyes, fine auburn hair—they could even sense her protective disposition, which he missed most of all. Chris, however, was the other Sicilian in the family. He got his father's hook nose, dark wavy locks, athletic ability, and his "temper," *(whatever that means)*. And when Chris at last fixed his shifting sight onto Victor, he felt as if he were looking into a magical mirror that could show the terrible future, even minus the horns.

"I was named Angel of the Week," Janey said without a hitch. She pulled her trademark ponytail across her chest and appeared ready to take a bow.

Again with the angels. His suffering was never-ending, too.

Victor dragged his gaze from Chris, then quickly fastened it on Janey. "Angel of the Week, huh? What kinda nonsense is that?"

"It means I get to keep the attendance book."

"A little girl like you...in-charge of roll call?"

Janey shook her head and repeatedly stroked the ponytail. She was frightened of him, always frightened. That he knew. But she refused to give in, for the sake of that better life. And that he admired, too. "Mrs. Commerford does that. I watch the class when she leaves the room. I think she goes outside to smoke. She always smells like a furnace when she gets back. What a bad habit. If anyone starts talking while she's gone, I put a red check next to their name. Jenny Mayer got a lot of red checks today. She just can't keep her mouth shut. I mean, she knows I'm watching her. But she still keeps on talking. And then she gets mad at me when Mrs. Commerford makes her stay after school. I don't know what her problem is. I think she needs therapy."

Victor shoveled some chili into his mouth and chewed slowly. He seemed to contemplate each of her words, trying to figure out, as always, any hidden meaning. "Aren't you worried about becoming a snitch? That's not a good label, if you know what I mean."

"Like on a bottle?" Janey said.

Chris allowed his eyes to brighten ever so slightly. Now it was Victor's turn to act cool when he wasn't. He set his fork on the table as if it were a card, and he were playing poker with a most formidable foe—which, of course, he was. He leaned forward on his elbows, intertwined his busted fingers, and crunched his hands over his plate. Then he stared at Janey with those all-seeing eyes—directly at the consequences of his womanizing, unwilling or unable to be responsible for his actions, wishing he could take it all back, and knowing that he couldn't. There was a time Victor smiled, back at the old bungalow, when he was just starting his family and career, when he convinced himself, and them, that everything they wanted would come their way, if they just believed in him. No longer. Now it was all over his face, constantly. He wanted out. They wanted him out, too. But not the way he desired. "Tattling on people isn't going to win you any friends. Like you said, it only made her angry. Anger's not a good thing, wouldn't you agree, missy?"

Janey stared incredulously at him. Incredulously. "Too bad. She knows better. She needs to shape up."

"Shape up or ship out, eh Janey?" Victor said.

"Egg-zactly," she said with a forceful nod.

Victor eased back in his creaking chair and reloaded. "I can arrange that."

Janey folded her arms and just stared, like Victor.

The battle was on, and Victor was not a man who easily accepted defeat—not when someone attacked his character or "lifestyle." Victor knew where this conversation would lead. He engaged her in it often, and it always ended the same way. Still, like the salesman that he was, Victor persisted, looking for weaknesses, and hoping to wear her down. "How's St. Boniface working out for you? Everything going okay?"

"Yep," Janey said.

"You like your classmates, your teachers?"

Janey nodded repeatedly and tugged on the ponytail. "You know I do."

"No, I don't."

"Sure you do. You ask me all the time."

Victor grumbled but kept his composure. His mind seemed to focus on the canned presentation in his head. "Classes aren't too hard for you?"

"Haven't you seen my grades? You never miss anything in the mail."

"Because if they are," Victor said, briefly raising his voice, "you don't have to stay there."

"I know."

"I went to public school, got a good education—and it cost a lot less."

"Yes, you told me that."

"You'd save us a lot of money if you transferred. I'm already paying for those schools with taxes."

"You've told me that, too."

"We could do a lot with that money."

"Like what, exactly?"

"Furnish this damn house, for one."

"And whose fault is that?"

"I'm doing my best."

"No, you're not—not even close. You don't try. It's like Mom said. You're afraid to, like you know you're gonna fail."

Chris tried to suppress a sudden laugh, and nearly coughed. He recalled those Sandra words, spoken to no one in particular when she folded laundry or peeled those famous potatoes. Suddenly, Victor flashed Chris a perturbed look, which always made him cower.

"Mom wants me to stay there," Janey said.

"Your mom's not here."

"Yes, she is. She's watching over us, just like she promised. She sees everything that's happening, even now. And I don't think she likes what she's hearing."

The thick vein in Victor's wide neck throbbed. Threatening words or behavior were never used directly on Janey, not while he was sober. That he saved for Chris. "You really believe all that nonsense?"

"I do, and so does Chris—don't you, Chris?"

Chris felt the lightning bolts in his head, and cleared his throat. He should have been prepared, once the word "believe" was spoken. "Yeah, sure," he said, "I believe." But not the way she thought.

Victor stared at Janey and slowly shook his head. "You're just like her—gullible to the end."

Janey threw her ponytail aside and popped up in her chair. "That's me!"

"I gotta get you out of there before your brain turns to mush."

Then her expression grew stone hard as she leaned forward. "I appreciate your concern, but I'm not going anywhere."

Victor grew flustered. His eyes darted back and forth. But he did not explode, which was a good thing for all of them, even though his ego had taken a direct hit. Still, Janey had become secure in her position, knowing there was little Victor could do to force her from St. Boniface. Janey would have to do that mostly on her own, either by choice, or through failing grades. And there was no chance in Hell of either scenario happening.

Victor kept his focus on Janey. He was analyzing, and plotting, and not giving up, for which Chris felt a sudden guilt. Then...a cool inspiration overcame Victor. "I was talking to Pommerance the other day," he said, "checking on the balance, and I heard some interesting things."

Pommerance the traitor-lawyer, found at the courthouse, begging for work, after Sandra attempted her one and only inquiry about a divorce. The night following her funeral—after Pommerance informed Victor that Sandra not only had a will that cut him out, but also had been skimming just enough each month for years to pay for a hefty term policy—had been his masterpiece. Victor's *capolavoro*. Victor didn't "believe" in insurance, and bought it only when the law or a bank forced him to. It was as if Sandra knew her fate, despite the clean bill of health the required medical exam gave her. Pommerance had also mentioned "sundry items" despite promises not to (hence his need to beg). No doubt, the slip-up helped summon the Monster that night, though his father, until now, never pursued "the treasures" openly. Had the traitor-lawyer inadvertently done it again?

"Really?" Janey said, after a mindful delay. "What kind of things?"

Just like that, Victor had slipped through that otherwise well-guarded Way and was in her face. Chris kept his head down but listened carefully, trying not to show his concern.

"Things of value, little girl. You might call them treasures."

Chris wanted to scream, to end the inquiry now. But that would only tip Victor off. The Monster was looking for a sign, for any small twitch on Janey's face, or strain in her voice. It was telling that Victor thought Janey was the easiest route. But Chris had little doubt that he'd be the one to flinch if pressed. Through it all, Chris had to wonder: why hadn't Victor asked before?

"What kind of treasures?" Janey said. She was talking to a stranger offering candy. Her tone was clear and innocent, her eyes bright and full of wonder.

"Oh...you know, things she may have left you. You know Pommerance. Even though he is a pansy, he'd never lie. Would you?"

"But you call him a liar all the time!" Chris said. "He's a lawyer!"

With eyes aglow, Victor snarled at Chris, then tried to plaster over the nastiness with a smile. He loomed closer to Janey. "Well?"

"I don't want to sell her paintings," Janey said.

"I'm not talking about those goddamn things."

"What, then?"

"Other things we could sell."

"You know what she left us. There's nothing more."

What a great liar she's become, Chris thought. He didn't know if it were a good or bad thing. He always looked at her as his counterbalance.

"You're putting me in a bad spot," Victor said.

"I'm not doing anything."

"You think money grows on trees?"

"It does in Heaven."

"We're not in Heaven, missy!"

She had seized control by steering him away from the script. And now, an opening that Chris could only dream of, not that he'd take it. But Janey handled it in her own expert way, and with a smile: "See, you're not wrong all of the time!"

Victor's anguished sigh signaled that the first part of the battle had ended once again in defeat, their secret safe. Chris struggled to stifle his joy. He admired the way Janey spun Victor into the ground where he belonged—all so innocently. Money...in biblical Heaven. *Jeez, Janey.* Now it had a treasury department? Who, or what, was on the dollar bill? It was her own idea of Heaven, of course, which Chris had dubbed "Janeyland" (in his diary, not to her face), and nearly everything she needed grew on trees. He

15

had to admit, he liked the idea. If only it were true in this world, then maybe Victor wouldn't be Victor, but the celebrated opera star. And they wouldn't fear for their lives.

But now, as Victor returned his gaze to Chris—the horns momentarily sprouting and curling, the hairy nostrils briefly flaring—it was Chris' turn to defend himself, and his situation was much different. Though Chris also received a trust from his mother's will to continue his parochial education, his stipend wasn't seen as a potential cure for the family's money woes. Football—and the status it could bring—had everything to do with that twisted view.

"Well?" Victor said to Chris, his tone a bit more sour from his stinging defeat.

"Well what?"

"What's going on with tryouts?"

"Nothing."

"What do you mean, nothing? You're still going, aren't you?"

"You really don't know?"

Victor jammed some mashed potatoes into his mouth and swallowed hard. "This is what I get for letting your mother raise you. Wenzel's a tank. You should've left him in your dust by now. What's the problem? Not enough motivation? I can turn up the heat, if you want."

The flames of Pandæmonium roared to life within its pillared halls. Chris was tempted to lie, but that would only stiffen the consequences. Victor was a de facto member of the Holy Cross Men's Club. Though he no longer subscribed to the "nonsense" and didn't attend their meetings, Victor drank and played sports—and drank—with many of the Horde's fathers, who were members. They talked about their sons as if they were miniature versions of themselves. It was important to know how their male offspring stacked up against the others, to know that they dominated someone—anyone. The bigger the list, the better. "Coach doesn't like me that much," Chris said finally.

"Which coach?"

"Woz."

"Wozniak, you mean—not Woz. Are you causing trouble again? I'll say it once more: go along with the program and do as you're told. I had to ask some big favors to get you that tryout. It's not easy hiding things. You brought nothing but shame on this family."

"Me?"

"I doubt that your mother could have ever forgiven you. Now we gotta deal with it."

Victor loved playing that guilt card, too, not that his father gave a damn about the church—or anything else but himself—anymore. Chris resented him for the play. "I'm not causing trouble."

"Don't you lie to me, too."

"I'm not!" And Victor was not a forgiving man. Just the opposite. The Church Incident (*and that's all it was—really!*) happened last spring. Chris was doing all he could to make amends, though he still had few regrets. If anything, it made him all the more obstinate. But Victor was still jabbing at him, still punishing him. In his father's mind, it was always good to have someone in the family fail more miserably at life than he did.

Victor drew closer. "You know the terms."

"He'll make it," Janey said.

"He's gotta do more than just make it, little girl. He knows the deal."

Just solve all their problems, in a few days or so.

"He might be a poopster," Janey said, "but he's a good little one. I'm always praying for him."

Stunned by her betrayal, Chris glared for a moment at Janey, but then he extended his hand toward her and nodded. "There, you see? It's preordained—by the angel of the month."

"Week," Janey said.

Victor wiped his mouth with a napkin and tossed it on the table. "Don't screw this up, Chris—I mean it. It's your last chance. Or you're gonna end up like that Cavanaugh punk. And there's nothing in that will that says I can't do it."

Straight to Hell, no doubt. Chris sighed once more, but this time in defeat. This warning was taken seriously, despite Sandra's attempt from the grave to protect them. (Nothing terrified him and Janey more than being separated from each other. Not even the Monster.) It had always been a contentious subject with Victor, having so much money within his grasp, but forbidden to snatch it. And he could never let that tormenting thought go. Regarding the wording in Sandra's will, Victor was right. No words forbade him from transferring either of them to another private school, not that it would matter. But he'd do it because he could, just to get back at all of them. It was the one mistake Sandra had made before she died. But Chris had long ago conceded that he only had himself to blame for his predicament.

Victor slowly rose from his chair. "I gotta go pay bills—*school* bills."

But Chris knew that was a dig, and a lie. Pommerance the traitor-lawyer handled that task, too—yet another contentious point. "Can I use the telescope tonight?"

"Just don't go wandering off."

"Like you do?"

"Don't push me," Victor said. He snatched a stack of mail from the credenza and stared at the digital thermostat on the wall. He seemed surprised that Chris had not lowered it from its permanent summer setting of eighty-two degrees. He flashed an annoyed look at Chris anyway, then retreated, with the chain dragging, to his study. He closed the door.

Moments later, Chris heard the clinking of ice cubes in a glass, like a fire alarm. Then the Italian opera music (*always Italian, and who cares about the titles?*). He looked at Janey as a bolt of pain shot through his head, and they both sighed. The Story was awakening, the Storm clouds brewing. Bill-paying was always an adventure. More bills than money—the usual case—made for a potentially volatile night. Money problems often demanded great quantities of potion, demonic chants, and sacrificial lambs. And then the late-night atmosphere, so threatening and mysterious, would be ripe for the Monster's sudden appearance. Chris finally wiped his brow with a paper napkin. He stared at Janey. "Have you ever, ever, in your little-girl life, ever, ever felt that he was ever more mature than you—ever?"

Janey sat motionless and gazed back sadly. With all that wisdom imposed on her, with all of her Janey-isms always at the ready, she never, ever responded to this vexing question. She didn't dare hear it.

"I don't know why he ever got married," Chris said. "Come on, we'd better hurry up."

"Do I need to worry?" Their precarious future was always on her mind.

"No, Janey. I'll figure something out."

Janey smiled weakly and didn't say anything else. It bothered him that she didn't believe him—of all the damn irony. She expected failure. But he couldn't tell her about the tumult that was truly happening behind the solid façade of reality. He just couldn't. He'd simply have to deal with it on his own and come up with a real plan that would get them out of here for good, without placing Janey in peril.

Chris and Janey repeatedly passed each other to and from the kitchen while they cleared the dining table. Then Chris paused to stare at the painting on the dining room wall. It was his favorite of all Sandra's paintings: a lamplit village with its meandering stream, thatched cottages, towering pines, a steepled church, and stone-arch bridges, all lovingly frosted with snow. The Dream Village, she called it. (*Victor calls it "kitschy." He hates all her art—hates anything that brings us joy and reminds him of his failures—and he makes fun of it whenever he can. So he's out—with the rest of them.*) The Dream Village wasn't her best work, with all the sharp lines and primary colors and lack of depth, but it was one of her first. And that made it extra-special. Her first thoughts of rebellion, so vividly expressed on canvas for even Victor to see. The beginning of her escape, and theirs. As with all her paintings, it had the "dive-in" quality Chris admired and appreciated, and could not forget. Every time he stared at one, he wanted to dive in and stay there for a while, just so he could get away from the clomping thing—figuratively thinking, of course—and remove the suffocating pressure he often felt in his chest. Not until the night Sandra died did Chris realize why she had painted the Village. It had been part of her escape plan all along. The Sorceress Artist: Painter of the Magical Light. Maybe somehow (he hadn't solved that part yet, strange concoction that it was), but duly noted in his diary, Sandra was in that winter wonderland, painting in her Studio with those magical brushes and canvases—not drugged and emaciated and outrageously undignified despite her lifetime devotion, but healthy, beautiful again, and safe from the Monster, thanks to the Great Tree. The only problem was: she left them behind, and alone, to deal with a growing anger and a conflicting power.

    Chris glanced at Janey. Temptation again, now that he stood before an original that inspired so deeply. Did he dare take her hand, just so she might see? As Chris also noted shortly after the Monster's first appearance, looking for answers—after testing his hypothesis with a few trial runs and watching things vanish, according to the rules—it was Victor's threatening presence that helped Chris unwittingly tap into the Book's power over reality. To open wide a hole in this world—the *White Rose*—as the Way to escape. This controlling power, intended for protection and salvation, was indeed everywhere but unseen, except when a threatening sound like a slamming door or pounding footsteps or a snapped latch or the frantic ringing door chimes helped opened the Way.

    Or when he, The Man of Reason, Writer of All the Rules—and out of a former bad habit in times of undue stress—blinked-and-thought really hard where he wanted to go.

    Like into a painting.

    Like now.

    When the thunder died, the Studio appeared, its French doors wide open. Standing in the glowing ankle-high snow as the luminous flakes fell, and dressed in the flannel and leather of the required old-fashioned, Chris felt the delightful heat emanating from the well-lit space. A woman with dark, straight, shoulder-length hair sat at an easel with her back to him. She wore a black painter's smock, and worked carefully before a white glowing canvas displaying a half-finished blue sunflower. She gently dipped the dazzling tip of the brush into the radiant-paint palette resting on a wooden stool to her right. His heart raced again. But he never could approach her—not yet, anyway. He felt as if he were looking at a ghost. And he was looking at a ghost, after all. The last time he saw her face, she lay in a coffin, mummified. The last time they spoke, she uttered her last words in bed. The only sounds of her voice he had heard since then echoed from memories that haunted his mind. But now, she was painting before him, as if nothing ever happened. Would she really remember him? He wanted that so much from this ghost. It always pushed him—*pushed* him to confront her.

Chris started along the snow-packed walkway that split the slumbering garden in two—and past a line that he had never crossed before. He hoped she would hear his footsteps crunching the snow, so he wouldn't have to speak first, but she continued to paint the sunflower.

Still fearful, Chris stopped halfway. The woman turned her head to the right as if she indeed heard a strange noise. Then she spun around on her wooden stool to face him—at last!

Chris could not take his eyes off her astonished face. "Mom," he said with a surprising force as the thunder boomed.

"Don't be angry with her, too, Chris," Janey said, a mere echo.

He was violently yanked back, the particles whizzing past his ears. Feeling satisfied that what was his mother had seen him, maybe thinking that he were a ghost—if only for a false moment, now that the make-believe there had collapsed, and no longer a viable space—Chris watched his sister saturate the tabletop with the plastic bottle of cleaning spray that, since Sandra had so cruelly abandoned them, seemed to be on Janey's person at all times, like a concealed weapon. He still did not understand the science behind all the magic, or how the Other World remained accessible and intact, in its own ethereal way, like some flat spiritual recording that became substantive and three-dimensional only when he appeared in it. But that phenomenon, too, was undeniable. As was the light, flashing or otherwise, so important in the Story.

"You're not being fair," Janey said. "It wasn't her fault." She wiped the table with a paper towel.

But it was. All of Sandra's paintings that hung throughout the house had become part of that make-believe sanctuary for them. They had tied their wonderfully harrowing Story to those artworks, and others that, for better and worse, moved him deeply, which he also duly noted. And the tale filled their gloomy lives with light and magic and hope. Then one day, Sandra decided to quit the battle. And this loving young woman who cared for them so much got reckless and died, leaving them alone, and lonely, to battle the Monster. And though the Book and its magic still remained, for those selfish acts, there was no forgiveness, only consequences. This, too, had been duly noted, multiple times, on its own page, with the winds roaring, and the lightning bolts flashing.

Chris closed his eyes carefully, and let out a long breath. Time to beckon a true angel.

Chapter Three

Staring into Heaven

The late summer night was rapidly cooling but tolerable as Chris, defying the darkness, deployed the small, refracting telescope and its tripod on the back patio. A sliver of the Moon hung low in the sky, and the wondrous glowing cloud of the Milky Way—a roiling purple, and peppered with silver stars—revealed itself. It was so pronounced, like the giant backbone of some ghostly skeletal creature, Chris could feel its soft light upon his face. The night sky had gone through quite a transformation during the last two years. Once it had been a stage for heavenly creatures. Now it was a cold and voiceless expanse that offered no drama or comfort. But instead of white dots on a black backdrop, the tiny points of light became far-off places that begged inspection, and fueled his wonder. He was fortunate to have that inspection ability. And every time he stared at the stars, he was reminded of that great fortune.

To this day, the telescope was among the best Christmas presents he ever received (a designation that he kept to himself, fearing the consequences). Since Victor did not buy electronic devices for anyone but himself, of course—cable and Internet service for the house, other than in his den, were "out of the question," as were electronic games and cell phones—Chris and Janey only had their other books, their wild imaginations, and their mother's art to keep them entertained (the Book was definitely not for entertainment). The telescope came from Dr. Samuel as another hand-me-down. But this one was special. The doctor became an avid stargazer to clear his mind of the medical riddles that often kept him up at night. From time to time, he would invite Chris over to peer into the eyepiece. When Chris first saw the rings of Saturn, he became hooked. But after lamenting that the telescope wasn't powerful enough to see the galaxies, Dr. Samuel had a roll-off observatory shed built in his expansive backyard (*because he could*). Then he replaced the refracting telescope with a much larger reflecting telescope. But the doctor, a hospital internist, often worked long hours, and rarely made it home before Chris' imposed bedtime of ten p.m. Invites to the observatory were limited. So on Christmas Day two years ago, just after Sandra's death, Dr. Samuel's only daughter, Catherine, their once-frequent babysitter who helped Sandra develop her love of art, showed up unannounced at Chris' front door with a red bow around the old telescope. Chris had been using the magical device on a weekly basis ever since. Now with Victor in charge of the holiday festivities, Chris knew another such treasure would never come his way.

Chris lowered his gaze to Dr. Samuel's two-story Tudor, its trimmed boxwood hedge separating their backyards. The doctor's estate was part of the original development built decades earlier. These older homes were much larger. Each sat on acres of land with mature trees, and some, like the doc's, had natural ponds and streams. A land speculator, who saw Victor coming, snapped up the farmland that surrounded the old development and quickly built rows and rows of drywall boxes, one of which was theirs.

All the lights were out in Dr. Samuel's home. Not a surprise. But Chris' heart sank just enough to force a sad smile. It was always joyous and comforting to see Katie's home, to know she lived there, that their backyards touched, just as there was joy in writing and whispering her name. And sweet soft waltz-like music that automatically rose up with that name, playing somehow not inside of his head, but all around him—the kind of tune that Sandra used to hum glassy-eyed and with a girlish grin as she whirled in her fineries with Dr. Samuel in the gilded halls of her unattainable, old-fashioned, Victor-less world. Chris would dance and smile with Katie, clutching her tight, holding her dainty free hand just so...if he ever got the opportunity, even though he really didn't know how to waltz. Maybe he did know how...there. But tonight, as the music died, it seemed that a chance meeting with her would not materialize, not that it mattered. She hadn't come over in quite a while. The small break once worn through the hedge had nearly grown over, and she was missing out on the entire love story, with the full soundtrack, always playing somewhere outside of his mind. Naturally beautiful Catherine...Katie Cat Kate...so close...and so beguiling...in every impossible way... And make you do things you wouldn't normally do, in happier times. "Here, Katie Cat Kate." He closed his eyes briefly and took in a steady breath. Deep down, he knew why visits from the immensely popular, older beauty had ended. In accordance with family tradition, he just couldn't admit it.

Chris chuckled at his self-pity, then, ignoring the shadows as they judged and hissed at him, he squinted into the eyepiece. He tried to focus on the yellowish point of light, suspecting it was a planet. He didn't need anymore books to control him. But when his vision would not clear, he withdrew from the lens and rubbed the troublesome eye, careful not to push too hard, giving it enough time to refocus. Concentrating on anything, especially his studies, had been a difficult task since Sandra died. He could stare at whole pages sometimes and not recall one word. Most of the time, he just didn't care, and his grades suffered. Even now, as he often noted, he felt as if he were roaming in the Kingdom's persistent fog.

The sliding patio door opened and a set of light footsteps approached. He heard his sister whistling a happy tune. Chris gazed into the eyepiece and tried to suppress his smile, but couldn't, though he was perturbed with her. "The whistling pixie," he had called her, before she was cast in her new role. The whistling, more like a warbling tenor trying way too hard to impress, was an accurate health-barometer. Janey often whistled happy songs when she felt good. When she didn't, he grew concerned. Janey put on a good show, much better than he ever could. But Sandra's death had shaken Janey's once-indomitable spirit, though she refused to admit it. As with himself, he suspected she suffered bouts of depression, what little he learned of its symptoms. Some days, it was hard for her to get out of bed (*I know the feeling*). And she would complain now and then about exhaustion and just feeling "icky" (*that I know, too*). Still, Janey had come very far since the Monster smashed Chris' bedroom with its bloody hand and chain. Instead of cowering before him, Janey kept fighting back.

"Whatcha lookin' at?" Janey said.

"Your kinfolk," he said, still squinting into the eyepiece. "You know, the ones with the halos, big wings, and red pens."

"Very funny."

"You're funny-er," he said.

"You're funny-est."

Chris turned the focus dial. "Well, that's Heaven up there, right past the Moon. Isn't that what you're always telling me? Or is it past Jupiter, Neptune, Pluto? No? I forgot." He gripped the focus tube and began moving the telescope wildly in all directions. "Maybe its just past Polaris, Andromeda—M87! Where is it, Janey? Where did it go? I...I can't seem to find it? Oh no, we're doomed. *Doomed!*"

"Don't you worry," she said. "I think I can still get you in through the back gate—maybe. If you behave yourself."

Skewering the biblical Heaven and the associated beliefs while experiencing his own intrusions into the New World wasn't a tough task. Both were fictitious. No doubt. None at all. But they had major differences, which he knew well, and caused all the arguments. Chris stood up, shook his head, and sighed as he glared at her, because that was what he had to do. "What were you thinking in there?"

"What do you mean?" She was still in her jeans and pink sweater.

"You called me a poopster."

"Well, you are a poopster—but a cute little one."

"Yeah, nice try."

"Aren't you the one who's always telling me to be realistic about things?"

"Not in front of him. All you did was give him another bullet. You knew he was going to be all over me. So what did you do? You took his side. Victor. You *do* recall who he is. I thought we had a pact—right? I take care of you, you take care of me? That's the only way we're gonna survive."

"I was only telling the truth," Janey said.

"Oh, all right—fine! Pour gasoline all over me, light a match, and send me straight to Hell, Sister Mary Janey. I'm guilty—guilty as charged. Of everything! At least I won't have to shovel snow anymore—you know how much I love doing that. And the hot dogs—your favorite...mmm, mmm, I can roast them whenever and wherever I want. Can't wait."

"You're such a drama queen."

"King," Chris said. He sighed once more, and then tried to collect his emotions. That was difficult, these days.

"I'm worried about you," Janey said. "You've been so crabby—and for a long time, now."

"Well, don't I have every right to be?"

"So do I, but you don't see me losing it. Bad enough we got him scaring away everyone. You keep this up and you'll become just like Victor."

"Now you sound like Mom."

"Well, it's possible."

"May I remind you that I am fifty percent Sandra?"

"Amen to that," she said.

"You're fifty percent Victor, too, you know. Aren't you a little worried about yourself?"

"I'm not out to destroy myself like you are."

"*Who* says I am?" He saw in her widening eyes that his shouting and threatening posture had frightened her, and he became subdued by his sudden guilt. Hurting Janey was a no-no. Chris also worried about the persistent anger. He had never experienced such an intense emotion before. It felt like something else was in him, something bad, ready to burst. That he had, like now, difficulty controlling it only made it more worrisome, because of the Power. But until Sandra's passing, since he had been so invincible, death had only been something that happened to old people he did not know or care about. Now he was forced to think their thoughts, about mortality, and the hereafter. If he could just ditch the anger, and the incessant anxiety that accompanied it, then he could be somebody, and do wondrous things. "Look, I'm not mad at you."

"I know."

He paused to soften his emotions and tone. "So how are you feeling? I haven't asked you in a while."

"I feel good."

"You're not run-down? Depressed? Getting enough sleep? I'm worried about you, too, you know. You're not as strong as you used to be."

"That's Dr. Sam talking. Maybe you should talk to him. He's pretty good at that psychology stuff—remember?"

"I remember him being kinda sarcastic and...what was that word Mom always used? Oh, yeah—'straightforward.' There's a funny word. 'Rough' is more like it."

"Like you?"

"And you. I don't want talk with him, if it's all right with you."

"Okay, Victor. Anything you say."

"Janey—"

"Well? So what about singing?"

"Singing? Where did that come from?"

"I never hear you sing. Even you-know-who does that. It can make you feel better. I'm sure that's why he does it."

"He does it because he hates himself and his life—and us—and he wants to be someone and somewhere else—without us."

"And do you—"

"I don't want to sing, Janey, okay?"

"Why not?"

"Because I don't feel like it, that's why. Is this your version of Doctor Sam?"

"Ever try crying?"

"Crying?"

"Yeah, clears out all the yucky feelings."

"What—on demand? You make it sound like vomiting, and I can't and don't care to do that either. That's a girl thing."

"So how about whistling?"

"Again, your department."

"You can start going to church with me again."

Chris sighed, but said nothing, and let the statement die. He felt guilty about not taking her to church on Sunday. Not because of the rules, but because Janey still believed her way and wanted to attend Mass, but couldn't—not when the weather was bad, like in winter. Victor didn't go to church anymore, either. He didn't encourage it, and he no longer offered to take her. Even Katie, who used to attend with them when Sandra was alive, didn't stop by anymore to give Janey a ride. Apparently, she was too busy with her new life, and the young men who populated it. (*If that's what she wants—fine with me. She'll be sorry, too. Probably is. No doubt.*)

"What about confession?" Janey said.

"Confession? Oh please, I'm so beyond that."

"Then why don't you try praying? Maybe your guardian angel can help."

"Guardian angel? Jeez, Janey, don't you have homework to do?"

"I did it on the bus."

"Of course," he said. Janey, like Sandra, was relentless with the holy advice and the finger-wagging. "Look, we've been through this. It doesn't work, and they don't exist."

In the rarest of moments, Janey retreated inward. He knew what she was thinking: the standard old line she always gave him during their heated arguments. She was sad, of course, about Sandra's death, of course—but accepting (*of course!*) as part of God's Grand Design for them all. Just like the storm that swept them into the Chambers of Doom.

"I hate what they've done to you," she said. "You can't stop believing, Chris."

He defiantly put on his science cap, sensing her doubt, and his victory. "Believing, huh? You mean thought structures?" There had to be science behind all this weird stuff. There just had to. The Grand Experiment had showed him that. And his search would continue despite the pabulum of lies that Holy Cross spooned him.

"I still don't get that," Janey said.

"Sure you don't. You're not programmed to."

Janey scowled. "Call it what you want. If you destroy them, you'll be left with nothing. And I'm just not going to allow that. You saved me twice. Now I'm gonna save you."

"Is that right?"

"It is. Just like the One your name says."

But Chris didn't like his name. He found it embarrassing, and made him feel self-conscious, now that he no longer believed in that old junk. "So who died and made you boss?"

When Janey raised her brows and stared apprehensively at him, he realized just how foolish his stock and insensitive comment was, and he decided to end the debate before he got too emotional and caused his sister more pain. It was a battle neither one could win. "You know, you did good in there tonight, standing up to him. And you didn't fall for his tricks, either."

"I know," she said.

"I wish I were as smart, and strong."

"It's all right. You don't have to be. I can handle him for you."

Chris shook his head. "Do you know what the Horde would do if they knew my sixth-grade sister was tougher than me?"

"Uh-huh!" she said with her cutesy girlish voice, infused with impossibly high tones. "They'd kick you in the pooter."

That cutesy voice was intentional. She knew that he knew it was intentional. She didn't use it often, just when she wanted to win an argument, or melt his cold heart. It worked every time. He hated and loved her for it. "Thanks again for your honesty."

"You're welcome."

"Just do me one favor, okay? Don't ever, ever, call me a poopster in front of my friends, especially from school."

"But you don't have any."

"Yeah...well...and whose fault is that?"

"Yours."

Chris gazed at her, thoughtless. "Well, if I ever do and someone does come over to this Hell-hole, just keep that Janey-ism to yourself, please. If the Horde gets a hold of it, kicking will be least of my problems."

A light flicked on in the corner window of the second floor. Chris saw Victor's dark figure standing there like some specter, on the ledge of the Terrible Shrieking Mountain. Victor rapped on the window, then pointed to his watch. At least his father, for the moment, was where he should be, though, in truth, he was feigning parental duty. Victor was all about control—controlling them—hiding things from nosy neighbors, child advocates, and prying eyes. He was probably on his way out to see the perfumed giggling one who liked to smoke and thought that Victor was worth all the trouble. *Whatever.* Tonight, with some luck, that nasty thing from the Story would not show up, slip past the defenses, and sit on his chest while he slept, and he would rest. "Time to get your jammies on. And I suppose you'll want some grammies, too."

"It's your job, isn't it? Part of the Pact? And don't forget the milk—two percent, if he bought more." She headed for the hedge.

"Where are you going, little girl?"

She hiccuped, and sounded like a squeaky toy. "I just want to check."

"Janey, they're not there."

"Are you sure?"

"Would I lie to you?"

Janey whirled around and folded her arms across her chest. Then she stuck out the tip of her tongue and rolled her eyes from side to side. She was thinking hard, gathering evidence, and Chris suddenly realized the grave error of his habitual and clichéd response. He was about to get it, both barrels. He wasn't the only one in the family with "the gift."

"Yes," Janey said finally, the tally completed. "Yes, you would. Yep. No doubt. You betcha. Definitely. Uh-huh. Without question. Yeah...yes...yes, yes, yes. Yes."

"Janey—"

"And that's just this week."

Chris smoldered in silence, and ended his rebuttal. He did not care to hear every word of the account, including the dates and times, which she would eagerly provide—even if he didn't ask.

Janey stood by the hedge break and gazed into the darkness where Dr. Samuel's aerated infinity pond lay. The doctor called it "infinity" because of its figure-eight shape. (*Victor calls it a swamp.*) The many Canadian geese that once populated the pond were gone. To keep the "infernal creatures" away, Dr. Samuel recently added a boxwood hedge around the pond's perimeter, which eliminated nesting areas and discouraged landings. The only access to the water came from the small, stone bridge that arched across the narrow center. Before the hedge was installed, Katie—much to the doctor's dismay—often fed the geese from that bridge, especially in winter when food and open water were hard to come by. Years ago, Janey took up the cause and became Katie's self-appointed assistant. Though Sandra often featured the bridge and the geese in her paintings—she even depicted a girl with a bag of crumbs in one version—Sandra forbade Janey one winter from any future visits after Janey crashed through the brittle ice while attempting to hand-feed the filthy, noisy things. Of course, Janey ignored the edict until the hedge was installed, citing "humanitarian" reasons. But to this day, she remained vigilant.

"Satisfied?" Chris said as Janey approached.

"Just wanted to see. I don't know why he did that. They weren't bothering anybody."

"Ha! Geese are people too, huh, Janey?"

"I thought they were cute."

"You thought they were cute because you're ten times bigger. If you weren't, they'd chase you out of the neighborhood."

Janey strode defiantly past in an obvious refusal to engage him in a science debate. She knew better. "I'm going inside, now. It's chilly."

"Thanks for the weather report."

"Don't forget the cookies."

"Aye aye, sir. Wait—cookies? I thought you wanted grammies?"

She kept walking. "Can't I have both?"

"I'm going to put that on your headstone, you know."

"The way you're going, I doubt I'll die first."

Chris grumbled like Victor, then fell silent.

Janey dodged her nemeses—the "gross, disgusting" bugs swarming about the spotlights—and slipped through the sliding patio door before closing the screen. Chris loosened the bolts on the tripod. Then, moments later, as she had the most annoying habit of doing, Janey began talking to Chris as if he were standing next to her. But all he could hear was a mumble of angry words.

"What?" Chris shouted. He struggled to lift the telescope, which felt like a million pounds. Football was just killing him.

Janey returned to the patio screen. "I said you washed my blouses and your underwear in the same load."

Exasperated and breathless, Chris set the telescope down. "So? They're white, aren't they?"

"They're delicates. I don't want them to shrink. Don't you ever listen?"

"So don't throw them down the chute with everything else—Sandra!"

"You're all so much alike," Janey said. She turned away.

"I heard that," Chris said.

"I heard you, too!"

Chris drew in a slow, deep breath. Then, for salvation, he took one last look at Dr. Samuel's house and implored Katie's appearance, hoping that she wasn't with *him*. Finally, he gazed up at the sky. Stars, galaxies, the universe. Stupid words, actually—so *stupido*, they made his diary's List of the dumbest words in the English language. They were part of something far grander than just the universe. He saw it in the Book, despite its magical ways. He saw it in the Story, despite its roots in legend. And he saw it before him wherever he looked, especially now, in the darkness—millions and millions of tiny universes, like glowing orbs, swirling around a flashing black hole. There was a reason, one single solitary reason for this world. One day, he would figure it all out. Then he'd have a nice, long "talk" with all the other *angeli* who couldn't adequately explain why so many bad things happened while He was on His loving watch.

And they'd tremble with every word.

Chris set telescope inside and, after securing the patio door, he and Janey scampered past the storeroom, making damn sure its door was still barricaded with heavy boxes, before they turned off the dome light and scrambled up to the stifling loft. She closed her bedroom door and connected the unauthorized chain to its track. Victor remained in his den just below them, singing his opera with abandon.

Chris retreated to the kitchen to gather up the promised bedtime snacks. Once in the foyer, he passed the basement door, making sure it was shut. When he returned to the loft, Janey's door was already opened just enough to see her perspiring face. He handed her the plate and glass of milk.

"I'm sorry I doubted you today," Janey said.

"It's okay, Janey. I deserve it."

"No, you don't."

"You know what your problem is? Always looking for the good in people, no matter what they do or say."

"Sorry," she said, briefly bowing her head. "I miss Katie. I wish she'd just come back to us."

"Yeah, well..."

"I didn't want to say anything before..."

"It's all right. I get it."

Janey smiled sadly. "Do you really think you can do it?"

Chris smirked at her sudden flip-flop, sensing her hope in the promise of escape. Felt hurt, too. "Yeah...I do." Involving real things that he could hold.

She nodded repeatedly, but still looked concerned. "And should I worry? About tonight, I mean."

"No, Janey, I told you, it's just a story."

"And football?"

She was going down the checklist, before she could think of sleeping. "No," Chris said.

"I don't want him to take you away."

"I'm not going anywhere, Janey. I'll make it, you'll see. And then things will change."

"God bless you, Chris, whatever happens."

"Yeah-yeah, you too, Janey." Then he echoed Sandra's words: "Pleasant dreams."

Janey smiled, brightly this time, which delighted him. Her door closed once more, the chain rattled...and finally, the towel, stuffed ever so carefully, blocking out the strip of yellow light at his feet, leaving no way in—not even for the smallest and deadliest of creatures. He sighed, but couldn't blame her for her doubt or fear. In a way, this nightly routine was his fault, too—and all the creatures, really. It made him more determined not to fail her on the football field, or with his promises of salvation.

After bathroom routines, Chris entered his room and shut his door—then opened it and checked the hall, just to be sure. He stood there for a moment and listened to the grandfather clock ticking in the foyer. How could he not? The shadows remained stable, diffused, but he still felt something watching. *Childish child, fearful child, childish childish nonsense. Will you ever become a man?* The opera had ended, but Chris suspected that Victor was still there, sitting in the dark, thinking. Funny thing about that Book: it wasn't so discriminating. And just like Janey feared, despite his reassurances, Chris couldn't stay vigilant all night, and never really knew when any of the creatures would return, if only for a time. Fictitious or not, they had to be confronted. Always a frightening task. How could he make them finally go away?

Chris closed the door for good. But he made certain that his chain was secure, his towel stuffed in its proper place. He looked to the window, making sure that the drapes were closed, its rod mended with duct tape, which he always kept handy. Then, off to the closet, reaching to the top shelf to retrieve the diary, buried under a stack of other banished childish things: his Comics. Bauerneinband, full vellum, with gilded spine and borders. Chris ran his fingers over the cover's stamped lettering. *Wotan id est furor*, the very first words said within. Written by one of his ancients who still believed in such things when they made the Book to summon Him in a time of rage, in the land of the Woods and the Mountain that they honored and feared, where the glimmering Temptress beckoned the young and old to join Them, revealing her alluring spectral form so they could feel her deadly thrill. And the foolish Sentinel, dressed in rotted black, warning of horrors much too late before he fled the wrathful Storm. In Baden. Sandra's Baden. Noble Baden. Bad, bad Baden, burnt to the ground by the Turks who wanted the Book for their own evil designs—forever part of her being, and his. Now he was touching the very thing his ancestors touched, and buried, way back then, just before the Turks invaded. He felt its Power flowing as it numbed his hands. All for him to use...when he needed to.

Chris sat on his bed and stared at the Book, now feeling Janey's piercing doubt. Judgment Day was coming. It would be sudden, no warning at all, and he'd have to face it. He sighed once more, feeling constricted, then he stuffed the Book in its traditional hiding place.

After undressing, he slipped into bed and reached up to turn off the lamp. The clock radio was silent, but its red light glared. Power on, and transmitting those recordings. But to where? *Nowhere, nowhere at all.* He opened the drawer and, in the jumbled collection of ink bottles, half-used notepads, and dried-out pens, found the roll of duct tape. He carefully placed a torn strip over the indicator. But he decided to leave the protective lamplight on as he listened for those telltale sounds...

Chapter Four

Judgment Day

The next afternoon, Chris approached the equipment counter. Coach Joe checked off a roster name. Chris prepared for his usual greeting, and the stabbing humiliation that followed. But the coach seemed unusually glum. He retrieved Chris' equipment basket and shoved it forward.

"Here ya go, Chris," Coach Joe said. "Good luck today."

Chris stood there for a moment, stunned and frowning. So did everyone else in line. Head-pounding ritual was important to all at Holy Cross High School. Removing it without notice sent up warning flares. So that was it? No mangled Italian? No joking around? Good luck today? Chris grabbed the basket and started for the locker room. He heard the shadow figures in the tunnel hissing their joyful little laughs. Was it his imagination, or did he just receive his last rites, too? Suddenly, Chris felt like he was carrying his remains to the grave. Something definitely was up. So were his defenses.

After he arrived on the playing field, Chris realized that his suspicion was justified. This would not be an ordinary practice. It would not revolve around a scrimmage between the first-team offense and defense. Instead, Coach Woz divided them up according to position—quarterbacks, running backs, and so on. Then, all evening long, Chris faced the Weasel in a strange assortment of competitions.

The first was a strength test with a two-man blocking sled, located on the backline of the end zone. Not the sled in the Story. Nothing joyous or magical about it. Woz stood on the sled and behind the blocking pads, clipboard clutched against his chest with the ever-present whistle hanging around his neck.

"Ready?" he called out.

In a three-point stance, Chris and the Weasel faced the sled. Woz blew the whistle, and the two combatants threw themselves at the blocking pads before falling to the ground. The lightning bolts flashed. He tried to stay calm and thought of nothing. The Horde, which had gathered around, let out their howls for the Weasel.

"Ready?" Woz said quickly.

The whistle sounded. Again, they sprung at the sled. Then again. And again. Crackling. Flashing. While Chris bounced off the pad each time, Wenzel's powerful lunges made his blocking pad's metal springs scream in agony.

"Come on, Russo—hit that sled," Woz said. The Horde groaned and booed at Chris' effort while cheering on the Weasel.

Chris could tell he was losing this contest. The Weasel's side of the sled was farther up the field. Chris grew faint with each lunge. His head felt as if it were splitting open. Even worse, because he had to use his right shoulder for blocking (the arm and hand strength just wasn't there), it felt like it was tearing off. Speed and agility were his talents. Weight room work and summer practice were paying off for the Weasel.

Finally, Woz blew his whistle in a series of rapid bursts. The competition had ended. The Horde cheered. Victory for the Weasel. Woz jotted some notes, then said, "Quarterbacks—you're up."

"Way to go, Cristofori," Fitz said as he lined up before the sled. "Shoulda bet it all on you. You're done."

Chris looked at Coach Joe, who stood among the Horde. He saw the black death spread on the coach's sullen face.

⁂

Chris' next competition against the Weasel involved a punt return. This was the most terrifying test of all. Chris and the Weasel stood at the ten-yard-line. Past midfield, Coach Joe removed his fanny pack, then paced side to side with ball in hand. He waited for Woz' signal. Koch and Dahlberg stood on either side of Coach Joe. They were ready to charge toward Chris and Wenzel. Chris hoped the Weasel would receive the punt, but Chris knew Coach Joe would kick it to him. He needed the points.

Problem was: Coach Joe was a former college punter who almost went pro. Those powerful grizzly legs could kick the ball to the Moon. There was no way in Hell a high school freshman could prepare for this manly experience. After all, Chris had been practicing with his pubescent peers. He was onstage again, where the entire world could witness his humiliating failure.

From the bench area of the right sideline, Woz blew the whistle. Coach Joe performed his quick and powerful punting motions. He sent the football spiraling upward with a loud boom! The Horde let out a roar as if watching fireworks on the Fourth of July.

The ball turned into a speck in the yellow sky. Just looking at it made Chris feel wobbly.

"Oh, Hell," Wenzel said, "it's yours, dago!"

Regardless of the Weasel's insistence that Chris take full responsibility for the utter disaster that would eventually descended upon them like a nuclear warhead, Chris quickly realized that there was no sense in turning from his moment with destiny. He saw the entire trajectory, a bell-curve line from Coach Joe to himself. The ball was headed Chris' way. But he had to catch the damn thing first. If not, the ball would land with an embarrassing thud, bounce high into the air, and be snatched by one of the two devil-dogs charging down the field. Ultimately, Chris would be blamed for the fiasco, and he would fall farther behind in the contest—his confidence, already in short supply, crumbling to dust, the Book's controlling power becoming edgy.

Chris stared past the top edge of his opaque facemask and tried to decipher the exact trajectory of the ball, which was just now re-entering the upper atmosphere. Keeping his eye on the football, Chris stepped forward a few paces—then determined, much to his dismay, that the ball would land somewhere behind him. Chris backpedaled, slowly at first, then faster and faster as he realized just how far Coach Joe had kicked it. Chris lunged backward—but the furiously spiraling ball streaked through his outstretched arms, singeing them. He looked down in horror, expecting the worst.

The ball bounced into his gut.

Chris clutched the football and turned to see Koch and Dahlberg thundering toward him, kicking up dirt and grass. Chris gazed at the Weasel, who stared back in amazement at Chris' good fortune. Then Wenzel turned up field to try to block the devil-dogs. Chris quickly followed as he sized up his attackers.

What happened next took but an instant. But to Chris, time halted, freezing everyone and everything in place, as if he had hit a universal pause button. The practice field became a chessboard. The players became chess pieces. He saw everything from high above. He could rearrange the chess pieces and try different strategies. If they didn't work, he'd put everything back and try again. Patterns, connections, frozen orbs and particles—he saw them all. When he was confident he had chosen the right set of moves, Chris hit the start button, and the entire universe hummed into normal motion.

The four converged at the ten-yard-line. The Weasel struck first, as expected, taking Dahlberg out with a vengeance-filled body block to the crazy kid's knees. Dahlberg cartwheeled to the ground. The Horde howled its approval.

That left Koch to zero in on Chris.

Chris ran straight at Koch—so close, he saw his beaming eyes. The Horde screamed and hollered, anticipating the violent, one-sided collision between the brute and the wimp. Just as Koch was nearly upon him, Chris took a step to the right. But Koch didn't flinch, and kept coming. Chris juked left, planting his left foot near the sideline. This time, Koch took the bait and shifted his line of attack, refusing to slow his powerful charge. Now

Chris, with much less mass and force, had Koch right where he wanted him, according to plan, turning a negative into an advantage, the laws of physics (which he doubted they knew existed) in control. Koch leaped at him. Chris stopped and spun on his right foot like a turnstile. Koch flew past Chris, brushing his shoulder, then tried to slow his momentum. Instead, he tumbled to the ground. The Horde groaned as Chris streaked past Coach Joe toward the opposite end zone, the flat brown expanse of the empty field in his triumphant view. How he wished he could keep on running.

"That's uh-my little bambini," Coach Joe shouted. "Fantasti-*cato!*"

Woz' frantic whistle ended Chris' temporary flight to freedom.

Woz motioned with his arm for Chris to return to the right sideline. "Come on, kid," Woz hollered, "you're holding things up."

Chris sprinted to the bench area. There, the Horde congratulated the Weasel for his block on Dahlberg. "Payback time!" Fitz said to Wenzel. They bumped fists and high-fived each other.

Woz offered a rare praise. "Nice going, kid," he said to the Weasel. As the Horde began to sing that horrible Amore song, Woz looked at Chris. "You're lucky."

Chris was shocked at the cool response. Despite his triumph on the field, he had fallen farther behind Wenzel—down, and almost out.

So this is it—the final test, Chris thought on the sideline while Coach Joe spoke to the silent Coach Woz at midfield. It was dusk. The vapor lights on Pine Street had just flicked on and buzzed as if in his ears. One last chance to make an impression, score some much-needed points, and somehow beat the Weasel. But what kind of a test would it be? Even if he won the last contest, Chris doubted it would be enough to overcome Wenzel's two victories. Chris needed a miracle. Otherwise he would have to face his father. Forced into that perilous situation, Chris doubted he could hold it back.

Coach Joe broke away from Woz and headed for the end zone. He brushed past Chris, and knocked him slightly off balance. Chris turned to see Coach Joe flash a look of warning. Then, positioned at the orange pylon where the goal line and right sideline met, Coach Joe withdrew a stopwatch from his fanny pack. On the left sideline, at the other pylon, the trainer stood with his stopwatch. This was going to be official. Then another sign: Coach Joe nodded at Chris with a knowing grin.

Chris' eyes brightened, and he shivered with anticipation. The buzzing stopped. He couldn't believe his sudden fortune. This kinda stuff only happened in the movies—and never to him. Would he choke?

Woz blew his whistle. "All right—running backs," he said, "take your position on the forty-yard-line."

Some of the Horde let out their bays. The others kept silent, and not so sure. When it came to the so-called skilled positions, the running of the forty-yard dash was the gold standard, the ultimate contest. Forget craftiness, weight room dedication, team spirit. Deep down, everyone knew those traits were minor compared to blinding speed. Who could run the fastest? Breakaway speed. That's what really mattered. Woz, Coach Joe, the Horde—they all knew it. Just like they knew who was going to win the race. If he didn't screw up.

And so now, suddenly, one by one, the cheers began to falter. Feeding off their fear for once, Chris slammed on his helmet and jogged to the center of the field. He took his position on the forty-yard line and glanced to the sideline. Koch shook his head, while Fitz gritted his teeth and tightened his right fist. Even Woz seemed resigned to the outcome. Payback time, no doubt. But he still needed a miracle.

The Weasel joined Chris at the forty-yard line. He looked worried.

"Good luck," Chris said. Just for a moment, he was back at St. Boniface, standing at one end of the asphalt playground, victory waiting for him on the other side.

"Yeah," Wenzel said, already deflated.

"Get ready," Woz shouted. He grabbed his whistle.

Chris crouched just behind the chalk line.

"Get set."

He thrust his right hand down to the moist grass, assuming a sprinter's stance.

Then Woz blew the whistle.

For a split second, the Weasel took the lead as Chris slipped out of his stance. But that was the extent of Wenzel's moral victory. Chris had always been a slow starter in most everything he attempted. But once he reached his stride, Chris felt as if he were running downhill, almost weightless, with rocket engines roaring.

"*Andari, andari!*" Coach Joe said.

Chris also heard the hopeless calls from the Horde, urging the Weasel to give it his all. It didn't matter. Chris quickly pulled away. He widened the gap with every half-second. The cheering sputtered as Chris flew past the goal line. The Weasel chugged ten yards behind.

Chris spun around the goal post to slow himself down. Gasping for breath, his hands on his hips, Chris saw Coach Joe and the trainer converging in the end zone, comparing stopwatches. Then they stared at each other in disbelief. Coach Joe charged toward Woz. He held the stopwatch high in the air.

"Four-three-seven," Coach Joe said, "four-three-seven!" He held the watch to Woz's disbelieving face. Woz' eyes flared before returning to their normal suspicious stare.

"That's a school record," Coach Joe said, almost breathless. "Jesus Christ, Coach, I never saw that in college! You know what you got on your hands here, don't ya?"

Woz turned a burning gaze on Coach Joe.

Coach Joe lowered his head slightly and turned down the enthusiasm. "You gotta do it, Coach. You gotta."

Woz nodded, but looked befuddled. He waited patiently for the uproar to settle, thinking hard. Then he stared at Chris for what seemed to be an eternity, regret now dominating his expression. "All right, kiddies, it's getting late. Let's huddle up."

Chris jogged to the bench area. The Horde, shrinking and cowering, parted like the Red Sea. Everyone was in shock. Not even Fitz dared to look at him. For once, Chris felt proud, like a man among boys. A strange sensation, no doubt.

"When I call your name," Woz said, "take your position on the fifty-yard line."

Then Woz began naming the starters for each position, slowly assembling the first team at midfield. Applause and shouts rose after every announcement.

"Jim Koch," Woz called out. "Thomas Fitzgerald."

Koch took his place at left end while Fitz stood behind the center, each greeted with ape-like grunts and fists held high.

One last spot remained.

"Christopher Russo," Woz said, stuttering, as if he were forced to call out the name.

Chris ran out to take his place behind Fitz. A mild applause with a smattering of boos filled the air. Didn't matter. He was happy, for Janey. It was a strange feeling. After all, he had accomplished his goal.

"All right...men," Woz said, "I'll keep this short. I want to congratulate the starting team for their fine work and effort. But we have a lot of work to do next week. Mount Carmel's going to be a tough test. They're bigger than we are—but we have grit, cunning...and speed. And I expect we'll have them in tears by halftime."

The Horde began howling in that animal way that was forever inscribed as part of their destiny.

Woz held up his right hand to silence them. "Rest up tomorrow. But I want everyone on the field one hour early the next day. We've got some new plays to learn."

Woz said his closing prayer, then everyone broke the huddle and headed for the locker room. Chris jogged with them, helmet in hand. He saw everyone parting around Coach Joe, who stood on the sidelines holding the watch as if it were a souvenir. He waited for Chris to approach. "I know, I know," Chris said, maintaining his pace. "You really don't have to call me your little bambini anymore."

Coach Joe jogged alongside him. "Damn right I don't, not after what you did out there. Do you know what I'm gonna call you now?"

Chris shuddered to think. He and Coach Joe stopped. Then the coach held up his hairy arms and slowly moved them independently as if they were two spotlights shining on a theater marquee. "Tonight, you became Cristofori Russolini, football *dio-missino*. How does that sound? Amazing, huh?"

"Yeah, Coach," Chris said. "That's exactly what I was thinking."

Coach Joe slapped Chris on the shoulder and laughed robustly, nearly knocking Chris over. Then they ran with the team toward the locker room. It felt funny, running with the Horde—with all the scary things that escorted them, their dagger-like teeth, curly black claws, and featherless wings. Immersed now in their fantastic numbers, treading on the great Boiling Black Cloud, Chris could feel their seductive power, their terrible invincibility. But he didn't see how he could stay with them, knowing what could be their fate, if he wanted it to be so.

A football god, Chris thought as he sat in front of his locker. *For winning a foot race? Talk about stupid. What was wrong with people? Why was this a big deal? Was everyone at school suddenly smarter? Better looking? Healthier—just because I ran a four-three? What?* He settled his thoughts, and allowed himself to grasp a little joy from his victory. Maybe now Fitz would be kept at bay. Even better, Victor would be off his back—until Chris failed to fulfill some other grand expectation. But now he had to commit to the honor. And perform in a game that counted. What if, with all those bright lights and cheering crowds—with all those teachers and students and parents thinking he was really good—what if he short-circuited? Forgot all the plays? Or even one? And Fitz pitched the ball to someone on a power-sweep right, but that someone wasn't there because sometimes in his flip-flopping mind left was right and right was left and he had turned the wrong way when everyone else went the other? And the ball just sat there on the damp field with all those lights shining on it. And all those people in the stands with their mouths wide open, wondering what in Hell is going on? And the other team scoops up the ball and runs it in for a touchdown? And that one missed play becomes the difference in the game? And they lose the first of many games to come—games they're supposed to win because he's so talented? And it's all his fault? That was possible—no, probable. No, it was going to happen. Always did, under those circumstances. *Damn.* He hadn't won anything at all, just another set of problems he couldn't handle. Life was never more confusing, or frustrating.

"Hey, dago," Fitz said as he approached from the right.

Chris slammed his locker door, then stood to face his quarterback. Chris saw the fur standing on Fitz's scalp, his evil brown eyes shriveling into black sockets.

"We need to find a new name for you after that performance, don't ya think?" Fitzgerald said.

"What do you want, Fitz?"

"Maybe the dago flash? Or how about the dago thief? Yeah, that's better—says everything, don't you think? We both know you stole that spot from Wenzel."

"I didn't steal anything," Chris said.

"Weasel was way ahead before that bogus forty-yard dash."

"Bogus? You're whacked. I coulda done better, but I slipped."

"How much did you pay Coach Joe to stage that, huh? I mean, why's he so obsessed with getting you that starting position?"

"Maybe I'm a better tailback."

"Yeah, and maybe it's your tail. You doin' something for him that you shouldn't, butt boy?"

Chris felt a chip of his mind flying off. "Go away, Fitz. You lost. Again."

Fitz drew close and pointed a finger at Chris' chest. "How about this word?" he said. "*Busone.* Ever hear your old man call you that? I know he has. My old man told me. Yeah, he did. Vittorio knows what you're all about. We all do."

Chris' teeth clenched. The thought of Victor collaborating with the Horde and insulting him behind his back—his own offspring!—made his blood boil. It shouldn't have surprised him, and he shouldn't have cared. But he did.

And then Fitz drew even closer and got real nasty-looking, showing his blackened teeth. "You think this is over? You think you won?" He shook his head. "You might have fooled Woz, but you can't fool me. I know what you're made of. I went to Boniface—remember that little fact? So I know sure as Hell that you're no football player. You coulda stood on the sidelines with your helmet in your hand like all those other second-string losers, fetching us water when we wanted you to. But you just had to show me up, didn't you? Had to prove—once again—that you're smarter than me, that you can beat me. Well, you're not, dago—and you can't. This is my team. I make all the rules. Weasels' gonna be the starting back. And you're the one who's gonna get a beating."

Chris shook his head in disgust. Fitz was doing his best to revive old memories and resentments. But the villain in Fitz' version was much different than the one in Chris' mind. That was the heart of the problem between them: St. Boniface. And not just the Church Incident. The Grand Experiment really irked Fitz. That had made him feel inferior, made him feel left out. And he was particularly jealous of Chris, who had worked his way up, just like on the football field. Chris searched for a clever response, and snatched one from a deposed ally. "Why don't you let all of that go, Fitz, okay? Just let it go."

"Oh, now you're a shrink? Dumb—really dumb. You see, I already know what's going to happen to your glorious football career. Ain't gonna have one much longer. And do you know why?" Fitz opened the locker and reached up for Chris' playbook. But before he could snatch it, Chris slapped at the door. Fitz was fortunate to remove his hand before the door slammed shut.

"You're not taking that," Chris said.

"Oh, we're not going to take it. You're gonna give it to us. That oughta make that drunk you call a father real happy, huh, momma's boy?"

Fitz shoved Chris, knocking him a step backward. But Chris quickly regained his balance. He was scared and angry at the same time.

"Want to call your mommy?" Fitz said, looking encouraged, his aggressive tone escalating. "Oops, sorry, I forgot. You ain't got no cell phone, do you?" He laughed. "And you ain't got no *mamma mia*." He laughed even harder, and longer. And nothing about that joy seemed insincere.

Chris' temper flared, and he tightened his right fist, tempted to strike. There was too much bad blood between them, too much hate, for Chris to back down completely. This was one jerk Chris would fight, if he had to, regardless of the obvious and painful consequences. But he didn't retaliate. That's what Fitz wanted. Again, there was a higher power at work in Chris' mind. *Might as well be wearing a collar and some jingling tags*, Matt had said about their nemesis. *Stay cool. That'll get him.* The Power could, too. "You'll have to catch me first," Chris said to Fitz. "You've never been good at that."

"We're not in grade school anymore, *goombah*," Fitz said, holding up his oversized fist. "You're battling real men out there."

Chris saw the thick, dark hairs on Fitz's fingers, how they looked like quills. "Coach Joe won't go for it." He heard the hint of fear in his words, could feel himself slipping. That stoked his anger once more, and his eyes flared as the last of his wariness evaporated.

Fitz laughed boldly. His fist fell to his side. "Yeah, dumb-dumb Joe. He never could hack it. That's why he's here, asking for more. He won't have anything to say—not a thing. He's a fool, and a tool, just like you."

"Wrong again—Fitz. Aren't you getting tired of that?"

Fitz tried to shove Chris once more, but Chris snatched Fitz' wrist. The anger stood firm. He was ready. Consequences still didn't matter, nor did the Vow. They hardly came to mind. Only his Story, and the roles they both played. Chris stared intently, confidently, as Fitz began to frown. Chris saw his angry reflection in Fitz' glassy wide eyes, felt the Power crackling all around him, tingling his skin. He had had enough. "Åsgårdsreien!" he roared with a power and depth that he had never heard.

The lightning flashed...

...the thunder boomed.

And then?

Climbing a bed of broken rocks, they burst through the boiling blanket of fog to gaze in awe into a harsh new realm, dark and wild and forbidding. The Terrible Shrieking Mountain, which from a distance, within the Village, always looked smooth and placid with the drifting clouds at its benign peak, now showed its monstrous side. The full Moon, high above the vent, shined a harsh and glancing light on the Mountain's scoured face where nothing dared to grow, and cast shadows in the deadly chasms from which shrieking and moaning and a thunderous pounding rose. The vent was gaping and angry, frozen in an eternal roar. And a flaming orange glow illuminated its scarred inner walls. Chris looked at Fitz who was dressed in his black robe, his hideous face partially hidden in the darkness of his hood. "Home sweet home," Chris said.

"What in Hell...?"

Another flash, another boom, and they stood firmly on the concrete floor of the locker room. The shadow figures scattered. Fitz stared back, his expression twisted, his eyes afire. He yanked his arm from Chris' grip. "What in Hell, dago?"

"Happy now?" Chris said as the thunderous echo waned. Fitz would recall the flash, for sure. And maybe, within that flash, something more. Chris studied Fitz' confused expression, looking for signs. *Lucky, lucky Fitz.*

But Fitz, being Fitz, quickly regrouped. He snickered at first, then hesitated as he, too, seemed unsure about what had just occurred. Finally, he grinned in his rotted, sickening way—the way he would have every day.

If Chris had made him a lie.

"Okay, flash," Fitz said, his angry tone crippled as at last he stepped back, "see ya on the practice field."

"Sure, Fitz," Chris said. "Anything you say."

Chapter Five

The Fallen

With backpack in hand, Chris found his way to the bike rack as the last bands of the pink and orange sunset melded with the encroaching mass of deep blue just above the treetops on Pine Street. This evening didn't seem as scary, even with the lonely trip ahead of him. But the good news he carried did little to stop Fitz's threat from bouncing around in his head, and he renewed his will not to give up. Not just because of Janey and the lessons she taught him. He couldn't let Fitz and the Horde win. That catastrophe would not make the world a better place, no matter what form they were in. Maybe that little detour to Hell had helped, if Fitz saw or recalled it. But now that his anger had subsided and a cool reality set in, Chris saw the danger in this decision. It was too easy for Chris' scrawny body to get hurt playing a game that reveled in the violence that he was so against. Accusations of foul play after-the-fact would be useless. He could go to Coach Joe and reveal the threat. But as Fitz had correctly pointed out, what could the coach do without proof?

"Chris, is that you?" a familiar voice shouted. "Hey Chris, wait up!"

Chris slipped on his backpack, and then turned to see a stocky figure approaching from the cafeteria doors where a handful of scoundrels sauntered from detention into the dusk. "Hey," Chris said with reservation to Larry Witosz, taking note of his former friend's navy-blue tie, how the narrow blade was tied much longer than the wide one—no doubt, intentional. Chris scanned the parking lot for potential spies and demons before returning his gaze to Larry. "What's up?" He really didn't want to know, but felt bound out of a former loyalty.

Larry grabbed his rusty bike and walked it toward Chris. "Maloney let us out early. Guess he was feeling sorry for us."

"I doubt that," Chris said. He marveled at how much Larry, with his permanent five-o'clock shadow, looked like Coach Joe, only smaller, and dimples in his baby-fat cheeks. The coach had tried to get Larry interested in football. But when Larry, who with his stout frame certainly looked like he belonged, spewed his smart-ass reply—"I don't hang with Neanderthals"—Coach Joe nearly fainted.

"Where ya headed?" Larry said.

"Home. I gotta get going. Janey's waiting for me." And Victor.

"Mind if I tag along?"

Chris shrugged, but he wanted to say "yes." "Let me start out first. You can catch up. But if you see an old, black BMW—"

"I know what to do," Larry said.

Clomp, clomp, clomp.

Chris looked to his right at the lifeless church, then squinted into the growing darkness. The returning sounds didn't surprise him all that much, considering what they had just discussed.

"Problems?" Larry said, not sounding too concerned.

Clomp, clomp, clomp.

"Let's get going."

Chris headed south on Pine Street, passing along the crowded row of lamplit bungalows, refusing to look back. Larry caught up with him at the next illuminated intersection, well away from the parking lot.

"So what have you been doin' with yourself lately?" Larry said as they continued riding, his tie flapping over his shoulder. "You never talk to me anymore."

"I can't."

"Still reading those loony Ragnar novels?"

"They're not Ragnar novels. They're fantasy stories." Chris hadn't read one in a while. Sandra used to buy them for him, and they helped him write the Story. And like that story, fantasy novels offered him an escape, however edgy they might be. Now, to get the latest greatest, he often had to put his name on a waiting list with all the other cheapos at the public library. More embarrassment.

"Never could understand why you went for that sword-and-sorcery crap," Larry said, "you, of all people."

"Yeah, well, tell me you don't feel like you have to draw your sword and start hacking away the minute you wake up." No swords in the Story, though, or knives. Not anymore. Personal reasons. Larry giggled, but Chris was serious. "You don't live my life, do you?"

"No?" Larry said. "How soon we forget."

The dust from the past settled, and they continued on through the darkness, legs pumping, wheels spinning, a warm breeze ruffling their hair.

"I heard you made the team," Larry said. "First team, too. Oh yeah, and something about a school record."

Larry had a special talent to make vaunted accomplishments sound foolish. "Yeah, so? What of it?" Chris said.

"Nothing."

"Yeah, right. Go ahead and say it."

"Say what? You made the starting team. Goody-two-shoes for you. That's just AWE-some...*dewd.*"

"Stop."

"What?"

"You know. I don't want to be awesome or dude."

"So what's next? A baseball cap on backwards? How about a nice flame tattoo across one side of your face? That'll open the doors. Nothing like advertising how desperate you are for attention and acceptance. Or—hey!—maybe a goatee."

"You don't have to worry about that last one any time soon."

"Yeah, well, I never thought you'd fall for all that mindless rah-rah stuff either."

"It's not rah-rah stuff—"

"Right."

"—and I didn't fall for anything."

"Then why in Hell are you rollin' around with those apes?"

Chris slammed on his brakes. They both skidded to a halt in another lighted intersection and faced each other. The long, deep shadows on Larry's face made him appear decrepit. "Look, not all of them are apes—and you know why."

"Yeah—but first team? 'Going the extra mile?' 'Winning one for the old Gimpster?' That's Horde-speak, man. Fitz talks like that. You don't—at least I didn't think you did. What happened to you, Chris? You sure have changed."

"Fitz pissed me off, so I got back at him." It sounded reasonable. And tough.

"Fitz? Well, there's a surprise. So why don't you just quit?"

"I can't."

"Sure you can."

"No—I can't."

"Why not?" Larry said.

Chris sighed. Though Larry's old man—a baker—had him by the balls as well, Larry was still in the St. Boniface experimental mode, using a simple but effective argument technique to make a quick but profound assessment of Chris' situation. "Look, I'm sorry." Chris said. "I know what you're trying to do. But the old gang is dead. And I can't come back."

Clomp, clomp, clomp.

Chris gazed north again, past the bug-infested cone-shaped islands of lighted intersections—and once again to the darkened church. *Maybe that's where they hid. Certainly would make sense.*

"What?" Larry said.

Clomp, clomp, clomp.

"It's nothing." He was certain that Larry was unaware. The hoof beats were much too faint, even in the dusky stillness. Only an expert ear could detect it. But Chris' heart raced a little harder. Though slow, the clomping was drawing near, and did not cease.

"Then don't keep doing that!"

They started riding—faster this time, to distance themselves from the creatures, which seemed bent on contact, in the dark, when he was most vulnerable. All he had to do was look at them to give them the substance and the power that they craved. Chris didn't want to give them the chance—certainly not now, with Larry looking on—but kept mindful of their approach.

When they finally reached the point where the troubling sounds ended, Chris turned his attention to Larry. He felt sad for his old friend. High school was much more difficult for him. Plucked from the nest, tampered with, then betrayed, Larry was let loose without re-indoctrination on the unwitting freshman class of Holy Cross High School. Even the faculty didn't know what to make of his belligerence. More so than Chris, Larry was isolated from the herd, shivering in the cold, and slowly starving. Maloney, the school's ever-hovering sergeant-at-arms, often picked Larry off—in the halls without a pass, wearing jeans instead of creased blue trousers, or just for being late for school. Larry was on the fast track toward expulsion again. Victor had warned Chris many times to stay away from his former "degenerate" friends. Victor knew all about that word. And it was part of their agreement. Larry had no role in the Story—none of his former friends did. He liked them too much, still thought of those days fondly, to do such a thing.

"He's coming back," Larry said.

"Who?"

"Cavanaugh."

Chris felt uneasy, but intrigued. "When?"

"Around Thanksgiving."

"How'd you find that out?"

"The turd wouldn't return any of my calls or letters, so I went to see his old man."

"How'd that go?"

"Fine. He was cool. Almost seemed happy I stopped by."

"That's hard to believe."

"Why?" Larry said. "We didn't do it."

"Yeah, but we were there."

"So?"

"So? Look at us now. Life treating you okay?"

"Well, let's see," Larry said. He rubbed his chin stubble. "I get up every morning at two-thirty—two-thirty! Hell, we used to come home sometimes by then. And the next thing I know, I'm up to my elbows in unbleached flour. It's like dust, and it's all over the place, like a frickin' cloud. You know what happens when you breathe in that stuff all morning long? It starts coating the inside of your nostrils like snot—all gooey and sticky. Who knows what it's doin' to my brain? Might explain a lot of things, right? And my old man thinks I'm gonna take over the business. Of course, we have lots of old ovens...and insurance. Maybe I can get you to rig something up for me. Your brain's good at that. I'll even give you a percentage." Larry smiled and wiggled his eyebrows.

"Oh, man," Chris said. He slowly shook his head.

They looked at each other—and, suddenly, they began to laugh half-heartedly. And just for a moment, the tension between them melted, and they were back atop their little world, back in the days when they were cooler and smarter and so much wiser than everyone else, and could get away with anything. But when the laughter ceased, the crushing silence returned, and they continued their ride without speaking another word. Chris knew that Larry secretly wanted that old life back. Being a rebel had its serious consequences, just as Matt had warned them. But Larry, like Chris, was too stubborn to admit it aloud.

They reached the four-lane highway that ran parallel to the elevated railroad tracks. Then they turned into the poorly lit parking lot of the Lowenbach Funeral Home where Sandra's wake had been held. Instinctively, Chris' eyes locked on the building's portico, and for an instant he saw her casket being shoved into the back of the hearse. His mind began whirling as a kaleidoscope of more related sights and sounds vied for attention. The shadow figures seemed intrigued.

They stopped near the curb. "You okay?" Larry said. "You look like you're going to hurl."

Chris' head still felt as if it were dancing. This particular point in the universe was always a tough place to be. "Yeah, sure."

"I gotta hand it to ya. I don't think I could come by here if I were you."

"Yeah, well, I don't have a helicopter, so you get used to it."

"So what are ya thinkin'? Anything you want to share, or should I keep my mouth shut for once?"

"What this all about?"

Larry shrugged, and tried to look innocent. "Just talking."

Too humble. Too caring. Still trying to worm his way back in. "It's nothing."

"Bad memories, huh?"

"Not really—just something Matt said to me when she was dying, something I think about a lot."

Larry nodded. "More pearls of wisdom from our fearless, incarcerated leader? I can't imagine he said anything that helped, not that I could."

"It's not what you think."

"It's not, huh?"

"We were in the church, looking at the paintings—"

"Uh-oh."

"—and we were talking about magic."

"Magic? You mean like capes and wands and flying broomsticks?"

"I was complaining that there wasn't any."

"Complaining? Jesus Christ, starman, we're on a spinning speck of dust orbiting a giant fireball of gas that's traveling at seven hundred thousand miles an hour through an endless frickin' vacuum—and you're looking for magic? Really?"

"I know, I know," Chris said. Larry's observation was common among the Hotshits.

"You gotta stop reading that kiddie crap. Don't you think he's right, that it really matters what's in your head? You're not a Butthead, you're a man of reason. I thought you were on-board by then."

"I was."

"I guess dealing with reality can be tough. Look what it's done to Fitz." A smile spread on Larry's face, but Chris did not respond to his shatter-the-gloom attempt. "So lay it on me. What'd he say?"

Chris shrugged, still hesitant. "He reminded me of a lot of magical things, just like you did."

"Yeah, such as...?"

Chris paused to scan Larry's stout face. There didn't seem to be any insincerity in his friend's baggy eyes. Chris raised his right hand and pinched his thumb and forefinger together. He saw a speck of dirt beneath his index fingernail. "The universe was once this big."

"And that's what mesmerized you? What does that have to do with your old lady dying?"

Embarrassed for letting his guard down and allowing Larry a rare look into his troubled mind, Chris lowered his hand and retreated inward. Old ways died hard in them both.

"I gotta tell you, Chris. I think I'm weird—but, man, you got me beat by a mile. Maybe you've been staring into that telescope too long." There was no real contempt in his words. Larry was that unwittingly insulting to all his friends, what little, if any, remained. It was...Larry, toxic byproduct of the Grand Experiment. He glanced left and right as he prepared to cross the four-lane highway. "Good luck with that football thing. Maybe I'll see you in the cafeteria some evening."

"I hope not," Chris said, "or you'll see me here, too."

Larry shook his head. "Not allowed." Then he slipped through a break in the traffic and crossed the road, disappearing like a phantom beneath the darkened viaduct. Chris' line of sight shifted higher. Just beyond the tracks loomed the abandoned wood-cribbed grain elevator made famous in one of Sandra's paintings, and infamous by one of Matt's ill-fated get-rich-quick plots. Chris stared for a moment as it drew him in, the Power buzzing and crackling. A great place to hide things, if they needed hiding. He thought of what might have been, then quickly turned away.

Chris was about to head up the wide, concrete sidewalk that ran past the small illuminated shops along the north side of the highway. But then he gazed back once more at the glass doors of the funeral home, and fell into a morbid trance. A school day did not pass when he couldn't think of himself standing in stunned silence over her as she lay in that coffin. Dead. They knew that day was coming. He was certain his tears would flow, as they did from Janey. But then, when it happened... There had been plenty of flowers delivered, complete with sympathetic notes on tiny cards. But what about all those empty rows of folding metal chairs? Sandra had only one sibling, an unmarried sister named Monika. But she had died suddenly years earlier. *Dead dead dead.* Still, there was church and friends. Where were they? Why didn't they come? But he knew who to blame. He chased everyone away—especially first real loves. So on that horrible day, reality slapped him hard across the face, and Life was added to the list, as the word ceased to make any sense to him. As for death, it now seemed to be everywhere, affecting everyone—it's a miracle anyone's alive. And it caused him to ask many strange questions for which he received much scorn, but for which no one had any satisfactory answers. That only made him all the more frustrated and angry, and had put him on his quest to figure it all out on his own. For thirty-eight years, Sandra had been a living, breathing human being, creating thoughts and beliefs, collecting memories, the body being just the device to keep all the information flowing and churning. So where did it all go? Couldn't have just disappeared. That, he had read outside the classroom, was impossible. Once information is assembled, it can't be destroyed. It has matter, it has mass. And energy. Dead, he decided back then, was a supremely stupid word. Who would think of such a stupid thing? Like all the other words on the ever-growing list, it explained nothing. It was an empty term—a drug, used to try to pacify him, and give those who used it on him a power over him that they did not deserve. Well, we don't really know where all her thoughts and memories went. Those structures just disappeared. Like information swallowed into a black hole. But she's dead, all right. Dead as dead can be. Not satisfactory? Have you tried the word spirit? How about Heaven? Those are a couple of oldies but goodies.

Dead. *Morto.* It had rightfully earned its placement atop the list, duly and angrily noted with those roaring winds and damn lightning bolts.

Chris put his right foot on the pedal and prepared to ride away. But then he heard it again: the steady *clomp clomp clomp*—horseshoes on asphalt, still trotting toward him along Pine Street. Chris squinted into the dusk and caught the movement of something ghostly white, like a wisp of fog condensing in the folds of the boiling darkness. Chris shut his eyes tightly, sparking the flash, then opened them again to the rumbling thunder. But just like the night the Monster appeared, he could not alter this dreadful reality, and the mare trotted closer and closer. There was little doubt now, they had slipped through and—even worse—were becoming permanent without his cooperation, hiding permanently in the folds, and refusing to evaporate. His heart thumped wildly, up into his throat, but he would not give in to his fear as he continued to stare. He felt curious and brave enough to allow them closer, determined enough to face them, and maybe shout some anger, to try and scare them away. He saw the mare's round and pupil-less cue-ball eyes, its awful human grin. A furry little beast with the cat-like ears and a flattened nose and a fedora rode atop the horse, clutching the long and wild mane. And then came the laughter—like an old man's laughter, low and steady, but delighted by his fear. It trailed off as all went silent, then burst back louder, even more delighted and menacing. Chris knew where these nightmarish creatures ultimately came from, the awful things they could do, just as he and Janey knew how to combat them. *Janey!* Time to leave them in the darkness, and prepare.

Chris streaked past the lighted shops along the highway, then pedaled furiously through the spotlit entrance of the Lone Oak complex, listening to his tire treads rumble over the warm asphalt, certain that the mare was charging, closing the gap, and laughing all the way. He dared not look back until, out of breath, he turned into his driveway and leaped from the bike, running it into the safety of the dark but open box-filled garage, where he let the bike crash against those boxes as he spun around. But there was no sign down the lamplit street of the mare or its freakish rider, and no clomping hooves, just an occasional passing automobile with headlights on, and the sound of the tumbled bike's spinning front tire. And a moth, just a moth, all by itself, fluttering around the streetlight. *Not real, fictitious. Make-believe. Breathe. Breathe.* But as he finally pushed the button and watched—with a saving light now on—the garage door sections rattle one by one down the track, Chris, thinking of the Story, had to wonder: *Why are they after us?*

Chapter Six

Banished

The following Monday, Chris found the halls of Holy Cross a foreign world. Those who had shunned him before his great athletic feat now wanted him to know them by name. He never knew he had so many friends. Even his teachers looked at him in a new way—some with puzzlement, others with respect. Skinny, unknown freshman he was not (not the unknown part, anyway). As the first-team tailback and school-record holder, Chris was suddenly cherished as a rare commodity, just like the Book and the Orb. He had done something that no sports heroes—their photos enshrined in the lobby's glass trophy cases—had accomplished. And the second-best time wasn't even close, not in the nanosecond world. A miracle, it truly was. Now a blurb about his accomplishment, printed on an index card, rested next to Coach Joe's stopwatch, also encased. Word was planned for the school newspaper and the alumni newsletter. Toward the end of the school day, even Chris was convinced once more of his greatness (*that roller coaster ride is always wild*). And he indeed walked the halls like a man—make that a giant!—among boys, his skin tingling with a new kind of power: pride. Football was actually tolerable. Once again, his thoughts returned to the conundrum: Could he really be—willingly—an important part of this condemned team?

Victor's reaction to the news wasn't surprising. There was no congratulatory offering, just a dark reminder: "Don't screw up."

There was always that chance, since Chris really didn't care. And Woz reminded Chris of this possibility later that Monday evening on the practice field. "We didn't see you in the weight room yesterday, kid. Where were you?"

"I had lots of homework, coach," Chris said, though it was a lie. He didn't want to face Fitz and the Horde any sooner than he had to.

"Members of the first team are leaders," Woz said. "You need to be a leader, kid."

In the huddle, Chris didn't hear any signs of the threats voiced the previous Friday. Fitz called the plays that Woz prescribed. Often, they involved Chris. And with each run, Chris felt increasingly confident that

Fitz's plan would not materialize—at least, not under the watchful eye of Coach Joe.

But then Chris started seeing the conspiracy develop. On a left end sweep, Koch "missed" his blocking assignment. That gave Dirty Dahlberg a clear shot at Chris. Chris cut inside, but Dahlberg struck low and hard with a shoulder tackle on Chris' left thigh pad, knocking him to the ground. Each time Chris ran to the left, Dahlberg was waiting for him, unblocked. He struck low again and again like a sledgehammer on the left thigh pad.

From time to time, Woz and Coach Joe admonished Koch. But just as Fitz predicted, neither coach suspected anything. Dahlberg was a talented player. And Koch often had trouble blocking him. Chris was surprised that Dahlberg, who answered to no one, had joined forces with the Horde. Yes, there would be consequences.

∽

All week long, the trend continued. Dahlberg seemed to be everywhere, shadowing Chris even when he didn't get the ball.

"Are you trying to kill me?" Chris said one time after running a safety valve pattern into the left flat.

Dahlberg, all over Chris, in his face, just kept on grinning.

Finally, on Friday, it happened—but not from one of Dahlberg's sledgehammer blows. Rather, it came unexpectedly—while running sprints at the beginning of practice. Woz blew his whistle and Chris sprung out of his set position. His left quad tightened into a burning knot. Chris screamed in pain and clutched his leg as he hobbled about.

Woz approached slowly. "What's the matter, kid?"

"My leg, sir," Chris said as he tried to walk normally. But his thigh muscle tightened and burned even more, and soon Chris had to sit on the ground.

Coach Joe rushed in. "Charlie horse," he said to Woz. "He'll be all right."

Coach Joe helped Chris to his feet, then guided him to the bench where he handed Chris a paper cup filled with water. Chris chugged the contents, and then saw Wenzel take his place in the backfield.

"Dahlberg," Coach Joe said. "They put him up to this."

∽

All through practice, Chris tried to walk off his thigh cramp. But each time Chris tried to run, the muscle seized into that hot and painful knot. Woz grew concerned. The Mount Carmel game was Sunday, and his starting tailback was hobbled. He sent Chris to the training room where a large bruise on Chris' thigh revealed itself. The trainer wrapped an icy compress around Chris' leg, which was then elevated for a time. After practice ended, Woz entered the training room and was informed of the injury.

"Fine time for a stunt like this," Woz said. "Go home and get some rest, kid. We're walking through the game plan in the morning, if you care to join us."

"He'll be there," Coach Joe said.

༄

Coach Joe gave Chris a ride home in his old, black pickup truck that smelled of hot vinyl. They tossed Chris' bike in the open bed. Chris gave him the directions.

"I'm sorry, Chris, I should have seen this coming," Coach Joe said. He shifted the gears as they headed down Pine Street. "Fitz can be a real devil when he wants something. But that's why he's our quarterback. Gotta have guys like that steering the ship."

Chris sat in silence with the backpack in his lap, his left hand slowly rubbing the injured thigh muscle. He cringed to hear Coach Joe sanctioning that insanity.

"What I can't understand is why he hates you so much. That's not too strong of a word, hate, is it? Yeah, sure we all know he wants Weasel to be the starter. But Fitz's an athlete. He knows you're the better runner. But instead, he's trying to get you killed. I don't get it."

"He's never liked me. Not even in middle school."

"You two were classmates."

"Yeah."

"Did you have a fight or something?"

"No."

"So what happened?"

"I got promoted."

"Promoted?"

"Yeah, to the 'Hot Shots.' " Chris substituted an "o" for the "i," just to be safe.

" 'Hot Shots,' huh?" Coach Joe said before he laughed. "Were you in a gang?"

"Sort of. My school divided the eighth-grade class into two groups—smart kids in one, average kids in the other. Fitz and I started out in the average group."

"But you got bumped up."

"Yeah."

"Makes sense. You're a smart kid. I saw that from the first day. You got the ability to see everyone on the field all at once. And you know how to react. Don't see that too often. Quite a talent. Being fast as Hell doesn't hurt, either, huh?"

They reached the highway. Coach Joe downshifted, rolled slowly through the stop sign as he looked left, then turned right and accelerated. "So this war between you and Fitz, it all has to do with jealousy?"

"I guess."

Coach Joe shook his head as he stomped on the clutch. "That's our quarterback." When the truck settled into third gear, Coach Joe said, "I gotta do something about this. Maybe have a little talk with Dahlberg, too. We'll get Fitz to call off the dogs."

After a few miles, Coach Joe turned right into the Lone Oak development. A fountain and a sign with cursive writing chiseled in stone welcomed them. The coach followed the meandering street. "Lone Oak, huh?" Coach Joe said, examining the proliferation of tightly packed two-story brick homes on grassy lots. "So they left one standing?"

"Not in my yard," Chris said.

They arrived at Chris' house. The garage door was up, and Chris saw his father's BMW parked between the stacked cartons. Coach Joe parked in the street, then helped Chris remove the bike from the open back.

"Remember to keep icing that leg," Coach Joe said. "And another thing—don't give up. I know what you're going through, son. I was a skinny kid my first year in high school—yeah, me, can you believe it? That's a whole other story. Funny how things can change so quickly." He grabbed two handfuls of his belly that stretched his black T-shirt and laughed, only briefly. "But that's my point. I got pounded every time I got the ball. It was tough. I wanted to walk away lots of times. But my old man kept after me. He always told me: 'Wake up, son, you can't run away from your troubles.' Simple lesson, I know, and I'm sure you've heard it before. But it's true, and it bears repeating. You're gonna run into a lot more Tom Fitzgeralds in your life. Sometimes, you gotta fight back." His expression grew muted. "And those others...stay away from them. They might be worse. Making fun of you and the things that, way down inside, you know you really want. Always criticizing, tearing things down, groping for your sad company...telling you that you don't look the part, and can't make it. It's so easy and safe not to try anymore, to save yourself from the pain of failing, and having to try again. You can always blame others for your misery, how they plot against you. The rest of your life, if you want. That's safe and easy, too. Real easy." Coach Joe came of his mini-trance slightly flushed. He smiled, then laughed a sad little laugh before his forceful words exploded the pity-portrait. "Just make sure you don't quit."

"I won't," Chris said as he stood next to his bike. *I can't.*

"Buon-*issimo*." Then Coach Joe hesitated. "You gotta understand something. The coach is under a lot of pressure about this tailback position. He'll be challenging you every chance he gets. If you crack, you'll lose out, got that?"

"Yeah, but I'm hurt. What am I supposed to do?"

"I know. It'll heal. He knows. So don't get discouraged if he starts doubting you. Make sure he understands you want to play—no matter what he says. Keep reminding him of that. Your talent will win out. Always does. So rest up, and I'll see you tomorrow."

"Thanks, coach."

Coach Joe got into his truck and finally started the misfiring engine.

"Hey, Coach?" Chris said.

Coach Joe poked his head out the window. "Yeah, Chris?"

"There's something I've been meaning to ask you..."

"Sure, son, whatever it is."

"That language you speak—you know, your Italian."

Coach Joe's round face brightened as he smiled. "Ah, *si*—the food, the ladies—and the food! Magnifi-*cato!*"

"Yeah, well, you know, your translation...it's kinda...kinda..." He paused, fearing miscommunication.

"Yeah?" the coach said, still looking cheerful.

Chris decided to go right to the heart of the issue, as he saw it. "You really want to be Italian?"

Coach Joe looked on in bewilderment. "Doesn't everyone?" He laughed heartily—with his fat hand jutted out the window, and waving—as he drove off in a cloud of exhaust.

Clueless is he?

After Chris entered the house, Victor greeted the news of the injury in his usual way. "Are you sure about this?" he said as they sat opposite each other in the den.

"Do you want to see the bruise?" Chris said.

"I want you to start that game." Then he slammed his fist on the desk. "Damn it, Chris, when are you gonna man up?"

"I'm not faking it," Chris said.

"You've pulled this crap before," Victor said. "I don't believe you."

Chris shot from the chair, but came up limp. "There—happy now?" He turned and started out.

"You better not quit!"

Chris hobbled up the foyer stairs and entered his bedroom. He slammed the door behind him. Then he pounded his fist repeatedly on the mattress before lying prone on the bed, hot and vengeful thoughts filling his brain. He was sick to death of it all: Victor, Woz, football. Once again, he felt the urge to flee—to burst through his bedroom window like some fantasy hero, and hit the ground running, slashing sword in hand, seeking vengeance. But there was nowhere to go and nothing he could do—not while he existed in this world, and had to depend on his father for survival.

Chris took some deep breaths, propped his head up on the pillows, then stared at another of his mother's paintings that covered a hole in the wall opposite his bed: The Artist's Studio, on loan from the rest of his mother's collection kept in the spare bedroom (her former studio) and managed by Janey. It depicted the snow-covered stucco Cottage that sat atop a bluff, with misty, purple-and-blue mountains in the backdrop. A solitary dwarf evergreen frosted in snow glowed unnaturally in the foreground. There was a low stone wall with an arched gateway that ran from the right side of the Cottage and surrounded a small courtyard. And in the back of this courtyard sat the lamp-lit glass-façade Studio, those French doors wide open, revealing the easel and small wooden stool. Oh, yes, she had planned her escape very well. Judging by the number of paintings that hung on the long back wall of that Studio, Chris saw that she intended to be very busy, happily painting more scenes in that new life, further distancing herself from them in this world—maybe into another, then another.

Chris rolled from his bed, then stuck his hand between the mattress and box spring to retrieve the Book. Sandra had given it to him one Christmas, under strict orders to keep it a secret, even from Janey. It was a strange book in its own right, even without the bestowed Power. For "the family," a kind of fear-and-anger registry, containing anonymous entries over the centuries, written in Latin and then Bavarian and in all kinds of cursive styles, to summon the Legendary in the fight against those Turks and, later, the French. Sandra had hoped that Chris would use it "to collect happy thoughts," and to save his soul from the same anger that ravaged Victor. But just like his ancestors, he had used it to record every rant against his invaders—even what he would and would not accept as good or truthful. And then there was the Story. She wasn't the only one who could build new worlds.

Little did she know what she truly had done.

How it would open the door to her World.

She'd know soon enough, when she became a permanent lie.

Chris flopped onto the bed, removed the time-worn ink-stained wooden dip pen fastened by a loop on the inside cover, then withdrew an ink bottle from the drawer and set it on the nightstand. He collected his thoughts for the day. He flipped to the back of the diary and, after dipping the pen into the well, added *football* to the list of stupid words, underlining it twice, the lightning bolts flashing from the steel nib. And then he found his latest entry and wrote another just below, condemning them all to *Åsgårdsreien*— every single one of them.

The next morning, while the rest of the team was slowly drifting onto the practice field, Chris decided to test his sore leg. He had survived the night with little pain as the continual icing and aspirin had done the job. And after he got dressed, descending the stairs was uneventful. Chris' hopes were high that his leg had healed enough to resume practice. But he didn't dare try to run until after Victor dropped him off at school.

After a lengthy session of stretching, which helped to postpone the inevitable, Chris stood at the goal line, then started running toward midfield. His leg seized up after a few strides. Limping back toward the end zone, he saw Woz and Coach Joe approaching.

"Ready to go, Chris?" Coach Joe said.

"I'm still having problems with the leg."

Woz looked more annoyed than usual. Then he flashed the same suspicious look Victor had given Chris the night before. "Okay—Wenzel," Woz called out, looking around, "where are you, kid?"

Wenzel charged up from a group slowly approaching the field. "Yes, sir?"

"You're first team until further notice."

"Yes, sir, coach. Thank you, sir."

Woz brushed past Chris as the Weasel broke the news to the Horde. They raised their helmets and cheered. And then: " 'When the Moon hits your eye like a big piece of pie...' " They laughed at him and poor Coach Joe.

Chris grew bitter at the sight of them, and resisted a calling. When they got older, had families and well-paying jobs, when they gathered at one of those highly anticipated reunions and reminisced, the Horde would cheer and sing once more for their fine accomplishment. After all, they had won. And that's really all that mattered to them.

❧

After practice, Woz called Chris into his office. Chris sat in a steel chair opposite the coach's deep metal desk. Woz had the same severe look he had shown earlier. Chris felt as if he had just committed a heinous crime, and had been brought downtown to be interrogated in some harsh and sterile environment.

Woz put his hands behind his head and looked up at the suspended ceiling. "You know, there are lots of kids out there playing hurt. Sprained wrists, jammed fingers, cuts, bruises—"

"I didn't make this up, sir, if that's what you're thinking," Chris said.

Woz sat up in his chair and folded his hands on the desk. "What are you doing here, kid?"

Chris was confused. "You called me here, sir."

"You don't want to be part of this team, I can tell. I've seen hundreds of kiddies like you come and go. You razzle-dazzle your way onto the roster—and then you give up, on to something else. You don't put in the extra time. You weren't here for summer camp. You don't go to the weight room. And now you get hurt. I don't need players like that. I can't win with players like that. You just don't fit in."

"I didn't give up—"

"Look, kid, I stuck my neck out for you. I told Przybyszewski you weren't right for this team. I told him this would happen. But I gave in. School record—yeah, yeah, yeah. Great. Now look at the spot I'm in. Wenzel's not ready for tomorrow. What am I supposed to do?"

"I don't know, sir."

Woz rapped his knuckles on the desk. "You don't want to be here, do you?"

Woz was pushing him hard, real hard, just as Coach Joe had warned. But Chris kept silent.

"Come on, kid, be honest. Do you like football, or do you want to be doing something else with your time? It's okay, kid—really. You can tell me. I'm not going to bite your head off."

Chris shrugged. "No, I'm fine with it."

"Fine with it?"

"I don't want to quit, sir, if that's what you're asking."

Woz nodded slowly, sternly. "Okay, kid, I gave you your chance. I wanted to spare you the embarrassment. But now I'm gonna lay all the cards on the table. I got a call from a booster last night. Do you know what a booster is, kid? And I'm not talking about a shot or a chair."

Chris was stunned. "Yeah?"

"I gotta tell you, kid, I couldn't believe what I was hearing. I've seen and heard a lot of bad things, but I've never heard of a kid do anything like this. Do you know what I'm driving at?"

Chris remained silent. The hot blood rushed to his head, which began to pound in pain.

"A church? You vandalized a church? The House of God?"

"Well...I was there—"

"You were there? Christ Almighty, kid, what in Hell were you thinking? And now you expect me to keep you on a team that represents the Lord Himself? Do you know what kind of a fool you made me out to be? Wenzel's dad is a big contributor to this school. It was going to take somebody pretty extraordinary to push his kid out of the starting spot. Coach Joe convinced me I had my man—and it turns out, you're just a hoodlum. I'm a forgiving man—but this?" He shook his head. "The word's getting around now, kid. Not only am I getting calls to kick your butt off this team, the principal's getting calls to have me strung from a tree. And I'm not about to lose my job because of some degenerate like you." He leaned closer and folded his hands on the desk. "Let me ask you another thing. Aren't you afraid you're gonna burn in Hell for this? I mean, really—a church? I can't get over it. I've never heard of anything so goddamn irreverent."

The shame and the guilt Chris felt during the tirade quickly changed to anger. Everyone was so quick to pass judgment, yet no one knew all the facts. Guilt by association. His punishment, no doubt, would be eternal. Now he understood Fitz's threat, Dahlberg's attacks being just a sideshow, to keep Chris distracted from the painfully obvious and deadly main event. Chris had been all wrong about his nemesis. Fitz thought in ways that were foreign to Chris, a way that only the most cunning adult could understand. He never saw this coming. But he should have. It was much too easy, for Fitz. And bad stuff always happened even when just a bit of the horrible truth leaked out. He was tempted to disappear—and take them all with him. But he knew it wouldn't last, not before the Holy Season.

"Let's end this little charade so you don't waste any more of my time, or yours," Woz said. "Turn in your playbook before you go."

Shock seized Chris as he continued to stare at the coach's stern, unyielding expression. His flesh quickly blackened and shriveled, revealing patches of his tarnished skull. But those glaring eyes remained in place. Chris was so stunned at the dramatic turn, he felt as if he had just been shot, his anger evaporating. But he could not maintain eye contact for long, now that the coach knew. Chris looked down. The will to say anything more just wasn't there, not even with those incessantly nagging words hammering his brain—*you can't! you can't! you can't!*—or visions of the Monster Victor, towering over him with its chain, ready to capture him. Chris was never good at fighting for something he did not want or believe in. And a seductive relief immediately sprang up as it always did after a sudden failure, briefly clearing his mind of the horror. No more practice, no more charade, and Tom Fitzgerald. And he wouldn't have to perform, and fail, after all the hype, in an actual game. It's not like he quit. Forced to do it. Out of his hands. Chris could even blame Victor's betrayal, if he dared. So why did he feel like throwing up? Fitz had used the Church Incident, for which Chris was culpable. Couldn't hide Fitz' maneuver from Victor. He probably already knew, the phone call received, and would be waiting. So much for the relief. But there was no fight left in him.

Chris returned to his locker, grabbed his playbook, then set it on Wozniak's desk. The coach, at a grease board, contemplating Xs and Os, didn't turn to acknowledge him.

Once outside, Chris walked in a daze toward the bike racks—and saw his father's idling import parked on Pine Street by the parking lot entrance, the woolly black figure within growing and bursting through its silk suit, its horns curling out through the windows like black snakes. Like everyone else in the universe, Victor had received the call. The school complex, the houses, the trees—everything was falling into that swirling black hole, light flashing all around its event horizon.

"Chris!" Coach Joe shouted from behind. "Christopher Russo, wait up, son."

Sickened, Chris turned to face Coach Joe. He saw the panic in the coach's eyes. Even he seemed to be rotting.

"I just talked with the coach," he said. "What in Hell happened?"

"He kicked me off the team. He doesn't want me around. None of them do." He knew the sound of self-pity. But he couldn't stop himself.

Coach Joe grabbed Chris by the shoulders. "Why did you give him your playbook? Why? You promised me you wouldn't give up."

Feeling ashamed, Chris looked down and said nothing.

"Damn it, Chris, it was just a test—don't you see? He's always playing games with you kids. All you had to say was 'no.' Why didn't you say 'no,' Chris? Why didn't you fight him?"

"I did something this past year," Chris said, "something I shouldn't have. And now I'm paying for it. You'll hear all about it, I'm sure. I'm sorry. I know I let you down. Thanks for all you've done."

"So that's it? Just like that? After what we talked about?"

Chris struggled to look at Coach Joe, who was fraught with confusion. This was how it always worked. Coach Joe knew that. "I don't want to fight. I'm tired of fighting. The coach is right. I just want to go home. Just go somewhere…"

"But Chris—"

"I'm sorry. Really. But I don't want this. He does."

"He?" Coach Joe froze for a moment, then the fight seemed to leave him, too, and he nodded. "Okay, Chris," he said as he let go. "Okay. I'm…I'm sorry, too." He sighed and shook his head once more.

"Yeah, no doubt." Chris turned to face his father's harsh gaze. He saw in an instant that the Monster—with the terrible chain twirling—was ready to carry him away from Janey all the way to the flaming halls of Pandæmonium. He didn't know how he could resist.

PART TWO

The Holy Season of Magic

CHAPTER SEVEN

Resurrecting the Tree

"One step at a time, Chris," Janey said as they struggled up the basement stairs with the artificial Christmas tree. "Don't go too fast! This isn't a football game."

"Don't ever say that word to me again—ever," Chris said. "It's on the list!"

"What word?"

"You know which one."

"What list?"

"Don't give me that."

Janey was a few steps from the foyer. She guided the top of the tree while, farther down the stairs, Chris gripped the metal stand, still attached to the wooden pole that served as the trunk. Even though the tree was wrapped in a sheet to keep its artificial branches from straightening out, it barely fit in the stairwell. Bringing the tree from the basement was always a difficult task. Nearly all the weight was on Chris' end. Being the big, strong ex-football player, he shouldn't have needed his little sister's help. But since he tried to carry as much of the load as possible, sparing Janey any agony, Chris puffed and sweated with every awkward step, as if he were back on the practice field. Even worse, he could still feel the pain in his thigh from Dahlberg's sledgehammer blows, and his quaking leg felt as if it were about to buckle.

At least that nightmare was over. Since he was cut, Chris hadn't seen any curling horns or rotting flesh, and no more clomping horses. *Very weird.* The shadows were benign, the clock radio unthinking. Even the blinking-flashing thing had disappeared, which disappointed him, in a way. It had been comforting, consistent, always there. It was as if the dark power—now with a small "d" and "p"—had retreated all the way back to Pandæmonium, the *White Rose* had completely closed, and the book—small "b"—was storing its energy, waiting patiently for the holy season of magic—small "h", "s", and "m"—and giving him the rest he would desperately need before everything exploded out of control.

Like last year.

Or not.

Maybe the book's controlling power was gone for good. He had to seriously consider that part. The evidence was overwhelming, and he couldn't deny the facts, which was why the book had returned to being just his diary, its original intent. Not banished to the top shelf of his closet or sealed in plastic wrap, to keep it from oozing, as he once considered. That would mean it was still a threat. More like retired, useless, like the legacy and the legends and the religion. Chris was proud that his scientific ways seemed to have won the battle. The book and its power had been creeping back into his life, threatening to control him. But in the end, truth overwhelmed the lies, as it always should. (*How ironic I have the horde to thank for that. And Victor. I HATE irony!*) And with every passing uneventful day, truth became the new power. It felt good to breathe so normally for so long. So now, the day of reckoning was almost upon them—the first Sunday after Thanksgiving, on God's day (Janey's insistence, to coincide with Advent, which he let slide), the official beginning of their holiday season, and the final test. He had no intention of interfering with the healing process. Still, tomorrow—at midnight—couldn't come fast enough. He couldn't wait to hear the tolling, so he could at last drive a final "truth" stake into the heart of the book, and kill the power completely.

During this odd but welcomed respite, the horde ignored him at school, which was just fine with Chris. He concentrated on his studies, which needed concentrating. His school record stood, but was hidden somewhere in their books. The stopwatch and the notecard had been quietly removed after hours. And he went about his academic days like the unknown that he once was—with the badge of "loser" pinned to his chest, silently scorned for having the talent but no will, and branded again across the forehead as a failure. Janey was disappointed in him, though she never said it. But he could tell by her long stretches of glum silence, like Sandra used to show when she realized that her escape plans would never be fulfilled. Chris felt it whenever he was around Janey, despite her faint smiles and his efforts to pack the guilt tightly with all the other failures in his life. And then there was his promise of their escape, still unstructured with no safe conclusion, but always on his mind, with Victor lurking. Janey never talked about it. Neither did he. Victor hadn't gone through with his threat to ship Chris off to some military school. That required even more money, and work. And there had been no violent eruption, no angry beating. This football failure was expected, preordained, in the cards, as always, so no real surprise there, after all, not even to his father. But Victor had nonetheless tightened his grip on Chris—early to bed, and lights out—and the house became even more of a prison. At least Chris reacquainted himself with some of his favorite fantasy novels, read in appropriate candlelight. Their strange worlds had never been so comforting. But on the down side, the telescope became off limits, and Victor had unknowingly cut the one weak link Chris had with the ever-elusive Katie. Their breakup anniversary was coming, too. No telling how he'd react to that.

Suddenly, the tree refused to move. Chris nearly lost his footing. "Janey?" He had reason for concern. She hadn't been whistling much these past few weeks. And Thanksgiving had been a total bust, again. But today, given what it represented in their lives, Janey seemed to have much more energy. At least her take-charge attitude had returned. There was no way she was going to skip out on this highly sacred and much anticipated ritual. Not only was it the beginning of The Holy Season of Magic, it was the start of Janey's birthday month. Since she was born on Christmas, holiday gifts often doubled as birthday gifts. Feeling "gypped," she quickly remedied the problem, allowing the flow of presents and special favors for an unreasonably-extended time.

"I'm fine, thank you," Janey said at last.

"So what's going on in that girl-brain of yours? Why are we stopping?"

"You sound like you're having a heart attack."

"Well, it is a little heavy."

"Do you want to stop and rest?"

It came out of nowhere: *In the suffocating tunnel that leads to Pandæmonium?* Chris heard a distant boom echoing up behind him. He turned and looked down the darkened staircase.

Nothing.

Out of habit, Chris closed his eyes briefly to reset everything on a black canvas. "Just keep going," he said finally. "Get us into the foyer." Chris pushed the tree up the remaining steps and through the doorway. In the foyer's level openness, he caught his breath. All was calm, now. The tree felt much lighter and easier to handle.

With both hands clutching the sheet, Janey grunted as she walked backward, guiding the top of the tree down the one step into the living room. The grandfather clock struck five. The evening light was growing dim.

Chris followed her lead across the hardwood floor. "Now let's stop and rest," Chris said. "You're the one who looks like she's having a heart attack."

"That's not necessary," she said. "Keep moving, please."

Raising the tree the weekend after Thanksgiving became an act of defiance their first holiday season without Sandra. The sooner the tree came out, the better, Chris had decided after that turkey-less day. Victor hadn't helped with the decorating. He never did, not even when Sandra was alive, which, as it turned out, was to their distinct advantage, and his great financial loss. Infusing the holiday spirit into their home had been Sandra's great passion. So last year, Victor, having left the house for a while, was surprised upon his return to see the tree decorated without her presence or his consent—and that there would nonetheless be light and joy once again in his chambers of doom. Victor was so shocked, in fact, that he seemed afraid and powerless to stop it. Chris duly noted Victor's reaction, and he and Janey incorporated that fact into the story, which they still kept a secret, only to be retold when they needed power and revenge. So Christmas, which Chris had angrily considered banishing with all his other old and tired religious beliefs and icons, remained his favorite time of the year. It was a time when the laws of physics were temporarily relaxed, allowing the magic of his sister's world to coexist, side by side, with the numbers and formulas and scientific theories that now governed his. But in their house, even the power of Christmas had its limits. Appropriately, on Epiphany, when the Twelve Days were officially over, the magical world departed and order and reality were restored as the tree was dismantled, wrapped in its shroud, and buried in its basement tomb. Victor, of course, insisted on this.

    Before his transformation was completed, Chris and Janey had been holy compatriots. He was a fearless and mighty warrior, never defeated, always respected. And she was an angel, having selflessly given up her human life—if only temporary, until their task was complete—to acquire indestructible heavenly powers. They could leave the protection of the Village, created by the benevolent Sorceress artist, and plant the Sacred Trees all the way to the entrance of the Terrible Shrieking Mountain's Chamber of Darkness that contained Pandæmonium. This brave act secured, using God's pure light, the Boiling Evil within—and guaranteed the safe arrival of the Child Savior born on Christmas Day (Janey's "B-Day"). (*Because monsters should never be allowed to harm a child, not ever.*) But today, as they carried the artificial tree into the living room, Chris (now the nonviolent man of reason) and Janey (still the keeper of the sacred orb) became the two fearless allies, braving the perils of the kingdom of darkness to plant their apparatus that, when activated, would push all ignorance and lies away with the light of wisdom and truth. The grand decree, written in his well-hidden book of everything, stated implicitly that only the chosen could exist within the village for as long as the great tree stood lit. Their story, as he now saw it, and rewrote it in these tranquil times (unauthorized).

    They stood the tree before the bay window. The room felt cold, with the thermostat set at its permanent winter setting of sixty-five degrees. But Janey—in her traditional worn jeans and pink sweater, her wide eyes sparkling, and her smile gleaming—didn't seem to mind. So neither did he. Chris stepped back from the tree to see if it was centered. After adjusting its position, he stood back once more. Then, satisfied, he began removing the safety pins that held the musty old sheet in place. With the sheet gone, the tree stood like a shriveled relic, its artificial branches matted and bent.

"*Ish-ka-bibble*," Janey said. "It looks sad."

"It looks dead," Chris said. "Let's bring this thing back to life before he comes home."

Chris and Janey worked together in silence, each familiar with their tasks. Janey worked on the lower half of the tree while Chris worked the upper half, straightening the branches and brushing the matted needles open. After a while, the job was done, and they stepped back to admire the refurbished tree. It stood tall, but remained dark and slumbering.

Chris crawled under the tree and plugged in the dangling end of the string lights into the wall socket. Then he rushed to the wall switch by the foyer entrance. "Ready?"

Janey nodded. She, too, believed in their story of the tree's magic. So she also knew the dire consequences to their perception of safety should the tree remain unlit.

Chris flicked the switch. The tree's clear bulbs lit up like a thousand tiny stars and filled the room with the saving light.

"Yay!" Janey said as she clapped.

Chris was relieved. The magical glow, their safe haven, was back for another season. But the tree's full power was not yet restored. Other magical elements were needed. "Okay," he said to Janey, "let's go get 'em."

Janey rushed past him and back down the stairs.

"Hey, slow down." Chris walked quickly to the basement doorway and stopped briefly to gaze down the darkened stairway once more. Some years earlier, before the dark power invaded, this view brought on a creeping fear of dangerous things hiding in the dark, and eventually became the black heart of the chambers of doom. Now he smirked defiantly at the childish notion—forced himself to—then quickly followed Janey into the box-cluttered mess that was their storeroom (or, as she called it, the "icky room"), no longer barricaded. Chris wanted to make sure that Janey didn't go snooping around, and find things she wasn't supposed to see. Victor kept his outmoded rep samples here and throughout the basement (the newer stuff was jammed into the garage)—mostly sprockets, small generators, and those dreaded roller chains—and he never seemed to find the time to discard them. Illuminated by a solitary bulb with a pull cord, this room, Chris liked to joke, was more like a snapshot of Victor's brain, and offered great insight into how it worked. The brittle boxes of ornaments—some marked Friedrich (the great deniers), others marked Russo (the great liars)—were stacked near the idle furnace. Janey was already standing beside them. "Doesn't this room give you the creeps?" he said.

"No," Janey said. She began to sort the boxes into separate, smaller piles.

"It does to me. Always has. Never know what might be hiding in here."

"Just spiders," she said.

"Yeah, sure...'piders. Big, black hairy ones—you know, the kind that sneak into your mouth at night when you're snoring—"

"I don't snore!"

"—and crunch when you step on them. You know how much you like crunchy spiders. I think they might even have bones. And then there are the ghosts—and the winged demons."

She picked up a box. "There're no ghosts down here—Victor."

"Really? Well, now, there's a change of heart. I thought you believed in them."

"I do. But this house just isn't old enough."

"Oh, is that the rule?"

"Uh-huh!" she said before smiling.

"Well, if I were you, I'd stay clear of this room. I know I do."

"Something in here you don't want me to see?"

Chris placed his hands on his hips. "There's a lot of Victor's junk in here, Janey. I don't want it falling on you. If that should happen and I'm not around, you could be in big trouble."

"Okay, fine," she said, much too willingly. She held out the box. "Here, you take these. And—"

"Yeah, yeah, I know," Chris said, grabbing the box, " 'be careful.' Good thing you're here."

"Glad you admitted it."

"Are you sure you can do this?"

Janey seized another ornament box. "I thought you wanted to finish before he got home?" She pushed past him. "Will you please move those cans?"

"Excuse me?" Chris glanced at Victor's collection of half-empty paint cans and thinner at the base of the wall near the furnace. "I'll do it when we clean up."

"You said that last year."

"I won't forget."

"You said that last year, too. Do it today, as a present for me."

"Whatever." Chris glanced around, looking for signs...then quickly followed her up the stairs.

༄

When all the boxes had been carefully retrieved, Chris spread them around the tree according to heritage—Russo on the left and Friedrich on the right (*Friedrichs are always right, Janey says*). Then he removed the box tops,

66

revealing ornaments of different shapes and colors: stars, grapes, eggs, pears, teardrops, pine cones, and smooth orbs. Russo ornaments, most of which were red, were made of brittle glass. Some did not survive the journey. Friedrich ornaments were mostly blue. But some were made of thick glass with brass caps. And their silver linings made them reflective and shiny. "Kugels," Sandra had called them. They were all that remained from a rare collection handed down through the generations on his mother's side. "From Austria," she had said to them years ago when they first helped her decorate the tree, "where St. Nicholas came from." And the gilded book. And on that fateful day, she told a wildly foreign and amazing Christmas tale full of enchantment and foreboding, with odd names and scary creatures they had never heard of. Chris and Janey had, at the time, believed every word. And after extensive research, taking special note of all the associated famous artwork, ghoulish and frightening as they were, Chris wrote the story down in the diary. Soon the tale became part of the greater fantasy that he and Janey composed to deal with their fear and unhappiness. But after death not only came knocking but made itself right at home, after delving extensively into this tale and her heritage, Chris finally dismissed it all as a concoction based on pre-Christian Alpine folklore—a parent's clever attempt to educate her children on the origins of Christmas traditions while also trying to scare them into living good lives. And he had, accordingly, and without Janey's knowledge, altered the official version to suit his newly enlightened views and findings, and defiantly right the wrongs because he just had to, despite his pledge not to tamper with a single word without her input or approval. But then, the creatures started appearing, and he had to reconsider things once again and become more accepting, before they finally retreated with the dark power into the book. But this, he kept quiet, lest he seem unsure of himself, his beliefs, and his ability to accomplish things. Janey was still convinced that the spirits of the people and things in Sandra's story lived within the kugels. It was an interesting observation, Chris noted. He could see it. And he often wondered about the ancient faces and strange celebrations that, over time, had reflected off their shiny surfaces.

It was time to resurrect the tree to its full glory—kugels first. Per their ritual, Janey worked the bottom half, cradling each ornament in her hands as if it were a tiny bird, fallen from the nest. Then she carefully hung them on the branches. How ironic that these treasures hung in full view of a man so desperate for money, but who still, because of his disdain for the holidays, knew nothing of their value. Just as Janey liked to remind Chris often: *What better place to hide it than right under his nose? You know how men are!*

"Make sure you put them farther inside the tree," Janey said. "Not on the ends. I don't want you knocking them off."

"I know, Janey," Chris said.

"And don't crowd them all in one spot."

Chris stepped back to check their work. Apparently, they had different definitions of crowded. The "perfect" placement of her ornaments was inconsistent, leaving forbidden gaps in the tree. But he didn't dare move them, or even utter a critical word.

Slowly, the boxes emptied. At times, when Chris spied upon Janey, so intent on fulfilling the ritual, and so content, she appeared to be that small but determined angel of their story, wings and all. Once all the kugels were on the tree, they hung the rest of the blue Friedrich ornaments. Then they reluctantly dispersed the Russo ornaments. (Janey often objected to their use, as she considered them "evil." If it were up to her, the brittle red ornaments would not be hung at all. But since they were, they were often placed on the branch tips. Chris suspected that she would purposely dislodge them from the tree, and he even caught her removing them on occasion.) From time to time, they came across a cracked or shattered kugel. They treated each broken orb as a family tragedy, knowing that the supply was finite, and that once an ornament broke, so did a memory. Remnants could not be tossed into the trash. They were carefully picked up one by one and placed in a coffee can with the remains of past tragedies.

By the time the grandfather clock struck six, it was dark outside. But they had nearly finished decorating the tree, which was now all aglow and twinkling. All that remained was the placement of the treetop ornament, and a few other special accessories.

The topper was, by far, the most mysterious of all the decorations. Adorned with gold leaf, the ornament looked like a tower lopped off a Byzantine cathedral—a hollowed-out onion dome crowned with a twisting spire. Its history had long been lost with the passing of time. But it was silently revered, as if one day they would discover its importance. Chris had to stand on the bay window ledge so he could secure the topper on the tree's crown.

Special accessories added to the holiday magic. One was a snow globe depicting a chapel scene, complete with an altar on which the tiny statue of an angel and a Bible rested. Then the ceramic Nativity scene and its tiny wooden manger with bits of real straw, also in their story—the Child's ultimate destination—placed below the protective tree. And per that story, Janey appropriately set the ceramic figures of Joseph, Mary, and the baby Jesus on the mantel just above the living room's gas fireplace, well away from the tree. The figures would be returned to the Nativity scene at the stroke of midnight on Christmas, their traditional gift-giving time, after their storybook quest to save the Child from harm was officially completed.

But the most valuable accessory, by far, was the nineteenth century music box, made in Leipzig, that Sandra had given Janey on their last Christmas together. It was actually two boxes, the smaller inside the larger, which was—with its cracked wooden slats secured with rusty nails, and stenciled with the word "ornaments"—purposely made to look common so as not to draw attention to the gilded one within (*Janey's "phone booth," where she changes*.) When its lid opened, its chimes activated. Inside that box, encased in the red velvet liner, was the carved statue of an angel with a tiny white snowflake on her chest. Her arms were extended forward, and her hands were cupped to hold the small purple orb, no larger than a marble, also encased within. It was the orb that was the real treasure—a rare amethyst kugel (*"purple" to me—I'm a guy*). Sandra had kept it a secret from Victor, whom she feared would pawn it. ("You're its guardian now," she had told Janey.) In their story, it was the true source of the tree's power. Noticeably missing was the comparably valuable *Windrädchen*. Victor confiscated it last year after they left its candles burning, and, with its black riders, became his terrible war machine, entombed in the mountain. Chris doubted his father's concerns about a devastating fire—he would love it!—and only confirmed his fears about the purple kugel.

"Here," Chris said to Janey as he lifted the music box from the crate, "you hide it."

But just as she did last year, Janey placed the music box at the foot of the tree with the manger scene. Janey opened the outer box, removed the inner one, then closed the outer box lid before resting the smaller box atop it. Then she repeatedly turned a small brass crank, which wound the inner spring. When she opened that lid, the chimes activated. Janey set the angel in its stand and began whistling the song. Finally, she placed the kugel in the angel's hands. "I'll have to make up some words for it some day, so I can sing it to you."

"That's okay. I like it the way it is."

"But it's me—and it's my song. I want to sing it to you. It's my signal—in case I get in trouble."

"Changing the story, are you?" Chris felt glad, less guilty.

"Don't you want to sing it to me so I know you're on your way?"

Now Chris had to sigh. "Look, he's gonna open that thing one of these days."

"So? Even if he does, he won't know what he's seeing. Just like the kugels. But don't you worry, he won't come near it. He can't."

"I'm not sure he knows the rules."

"Yes, he does. He may not think it, but he knows."

He sure will. Chris and Janey stepped back one last time. Now the tree looked as big and proud as a mountain. They were ready for him.

"What about the candle bags?" Janey said. It was a tradition born at St. Boniface, which encouraged the parishioners to bring a candle bag to the outdoor shrine adjacent to the church, in remembrance of a lost loved one. Janey used them to line their driveway, not in the story.

"Let's wait till after he comes home. He might try to run them over."

⁂

It wasn't long before Chris heard the hum of the electric garage door opener. He hid the music box in its unassuming container. Then he stood next to Janey before the tree, hand on her shoulder, as they faced the darkened foyer.

With bowling ball bag in one hand and a fast-food cup with lid and straw in the other, Victor squeezed through the doorway beneath the staircase. He had been drinking. Victor didn't like soda pop. He used the cup so he could openly drink while driving. Victor paused as he stared at them. The light from the tree illuminated his stern face. He seemed irritated at the entire defiant scene, which was not unexpected. It didn't take long for the curling horns to appear. "At it again, I see." He quickly turned away, set his bowling bag on the floor and the cup on the small table next to the door. Then he removed his leather jacket and hung it in the closet. Victor approached the living room but stopped just short of the step. He gazed around with the same bewilderment he showed last year. "Make sure you put all those boxes away. And put a timer on that damn thing. I don't want it shining all night."

"Of course not," Chris said.

"What was that?" Victor said.

"We will," Janey said.

Chris looked at her and raised his left eyebrow. Her lying, it seemed, knew no bounds.

Victor retrieved his fast-food cup and headed for his study. The keys jingled, the handle turned, the door slammed.

Chris watched Janey as she stared intently into the foyer. Her smile slowly spread. He smiled, too. The tree had passed its first major test.

"It was the light," Janey said. "You know what it stands for."

"Logic," Chris said.

"Faith."

"Proof."

"Belief."

"Not in my village," Chris said.

"It's not yours. She created it."

"She only lives there. I let her in my story."

"Our story!"

Chris saw that her face was growing hard, that she was digging in. "C'mon, Janey, let's not ruin things. No lectures from me, no sermons from you. Let's just let the story do its thing."

"Well? It's just a thought," she said, turning down her emotions. "You should keep it in mind. I am the Way and the Truth and the—"

"Yeah-yeah, I remember how it goes." How could he not? Wisely focusing on the visual, Janey had placed a cross from his mother's casket and a Europeanized portrait of Christ the Savior in Chris' bedroom shortly after the assault.

Janey gazed at the glowing tree. "Good, you should. It's what this holiday is really all about."

"The Light?" Chris said. She had trapped herself in another famous Janey-ism. "It's not the Light, it's the Life."

"And the birth of it." She faced him, stuck out her tongue, then smiled.

"You never can admit when you're wrong, can you?"

"I got you to think about it, didn't I? That's all that matters."

"Yeah, sure. Let's finish cleaning up. You get the vacuum—as I know you're just itching to do—and I'll get the heck out of your way. Then we need to work on your letter to Saint Nicholas." Sandra had instilled that tradition, too. (*No Santa Claus allowed, even though they really are the same person—just ask the Dutch.*) Last year at this same time, because she had access to a car, Katie had helped him fulfill that list. Chris wondered if she would appear at his door this year. He could call her, of course, but he feared the response. Fear often kept him from action.

"I've already finished the list, thank you," Janey said.

"Naturally. Can I see it?"

"What for?"

"Maybe I want to add something."

"You do not." She looked past him as something caught her attention. Sadness swept over her face.

Frowning, Chris turned and looked out the darkened window. He did see something—some *things*—fluttering down.

"The angels...they're crying," Janey said. She ran into the foyer.

"Angels? What, again? No—Janey, wait!"

Janey was already outside by the time he reached the doorway. Standing in the middle of the slushy lawn, illuminated by the tree's light, Janey spun 'round and 'round with her arms extended from her sides. "Look, I'm the music box angel."

"Yeah? Where's your purple kugel, oh keeper of the sacred orb?"

"Oopsie, must have lost it. And it's not purple, it's amethyst."

"Not in my story."

"*Our* story." Janey tipped her head back and caught on her tongue one of the fat snowflakes that drifted down from the icy moonlit sky.

"I hate to remind you again, little girl," Chris said, "but you have to die before you can be an angel. And if I remember all the old junk correctly, human spirits can't become angels. Angels are created spirits. Never had bodies. Our story is breaking the rules."

Janey kept twirling.

Her momentary silence told him she was listening, but not happy with his words. "Don't get mad at me," Chris said. "I didn't write the rules. You'll have to file a complaint with the home office."

"See what you're doing?" she said. Her darting tongue caught another flake. "They can't stop crying."

Chris folded his arms and leaned against the doorjamb. "Really. And why is that?"

"Because you won't believe in them."

"Of course, it's my fault."

"I *know*."

"Sorry, I'm not giving in. You and your kind are frozen out of my world until further notice."

"It's not your world and, yes, you will be sorry."

"Hey, you've got your realm and I've got mine. Coexistence. Side by side." As he now saw it. He could sense that Janey was mistaking his confession for banter. She didn't fully comprehend what he was telling her, how he had broken a promise, or the specifics of that betrayal, but that was okay. He was still the man of reason. And he had to stick to his principles, express his true feelings, and rewrite the wrongs. He was certain that she would understand and forgive him if, by chance, she discovered the changes. At least the angels were still there. But he didn't see how that scene would happen, as long as she didn't read his diary. That he could not allow.

"I'll get you to change back, you'll see."

Chris shook his head, but smiled. It warmed his heart to see that she was feeling so well this special night. "You're gonna get dizzy."

"You should try this," Janey said as she continued to spin.

"I don't think so. You know how much I hate shoveling the stuff. If I had my way—"

"But the snowflakes are blessed. They will heal your soul, and help you see the light. When it is time, you *will* see the light. And I will be there for you."

Again with "the light." Just can't admit it. "I see perfectly, thank you. In fact, I see someone who's gonna fall down if she doesn't stop."

Janey ignored him and, though wobbly, kept on spinning.

"You know, I'd really be hearing it about now if I were the one out there without my coat and hat and mittens."

"But you're not," she said before giggling.

And then she tumbled to the ground.

Janey lay motionless on her back, her eyes closed. He couldn't see her breath.

"Janey?" Chris said. He pulled away from the doorjamb.

She did not respond.

"Janey!" He ran up to her.

Janey's arms and legs began moving as if she were doing jumping jacks. "See, you believed me. My plan is starting to work." And then it came, to remind him just how big of a dope he was: Janey's head-tipped, full-throated, mouth-wide-open laugh that sounded more like the jovial Victor when he was really drunk. The laugh was so loud and obnoxious, it seemed to rattle the neighborhood. And then the best part: when all of oxygen in her lungs used to expel those laughs had been squeezed out, she drew in a long, high-pitched wheeze. She sounded so cartoonish, so unbefitting of her angelic image, the laugh made her all the more human and charming.

But there was no way he was going to let her know this—not now. "Not funny, Janey."

"So guess who I am now?" The snow angel took shape.

"You...are...relentless!"

"It's my job."

"Yeah, well, I'm just about ready to fire you. Who do I see about that?"

"Sorry, can't do it. We have the pact." She stopped, sat up, then turned around to admire her work, the clumps of wet snow dropping one by one from the back of her sweater.

"Aren't you ever gonna give me a break with this angel stuff? That would be the greatest Christmas present ever."

"Not until you believe again and I save you."

"It's too late."

"No, it's not. It never is."

"More divine laws from Heaven?"

"Uh-huh!"

Chris extended his right hand. "Enough." Janey reached up and he pulled her from the slushy lawn. Then he brushed the snow from her clothes.

"Thank you," she said.

"You're welcome." She stared at their glorious tree shining in the bay window. "Look—isn't it pretty?"

"It sure is." Chris rested his left arm across her shoulders, and gave her a slight hug, which, because he rarely did it, felt weird but good. "Merry Christmas, Janey."

She turned and slipped her arms around his waist, pulled herself close, and looked up at him with those great, round, Sandra-hazel eyes. "It will be the best ever. You'll see."

Tomorrow at midnight, Janey. That's when we'll know for sure.

Chapter Eight

The Wish List

Nov 28. Back to my favorite topic—that famous equation—because Janey talked about it yesterday. (Well, sort of. She wants me to "see the light"—har har, science humor!) The equation is so small and simple, but so powerful, it keeps bugging me. Everyone thinks it's just for nerdy scientists to help them prove their whacko theories. But it's not. It's the key to the whole thing: matter is energy and energy is matter. Each can change into the other. Each IS the other. That's all there is in the universe. Nothing more, nothing less. (This equation should have made the Holy Book. On second thought, I guess it did—by accident. What did they know back then?) So every "thing" in the universe is "frozen" energy, including me. It just has a different formula that arranges the stuff. (Chris = light x Sandra + Victor? Sorry, can't do math.)

Light is energy. So it too can change into matter. Light is the fastest thing in the universe. Nothing can go faster, not even me (more humor!). But light can be slowed down. It can even be stopped and examined. Light is made of particles. It can carry information. Whoa! So if you freeze pure light, what does it look like? What gives energy matter and mass? I'm trying to picture this all the time, but it's so hard to do.

***Footnote: In case anyone ever reads this junk (that means you, Janey), every time you see a word underlined, it means it's a stupid word. And since I haven't explained that before, this is what makes me mad about all those words: they're just part of a cover-up, to make me shut up and run with the herd. But, hey, you can't just say, "It's light. Accept it and move on." What in Hell does light mean? What about the particles? What are they made of? And what are the particles that make the particles made of? Can they become matter? How? The connections keep going deeper, down and down, smaller and smaller, faster and faster. Where does it end? Does it ever end? If I could make myself small enough to be in one of those particles, what would the night sky look like? (I would need a sky. After all, I'm human.)

What about the other way? What is the universe? Is it just a particle? Is it part of something? Up and up and up—bigger and bigger, slower and slower. Does it ever stop? If I were big enough so I could pinch the universe *between my fingers, could I see my house? (Har har again!) Or would things move way too fast and be too small to see? And what would my night sky look like?*

So that brings me to this question, and I'm serious: Why isn't <u>dead</u> like light?

Chris lifted his dip pen from the diary and gave his pulsing mind a respite. Such intense and wild thinking about difficult subjects often made his head hurt. He closed his aching eyes and rubbed his temples, recalling how perilous that action once was. Then he looked out the window at Dr. Samuel's house, wondering, beckoning. A thin layer of snow covered the steep roof, but he could still see the outline of each slate shingle. A trail of smoke from one of many copper chimney pots rose slowly in the crisp blue sky. The Tudor was one of Sandra's favorite art subjects. Many variations existed in her collection. She often embellished the doctor's home, making it much larger and more elaborate than it already was. "He deserved it," she liked to say. Because of the around-the-clock care he extended to them after Sandra had been diagnosed with breast cancer, Chris and Janey gladly included him in their picture-world fantasy, further indulging him with servants. In that fantasy, Janey suggested pairing Sandra up with Dr. Sam, whose real-world wife had divorced him (ran away with the "lawn boy," Victor likes to tell us, though Katie never mentioned it) before Victor moved them to the Lone Oak community. But Chris was against this arrangement, for selfish reasons. That sound union made his dream-pairing with Katie unthinkable. He had never written any specific role for her in the story, other than hoping for what she once was. But his anger toward her betrayal was still there, and it was always tempting.

Chris thought he heard the doorbell ring, and he felt an impossible hope rising in his chest. He waited anxiously to hear it again. When the chiming repeated, Chris eagerly cast aside all doubt. He sprung from the bed and stuffed the diary under the mattress. Then he snatched the two folded pieces of paper on his dresser and bolted from his room. He ran past Janey's bedroom. Her door was open. He stopped for a second and peered into this unabashed shrine to all things soft and frilly and "cute," and saw her in Auntie Monica's hand-me-down canopy bed with her back to him, sleeping soundly beneath the pink daisy comforter. Perfect. He slowly closed the door, then flew down the foyer staircase, nearly stumbling. He paused to catch his breath, then quickly ran his hand through his hair. But his heart was still beating furiously. No one on this Earth had such power over him, could make him this nervous and crazy. Was she really here? He could barely stand the suspense. Chris gripped the handle and pulled the door open. A cold blast struck him, and swirled about.

With the sunlight at her back, a young woman stood in the doorway, motionless. The light was piercing, and he had trouble seeing her face. Then his eyesight adjusted as the wind died, and Chris—now feeling his joy die with those winds—could tell that Katie, too, seemed surprised that they were staring at each other. Even worse, Chris realized with much agony just how long it had been since they had seen each other. Katie looked different. She was taller than he remembered. And the young teen face that had occupied his endless fantasies had transformed. With hardly a hint of makeup, her lips were nonetheless fuller, her long-lashed blue eyes were larger, and her high, pronounced cheek bones and perfect skin gave her the intimidating look of a young and handsome woman. Yeah, she was not a lie. Way beyond fake, phony "girlie" pretty, and confident of those strong looks—and gently stepping away from him into her most beautiful and healthy years, knowing just as her father did that she could have the world, or whatever shiny parts she found pleasing. She even dressed like an adult from that rich world where she dwelled, just across their bottomless backyard void. Katie wore high, laced black boots and a long, shimmering white coat with soft white scarf wrapped around a fur collar as fluffy as new-fallen snow. Her hands were tucked into a large white muff. She stared down at him, and Chris suddenly felt like a child again, hopelessly inadequate and poor and foolish. Her shock confirmed his fears.
    Though Katie had been their loyal and ever-smiling babysitter, and never encouraged any of his budding romantic notions, Chris nevertheless had—because of her loving and gentle ways, which brought welcome relief and joy into his troubled existence—made the unfortunate decision to elevate her to sacred status. The perfect being, one of a kind, never to come along again. And he slowly intertwined fact and fantasy about her until she became an obsession. He recalled the pure thrill of seeing her face for the first time, when she stepped so unsuspecting through this guarded door of their prison, eager to fulfill Sandra's call for help—and how that moment forever changed his world for better and worse. Now he was paying dearly for that error.
    Katie may have sensed his fragile ego was crumbling, for she quickly summoned a bright, full smile with those perfect teeth. "Christopher," she said with her always surprising, made-to-order sultry tone, "how are you? I haven't seen you in ages, have I? May I come in?"
    Chris stepped aside. He never liked the way she called him so formally by his formal first name. Even with that wonderfully odd tone, both innocent and alluring, it sounded so...formal. And respectful. Like when old people talked to each other in church, fearing the lightning bolts from heaven, or when babysitters talked to their... He knew where that tone came from. Chris wanted her to think of him in a much more friendly way. Still,

his heart fluttered wildly as he stared at her so intently, and he could not look away even if he wanted to. It was hard to believe that she was finally here. "Yeah," he said, trying not to sound excited. Already, he worried about what to say, how to act, and could feel his throat tightening. Could she see him blushing? "Sure." How he hated his boyish tone, made worse by the throat tightening, which made him blush even more.

Once Katie entered the foyer, Chris shut the door, then stood in the warm, soft glow of her benevolent presence, his embarrassment cooling. This was one angel allowed into his protected, logical world at any time. Special dispensation granted, no doubt about it.

Katie removed the hand muff and set it on the foyer table. "You know me—always with the cold hands," she said. "But you know the old saying about that. I can't stay long, but I wanted to stop in and say hello. It's so good to see you. You're getting so tall and muscular—such a handsome young man. I hardly recognized you."

Having just received a compliment uttered in the sincere but unconvincing manner of his Auntie Monika, Chris suddenly wished—as always—that he were taller and more muscular and older than his present puny state. "Yeah," he said.

"I understand that you made the...football team?"

He was thrilled that she knew, that she found it impressive. "Yeah, I did."

"And the telescope?"

Sudden deflation. "Yeah?"

"Getting bored with it?"

Now, disappointment. "No, I've been out there." She hadn't noticed him standing in the dark like the lovesick fool that he was.

"That's good, I'm glad to hear that. I'll come out the next time I see you there, I promise. Then you can show me that star again—you know, the closest one to Earth."

Sudden encouragement. "You mean the Sun?"

"The Sun? Oh, yes, I suppose that's right. Of course." She covered her mouth and laughed. "I meant the next-closest star—what was it you called it? Alpha something..."

"Alpha Centauri?"

"Yes, that's the one."

"Actually, Proxima Centauri is closer. But we can't see either one from here. I think it was Sirius that we were looking at. In winter, it's the brightest star in the night sky—in the Winter Circle, just above the southern horizon."

"Yes, that was it—wasn't it? The brightest."

Chris suddenly felt stupid for lecturing her like some nerd, and he feared to say anything else.

Katie seemed to sense his embarrassment, and grabbed his arm with excitement. "Yes, I recall now. You told me the name, and I said, 'Are you serious?' And you laughed at my pathetic little joke. Well, that's what I get for trying to be smart about things my father and you care about. Whichever star you choose is fine with me."

Translation? You're still a nerd.

Katie removed her grasp, but he could still feel her electric touch, as if his skin had swelled—yet another reminder of the amazing power this young woman always had over him, one that he wanted to feel again and again, and never give up. Chris grinned and nodded, but he wondered why he never had enough sense to keep his mouth shut regarding things people didn't care about. Of course, it didn't matter, really. With this brief but eye-opening encounter, Chris realized that he would never be with her. And he conceded that his fantasies about her—like all the rest of them—had been silly, childish, and unrealistic. That was glaringly obvious to him. Besides being older and rich—something he could never overcome—Katie seemed happy and content with life. Sure, she was a "herd-running pagan" (as Matt, despite his radical religious views, liked to call all public-schoolers who reveled in its social activities). But those designations, combined with her beauty and popularity, which went hand-in-hand, gave her distinct advantages and benefits. She would—Hell, she already was having a different teen life than he ever would, going to all kinds of sporting events, parties, and dances, and thinking they were fun. Then one day, if he took no action, she'd be off to college and he'd never see her again, leaving him behind to fight his private boyhood wars. But this visit did help her cause. He decided to take more mental notes before he took up the pen.

"So how's your father?" she said cautiously.

Her mood turned gloomy, and the abruptness startled him. "He's still around."

"And Janey?"

"She's upstairs sleeping. Want me to get her?"

"No, no, leave her be. But my dad wants to see her."

Chris frowned. "About what?"

"She hasn't been to his office in a while—and neither have you."

"That's Victor's fault."

"I know, and I'm not blaming you. But you should make it a habit."

"What can I do? He won't take her."

"My father's always been there for you, hasn't he?"

"Yeah."

"You don't need to wait for Victor to do anything. Just bring her over to our house. In fact, you should do it today. He's home. He can take a look at her there."

"Well, I can get her now, if you want."

"Wait till she awakens." Katie smiled. "Now...you have something for me, I believe?"

"Oh...right." Chris handed her a copy of Janey's wish list, then stuffed his into his back pocket.

Katie unfolded the piece of paper. "Not much here again, I see."

"She knows not to expect much."

"But she still believes?" Katie said softly, as if Janey were standing here. Chris nodded.

"That's good, too."

Chris marveled at how her views reflected Sandra's—and Janey's, too. And though he no longer agreed with them, it gave him comfort to hear them. Katie had spent much time with Sandra as she taught his mother how to sketch and paint. With Katie's urging, they often discussed religion. Towards the end, Katie even attended church with them. Dr. Samuel tolerated the whole conversion process. But since he was a "man of science," they could tell he wasn't pleased.

Katie glanced at the list once more. Her forehead crinkled. "She wants you to sing?"

"Yeah."

The ends of her mouth began to curl up, but thankfully she did not laugh. "This is a special gift to her?"

"I guess."

"Are you going to do it?"

"I don't know. I might."

"I think you will."

"Yeah, probably. A Christmas song."

"Yes, on Christmas. I know you will—I just do." Katie smiled as her eyes returned to the list. Then she frowned. "It says here that she also wants you to cry."

"Yeah. I can tell you right now, I never, ever wanna have to do that."

"Not manly enough?"

"There's a little more to it. Something about breaking a spell."

"A spell," she said flatly.

"It's nothing, really. There is no spell."

She nodded. "You seem to be the main theme of her list."

"It's just part of her plan to save my wicked soul." Chris thought his clever, adult-sounding response would impress her and draw some laughter. But Katie just stared at him for a moment, looking oddly worried. "What's this next item? A...a vacuum cleaner?"

"Yeah, she hates dust bunnies. The vacuum we have is getting old. Just kinda pushes the dirt around."

"But it's Christmas. She's just a young girl!" Katie put her hand to her mouth. She looked as if she were about to cry. "I'm sorry, I keep forgetting." Then her eyes brightened as she read another item. "Horseshoes?"

"Yeah, for protection. It's a long story—something my mother told us. She shouldn't have, really. It just stuck in Janey's head." He intentionally left out the "Mine, too" part.

Katie appeared worried again, but seemed to understand. "What are we going to do about this?"

"I'll find stuff in the storeroom."

"The storeroom?"

"Yeah. Victor used to have horseshoe pits at our other house. I'm sure all that stuff is packed away. There's lots of old stuff down there, especially in the trunk. Real old. But there's some good stuff, too. I don't know what you call them. Heirlooms, maybe, I guess. I wrapped some up for her last year. Marked them From St. Nicholas. She really seemed to like them. Actually, she thought my mom left them under the tree for her. So I'm gonna do that again."

"The storeroom, yes—yes, I know." Tears stood in her eyes. "Oh, Chris, that's so sweet." She brought her hand to her trembling lips.

The car horn sounded.

Still visibly shaken, Katie withdrew a coin purse from her pocket, loosened the delicate drawstrings, and stuffed the list into the purse. Then she grabbed the hand muff and turned quickly to open the door. "I'm sorry, I have to go," she said as the cold air seized him. "Don't forget to bring her over later, okay? I'm going to bring her something, too." She headed out.

His heart thumped in his chest, but in a bad, aching way, tearing itself apart. She was leaving him, again. "Sure. Hey, wait, I didn't mean to—"

Katie turned to face him and wiped her tears. "I miss you two, do you know that? I wish I could be here more. But I have a different life now. So do you. I know you understand this."

The car horn sounded once more.

Chris was stunned. Her words punched a hole in the gloom. It felt strange and wonderful to actually hear her talk so lovingly about them, to know that she still thought of them that way, that he still mattered, even with the distractions, even though she was now with him.

"I know what you're going through. Every bit of it. I really do. And I'm so, so sorry that she's not here to help you." Katie touched him on the cheek. "You take care, okay? Don't ever hesitate to call me, for whatever reason. I promise I'll see you soon."

Chris wanted to say those words he longed to say to her but never did, but as usual, his emotions jammed, and he kept coldly silent. With the mix of polar-opposite emotions pulling at him, ripping him in two, Chris quickly brought his left hand to his face and pressed hard to capture the tear she left there. Then he stood in the doorway and the biting air and watched Katie as she climbed into the passenger side of the red antique sports car parked in the driveway, lined earlier with the candle bags. His gaze switched to the grinning, masculine face at the wheel, and he felt his jaw tighten. She waved before the car backed from the driveway. Then the car accelerated with a squeal, and she was gone, racing into another story separate from his.

Don't leave me—not again. Chris heard the chiming of his heart as it shattered like glass.

The hammering in his ears returned, as did the pressure in his chest. His throat tightened, and his eyes felt as if they were sinking into his head. What to do about her teardrop? It was her, on his cheek. If he removed his hand, the tear might disintegrate, and the precious gift would be lost. Still, he couldn't stand here for an eternity with his hand pressed to his face. He was certain the neighborhood had already erupted in gossip. Resigned to fate, Chris carefully removed his left hand from his cheek. He held it out, chest-high, and turned it slightly perpendicular to the porch so he could examine his palm in the daylight. The teardrop had, indeed, disintegrated. Its remnants trickled down through a line in his palm. But when the stream reached the right edge of his hand, a dangling teardrop formed. It separated into a perfect orb that seemed to suspend itself in the air, glinting in the sun, reflecting his astonished face, before the teardrop fell toward the cold concrete slab. When it landed, the drop exploded like a starburst, and quickly froze into a crystal before evaporating. He blinked a few times, but not hard, just to make sure he was seeing clearly. Then Chris looked down the street once more. Already, he wondered when—or if—she would return.

And then Janey screamed.

Shocked from his trance, Chris slammed the door and dashed up the stairs to Janey's room. Wearing a long-sleeve pajama top with white and pink hearts, Janey was sitting up but with her back to him, pointing to the sun-splashed window framed by white lace curtains on the far wall alongside her canopy bed. "The bug, the bug," she said. "Kill it."

Chris' eyes brightened as he watched the small white insect flutter against the window. The deadliest of them all. But it was supposed to attack Victor, not Janey. More fantasy boldly leaking out, becoming real as the hour drew near? *No!* Keeping his eyes focused on the window, Chris quickly skirted the bed. He felt his fear rising, but he wasn't going to admit it aloud. Besides, for Janey's sake, and his, sanity had to be maintained. "C'mon, Janey, it's just a moth, not the butterfly."

"No, it's not."

"That was just a story."

"I don't care—kill it!"

Chris held his hand out, watching intently as the moth fluttered around. When it stopped, Chris slammed his cupped hand over it, making sure his palm did not squash it, giving it the power it craved. Then as he felt the insect's wings beating furiously, he slowly closed his fingers around the dreaded thing until it could only squirm. "There, no more moth," Chris said. He turned away from the window so he did not have to face her.

"This isn't time for a bug rescue. Did you kill it?"

Chris headed for the door, and wondered where he could release it. Had to release it, because if he didn't and gave in...

"Let me see," Janey said.

"Will you relax? I'm just going to flush it down the toilet."

"Let me see."

"Janey—" Chris turned to lecture her about her mistrust. But when he did, he saw the thick trail of dark red blood that ran from her nose and mouth, and branched out down the side of her face, matting her hair. And then he saw the dark red stain that covered nearly half of her white down pillow. A loud boom exploded in his ear like a canon shot, and with the storm of emotion howling in his head, the glowing black hole appeared before him. It was swirling and flashing, gobbling up the room. He closed his eyes briefly, hoping Janey's image would reset to normal. But seconds later, when he realized that nothing had changed, he trembled. Something was happening. But not the unworldly terror he feared. "Janey?"

With her mouth open and her brow furrowed, Janey glanced down to look for the thing she seemed to suspect was crawling on her. Suddenly, her head snapped to the left. And her eyes locked onto the ghastly pillow. When Janey returned her gaze to him, those eyes were lit with a horror she had never, ever displayed, telling him everything. Then she ran her fingers through her matted hair and stared at her bloodstained fingertips.

Chris closed his eyes again, and felt the thing in his hand transforming, no longer squirming, now the sting of its icy crystals. Then he gazed at Janey, bleeding so abnormally before him. *What? What?* While the fire crawled across his face and his ears began to ring, he thought of Epiphany, heartless Epiphany. Epiphany all over again. A voice he had heard only once before shouted outside of his mind: *What have you been doing? This is how you face your fears? You know what you did to her!*

83

The wild and beautiful fantasy, which he had painstakingly assembled all these years to tap into its power, to give him power so he could cope and not fail, popped into his mind all at once. A kaleidoscope of images that suddenly exploded, scattering like buckshot into the edges of the swirling, flashing blackness—everything, all of it. When the ringing subsided, it left an unsettling calm. Just like that, it was over, the power gone again, his mind clear and focused once more as he stood there in his burning shame. He could conjure nothing, only Janey, bleeding Janey—and then, bleeding Sandra.

The nightmare from which he could not awake.

They were still in it.

"Oh, Janey, no—no," he said, as if the words would make the nightmare go away. But when it didn't, Chris tightened his fist, and crushed the moth.

Chapter Nine

Treatment

After her funeral, Chris often walked his final days at St. Boniface like a zombie. In the crowded halls, his classmates pushed past him, desperately trying to get seated in class before the bell rang. He didn't care about bells, or the punishment doled out for not being on time. He felt as if he were pressed against the inside a drifting bubble, occasionally knocked about as the thundering herd rushed below, each member trying to sit next to the one he or she loved. But from that bubble, he saw past his youthful dreams of acceptance and adoration, past the older visions of success and empire that his father often boasted about, convinced it would all come true—all the way to the dark clouds gathering in the distance, no longer feeling eternal, or blissfully ignorant of their ultimate fate. Where there would not be another dawn for her or him, and they would no longer walk the Earth, or remember a thing, or have anything extraordinary—even magical—happen that would reveal an amazing answer to the biggest question of all.

And so now, this view of life remained as he looked upon Janey.

She sat in the reclined lounge chair and stared at the ceiling-mounted television as if it weren't there. A warmed blanket covered most of her body, except her right arm, which lay palm up atop the armrest. The dispensing gizmo, attached to the pole from which the clear chemo bag hung, towered over her. The machine made a strange grunting sound with every successful drip, as if happy to be in control.

Chris sat motionless next to her on a metal folding chair, pretending that he cared what was on the news channel as if nothing were wrong, afraid to emit any negative energy that might betray the panic coursing furiously within. He was stunned by the speed with which the peaceful day had turned into a tragedy. They both were. Neither had expected, or wanted, to see this room again.

But the events earlier in the day forever changed what was supposed to be their best Christmas ever.

Once Chris got the nose and gum bleeding under control, he called Doctor Samuel, who rushed over to the house. With a calm but concerned demeanor, the doctor took her temperature. Then he examined Janey as if he were at the grocery store, inspecting a tomato—then her teeth, as if she were a horse. Chris knew why the doc was acting so. But it still irked him. All the while, the doctor looked way too concerned for a man inspecting produce and livestock. Finally, Dr. Samuel asked her questions about breathing, stamina, and pain. Afterwards, he left the bedroom to make a phone call. Upon returning, he announced that they were going for a "ride" in an ambulance, just as a "precaution." But they had been through these precautionary trips before. They knew Janey's situation was serious. Ambulance rides were "outrageous," as Victor had often complained. But, out of legal ramifications, even he had agreed to them. So what did the doctor suspect? They were too afraid to ask. "Where's Victor?" the doctor also had inquired, but he seemed to know the answer.

Once at the hospital, blood was drawn. Then it was on to a sterile room filled with stainless steel tables and trays, hanging lights, tubes and wires, and a lot of strange machines that beeped and gurgled and buzzed. By now, Janey was in a hospital gown. Somewhere in the whirl, Chris discovered that Victor had consented over the phone to the next procedure, in which Chris participated.

Janey lay face down on a table. Chris held her hand. A needle was inserted as if it were a corkscrew into her pelvic bone to extract the marrow. "Ow-ie" was all she said. But she nearly crushed his hand. He wanted to smack the doctor for causing her such pain.

Then suddenly, they were whisked into a sterile common area, its rooms separated by curtains. There, they looked at each other in confused silence as they listened to all the other medical dramas around them, wondering when definitive news would come. While they waited, some well-intentioned nurse poked her head in and happily assured them that Victor was on his way to provide support and comfort.

And then Dr. Samuel entered into the room, suddenly there, in all his greatness. He always had a professional intensity about him that Victor could never achieve: straight, jet black hair trimmed and parted neatly on the right, fine clothing clean and pressed, black shoes polished. He just reeked of power and confidence. He knew what he wanted out of life, had the intelligence and temperament to get it, and that "it" would be enduringly satisfying. But accompanying that power was a prevalent sadness that Chris couldn't fully understand. Did he miss Sandra more than Chris ever knew? Was he, too, dealing with bad memories of this place? The doctor seemed oddly flustered, and apologized for not remembering when human biology was taught in school. Then he told Janey about her blood. "Some of your white cells aren't normal," he had said. "And when you have a lot of white cells that aren't normal, it can make you real tired. Not enough red cells, you see. But, we can start fixing this—

today. Typically, leukemia patients have an eighty percent chance of beating this, Janey—eighty percent. That's a real good number." But Chris saw that same doubt in the doctor's eyes that he displayed when giving his required pep talks while Sandra was dying. There was more talk of using part of the insurance money to pay for the chemo. Dr. Samuel told them that Victor had already tried to secure control of these emergency funds, but Pommerance refused. Chris suspected that the doctor had already decided to pay for everything, to calm Victor and keep things moving forward. Finally, a nurse advocate took over and gave a hasty, smiley-faced child's version of chemo orientation before Janey landed in the reclining chair.

Now Chris wanted desperately to say just the right words that would make her smile, if only for a moment. But the anger and the guilt and the gnawing questions kept him silent. Leukemia? Where did this come from? And then suddenly, miraculously, the perfect words welled up from his heart. "I'd switch places with you in an instant if I could," he said.

Janey looked at him with big, shiny eyes. He knew she wanted to say something sassy and clever to comfort him. But the extraordinary events of the day inhibited their typical banter. She couldn't even smile. Instead, she returned her empty gaze to the television.

Feeling helpless, Chris looked around the room. This certainly was no place for a young girl. With its row of tightly packed lounge chairs that rimmed its windowless perimeter, the chemo room looked like some morbid salon, all decorated for Christmas. Most of the patients were old. Some were bald. Others were bald and ashen. Many would beat the odds, and receive applause—and a new life—for their efforts. But Chris could tell which patients wouldn't be around much longer. He wondered which camp Janey was in.

∽

They sat there for hours as each clear plastic bag slowly collapsed and shriveled, its contents draining through the IV and into Janey's body. When that "protocol" finally ended (*doctors like words that lie, too*), the nurse stopped by with a new round of warmed blankets and a large needle-less syringe filled with a pink liquid, which she attached to the IV. Then she put on a smile and talked pleasantly to Janey as she slowly pushed the plunger. But Chris sensed a hint of apology from her as well. He knew this stuff would make Janey nauseous, and eventually cause her hair to fall out in clumps.

The hair thing was the next big hurdle. Sandra had experienced it, too. She had claimed that it would be "no big deal" when it happened. But when it did, her world crumbled—reminded constantly afterward, every time she looked into the mirror, that something was terribly wrong, that she was battling for her life. With the powerful drugs Janey was receiving, the blessed event would take a week or so to occur.

When the nurse finished injecting the drug, she gave them a friendly reminder about the next chemo session a week from this day. Janey received about a half hour to "rest." Then Victor made a sudden appearance.

"Poor kiddo," he said as he stroked Janey's head with those busted, crunching fingers. "That wasn't so bad, was it? You're a strong one, aren't you? No surprise there. Sam thinks you'll tolerate this well. Better than your mom, huh?" He was singing a joyous opera.

"Sam," Chris thought. Like now they're best buds. It's not gonna work.

Janey squirmed and kept silent.

"Can we go?" Chris said. Victor was always happy when someone else paid the bills.

Victor looked at Chris as if he were in a bar and wanted to fight. "Yeah, sure, no problem. One big happy family."

⁂

Chris didn't say much to Janey on the way home—just an occasional check on her health status. She would nod or shake her head, but still refused to speak. Otherwise, Janey slept most of the time. Victor kept quiet, too. But the well-oiled wheels inside his seething brain seemed to be turning fast in much different directions as he plotted a new and devious course.

Once they arrived at the house, Chris helped Janey into fresh pajamas and put her to bed, linens already changed. When he attempted to turn off the light on her nightstand, Janey finally spoke: "Leave it on, please."

He knew where that came from. "Okay," Chris said, encouraged by her tone. "Anything else? Some grammies, maybe?"

Janey rolled onto her back and looked at him. In a rare moment of weakness, tossing Heaven aside, she said: "I want to stay here with you."

Her words pierced his heart and burned onto his brain, and Chris saw the fear in her eyes. Chris nodded rapidly, repeatedly, and he did all he could to keep his tears from flowing. As usual, his better emotions fizzled, and the words got stuck in his throat. "Yeah...yeah, okay. Yeah. Good night, Janey. Pleasant dreams." His declaration of worthlessness—even his own words disgusted him. So he did something he had never done before: he bent down and kissed her on the cheek. Her fragile smile told him he should have done this long ago.

When Janey closed her eyes to say her prayers, Chris slipped from the room, carefully shutting the door behind him. He closed his eyes and sighed, and it became hard to breathe. It really was happening again. Then he saw Victor standing in the darkened foyer, the glow of the hated Christmas tree illuminating his backside. Victor reached up with a clenched fist, then beckoned Chris with the repeated curl of a thick forefinger. Chris descended the stairs and followed his father into the forbidden den, its wooden shelving crammed with trophies, past and present. Victor closed the door and poured himself a drink at the wet bar. Apprehensive, Chris plopped down in the shabby upholstered chair opposite his father's desk.

"Your sister's very sick," Victor said. He eased himself into his high-backed vinyl chair.

"Yeah, I know."

Victor took a sip of his drink, ice cubes clinking. "No, I don't think you do."

Chris tried to gauge his father's odd mood. Was he happy? Was he sad? Was he worrying again about what all this would cost? Through it all, money still didn't seem to be an issue, as it had with Sandra's illness, verifying Chris' theory about Dr. Samuel's benevolence. So what was the point of this meeting?

"Sam thinks she might have A-L-L," Victor said. "Acute lymphocytic leukemia. Know what acute means?"

"No."

"It means she's in deep shit. Her illness is in a severe stage—and it's rapidly progressing."

"And whose fault is that?"

"Not mine, damn you," he said, coolly. "I'm not taking the blame for this." He took another sip. "I knew you would get around to that. You're always blaming other people for bad shit. Where in Hell does that come from, huh? Never mind. That's why we're having this little chat. If you want to blame someone, blame your mother."

Chris rolled his eyes. "I don't believe this."

"No? Would you believe Sam, then?"

Chris frowned.

"Yeah, he's the one who gave me the news. I know he fucked up—fucked up big time. Should have been watching for this. Could sue the son-of-a-bitch, I suppose. We'll see. Might be hard to do. And you know how much I love getting in bed with those parasites. Depends on what happens to your sister. I'll let him dig his grave for now." He paused as those thick dark brows lowered and his narrowed eyes flared. "Shouldn't even be her doctor. Specializes in adults. But that's your fault. You called him. Don't ever pull that crap again."

"She doesn't want anyone else," Chris said.

"Yeah, well...we'll see about that." Then his expression softened, as if pleasant thoughts appeared. "Anyway, he thinks it may be genetic. Don't ask me how. I don't get all that bullshit. He was babbling on and on about subtypes, translocation, and—oh, yeah—a specific gene modification. Like I know what in Hell that means. You know how he is. He's your buddy. But he says he's going to look into it." Victor laughed, though it sounded threatening. "A little late for that. You see, little girls don't get leukemia from walking to school without a hat. Nine times out of ten, it comes from a parent—something like that. Your mom's the one with the cancer. She probably got it from someone on her side. And now she's passed it on to Janey. What do you think of that, huh? Some Christmas present."

"You make me sick."

Victor laughed again in his aggressive way. "Oh, yeah, I know—I'm such a meanie. Don't you just wish I'd shrivel up and blow away? I know what you two think of me. I hear you talking. I remember everything. But you know what? I don't care. You have a roof over your head. I'm still paying the bills. You'd be nothing without me." He sounded remarkably in control and confident—too confident, for Victor.

"You want her to die, don't you?" Chris said.

"You're nuts."

"You'd get all her money, wouldn't you?"

"Your mother didn't see this coming, did she? Serves her right." He took a congratulatory sip. But then his eyes glazed over, and his expression hardened. "First she robs me blind and then she gives it all to you. I'm her goddamn husband. I put up with her crap all those years. Why shouldn't I get something out of it? Why shouldn't I get it all? Christ, she even stuck me with that lousy burial tab."

"She paid for that."

"With my money!"

Feeling the heat building across the back of his head, and the urge to kill, Chris sprung from the chair and started out.

"Keep this conversation to yourself," Victor said. "She's got enough worries. You'll only make things worse, like last time. Then you'll have another death on your hands."

Chris slammed the door behind him, then stopped. The anger—there was so much of it coursing through his veins, he could hear it rushing past his eardrums, building intense pressure in his chest and head, hammering in his ears, sparkling in his eyes. He grew light-headed and weak, and the hallway shifted around wildly, appearing randomly before him like framed pictures, a movie without cohesion. Chris closed his eyes and took some deep breaths to stop the shifting and quiet the growing nausea, then he slowly ascended the stairs and entered his room. Jamming his hand beneath the mattress, he gripped the diary and yanked it free. Now he stared at the title, and snarled. *The Book of Everything, or the book of nothing? Happy thoughts, and childish stories. Yeah, yeah, I'm awake.* He whirled to his left and slam-dunked the accursed book into the bedside trash can.

Chris returned to the foyer and opened the closet's bi-fold doors. With his strength restored, he felt like a caged animal. He needed to run. He found his old black ski jacket and hat, and slipped them on. But the fire in his brain remained, as always, and made him think of things he, in happier times, wouldn't consider.

Once outside, Chris looked about the silent neighborhood, covered in white, noting all the lights and decorations on the houses and lawns, everything oblivious to their plight. Then he turned and looked at the tree in their window. He could not believe how the joy had been snatched from the glorious scene played out the previous night. *Best Christmas ever.* Deep down, he knew it was his fault. All of it was. It fit the pattern. He, like the doctor, should have seen this coming. Yesterday had been much too pleasant, had taken him much too high—like the roller coaster, and the bell curve—as he floated in the clouds of his childish fantasy. Now it was time to crash and burn in this heartless creation, as he was never really allowed to experience any lasting joy. It was the Curse, after all. Everyone he loved died, and everyone he hated thrived. Well, he had had enough of this unjust punishment. They had already been pushed to the limit—far too many times. And now this? *Sometimes, you gotta fight back.* An ultimatum needed to be shouted with rage and with clenched fists raised to the heavens. But not here, where the heartless and the gossips could hear him, or the spiteful Deity could hide behind thick clouds and pelt his face with ice. He needed to return to the source of all his torment...to the home base...to the scene of his crime.

Chris scooped up one of the unlit candle bags, then headed for St. Boniface.

Chapter Ten

The Church

Sometimes, when Victor got really drunk and convinced the unsuspecting that taking him to her place was a really good idea, he would lose his car keys. No matter. He had the ability to walk tremendous distances—sometimes all night, in all kinds of weather—and find his way home before the dawn. What he thought about (*if he thinks at all*) was a mystery to Chris. All he knew was that Sandra would willingly, without uttering a protest, take Victor back, with spare keys in hand, to the bar at which he had hatched his conspiracy so he could drive off to "work." This part, he never understood.

So Chris found it ironic, and a little unsettling, that he was walking late at night in the snow and sleet through the old Cottagewood neighborhood to St. Boniface. He had to, now that he decided to throw down the gauntlet. Another oasis of tranquility before the developers arrived, Cottagewood was sandwiched between Lone Oak and the church. In the summer, it was a leafy neighborhood with winding streets, a meandering stream, and small but well-crafted houses of stone, stucco, and wood that—because she always wanted to live there—helped inspire Sandra to paint her cozy cottages and dreamy villages. More than that, it had been the inner circle's stomping grounds, where Matt Cavanaugh lived, where they strolled idly and discussed all that mattered to them, and where they (mostly Matt) learned to flirt with older girls.

Chris trudged ever closer to the church, sloshing through the snow. The memories of happier times returned, and Chris was surprised how his journey through the sparkly, sleepy neighborhood calmed him, if only temporarily. But by the time he reached the stone arch bridge at the western edge of the neighborhood, the gloom and the anger returned, and he still found it maddening and impossible to believe how his sister was thrown, without much warning, into a battle for her life. A black nightmare had descended upon him again, enveloping him, and now he was trying his best to punch out of it.

St. Boniface was only a few blocks from the bridge, and when Chris arrived at the church's wide front steps, he gazed up at the looming, twin-tower façade. The giant rose window was shining from the light within, but Chris knew that, at this late hour, the massive front doors were locked. But there was a way in. Every current and former altar boy knew that the door behind the right bell tower remained unlatched so that the most-devout had permanent access to the warm but humbling environment within. It was the same door through which he and Matt and Larry entered during that fateful lunch hour last spring. He had not been back since his mandated confession.

    Chris skirted the tower and entered the courtyard and old graveyard that connected the church to the school. A shrine to the Blessed Virgin, covered by a white pergola laced with thick dried vines and attached to the church, stood in the courtyard's center. There, the parishioners crowded their candle bags before a manger scene, complete with real straw. Chris approached the manger, reached down to grab a candle from one of the many bags, then used it to light his own candle before adding the bag to the scene. He thought of Sandra and muttered a rusty, half-forgotten prayer that drifted away with his smoky breath. Then he slowly and reverently backed away until he reached the bell tower. Brushing the snow from his coat, Chris slipped into the small chapel in tower base, where Janey had been baptized. (*Janey calls it her private chapel, where its altar tomb became her gilded box.*) He pulled open an interior door and entered the main vestibule, lit by the many brass picture lights that lit the extensive art collection hanging within ornate frames on the plastered walls. Now, his attitude had changed with the warming temperature, and once again he felt rebellious. He had spent many hours with Sandra and Katie in the vestibule, studying the carefully selected Renaissance and Romantic-era reprints by Caspar David Friedrich (no relation, he was assured), Gustave Dore, Pieter Bruegel, and John Martin. Sandra did not intend to copy their style or subject matter, nor did Katie encourage it. But both admired each artist's ability to grab the viewer and instill a sense of awe, dread, and humility. These were qualities that did not go unnoticed by the old and fiery Irish pastor, Father O'Hara, who selected them for a dastardly purpose, or by Chris, who became enthralled by them. Chris wrote about each sketch or painting extensively in the book, and used them in the story, particularly Dore's *Lucifer, King of Hell* (selected "to inspire fear," Sandra had explained— what awaited them in the fiery mountain chamber of darkness), the *White Rose* ("to inspire hope"—the portal in and out of the former and nonexistent Heaven), and Bruegel's *The Little Tower of Babel* ("to show man's arrogance and folly"—part of the monster's terrible war machine, as a fitting artwork). Seeing the paintings now, with Janey's questionable future weighing so heavily on his throbbing mind, only made him angrier. It was, as Victor liked to say, "a bunch of nonsense."

Chris made his way to the center-aisle doors, gripped the handles, and flung the doors open. He caught a whiff of incense and votive candles. Then he walked boldly into the dimly lit nave and scanned the long rows of wooden pews for signs of the faithful, his boot steps on the marble floor echoing throughout. The church was empty. He kept on walking down the main aisle as his gaze found the main altar, far ahead. Twenty-foot balsams, twinkling with tiny white lights, flanked the sanctuary. Then he glanced to the left at John Martin's blazing *Pandæmonium*, which he dreaded the most, strategically placed above the confessional as a reminder to them all where they would go if they didn't repent. Even now, with his anger never greater, the painting gave Chris the willies, knowing how he used it, and that it was possible to spend an eternity in such a terrible place, even if it were a lie. He couldn't help recall the day Fr. O'Hara—upon hearing Chris' required and humiliating confession—yelled at him so loudly from the confessional's center stall, the others in line ran away. No more running. Not tonight.

Reaching the center of the church, Chris turned around and examined the choir loft, searching for more signs of unwanted onlookers, noting how odd it felt to be back again, recalling the days that Victor himself, before his anger destroyed him, had sung up there during Mass, everyone hearing that dominant and magnificent tenor voice, turning to admire him, if only that hour. Finally, Chris shifted his fiery gaze to the vaulted ceiling and stared at the faded angelic frescoes. They seemed to be cowering, no clouds in sight.

"Hey, remember me—the heretic?" he shouted. Beads of sweat formed above his upper lip. "We've gone through this before. Haven't You had enough? Why do You keep doing this, huh? What do You need another angel for? You heard her. I know You did. She doesn't want to be with You. She wants to stay with me—me! Not on Your ceiling. I don't want to be alone!" His words echoed throughout the church, rattling the windows, shaking the dust from the beams. Then Chris reached into his back pocket and withdrew the folded piece of paper. "Here, see this?" he shouted once more at the now indifferent pudgy faces on the ceiling, waving the wish-list like a white flag. "Well, I'm adding one more thing. You know what it is. You have twenty-seven days—twenty-seven! If she doesn't get it, I'm coming back here—and not a second late. Then I'm really gonna show You what I think of Your Grand Design."

"Here, here, now," a man's raspy voiced called out from behind him. "What's all the shouting about? No shouting. No!"

Chris whirled around to see a bearded old man in a blue uniform standing in the vestibule, his knobby hands clenching the handle of a mop submerged in a wheeled metal bucket.

The old man, missing his right eye, squinted his left one—and then it shot open. "You!" he said. "What are you doing here? Lord, save us. Not good—not good!"

Chris recognized the man immediately. It was "John the Janitor," as Chris' snickering first-grade classmates had dubbed him. John was impaired, and of course had a hard time seeing. And he couldn't hear very well, either. Chris remembered him as a quiet, slow-moving man who moved about the school like a ghost, but who never complained about having to clean up lunchtime rubbish, or vomit from a desk or classroom floor. It was easy to pull pranks on him, which they did often—making more messes after he cleaned up, getting him into trouble for his "lackluster" effort. Had he heard every angry word? The promise? Chris had to find out. "I'm sorry, I didn't mean to shout. I just came to say some prayers." Even Chris could tell his own statements were insincere, for they were laced with anger.

The old man's expression turned placid, and he began moving his head about as if he could no longer see. " 'Prayers,' you say. Yes, praise the Lord Almighty. Maybe you should try confession...you know, to help cleanse your soul. That's what I would do, if I were you. If I were you."

The suggestion, one Chris always resented, triggered an emotion and response that he could not keep tethered. All these foolish finger-waggerers, telling him what to do. "They already made me do that. I don't need anymore cleansing. Isn't that your job?"

Thankfully, the old man seemed unfazed by the sarcasm—as if he even knew what it was. He held onto the mop handle as if it were a cane, desperately needed to keep his balance. And he continued to move his head like a blind man. "Yes, clean the floors, but be quiet about it. I will. I will. Thank you. How about a second chance, just to get things right? I can do that, if you'll let me. Please, I can. Thank you. While you're in here, maybe you should ask for that instead of shouting. No shouting. No. That's what I would do...if I were you. If I were you."

Chris nodded slowly, his fears diminishing. He had forgotten just how feeble the man was. Perhaps he hadn't heard everything. Maybe nothing. Maybe he was still the same old John the Janitor. Very likely, he was worse, would remember nothing, or—even better—wasn't capable of convincing anyone what he thought he saw or heard. "Yeah," Chris said, "yeah, maybe I should." But the resentment lingered, and he just couldn't help himself. "Thanks for the stellar advice." It was always easy to feel superior to the feeble John the Janitor.

The old man frowned as his head stilled. "I think you should go, before you do something foolish. Come back when you're ready. You can come back. But not now. Yes, thank you. You're not supposed to be here, remember?"

"I remember. No one's gonna let me forget, I guess."

"Shoulda thought of that before you made a mess of this place. Always think of the consequences before you act. Always. Yes, I will, praise God. Terrible mess. Terrible. What am I supposed to do? But I'll clean it, scrub it hard, if you give me another chance."

"Yeah—yeah, sure, whatever it is you're trying to say," Chris said, staring quizzically at John, the anger retreating. It was time to go. No worries about this man. None whatsoever. Chris walked toward the janitor.

"Thank you, thank you," John said. He turned his head slightly and narrowed his one good eye. "You doing all right? You don't look well."

"I don't look well?" He scoffed, but this time held his tongue.

"Did you get into a fight or something? That's not good. No fighting. No. Bad for the soul."

Chris stood beside him. "You wouldn't understand."

A sadness swept over his ruddy face. "I know what you think of me. I have feelings, too. It hurts. And I do understand." Then, just as quickly, the sadness—and lucidity—disappeared. "And I see just fine. I really do. The Child is coming!" With his eye wide open, he now beamed with joy.

"Sure you do, old man," Chris said. Nothing worse than out-of-touch adults—who couldn't handle their own lives—giving advice. Victor had taught him some things. Still, Chris felt regret for his anger, that poor John the Janitor had the misfortune of stumbling upon the intensely emotional and private drama. But Chris offered no apology. He couldn't. Not this night. He pushed past John and out the main doors into the snow and cold, then slipped his hands into his coat pockets. His anger had been subdued, but it wasn't purged. His outburst had serious tones to it, and he intended to uphold his promise of retribution if Janey did not survive. But for now, he had another important task to complete. And he stormed off into the frozen night, hoping his sister was still at rest.

Chapter Eleven

The Gift

When Chris returned home from his trip to St. Boniface, he removed his wet hat and jacket and hung them on the vacant hooks of the coat tree beside the grandfather clock. Quickly slipping on a pocket sweatshirt to chase away the chill, he rushed up to Janey's room and carefully opened the door to check on her. The bedside lamp shined its protective light upon her, and she lay on her favorite side, facing him, her stuffed guards still crowded all around, though some had toppled over, helpless on the floor. The slow but steady rise and fall of the comforter told him that she was sleeping comfortably. He could feel a little fear emanating from her dreams. But there was also a strong determination to win, to stay with him, and her will inspired him, sparkling his mind with her magic. It was the perfect time to complete his task.

Returning to the foyer, Chris flicked on the wall switch for the basement light and without hesitation descended the stairwell. Then he opened the door to the darkened storeroom, which was directly below Victor's den (he could hear the constant thumping of the music, however muffled) and contemplated his next move. This was, after all, where all the evil once flowed from the hellish furnace, much like it did from the dark heart of Pandæmonium, in that other world. Much to his annoyance, despite the purge, that disturbing feeling still remained. The dome ceiling light of their partially finished basement was too far away to illuminate much of anything in here. Of course, there was a flashlight on his father's cluttered workbench. But that thing hadn't shined in years. He would have to stumble in the dark to find the pull cord. As he had confessed half-jokingly to Janey, stepping into this subterranean tomb had always been a somewhat frightful task. Even after his recent self-enlightenment, he suspected that the demons of their story lurked in every shadow.

Chris slowly pushed his way toward the center of the room through the rubble pile of stacked boxes as his right arm swung wildly in the dark in search of the pull cord. The furnace suddenly roared to life, startling him. Pandæmonium, no doubt. But now the row of flickering gas flames at the base of the furnace provided just enough devilish light to aid him in his search. He grabbed the cord and tugged it, but the light did not go on. He tugged it again, then again. Still no light. "Great," he said loudly, to inject some sanity into the room. The grocery bag of assorted replacement bulbs was here somewhere, probably inside a box that was inside another box. (He couldn't remember the last time he saw it.) But it would take him longer to find the bulbs than the chest. That he could not endure. So he decided to bravely press on.

With his distorted shadow dancing wildly across the floor joists above, Chris pushed the stacked boxes aside, clearing a wide path from the furnace toward the cinder block wall. Suddenly, there it was: the oversized barrel-stave trunk with all the ancient things.

Eager to complete his sacred quest and retreat from this eerie place, Chris knelt before the unlocked trunk. He flipped up the two brass latches, and flung the dome top open.

Something jumped out at him.

"Damn it!" Chris nearly fell on his back. He shielded his eyes with his right forearm as a musty smell overcame him. Then he sprung to his feet and turned away. The mask. He forgot that he had used it to set a trap.

Chris took some deep breaths to calm his racing heart, then lowered his arm to stare at the roaring furnace. How he hated that mask. It was the most hideous thing on the planet. And being such a thing, it was wisely kept inside the lid's drop-down compartment. But just last year, in a moment of perceived brilliance, Chris had hung the mask on a wire connected to the lid. When an unsuspecting victim opened the trunk, the mask would swing out in all its ghastliness, causing said victim to run screaming up the stairs (as he did when he first discovered it), thus protecting the source of St. Nicholas' wondrous gifts. But now, with his heart still pounding, Chris decided that maybe he hadn't exercised the best judgment, and that the mask should quickly return to its proper hiding place.

One last deep breath, and Chris turned to face this horror. He still couldn't stare directly at it for more than a few moments. He was afraid that its hideous image would burn into his brain, and that when he closed his eyes at night, that thing would still be staring at him.

The top of the mask was the most peculiar. A tuft of long white fur lay between a set of brownish-white ram horns that sprouted upward just above each menacing red eye. The horns curled backwards and out to each side. But then, two more sets of horns curled wildly from the top of the furry white cap, while long black-and-white fur draped from the sides and chin. To ensure its revolting ugliness, the leather face, stretched across carved wood, was shriveled and blackened with rot. A long, pointy, human nose twisted down and over the mouth, which was frozen in a gaping smile that curled freakishly up and over the eyes. The slack jaw was disproportionately large and lined with molars stained with decay and set in receding black gums. But the worst feature, by far, was the flat, blackish-red tongue that flopped out of the right side of the mouth. Chris could even smell its foul breath. The whole man-goat thing looked like road kill, flattened and left to rot. And yet, somehow, it managed to stay alive.

"That's a *perchten*," Sandra had said after scolding him years ago for his unauthorized rummaging. The mask was once used to scare away evil spirits, in the land of the shrieking mountains. But those beliefs, she insisted, had long since died. She kept the mask only as a "collector's item," and it was not intended for viewing by rascally children. Then she made Chris promise never show the mask to Janey, and to forget that it ever existed. Chris kept the first part of the promise to this day. But the last request was impossible to honor. From that moment on, the mask became the monster of their story, the demon with the terrible chain used to capture its victims, and relegated with all the other evil ones to the demon horde. And, once in the story, the trunk became the source of the dark power.

No doubt, to a young and active mind desperate to make sense of his father's violent outbursts, the mask and the trunk provided much-needed answers. After all, the steamer trunk was a Russo trunk, as Chris also discovered the day of his scolding. He found out because he had asked about the yellow-and-black lizard painted on a framed square plate inside the dome top. "That's the *lucertola del fuoco*," Sandra had told him. "The fire lizard." It was a reptile found in the Russos' native town of Termini Imerese, in Sicily, and served as the family crest. Victor's mother, Marie, had told Sandra that the Russos had royal blood. It was from Marie whom Sandra absorbed her limited Italian vocabulary, which she passed onto Chris. (After Sandra died, Marie—with Victor's silent blessing—had been stuffed, out of her mind, into some West Coast nursing home by Ted, the only half-brother who occasionally and without success hounded Victor over the phone for contributions.) Even more, the Russo family tree was rooted to the famous castle built there. And the lizard was chosen because it had a special indestructible power: it could live in the fires of nearby Mount Etna. But Chris had since discovered and noted that the claims were just lies. First, there was no castle in Termini Imerese. The closest one was in Caccamo, to the south. And it was Norman, not Sicilian. So much for the royal bloodline. Even the story of the lizard was a lie. Mount Etna, though still a threat to all, was not nearby. It rose on the far eastern side of the island. But Imerese did have hot springs. As for the "lizard" itself—it wasn't a lizard at all, but a poisonous salamander. How perfect. Probably chosen because the creature was indigenous and colorful. Lies, lies, lies. They helped explain how a rogue like Victor could trick a saint like Sandra into marrying him. She even apologized to Chris in one amazing outburst for having married Victor, claiming that the man had once been "charming," that she did not see his "other side" until it was too late. And that's when Chris discovered his mother's greatest fear—one that Janey liked to express: that Chris would one day become like his father. Chris held the idea to this day as a supreme insult, despite its logic. There was a pleasant irony about Termini Imerese. The town had numerous churches, one dedicated to St. Nicholas, another to St. Catherine.

So now, Chris had to deal with the smiling mask before he could resume his treasure hunt. The only thing worse than looking at the furry thing was touching it. With his distorted shadow still dancing wildly above him, Chris knelt before the chest and pinched between his right thumb and forefinger the tip of a curled horn. He did not want to risk getting bit or catching some incurable disease. With his left hand, Chris unfastened the leather strap attached to the flap of the lid's main compartment. The flap fell across the top shelf of the chest. Chris stuffed the mask into the domed cavity and held it there, then pulled the flap up and refastened the strap. The mask was secured and covered, except for some traces of fur and the ends of those wild horns. He sighed.

The chest's top shelf was shallow and removable. The age-stained, black-and-white photos of ancient family members were kept there in banded stacks, the Friedrichs to the left and the Russos to the right. Chris never met any of them, of course, though he had from time to time gone through the photos just out of curiosity. Of particular interest were the Austrians in festive "yodeler" costumes, as he once called them. It was especially funny to see how many of the old bearded men, particularly on the Friedrich side, looked like Saint Nick. Beach photos of short, stocky Sicilians were also amusing. Men wore swimsuits that looked like long underwear, while the women wore swimwear that looked like dresses. Many of the males had hairy shoulders. Their hairlines—just like Coach Joe's—crept halfway down their broad foreheads. Sandra had helped identify those whom she could. That's how Chris learned about Grandpa Sylvester. Victor's father had died while in his forties, before Chris was born. All Chris had were photos of the dapper man. A tailor with a gimmicky horse-drawn cart used for deliveries in the crowded big city, Sylvester had married twice, and had a penchant for fedoras, and the ladies. What a surprise. As a result, Victor emerged from a tangle of half-brothers-and-sisters who cared little about each other, and who drifted apart. No surprise there either. In one classic photo sought out often to stir up vengeful and riotous laughter, the baby Victor sat in shorts, suspenders, and floppy hat atop his father's white mare.

Chris lifted the top shelf from the chest and set it on the floor, revealing the jumble of trinkets, knick-knacks, and collectibles from each family. There was costume jewelry, tarnished silver candleholders, small gold picture frames, gold pocket watches, tiny silver crosses, holy cards, small statues—anything attached to a treasured memory. But just like last year, Chris found it difficult to find much that was appropriate for an eleven-year-old girl. It didn't really matter. Janey would gladly take anything she thought came directly from Sandra.

Settling for a simple but tarnished silver bracelet, Chris jammed the item in his sweatshirt's large pouch pocket. He replaced the shelf and reached up to close the lid. But as he did, he stared at the fire lizard, then thought of Victor sitting just above him in his comfortable chair, sipping his drink, and waiting for his daughter to die. His anger and outrage struck him hard—like a head-spinning slap across the face. Hit it, the gentle voice whispered in his ear. He punched the lizard.

The wooden plate shifted within its frame.

"Damn it," Chris said. He didn't need to give Victor another reason to boil over. Chris reached in to push the plate back into position. But when he did, it fell onto the trunk's shelf, revealing a dark leather pouch stuffed within a dusty, once-hidden compartment.

Wide-eyed, Chris hesitated, then grabbed the pouch and turned to face the roaring furnace. He loosened the leather drawstrings and stuck his right hand into the bag. Whatever was in there felt like...a pile of worms.

Chris withdrew the contents and examined them in the flickering light. A pile of worms, all right—no...leather shoestrings. But something was gleaming in all that leathery spaghetti, something small with lots of points. Chris closed his eyes for a moment to clear his vision. Then he pinched one of the shining pointy things with his left hand, pulled it from the pile, and held it up in the hellish light. It looked like a snow crystal with a hollow pentagonal center from which a branch extended from each of the five angles. The snow crystal appeared to be encrusted with diamonds. And there was another one in his right hand, though one of its branches had broken off. Both were simple pendants, no larger than a nickel. Chris inspected the pouch for the missing branch, but it wasn't there. Then he slowly rose to his feet, returning his gaze to the dazzling items.

This was serious, rich-adult-world stuff that he could imagine Katie wearing. He had never touched something so precious. What were these things doing here? And whose were they? Surely, the pendants didn't belong to the Russos. Victor would have pawned them by now, or given them to the floozy. But maybe he didn't know they were there—obviously, he didn't know! Were the pendants from the Friedrich family? If they were, Sandra had to have put them there. She was the only one from that side who would have known about the secret compartment. But if she knew, why didn't she leave word in her will? Financial matters and family treasures did not escape her.

Chris brought his hands together, unable to remove his gaze from the pendants. He was astonished at how well preserved they were. What a wonderful gift for Janey—how amazingly wonderful! What could be more appropriate for a snowflake-gobbling angel? And to think that Victor, of all people, was indirectly responsible for this little miracle. Chris savored the delicious irony, imagining with great satisfaction the shock that would, on Christmas Day, grip Victor's face upon seeing one of these pendants around Janey's neck. But that might set him off. Would he recognize it as a family heirloom? Or would he be blind to the possibility? There was a way to find out. He had to be careful, but there was a way.

The trunk's musty smell sickened him. And the constant flickering of the furnace flames made the room shift about. Time to get out.

Chris slipped the pendants back into the pouch and carefully slid it into the sweatshirt pocket. But before he left the room, Chris scanned the shadows, then glanced down at Victor's paint cans. "*Idiota,*" Chris said. With his foot, he pushed the cans away from the furnace. Then he picked up the canister of thinner and bounded up the stairs to his bedroom where he prepared to confront his father.

CHAPTER TWELVE

Shadows from the Past

Chris stood outside the den door, his right hand on the knob. Victor was still inside, listening to his goddawful opera music, and belting out those hated words. Chris hesitated. This was another room he dreaded to enter, even when he wanted to. Not even his vacuum-lugging sister dared to sneak in. It was Victor's world, a trophy-filled shrine dedicated to his supreme selfishness, through which the dark power, in the storeroom just below, flowed and condensed into the boiling black cloud in which the monster, and the others, roamed. It was also a place Victor could—as he did now—pretend not to be the miserable failure that everyone knew, but some cherished opera singer, whom everybody loved. Talk about a fantasy...

Chris pushed the door open. Victor sat in his desk chair with his back to Chris. Music blared from the speakers on either side of the entertainment center behind the desk, which Victor faced. In his right hand, which rested on the chair's overstuffed arm, Victor held a half-filled glass void of ice cubes. Apparently, he had decided to skip the formalities and drink his vodka straight, for quicker and greater effect. Standing in the center of the middle shelf among all the trophies was the confiscated candle pyramid, its fan and army of black-horse riders stilled from the lack of candlepower. But Chris could feel the dark power from below rising up...stirring the great and terrible war machine.

Victor did not move as Chris approached. He was far off in some immense opera hall or metropolitan square, dazzling the fans. Chris hesitated, then tapped him on the shoulder.

Victor snapped his head around, startled to see Chris standing there. Then his eyes narrowed as he hit the mute button on the remote in his lap. "Can't you knock when you come in?" he said, looking a little embarrassed. "What do you want, Chris?"

Chris did his best to act innocent. "You know that trunk in the storeroom?"

"You mean grandpa's?"

"It's your father's?"

"Yeah. Why? What are you doing down there? Don't be messing with things that don't belong to you." Victor didn't seem to be too alarmed, just his usual ornery self.

"I was just looking for things to give to Janey—for Christmas."

"Janey?"

"She likes those old things in there."

"No," he said. "You kids need to stay out of there. That's family stuff, not a toy box. Go find something else to give her." He hit the mute button and sank in the chair as the opera resumed with full force.

Chris raised his voice. "I found the jewelry."

Victor sighed and silenced the music once more. "What?"

"I found the jewelry. It was in that compartment thing with the lizard on it."

Victor stared at him blankly. "I don't know what in Hell you're talking about. What compartment? What jewelry?"

Chris held out the silver bracelet.

Victor looked casually at it, then glared at Chris. "Put—it—back." The opera resumed once more. So did the sipping, which now looked more like gulping.

Before Chris withdrew from the den, he spotted a glass ashtray on Victor's desk. A half-crushed but barely smoked cigarette, complete with lipstick stains, rested on the grooved edge. Gritting his teeth, Chris kept his eyes on the back of Victor's head as he quickly snatched the ashtray from the desk and stuffed it into his front pocket. Then he slipped from the den and shut the door, feeling a bit hollow, but a little joyful. The night had ended with one of those moral victories coaches liked to talk about after a hard-fought game that ended with a disappointing loss. The pendant would be retained, boxed and wrapped and hidden, and cheerfully handed out at midnight on Christmas, their traditional gift-giving time. But now, the battle for Janey's life was on. He wondered, with some guilt, if he could endure it.

Chris dragged himself up to his room to hide the pouch with his other secrets in his closet.

〜

Chris discovered during a quick detour to his encyclopedias that it was not uncommon for old barrel trunks to have chromolithographs or secret compartments. But the mystery of the pendants wouldn't be easily solved, now that Victor showed no knowledge of their existence. Chris couldn't even be sure that they belonged to the Russo family. He thought about thumbing through the stacks of old photos in the trunk to see if any of the ancients were wearing them, but he would save that for another time. Chris had to find a safer place than the closet to hide the pouch from Victor and

Janey. Chris would put the silver bracelet in the chest's secret compartment, as Victor requested, just in case his father remembered their conversation and decided to check it out. As for Janey, she would, in all probability, recover from the initial hit the chemo delivered and try to resume her normal routines for the remainder of the week. (Sandra had endured the treatments for months, nosebleeds and all, before she was finally bedridden.) And because Janey was such a neat-freak, she got into everything while lugging the vacuum and assorted dust and window rags around, or while putting away folded laundry. Not that she was cleverer with her favorite hiding place (her coat pockets). Still, hiding the pouch from her would be difficult.

Chris returned to his research. But his tired eyes caught a glimpse of a fuzzy light suddenly illuminating a window in Dr. Samuel's house. He blinked a few times to restore focus—then realized that it wasn't just any window. It was the casement of Katie's bedroom. Chris scooted from his bed and stood before his window. Someone was, indeed, in Katie's bedroom. But the sheer shade in her window prevented him from identifying the mysterious figure that moved about inside. Chris was certain that Katie knew by now of Janey's dire situation—just as he was certain of her sadness and concern. No doubt, she would stop by. Only the late hour prevented her from doing so tonight. Still, he fervently hoped she was alone, would see him standing here, and venture over nonetheless.

Suddenly, a snowball struck his window, knocking him from his trance. The slushy remnants slid down the spotted glass, leaving a watery trail. Chris looked out to see two dark figures standing out against the whiteness of his tiny backyard flanked on both sides by a planked fence. The intruders waved at him in a wild, obnoxious way that was all too common, as if flagging down a rescue craft. Astonished by the sight, Chris lifted the sash and stuck his head out into the cold night.

"Surprise, surprise," Larry said, a brimless fur hat with earflaps framing his fat face. "Look who just got out of prison."

"What's goin' on, me boy?" Matt said in a strange, deep voice. His torso was noticeably longer, as if he had been tortured on the rack. And though his chest was still flat, no pecs, his sharp shoulders were wider than Chris remembered, and his leather coat hung on him as if still on a very large hanger. It felt like years since Chris had seen him. Matt's coat collar was turned up, but in his typical winter fashion, so bent on being "cool," he didn't wear a hat, which was just plain stupid, not that Chris would ever say. His dark, curly hair that he once proudly displayed, with long sideburns, was gone, replaced by a buzz cut—a striking reminder of what had transpired this past year. The cold burned his scalp and ears with red.

Even though he could still hear Victor's opera music, Chris was frantic. "What are you two doing here?" he said in a forceful whisper. "You want to get us all killed?"

"Great to see you, too, Chris," Matt said. "Thanks for saying so."

"What do you want?" Chris said.

"What do you mean, 'what do we want?'" Matt said. "We gave you the signal. You opened the window. Hell, man, the game—it's back on."

"The game?" Chris said. "Are you two whacked? We can't do that anymore."

"Sure we can," Matt said. "The car's just down the street. Besides, I already found a party."

Chris could not believe his ears. Cruising Cottagewood late at night for high school and college gatherings had become one of Matt's favorite holiday traditions. He became successful at it, not only because he lived in the neighborhood, or because of his boldness and his father's stolen car, but because of those long sideburns, now gone. Larry's stocky frame and permanent five o'clock shadow didn't hurt their chances of successfully crashing parties, either. And since Chris was with them, he often passed through any resistance, despite his boyish looks and spindly physique. But that was last year—before Victor's edict.

"I can't go with you."

"Why not?"

"You know why."

"Is he home?"

"Yes," Chris said, followed by a fatalistic laugh.

"Is he drinking?"

"Does that matter?"

"Well, sure, if he passes out."

"If he catches me with you, I'm dead."

"He never caught us last year."

"I can't go."

"All right," Matt said, "we'll just stand here and whistle some Christmas songs—like Janey does—until you come down."

"Whistle?" Larry said.

Matt gave Larry a backhanded slap across the shoulder. Then the two began whistling separate tunes.

"No, stop," Chris said.

But the more he pleaded with them, the louder they whistled.

Fearing the volcano would soon erupt, Chris shut the window and dashed down the stairs. He stopped to make sure Victor's music was still playing, then continued on to the basement where he slid the patio door open. They didn't stop their disjointed serenade until he approached. Chris realized how much Matt had grown as he had to look up at him.

"Like the new do?" Matt said, brushing the top of his head. "They're letting me grow it out a little. Really makes a difference, don't ya think?"

"You guys shouldn't have come here," Chris said.

"We weren't really gonna stop," Larry said. "Just making the old rounds. But then we saw the lights on, so we said, 'What the Hell. Let's see if we can get him to come out.' And here you are, right on cue."

Chris saw the light go out in Katie's bedroom, and he gazed past them to see if she would appear from the house.

Matt turned momentarily to stare at the Tudor, then returned his gaze to Chris. "Is that babe still living there?"

"Yeah," Chris said reluctantly. He didn't like the idea of this man-child talking about her. Never did.

Larry smirked. "The babysitter—oh, yeah."

"She was our caretaker," Chris said.

"Caretaker, right," Larry said. He giggled.

"Quite a rack, if I remember correctly," Matt said. "It's amazing what thousands of years of selective breeding can do to a collection of atoms. Got it just about right, I'd say. If only we could factor out that 'talking' thing."

"Yeah, no shit," Larry said.

But Matt seemed to sense that his crude humor did not amuse Chris, and he softened his tone. "Still got a thing for her?"

Chris didn't answer.

"Maybe she'll be at the party."

It wasn't the selling point Matt strived for. In fact, it was a horrible thought, now that Chris knew he had no chance with her. Seeing her with her boyfriend would only crush his heart again, what was left of it, and stir his anger. He didn't want to feel that way about her. Seeing Matt flirt with her would be even worse. "I gotta go inside."

"Oh, come on," Matt said. "I haven't seen you in months. We've got lots of catching up to do."

"Janey's sick."

Matt's face lit with worry. "Janey? What's wrong?"

"Blood disorder," Chris said. It sounded less threatening, like the flu.

But Matt seemed to sense its gravity. "Blood disorder? Oh, man, what's going on in that house?"

"Fucking cursed, aren't you?" Larry said.

"Hey," Matt said, scowling at Larry, "you know where that word comes from, what it means—right? What's in your head? His sister's in trouble. Show some respect!" He punched Larry's arm.

Larry's smart-ass expression evaporated. He grabbed his arm and mouthed "ow." And suddenly, in Chris' whirling mind, they were back at St. Boniface, with Matt in command of their little rebellion...

Chapter Thirteen

The Grand Experiment

The rebellion seed germinated in what Chris described as the Grand Experiment. School administration decided to put the smartest thirty-or-so eighth graders into one class, which didn't go over well with the rest, labeled by the faculty as average or as unmotivated (*"the Buttheads," we're called, but we got even*). This new class (*"the Hotshits"—tah-dah!*) quickly developed a peculiar habit of turning up their noses and avoiding eye contact (as if we didn't exist) in the halls and elsewhere with those who did not get in, which really set nerves on edge, particularly with those whose physical prowess had put them atop the prepubescent heap.

The Experiment's premise was simple. This special, protected, and pampered class , with the world handed to them on a platter, was encouraged to question everything—anything—at any time so as not to hold back their intellectual development. No text, no teacher was infallible. Any two-year-old could appreciate its method. But it was supremely effective. "Why?" "Why not?" and "What if?" became the most common probes. These questions were fired relentlessly until the buried truth was reached, and no more questions could be asked.

At first, Chris was placed in the lower class. He had difficulty with math and reading. Numbers and letters just didn't sit still on the pages long enough for him to link together it from bit. And sometimes after reading entire paragraphs, he couldn't remember one word. But Chris quickly showed a peculiar ability in geography, art, science—any subject where he could capture, with the blink of a non-flashing eye, great gobs of information presented as a singularity, like pictures, photos, diagrams, and maps. And then, one day, when he put a book down on his desk after another failed attempt at reading individual words, Chris discovered—just by blinking—he had snapshots of an entire page of text in his brain. Then, after experimentation, he discovered that once the text picture was captured, he saw every word, and he could go back anytime at his leisure to access the information as required. (*The gift...from Sandra.*) This unique skill—the discovery of which he kept to himself—revolutionized his learning ability. Chris quickly outshone his fellow Buttheads. And he became the first—and only—to blast his way into the otherwise impenetrable and protected world of the Hotshits, which its members viewed as a birthright. Still, most of his classmates treated Chris like a celebrity. Some called him a genius, which he hated. This crown placed upon him had thorns. The camera in his mind didn't work sometimes, especially when he willed it to. And when that happened, and he stumbled, he was accused of laziness, which brought on an enormous guilt, and only made the camera malfunction even more. Still, the school administration made him the poster boy for their Experiment, attributing his success to an unforeseen motivational factor to "get in." But others looked upon him with suspicion, contempt, and jealousy, and he withdrew even more.

That's when his life's path crossed with Matt Cavanaugh's. Suddenly, he had entered Matt's world. Matt knew of Chris' existence. And they started to interact.

At first, Chris was accepted only into the outer circle of friends Matt loosely maintained. These were the hangers-on, those who wanted to associate with Matt because he was smart and cool and charismatic and didn't give a damn about what people thought of him. But since Chris and Matt lived within a mile of each other, their paths outside the classroom crossed more and more. They rode the bus together, rode their bikes together, walked to school together. And they talked (Chris did most of the listening).

The defining moment came one day in Mr. Kane's history class. Deciding to take a break from the usual dead topics, Kane asked his class to name the "coolest" person ever. Chris was wary anytime an adult used the word "cool." Kane was trying to be one of them, which he wasn't, and never would be. He wanted the class to let down their guard, to open up, and Chris was stunned to see the ploy working. One by one, the Hotshits voiced their enthusiastic opinions: famous actors, pop singers, rock musicians, and athletes. When it was Chris' turn, he hesitated, afraid to speak his true feelings. Pop culture? Going along, repeating things you didn't know about or believe, liking things you didn't like—just to show how smart and grown-up you really were, despite appearances, and be liked and accepted? This wasn't what the Hotshits were all about. Why did they take the bait? Now a bit angry, Chris took a deep breath and blurted out his answer.

Upon hearing it, Kane's eyes lit up. "Darwin?" he howled.

The class exploded with laughter. "What's wrong with you?" a girl's voice squealed. "What a doofus," another said.

Chris sank in his desk, his face burning. So much for being honest.

"Now, now," Kane said, raising his hand to calm the class, "there's no wrong answer to this question. I said the coolest person ever. Darwin certainly can qualify. . .somehow." He smiled, no doubt thinking he was cool and clever, and glad to be accepted.

But the class groaned their displeasure as more insults were tossed Chris' way.

When Kane finally gained control, he looked at Chris with a quizzical expression. "Darwin?" he said softly. "Really?"

"Yeah."

"Why?"

"Because he figured it all out—just by drawing and watching things. He wasn't afraid to tell people. His theory was simple. Everyone could understand it. And he described it with one word."

"Simple, huh?" Kane slowly nodded his head as someone giggled. "Okay, sound response. I can understand where you're coming from, I suppose. But don't think you have to appease me in any way by choosing historical figures. If I gave you another chance, what would it be?"

Chris hesitated again.

"Come on, Chris," Kane said. "Remember, no right or wrong answer. It can be anybody—anyone you admire."

He cleared his throat. "Galileo."

Again the class burst with hysteria.

"Da Vinci!" Chris shouted angrily through the laughter.

"Now he's just picking Italians!" said someone to his right. "What a goombah."

The rest of his deity (Einstein, Wheeler, Sagan, Wigner, Kaku, Dennett, Higgs, Susskind, Smolin, Linde, Guth, Pribram, and Polkinghorne) never made it from his lips. Chris sank once more as the Hotshits' laughter seemed endless. But as he drowned in his embarrassment, he caught a glimpse of Matt in the corner of his left eye. When Chris turned to face him, Matt just sat there nodding, and grinning. Chris saw that the king approved of his bravery in the face of overwhelming ridicule from the herd. Soon, Chris was invited to the inner circle reserved for only a select few. Chris was proud of the honor. He considered it his second major step toward adulthood.

Matt was different from all the other eighth graders. He seemed more like an adult locked in a child's body. And he wasn't afraid to test his boundaries. He tried smoking (*but quit*), he had lots of girlfriends (*he likes older teens*), he knew all about sex (*knows from experience, the rumors say*), and he always had a wad of cash on hand (*not daddy's money, but no one can say where this fortune comes from*). But he was kind, too, and loyal to the inner circle. He knew when to support fragile egos and sensitive feelings. But always—always—he would speak his mind.

And that's what started all the trouble.

The Grand Experiment worked well in nearly all the academic subjects. Traditional lesson plans, hewn to near perfection over the years, were often shot to Hell within minutes as teachers were pinned to the blackboard, struggling to explain theories, methods, statements, or procedures that were quietly accepted as fact by the other classes. Matt often led the assault.

But when it came to religious studies, the buckshot technique quickly showed its flaws. These teachings were meant to be taken as truths—no questions asked. They were meant for memorization, not debate. Questions were answered in ways that led to further questions. When those questions were answered unsatisfactorily—or not at all—frustration, confusion, even anger set in. Sometimes, these reactions were answered with discipline—extra homework, letters to parents, or detention. It was effective action on most of the Hotshits. But to the inner circle, discipline only stirred more anger and resentment and signaled clearly that something important was actually unknown or was purposely being hidden. That was unacceptable. The Grand Experiment had shown them the light. It worked. There could be no exception to the rules.

"All right," Matt declared one day to the inner circle as they gathered on the playground, "if they don't want to answer our questions, we'll have to find out for ourselves." Matt then asserted coolly and confidently that they could solve all the mysteries of life before the end of the school year.

But their journey, he warned, was not without danger. "If we want to know this stuff, we'll have to let the beloved herd run by. We'll no longer believe in whatever's popular so we can be liked and loved and accepted. We'll have to think for ourselves." They'd become outcasts, for sure, labeled as troublemakers, which in the "herddom" was the worst fate. Being alone and isolated was a serious survival risk. "And the girls," he lamented, "probably brand us as geeks. We might as well stamp a big 'G' on our foreheads."

Matt identified the "Book" as the main target. He was not interested in the nature of what was written, who said what when, who did what to whom. "All that noise doesn't matter," he said. "Let's find out who really wrote it." The Book, he was convinced, was the key to the whole deal. All encompassing, all powerful—and hanging to reality by a thread. All they had to do was cut it, and that Book would fall into oblivion.

Religion was not the only target. The nature of evil and violence, life and death—all the things that weighed so prominently and unfairly on their hungry young minds. That's when Chris discovered he disagreed with Matt. Because of his experience with his father, Chris detested the use of violence no matter what the reason. But Matt had another view. "Kumbaya is great when everyone's singing," he said. "But what if some doesn't want to sing? Then what are you going to do? Hit 'em over the head with the Book? There's a good use for it. Even they know that sometimes you gotta get a little beastly when someone forces you to." This view was an exception to the rules, and Chris did not approve of it. But he didn't challenge Matt, either.

In the end, the search for the Book's authors intensified the downward spiral. The information was easy to find. And in their minds, it cast serious doubts about its authority.

Matt confronted the poor nun in class one day with their findings, and he refused to back down when a "final" answer was given. "Hell, I can write inspired things, too," he said. "Why aren't my thoughts part of the Book? Seems like a lot of people just want to be God—and have all the perks that go with it. Why would I want to give anyone that kind of power?"

Matt's response drew a mix of laughter, applause, gasps, and outrage. Class was dismissed, and the rest of the school day went on as planned. But before he could step on the bus, Matt was whisked away by a number of the faculty who brought him to Mr. Bernard's office. For being "disruptive," a sentence of detention—with the threat of suspension, and after that, expulsion—was handed down. Matt kept his mouth shut for weeks. But Chris knew it was coming.

Chris sympathized with Matt during this unsettling time. Chris had, by now, finished reconstructing his own beliefs about the big questions, even while he thought he heard her begging him from the grave not to do it. The old convictions were, indeed, retired—rerouted and stored in dark, unused recesses, and nearly forgotten. New claims would be accepted only if quantified by math and/or scientific observation. Even more, because she was dead, and Chris felt much resentment and rage about the divine reasons given for her undignified and senseless demise. Something was definitely amiss with the big picture painted at St. Boniface. And the hypocrisy surrounding the Grand Experiment was appalling, and it affected Chris deeply. Matt had every right to have his questions answered correctly, and to express his feelings in his unorthodox manner.

On the fateful day, Matt, Larry, and Chris went into the church through the bell-tower door around noon to eat their sack lunches and play their usual game of tag (they had become bored with the cafeteria and playground scenes). The church was the perfect venue. Besides the banks of long wooden pews, there was the choir loft, crying room, coat-check room, and four sets of confessionals—plenty of places to hide or scamper to, to avoid being tagged.

The one big problem Chris had about the venue, besides being a church, was the rest of the church's art collection hung strategically throughout the nave—a collection Matt, fully aware of its purpose, openly despised but secretly coveted. Once, in one of his more rebellious moods, Matt had suggest that they abscond with a few of the paintings he alarmingly deemed "most valuable" and hide them in the old grain elevator, which Chris had long suspected was the nerve center of Cavanaugh Enterprises, though he never had the guts to poke around. (It was the one place Matt insisted much too often that they not explore, even though the abandoned complex was ideal for their youthful games and escapades. "Too risky" was the odd, almost laughable reason given.) But in a rare moment of unwavering defiance, Chris and Larry quickly shot down the art-theft idea, most fearful of the legal consequences, and the angry fists. Like the vestibule collection, the nave artwork was meant to be thought-provoking, and downright intimidating. During all their irreverent cavorting, Chris felt like he was being watched.

So on that portentous day, the game progressed as normal. Each player took his turn to be "it." Throughout the game, Chris was more than successful at avoiding detection, and he seized the moments to revel in his accomplishment. An hour later, the fun had run its course, and they exited the church quietly with crumpled lunch bags in hand to return to the school complex, certain as always that no one had seen them.

After using the restroom, Chris joined the other Hotshits in Mr. Lee's science class. Tired from all the scampering, Chris could barely keep his eyes open during the lecture about the periodic table of the elements which failed to mention how they were part of the Dark Power. Suddenly, the classroom door opened with a flourish, and Mr. Bernard entered the room with a furious expression. He clenched a crumpled lunch bag in his right hand. Busted!

"Cavanaugh, Russo, Witosz," he yelled, "get out here—now!"

A hush fell over the stunned classroom as Chris followed his compatriots into the hall. There, Fitz stood with his best choirboy expression.

"Are these the three you saw?" Bernard said.

"Yes, sir," Fitz replied.

"You're sure?"

"Positive, sir."

Chris was sick to his stomach. He was trembling. He had never been in this much trouble before. He didn't know if he could speak when spoken to, and he felt like crying. They had been so successful at their secret little game. Why did they have to get caught now?

"Who was carrying this?" Bernard said as he held up the lunch bag.

"I don't know, sir. They all were carrying something. I found it in the trash can, the one outside the school entrance."

Bernard turned his fiery gaze on them. "Whose is this?"

"I-I don't know, sir," Larry said. "We all had lunch bags."

"With a can of spray paint in it?" Bernard said. He withdrew the miniature can and held it in the air.

"It's mine, sir," Matt said proudly. "I did it."

Bernard's jaw clenched. "Let me see your hands."

Matt held his palms out. Black paint stained the base of his left fingers.

Chris couldn't believe what he was hearing and seeing.

"Why?" Bernard said with great disappointment.

"I needed to make a statement."

"Statement?" he shouted. His voice echoed down the hall, and seemed to rattle the far windows. "You make statements in the classroom—not by spraying an insolent word on a church wall!"

Matt looked down and said nothing.

"You realize the seriousness of your actions?" Bernard said as his tone grew calmer.

"Yes, sir," Matt said.

"Then let's go—all three of you. Fitzgerald, you go back to class."

"Yes, sir," Fitz said, and he turned to walk away. But Chris knew that, inside, Fitz was kicking his heals in the air, overjoyed that he had destroyed the core of the hated inner circle with one masterful stroke.

And so the brief but tumultuous age of the Hotshits had come to a sudden end.

Because Matt admitted his guilt, Chris and Larry were not expelled. But Chris could not dodge his father's angry fists. That night, Chris received a beating like no other, payback for not only making Victor's life more miserable, but for all the misery—all of it, imagined or otherwise—that had preceded. Afterwards, Chris thought he'd never be allowed to leave his room again. Larry's fate was not as brutal, but he, too, remained locked up for a long, long while. When he wasn't, he worked in the family bakery. Janey handled the situation her own way, quickly dubbing Chris the "poopster." And that was the end of it. But it marked the beginning of her quest to "save" him.

As for Matt, his actions forced a hasty meeting of the parish council, on which his father served. They quickly voted to expel the young rebel. And soon Matt was on his way to a life of sleeping in barracks, standing in formation, and daily inspections.

When Chris returned to class the following week, the Grand Experiment was over, and the Hotshits had been disbanded, scattered among the rest of the eighth grade classes. As Matt had warned, Chris and Larry were shunned by their classmates, and struggled through the rest of the year under the suspicious eyes of the faculty, who piled on impossible amounts of homework to keep their minds focused. Neither he nor Larry attended the graduation ceremony. They weren't invited. Instead, they received their certificates in the mail.

☙

"I was wrong to be such a follower," Chris blurted as they stood in the backyard snow.

"Say what?" Larry said, his face askew. "What in Hell are you—"

"I shouldn't have been a herd runner. I hate that."

"I never thought you were," Matt replied as if he had been watching the movie that had just played in Chris' mind. "Okay, maybe at first. But not later."

"You shouldn't have been expelled."

"Yeah, well, small matter of opinion. Amazing how paint gets on your fingers—damn cheap spray cans. Not very smart to dump it in the school trash. But I wanted out—really." He paused to smile painfully. "I wouldn't have lasted—you know that. They were out to get me. Besides, it was getting too crazy there."

"I'm sorry."

"Don't be. I'm in a better place. Lots of loony spoiled jerks like me with money to burn. The business opportunities are endless."

But Chris didn't believe for a moment that Matt was happy about his predicament. "Can you tell me one thing?"

"What's that?" Matt said.

"Why did you do it?"

He shrugged. "All things considered, in the heat of the moment, just seemed like the right thing to do."

The spotlights behind Chris burst to life. He whirled around and saw Victor pulling open the glass door, fast-food cup in hand. He had his bomber jacket on. Chris wasn't surprised that he had been caught, that he would have a face-off with Victor. But now he realized the magnitude of his miscalculation. Not now, not here, in front of the guys—in front of her!

"Uh-oh," Larry said, looking away as Victor approached slowly, arms extended outward for balance, as if he were walking a line.

Matt stood tall, refusing to move, as if ready to absorb an impact.

"Well, well, *well*, well, well," Victor said before taking a noisy sip from his cup. "If it isn't the three mus-ke-teers, back together a-gain. What a delight."

Victor was completely drunk by now. His eyes were like slits, and he spoke slowly and deliberately, trying not to slur his words. But that never worked. It was the jovial Victor—the one that everyone who didn't know him well seemed to like. The one who was an expert at drunk driving, and who—despite the countless chances—had never been arrested. *Oh, your father is so funny! What a riot. Why can't you be more like him?*

Victor squinted in the bright light at Matt. Then a laugh erupted from his belly as he pointed his cup's straw at Matt's head. "Got you by the short hairs, don't they, kid?"

"Yes, sir," Matt said. He was solemn but respectful.

Victor's laugh stopped abruptly. He stood tall and wide-eyed, his mouth puckered as if he were trying to whistle. "Oh, yes, sir—yes, sir," he said. He gave Matt a few mock salutes with his left hand. Then the wide-mouthed belly laugh returned.

Suddenly, Victor stopped laughing. "Oh," he said, as if an idea popped in his brain, "where's my man-ners?" He shoved the cup into Matt's face.

Matt flinched as the tip of the straw poked his nose.

"Have a drink, kid," Victor said. "You look like you could use one."

"No, thanks," Matt said. He carefully pushed the cup away with his right hand. "I'm drivin'."

Victor's tongue followed the swirling straw around as he tried to put it into his mouth. Then he took a long sip. "You will," he said, after gulping. "Someday, you'll all be like me. You just wait."

"I sure as Hell hope not," Matt said. "I think I'd have to shoot myself. Maybe you, too."

"Oh-ho-*ho!*" Victor replied. His jovial expression began to falter. "Getting all high and my-tee, are we?"

In a flash, Victor dropped his cup, whirled around, and slapped Chris' face, as if throwing a sidearm pitch. The force of the blow—and its suddenness—knocked Chris to the ground. Now on his hands and knees—not sure where he was, the left side of his face on fire—Chris touched his swollen upper lip and tasted blood. Just like that, the monster had reappeared.

Matt stepped forward, fists clenched. But Victor spun back up to tower over him, and Matt froze. Larry was bug-eyed and paralyzed.

"You want some of that, punk?" Victor said in a low growl. His arms were at his side, but flexed, and hands spread wide, ready to strike again.

Chris saw that Matt, though burning, wanted no part of this raging, drunk, athletic man who fought other men of greater stature in bars, and, because of that famous anger that knew no bounds, often won.

When Victor seemed certain that he had sufficiently intimidated Matt and Larry, he grabbed Chris by the jacket collar and threw him toward the house. "Party's over. Get inside." Even though intoxicated, Victor was careful not to roar. Experience told him that if he did, neighbors—or the police or social workers—might descend on him.

With his heart racing, Chris scrambled to his feet. He ran through the opened patio door and turned to see Victor right behind him. As if he had planned it, Victor grabbed the telescope and heaved it at Chris. Chris ducked to the side as the telescope and its tripod flew past and landed hard on the cement floor. Glass shattered and scattered like marbles as the telescope raked the concrete, then crashed in a loud heap against the storage room wall.

"Didn't I tell you not to talk to those two?" Victor bellowed. He slammed the patio door shut. "Didn't I?" With eyes afire, Victor rushed toward Chris.

Chris dodged his father's lunge, then sprinted to the left before bolting up the steps to the foyer. Slamming the door, Chris whirled around, uncertain what to do or where to go, refusing to bring the battle up to the second floor. He could hear Victor's deliberate steps pounding up the stairs. This was it. The storm clouds that had been gathering all this time had finally built into a tempest. All of the rage for all of Chris' misdeeds—the forbidden friends, the football tryout, the church—was about to hit in one thunderous strike. Once again, Chris feared for his life.

Instinctively, Chris backed into the living room and slowly made his way to the glowing tree. The basement door burst open, then Victor appeared, horns growing, red eyes flaming, the roller chain dangling from his right cloven hand.

"Don't you dare run away from me, you little shit!" he screamed as he slowly crossed the foyer floor. "Who in Hell do you think you are, huh? This is my house. I make the rules. And you—you're gonna obey them!" He stopped at the step and wrapped the chain tighter around his hand, making sure he had a firm grip. But the chain cut his fingers so they oozed, and added to the growing horror. Then he stepped down into the living room.

"Go away!" Chris shouted, nearly in tears. He backed around the tree so that it partially shielded him. "Leave us alone!"

But Victor kept on coming. "You think this stupid thing's gonna save you?" Victor said. He thrust his left hand into the tree, gripped its pole center, then threw the tree to the side. Its lights flickered, then went out, casting the room into darkness. The kugels bounced and cracked on the floor while other ornaments shattered as the tree rolled in agony.

"Go away!" Chris shouted into the howling winds. "Go back to your chamber where you belong!"

Victor's ominous shadow raised the chain high in the air as the boiling black clouds flashed and thundered.

Chris covered his face with his arms.

"No-o-o-o!" Janey's voice shrieked. "Stop it!"

At once, the raging storm died. All Chris could hear was a few of the fallen kugels rolling across the hardwood floor. The tree flicked back on, filling the room with its saving glow. Chris looked past Victor to see Janey standing in her heart pajamas at the base of the foyer steps. Even Victor turned to look at her. Janey was staring at the fallen tree and the broken kugels. And she was sobbing. Suddenly, blood trickled from her nose and across her lips.

"Janey," Chris said in a subdued but tense voice, careful not to frighten her. He walked quickly to her side.

"Why are you doing this?" Janey screamed at Victor in a guttural tone that he had not heard in years. "Why? What did we ever do to you?" Then she broke down, weeping.

Chris snatched Janey by the hand and refused to look at Victor. "Come on, Janey." He led her to the bathroom next to Victor's den and closed the door. He spun the roll of toilet paper, ripped the dangling sheets away, then balled them up and began dabbing her nose.

"The kugels," Janey said, her sobbing now down to a whimper, "he destroyed them."

"No, he didn't—maybe just a few," Chris said as calmly as he could, tossing the bloodied toilet paper into the wastebasket before grabbing another bundle. "Here, tip your head back."

She took the ball of paper in her hand. "What about my music box?"

"I'm sure it's fine," he said, guiding her hand up to her nose. She was still bleeding. "It's strong—like you. I've never met anyone so brave. I'll get everything cleaned up and put back in place. Don't you worry."

Janey held the toilet paper to her nose, and she seemed to calm a bit. But then her sad eyes grew alarmed. "Did he hurt you?" she said as she withdrew her hand.

Chris ran his tongue across his swollen upper lip. "I'll be okay. It's nothing."

She began sobbing.

"Come on, Janey," he said, helping to tip her head back, "we gotta stop the bleeding. I'm not ready to give you your Christmas present. We'll drown in here."

Janey shook her head and dabbed the trickling blood.

After a while, and a few more wads of toilet paper, the nose bleeding subsided. So did her sadness, slowly replaced by an ever-growing determination that blazed in her narrow eyes. Chris grit his teeth and smiled. "That's what I want to see, huh? Yeah, stronger by the second." Now it was time to face Victor once more—or whatever awaited them out there. "Ready?" he said to her.

She nodded. He did to. They both smiled. Then they put on their warrior masks.

Chris gripped the door handle. "Be strong for me, no matter what you see or hear. We don't want to let him win. Remember, just you and me. And don't stop thinking it."

Chris pulled the door open and they stepped hand in hand into the foyer. With slumped shoulders, Victor stood in the living room staring down at the massacre, chain still clenched in his right fist. He looked confused, as if he had been sleepwalking and just woke up to this terrible sight. Then he slowly raised his head. Chris and Janey met his confused gaze with all the resolve they could muster.

"This isn't my fault—none of it," he muttered. He rolled the chain into a ball. "I didn't want you, neither one of you. All this bullshit—the house, that ridic-u-lous tree, all the crappy artwork—this was her idea, not mine."

So now it was out: the world, according to Victor. Finally, Chris had the official answer. But they were the cruelest words he had ever heard.

Even Victor seemed a little stunned by his acid statements, but he quickly regrouped for one last horrible stab. "One of these days, I swear, I'm gonna burn this place to the ground. And you're never gon-na see me again."

Chris should have felt a spark of joy to think of Victor leaving them. Instead, Chris felt...hurt, and painfully so. It was amazing how a man who had used brute force most of their lives to harm them—a man for whom they had no love at all—could end up ripping their hearts out with such candid proclamations. Chris also felt a familiar alarm. It wasn't the first time their cash-strapped father had threatened to burn down the house. He had done it many times, even when Sandra was alive. In the aftermath of his tirades, she would try to reassure them that it was the alcohol talking, but Chris never fully believed her. And so Chris made sure he understood all the methods that such a desperate man would use.

So now they stood silently and in fear, watching his every move as he drifted past them like the demonic specter that he was, wondering if would spew more venom. Victor stepped into the foyer and mindlessly set the balled and bloody chain on the oval table next to the grandfather clock. Then he started down the hall. They didn't budge until they heard his den door close tightly. He would stay there the rest of the night, passed out in his chair. If only they could wall him up in there, forever. Chris swallowed hard, then looked down at Janey.

"Why doesn't he want us?" she said in a small voice.

Chris knew the answer. He had stated it many times before. But the hurt and despair in her expression were too much for him to bear, and he quickly looked away.

Chris led Janey to the stairs. They started up, but Janey stopped on the second step.

She looked up at him with red, weary eyes. "I can't," she said.

Chris scooped her up and carried her to the landing, and finally to her bedroom where he gently laid her in bed. "Try to get some rest," he said. He pulled the comforter to her chest.

Janey closed her eyes and kept them closed as she whispered her prayers. Neither of them could feign a smile. And the thought of uttering "good night" or "pleasant dreams" was laughable. They had been emotionally gutted. All that remained was a hollow shell—and the renewed fear for their future.

Chris closed her door, descended the stairs, and returned to the living room to assess the damage and try, as Sandra had taught him, to clean up, restore order, and hide the shame. (That was the strangest part. Despite all the hate he felt towards Victor, there was an overriding sense to protect honor and reputation—not Victor's, but his. After all, Victor was his father. To have a monster filling that vital role was the greatest embarrassment of them all.) Chris hoped most of the kugels had survived the fall. Bits of red and blue glass were scattered everywhere, sparkling like jewels on the floor, while some of the ornaments had survived but slid or rolled away to all parts of the room. He wouldn't know for sure until the tree was back in place. As for Janey's angel, that was another matter. If it hadn't survived, if it was beyond repair, Chris hated to think of what that news would do to her.

The terror wasn't going to end, really. It would go away for a time, here and there, but it was a permanent fact—on and on and on for all eternity. He still wasn't sure if the conflagration would ever transpire. Victor often vowed outrageous acts when drunk, things that he would like to do to clean his slate and start over. But he never had the guts to pull them off. Now Chris contemplated running away—the both of them, anywhere, just so they could finally be rid of his father. Strangely, Katie popped into his thoughts, but only briefly, as her vision was quickly beaten back by all his troubles. It was a rare time her image brought him no pleasure or comfort.

Chris went to the window and knelt down to secure the light plug that had loosened from the outlet when the tree had been thrown to the floor. Then he walked around the tree's corpse and pushed the topper into place. Slowly he lifted the tree upright. Glass fragments jingled like tiny bells as they fell with whole ornaments to the floor. He retrieved the scattered ornaments, doing his best to properly place them on the tree. Janey's music box still beneath the tree, and undamaged.

Once he rehung all the whole ornaments, Chris grabbed the dustpan from the foyer closet and swept up the shattered remains of the ornaments that did not survive. He dumped them into a grocery store bag from the recycled supply kept in the closet. Then he brought the bag upstairs and checked on Janey before he flopped onto his bed. He would add the remains to the coffee can tomorrow. Tonight, he just wanted to forget everything that had happened, that this world even existed. If only he could remove his aching brain and place it in a jar...

Chris rolled over to turn off the light. But before he did, he gazed at the book, still in the trash can. He hesitated, recalling its strange comforts and the approach of midnight, then retrieved it. Feeling its numbing Power, he clutched it to his chest. Now growing drowsy, slipping in and out of insane dreams, Chris—in a moment of utter exhaustion and defeat—silently hoped that he would not wake in the morning.

PART THREE

The Dream World

Chapter Fourteen

The Dream Village

Chris slowly awakened in a sour mood, as if someone had rudely nudged him from his sound sleep. He was on his stomach, still in his clothes, and soaked in perspiration. He felt hot and nauseous, and the vomit crept up this throat like lava. Though he didn't want to, he knew he had to get to the bathroom or risk throwing up all over himself. When Chris opened his left eye ever so slightly and looked out of its corner, he saw flames shooting up from the edge of his mattress.

Victor!

Now wide-eyed, Chris tried to push himself up. But as he did, the shadow figures charged in on him and leapt into the fire where they took on grotesque shapes. Small, clawed hands reached out to grasp his clothing and hold his arms and legs in place. The harder he tried to push himself up, the harder the gnarly hands pulled down. When he looked closely into the flames, Chris saw horned bat-like faces—dozens of them, all piled on top of each other—grinning back at him with sharp black teeth. There was no roaring of fire, or crackling or hissing of wood, yet an odd kind of black billowing smoke filled the room. It lacked any real soot, appearing more like a dark, bubbling energy, as if made of syrup, through which he could see. The devilish creatures were strangely silent. All Chris could hear was the ringing in his ears, and that awful pounding—and never worse, as if from the great and terrible war machine.

His defenses rose, and sensing the severity of the situation, he stacked up some of the heavy-duty thoughts from his arsenal of rationality. What this real? Another vision? Or was it just a lucid dream? Maybe it was real and a dream that somehow overlapped. Maybe he was sleepwalking. Maybe a false awakening. He knew all about that stuff, out of necessity. It could even be the flu. His mind often played tricks on him when he was getting ill. It wanted him to sleep and take action against the illness all at the same time. Maybe he should just go back to sleep, before this brand-new craziness got out of hand.

Then, beyond this waking nightmare, or whatever it was—movement in the doorway. A slightly bent white-cloaked figure with a floppy, wide-brimmed hat with white feather in its band materialized in the wavy amber fluid. Chris could not see the details of the distorted face, only the long white beard. But he had a damn good idea who he was. With staff in hand, the figure slowly raised his arms wide. The flames grew more intense, while the demons held Chris fast.

The heat was suffocating. Sweat poured from his brow. Nightmare or not, if he didn't free himself from the flaming bed, Chris knew the heat would overcome him.

The grandfather clock in the foyer began its methodical bonging. At that instant, an army of pudgy, naked creatures with tiny feathered wings descended from above. They, too, seized him by the limbs—even his hair—and began pulling him upward. The stinging pain was real. A tug of war ensued as Chris tried to free himself from the clutches of the fiery little demons. The struggle only incensed them. They beat their membranous, bat-like wings and snarled, revealing those sharp black teeth. But with each bong of the clock, some of the demons paused to cover their pointy ears before falling away into the flames, now diminishing. This lessened the heat and the downward pull, and gave Chris the opportunity he needed. With one mighty push, Chris helped the victorious *putti* extract him from the flaming bed as the twelfth bong from the grandfather clock sounded.

Now standing upright on the floor, Chris saw that the flames and the demons and the cupids were gone. So, too, was the white-cloaked figure. But in his place stood an angelic creature with long, dazzling hair and a glowing white gown. Her face shined so bright he could not see its details. A cool and seductive calm swept over him. That was her telling power. He no longer felt nauseous. Only the ringing and the pounding in his ears remained. The angel stood there a few moments longer, then turned and left the room.

Chris walked to the doorway, then gripped the molding and stopped. He just had to fight it with every ounce of reason he possessed.

But then, Chris stuck his head out the doorway. That was required, too. He looked down the hall, hoping that the angel was gone, and that the madness had ended. A shaft of warm light shined from beneath Janey's bedroom door and across the hall, as it should have, linking the scene with the sane. But beyond that, the angel stood at the edge of the stairs, waiting for him to follow. Now he had to see this through and push her from this reality.

Chris stepped into the hall and quickly approached the creature. He didn't bother to look in on Janey. He would do that momentarily, on his way back to bed, when everything was okay again. He followed the angel down the steps. The ringing and hammering in his ears intensified. She drifted into the living room, then dissolved, sparkling and chiming like broken glass, into the glowing halo of the tree.

Chris could have ended the night at that moment. The angel, or whatever he would decide she was, was finally gone. Now he could go upstairs, take his temperature, and rationalize himself to sleep. But there was one more detail that wasn't quite right, one more dazzling vision that caught his eye. It wasn't a cupid or a demon or some other sort of phantom. It was the tree topper. A beam of intense light was shining up from its spire. Even more amazing, all the kugels were glowing furiously, like miniature suns. And Janey's music box angel was twirling with delight as the chimes played the sweet and innocent song.

Chris drew close to the tree, and felt compelled to inspect one of the glowing kugels. The pounding and crashing in his ears, the iron hammering wood, was never louder, and kept time with his beating heart. He lifted his right index finger to touch a kugel—just to see if it were hot. But as the tip of his finger drew within a millimeter of the ornament's surface, the static electricity discharged with a loud pop. Only, it wasn't a pop—more like a clap of thunder, just like on the night the monster first appeared. A blinding flash enveloped him, and he felt himself falling.

Moments later, Chris was lying on his back, with knees bent. He breathed slowly but heavily, as if he had indeed survived a great fall. The hammering in his ears, so harsh and annoying, slowly dissipated into a soothing song, like the ringing of a fine ship's bell that chimed with the slow but forceful pulse in his neck, and with the rise and fall of his deep breaths. But the brilliant light still surrounded him. He blinked a few times to activate his pupils and squinted mightily. Then he felt a cool wind swirl around him, and he caught a whiff of pine. The rational narrative held firmly in his mind. Now what, another lucid dream? The same one? Or had he fainted and was just coming to?

With all his senses now functioning properly, the chiming drifted away. Chris sat up. He looked around, trying to orient himself—trying to recall the last image before the blinding light overpowered him. The Book! That's when he realized that he was sitting in something that did not belong in his living room, or anywhere else that was familiar—a spongy surface of sharp, stiff, needle-like objects that crunched beneath his weight. He still could not see a thing other than the blinding light, but also sensed that it grew dimmer to his right. He placed both hands on the surface and closed his fingers around what felt like straw. Then his hands crawled outward like spiders and found a sturdy narrow frame that ran parallel to him on each side, and dropped off beyond an edge. He swung his legs around to the right and his boots found a sturdier surface that still felt a little spongy and crunchy. He stood up quickly, and felt the weight of a heavy jacket and the tug of suspenders on his shoulders. Though strange, not foreign. And it disturbed him. He had to finally concede that he may indeed be in the vision that he had hoped would never haunt him again.

With his mind still whirling, and feeling anxious, Chris shielded his eyes with his right arm, then slowly backed away from the blinding glow. When the light dimmed, he saw his pointy scuffed boots, his iron-stiff cuffed and scratchy wool pants and plaid flannel jacket that resembled nothing in his wardrobe—that he had worn briefly many times before. But what really seemed odd, and a little encouraging, were his thicker fingers and larger hands—strong, farm-boy hands, calloused and cut—which he turned simultaneously palms up to examine as if they were growing before him. Beneath the jacket, the tug of those suspenders on his broader shoulders, suspenders that ran down over his jutting chest. This was something new. Maybe he was dreaming? A clarifying hope began to calm his mind. Now Chris realized he had backed up onto a narrow dirt path that cut through an immense field of giant red poinsettias. He stared back at where he "landed"—at the wooden stable filled with straw, in which sat a manger.

Chris lowered his arm and looked up. A mountainous pine tree towered over him, its great bulk of giant branches laden with millions of tiny white orbs, its own mini-galaxy. His jaw dropped. With his eyes still locked on the tree, Chris continued to back away from it along the dirt path until he saw the very top. The pine tree had a giant topper similar in shape to the one back home, but different in substance. It looked more like a natural part of the tree. A beam of light shot straight up from the tip of the topper's twisted wooden spire, while two other beams shot laterally and in opposite directions from two holes in the great hollow just below. The light from the hollow was so bright, he could not see within. The tree, he estimated, was at least five hundred feet tall. Never imaged this before—never been in this scene before. The cold wind made the case for vision as it howled in his ear and rattled the orbs. His cheeks burned and the fine hairs in his nostrils froze. This was not like dreams with their confusion of fuzzy images that he often had a hard time recalling once awake. In this one, the sights were exquisite and the sounds clear, like those chiming bells. And not since the days back in the old bungalow, when they used to cut a real tree and stand it, falling needles and all, in the living room window, had a pine scent smelled so fresh and intoxicating and real.

Chris tried to laugh at it all, laugh it all away, but nearly choked. He hadn't realized how long he had stood with mouth opened wide, how he had nearly stopped breathing, how dry his throat had become. When he tried to swallow, he felt as if he were gulping razor blades. Another case for the vision.

In a stunned silence, Chris reluctantly scanned the scene with trepidation. He gazed beyond the tree topper and up into the fresh, dark atmosphere. There was a moon—a full moon—with the same man-in-the-moon crater markings as on the real one. In fact, as he looked around at the stars, the entire night sky seemed the same. There was the Big Dipper, the Little Dipper, Polaris, all the familiar sights, all where they should be—and the Bethlehem star, almost directly overhead. Not good. Not good at all.

And then suddenly, as if on command, Chris' gaze fell to the horizon and onto the snow-covered village that sat in the forest valley before him. And just for a moment, he felt as if he were standing in his dining room, staring at his mother's painting. Only he wasn't. He was...here. He gazed at his strong hands, and frowned.

Chris began to realize the tremendous implications, and consequences, if it were the Story. Janey popped into his mind, lying sick in her bed, back home, without him. The more his willfully disbelieving stare focused on the Village, the more disturbing features he saw—his sight aided by the powerful glow of the Moon and the Great Tree. Plenty of telltale signs existed: pointy roofs, stone chimneys trailing blue smoke, and bright orange light from tiny windows. But then, another glimmer of hope for the just-a-dream scenario: the steepled church was missing. A white, meandering stream dotted with lamplight split the Village in half. Tiny white lights also shined from the many smaller frosted evergreens scattered throughout the Village. He saw an arched Bridge at the nearest edge of the village, but no roads or automobiles. Before the Bridge lay an ice-covered pond, some skiffs ashore partially buried in the snow, and a few bundled figures who glided on the pond's windswept surface, their blades scraping the ice. From there, the frozen stream continued into a snowbound meadow that stretched far to his left. And the cold wind howled once more.

The familiarity of the Village was haunting, chilling as the breeze, and undeniable, even though he had never experienced this scene before either. Yes, it was the Village. He didn't need to stare any longer to understand what he was beholding, just as he knew what may have sparked it all. But now he had to wonder: was she here, too?

Chris hesitated to take another step. Strange thing about the visions: they usually collapsed by now. So did his dreams—twenty minutes tops, the experts proclaimed. But it was the Holy Season of Magic, when things could run wild, and play for prolonged times. He dreaded the idea: giving in to the Power, living that life again, under its spell. And yet, with the scene still intact, beckoning him to continue on, showing no sights of quitting—where he could not only see her, but talk to her, and maybe even touch her—did he want to pass the opportunity? It was, possibly, a trap. What if, this time, he couldn't come back? That fear had always been with him, since the Monster first appeared, and ultimately steered him from the Book.

But if he were just dreaming...

Chris now feared that if he took one step, created one tiny crunch, the exquisite scene so vividly laid out before him would collapse in an instant, and he would fall back into the living room, and awaken to a great sadness. He decided to cast all fear aside and take the gamble, just to see.

Chris stared at the Bridge. He could feel his heart racing, his anticipation growing. The smooth but odd-sized river stones set in mortar, the copper lampposts tarnished with green, the wooden sign chiseled from a rough cedar slab—he could almost feel their rough surfaces. The details were so clear and precise and persistent, he couldn't contain his excitement. "Holy shi—," he shouted, clamping his mouth before the ugly word could echo across the meadow and ravage the beauty. He was stunned by the deepness in his voice, but dared not speak another word. He looked at the skaters. They hadn't noticed him.

I'll see you one day in the Village, yes? In the Village...

Yes, those famous words always drove him. Run, *stupido*—run!

Chris bolted down the path and quickly broke free from the poinsettia field. The cold air burned his face as his boots busted through the crust of the ankle-high snow. He was just as fast as ever, but felt heavier, and more powerful as his bulkier muscles flexed machine-like beneath that scratchy clothing. His noisy approach caught the attention of two older boys in heavy jackets and trousers skating along the near edge of the pond. They glanced at him, laughed, then kept on skating.

Chris ran up to the entrance of the arched Bridge and stopped to catch his breath. He was thrilled that the scene was holding together, that he was about to finally enter another of her cherished creations. But even this place set limits on physical endurance. More evidence for the vision. He bent to rest his hands on his knees and exhaled puffs of steam. Once composed, Chris glanced up to the right at the wooden sign next to a pot-bellied hydrant, both illuminated in lamplight. "*Villaggio di Sogno,*" he read aloud with pleasure but without much thought, as if he had expected these exact words. Then he stood up and glared at the plaque. "*Villaggio? DI SOGNO?*"

"Cristofori," a young woman's voice called out, "what are you doing?"

Chris looked down the embankment to his left. Besides the geese swimming in the small patch of steamy open water directly beneath the Bridge, Chris saw the handsome face of—Katie.

It...was...*Katie!* Katie? *Wait—what's she doing here?* Not part of the Story. Each word, each letter carefully selected and etched with lightning bolts into the Book—*no way!* Out of habit, he blinked a few hard blinks. She remained standing at the pond's edge in black boots with clamp-on iron skates, her hands in a fur muff clutched at her waist. Katie sported the same knee-length white coat she had worn the last time he saw her. She hadn't changed one bit. Could there be any doubt now? Could there? Oh intelligent, funny, lifesaving dream, grabbing wildly at all sorts of memories—hold together a little while longer!

Chris turned eagerly to face her. "I was just looking at *il segno*." His eyes shot open. He wanted to say "the sign" with that new, deep voice. Those were the words he had thought to say. But they came out translated. And he didn't even know the translation. Then another oddity hit him. "What did you call me?"

"Di Sogno," the young woman said irritably. "Yes, that's what the sign says, all right."

Chris frowned. "The sign?"

"*Pardoni?*"

Chris shook his head, and then he shook it a second time with more vigor. First it was "il segno," now it was back to "the sign." And she didn't even use the right word for "pardon." "You mean *pardoni*, don't you?" he said before laughing. *Perdono* didn't work here either. He couldn't be more encouraged.

The young woman mirrored his frustration. "Stop teasing. Are you going to skate with me or not?"

With you? Really? Then Chris realized that—*oh, yes!*—Coach Joe's mangled Italian and its insane rules, never part of the Story either, had infected the dream. This kind of crazy stuff always happened. It was the stuff of dreams! The evidence was indisputable, and the last of his fear concerning the vision evaporated. But then, a new fear: the mangled Italian might be a warning that the dream was breaking apart, or going off in a new direction—maybe even back to the practice field. That kind of stuff always happened, too, when dreams became nightmares. He started to panic. "I'm looking for someone."

"Looking for someone?" the young woman said, still annoyed. "What do you mean by that?"

"My... my *momma mia*." He had tried to say "mother," but now he fully understood that certain words just couldn't be spoken, and converted on their own, with no notice at all, becoming the norm.

Now the young woman was scowling at him. "Cristofori, get down here and put on your skates or I'll skate by myself—and you can go back and stare at that manger all night, if you want."

Chris approached the young woman. "Do you know her? I mean, is she here?"

"Who?"

"My mother."

She tilted her head and frowned. "All right, that's enough." She began to skate away.

"No, wait—please! I need to know."

The young woman stopped. Her irate expression slowly dissolved into one of concern. "Are you feeling okay?"

Chris stepped to the edge of the pond. "Listen to me—I don't have a lot of time."

"A lot of time?" The young woman gazed at him for a moment. Then her tone softened as she seemed to sense just an inkling of his extraordinary predicament. "Do you...do you need to go home, Cristofori?"

Her conclusion astounded him. "Yes, I do. As quickly as possible, please."

The two older boys who had spotted Chris earlier skated up to the young woman's side. Chris knew instantly who they were—and just like her, never part of the Story. But unlike Katie, each looked a little older and even more developed than the last time he saw them in the real world. No doubt, they had become young men, like he always viewed them. How perceptive dreams could be, too. Freud knew that. Good ol' Dr. Freud. An infallible genius—no doubt!

"What are you two yakking about now?" the tall, hatless one said, looking more handsome and rugged than he ever was. "What's the matter, me boy? You look sick. Aren't you going to skate with us?"

"He says he needs to go home...to see his mother," the young woman said sadly.

"Home?" the stocky boy said with a grin to the young woman, his baby-fat dimples gone. "To see his mommie? Why are you looking so scared. Don't you know when someone's messin' with you? He's the master." He turned his cocky gaze to Chris. "You don't like us anymore, Cristofori?"

But Chris ignored the stocky boy and kept his eyes locked on the young woman. "Will you take me there? Now?"

She stood motionless, unsure.

"Are you two plotting against us?" the tall one said. "Come on, Cristofori, you see Caterina all the time."

Caterina—yes, that was the correct translation. Her new name sounded even more delightful. "Please," Chris said to her, "there isn't much time."

"Wow, he really must need it," the stocky boy said to her. "Is he always like this?"

"Hey," the tall one said, slapping the stocky boy on the shoulder, "what's in your head? Show some respect."

"What's the big deal? It's just sex."

"This is no joke, Lorenzo," Caterina said. "I really think there's something wrong."

The two young men looked at her with a fresh apprehension, then turned their attention to Chris.

"What's going on, Cristofori?" the tall one said.

"Are you Matteo?"

"Am I Matteo? What kind of question is that? Don't you recognize me?"

"I do."

"So what's the problem?"

"I have to see my mother. Now."

"Why?"

"I don't have time to explain. Please, just take me to her."

"You don't know where she lives? You—the man who remembers everything?"

"I have an idea. But I don't know how to get there."

Looking perplexed, Matteo glanced at the others. No one seemed to be in a jovial mood.

"He's not joking around, is he?" Lorenzo said.

Matteo nodded. "All right. We can do that. Just give us a minute."

They sat in a tense silence in the snow pile along the edge of the pond where they began removing their skate blades. Chris took shallow breaths so as not to disturb the fragile makeup of his dream. Then he gazed down the frozen stream at the cottages and small shops of the Village, all decorated with pine garland and bowed wreaths frosted with the latest snow. He still could not believe where he was standing. Like Matteo and Lorenzo, the Village structures were a little different than he remembered and described in the Book. Different, but better—sturdier, with the large-pegged mortise and tenon joints of the timber framing visible, just as he recalled reading about. The most noticeable change, other than the missing church, was the roofs. Instead of thatch, they were covered with thin sheets of slate shingles, fastened firmly to timber battens. Along the lamplit walkway on each side of the stream, stately men in top hats and calf-length topcoats strolled arm-in-arm with young ladies in bonnets, long jackets, and billowy skirts. Farther down, he saw a few more arched bridges and their tarnished lampposts. The haunting smells of baked breads and pastries from Christmases past filled his nostrils. He could hear soft, festive music—stringed instruments and piano, without singing, the kind she liked—and occasional laughter. He had never imagined such amazing details when staring at her painting, and he was pleased that his dream had granted such an experience and

perspective. How he wished he had time to explore. *Stay focused on Sandra,* he reminded himself once more. *Don't let your mind wander, or the dream will fall apart.*

With their iron skates bound with cord and slung over her shoulder, Caterina walked up to him, right hand extended. He eagerly reached out and pulled her up the slope. And though her hand was cold, he took great delight in touching her. Even better, Chris realized that he was taller than she was. He removed the skate cord and draped it over his shoulder before she locked her arm in his. He tried to coax a smile from her with his own feeble grin, but concern remained firmly on her face.

"Come on, Cristofori," Caterina said as her hand returned to the muff, "let's take you home."

The familiarity with which she treated him surprised him—and thrilled him. Chris looked at the Village once more and smiled. Home...to finally speak with Sandra.

If he could hold the dream together.

Chapter Fifteen

The Artist's Studio

"Are you and I...are we, you know, together?" Chris said to Caterina. They followed Matteo and Lorenzo along the lamplit path that angled up the bluff to the left of the Village.

"You don't remember that either?" Caterina said. Their arms were still locked together as she clutched the hand muff.

"That makes me happy. You don't know this, but I always dreamt of us this way."

"This is not a dream, Cristofori."

"Yes. It is." Chris glanced down at her—then realized, once again, that he was glancing down at her. The creative power of his dream state made him smile. But he saw that she was worried, and he did not doubt that she felt its pain. "I'm sorry. I don't mean to scare you. There's really nothing wrong. All of this will be over soon."

"Please don't talk like that. You're a little overwhelmed with emotion, and memories. You just need to lie down for a while. I'm sure of it."

"Ah—Doc-speak," Lorenzo said, turning slightly as he continued on. "Better listen to her, Cristofori. She ought to know."

Matteo faced Lorenzo. "What happened to him? Did he fall and hit his head? Maybe he slipped in the snow."

"I don't know," Caterina said, "I didn't see anything. He said he needed to go to the Tree. And then the next thing I knew, he was standing by the Bridge staring at the plaque."

"I didn't hit my head," Chris said.

"What's with him and the Tree, anyway?" Lorenzo said.

"You really need to ask that question?" Matteo said.

Lorenzo adjusted the skates draped over his shoulder. "It's just *L'albero*."

"That's just a tree?" Chris said. He glanced at the towering evergreen. But he now understood from their vacant expressions that this Tree, though spectacular and powerful, was no more wondrous or unusual to them than the Sun.

"Did something happen to you, Cristofori?" Caterina said. "Did you fall down?"

"No, I didn't fall. And I didn't hit my head."

"Well something had to happen," Lorenzo said.

"Yeah," Chris said. "Something did."

"What?" Caterina said.

"You don't want to know."

"Of course we do. Why wouldn't we?"

"It's just too weird."

"Weird? What do you mean?"

"I told you, it doesn't matter. All this is just a dream."

"Why does he keep saying that?" Lorenzo said. "Is he sleepwalking or something? Maybe he's flipped his *parrucca*. Come on, Caterina, you should know."

"I'm not the doctor in the family, Lorenzo."

"Just tell us what happened," Matteo said. "It's okay."

"All right, fine." Chris said. "I warned you." He stopped in a beam of lamplight, turned abruptly to the Great Tree and cringed, fearing teleportation, even destruction. But when the dream persisted, he decided to speak the truth, because it didn't matter. All he wanted to do was see Sandra—as quickly as possible. "You're right, Lorenzo. I was looking at the tree. But this tree was in my house, in my living room. I touched one of its ornaments, and I got a shock. Then everything got real bright. Don't know if I fell or what. The next thing I know—zap—here I am. And you know what else? Caterina lives behind me. She used to be my babysitter. Yeah, I said it—my babysitter! And you two are my friends, sort of. I go to school with you—one of you, anyway. That's another story. Even your Village is part of my world. It's from one of my mom's first paintings. And it's hanging on our dining room wall. She even gave your Village its name. And this crazy language you speak—well, you wouldn't believe the story behind that. I'm dreaming all this stuff up, you see—even you, sorry to say. That's why I'd like to talk with my mom before I wake up. I know nothing around here is real—but it's awfully damn close, so I'll gladly take it."

They stood motionless, staring, with mouths opened wide.

Chris was surprised, too. He couldn't recall voicing in his lifetime so many sentences in one outburst. He sounded like Janey when she got excited, or wanted to win an argument. "Anything else you'd like to know?"

With a burst of energy, Caterina dragged Chris up the path to the top of the bluff with Matteo and Lorenzo in tow. The uneasy silence remained. The glow of the Great Tree and the full Moon illuminated the snowy mountain-meadow landscape, with its giant boulders, outcrops, and groves of flocked fir trees. They followed a footpath that snaked around the boulders, then opened to a meadow where the long spring sails of a stone windmill slowly turned in the breeze. Suddenly, they came upon a Cottage, sitting on the edge of the bluff, the dark mountains looming in the backdrop. He recognized it immediately, and he smiled, nearly shouting his joy. The dwarf evergreen, covered with tiny white orbs, was where it should be, glowing just to the right of the purple arched front door. Even better, he was about to see this through, and confront her.

Caterina led Chris along the path that swept right of the evergreen and along the low stone wall. They stopped at the arched entryway. There, before him, was the Artisit's Studio, right where it should be. And sure enough, the French doors were wide open. The delightful heat emanated from its well-lit space. The woman with dark, straight, shoulder-length hair was sitting at an easel with her back to them as she was supposed to be—in her black painter's smock. She worked carefully with the dazzling brush and luminous paints before the white glowing canvas displaying that half-finished blue sunflower. And then all the emotions and physical reactions came rushing in on him as they were supposed to do—including the racing heart. The scene, experienced over and over again, as he remembered.

"Come on, Cristofori," Caterina said as she tried to pull him along, "it's all right."

They started along that snow-packed walkway that split the slumbering garden in two. And as he did before, he hoped his mother would hear them approaching, so he wouldn't have to speak first. But like last time, she continued working on her painting. He stopped again halfway. The force that maintained all this imagery remained strong and determined. He was amazed at how the scene played the same way.

"Alessandra?" Caterina called out.

The woman spun around on her wood stool to face them. His time with her had come, and it did not falter.

Chris zoomed in on her bemused face. Alessandra, yes—but Sandra? Once again, something was a little different that confirmed his dream argument: her longer lashes on thinner lids, darker and narrower eyebrows, fuller lips, and everything set in just the right spot on a slightly narrower face, all the imperfections from the real world now gone. Despite the subtle changes, and awareness of the dream, his mind had accepted her image as real. She was beautiful and healthy again, like he wanted to remember. It felt so strange as always to see her immersed in this scene, as if she had existed here forever. Suddenly, Chris realized that he had another strange new problem that he did not know how to handle: tears.

"Cristofori!" Alessandra said. Even in dreams, she knew him well.

The sound of her voice astonished him, though it had changed slightly, too.

She sprang from the stool and rushed forward.

Chris pulled the cord from his shoulder and let the skates fall to the ground. Then he opened his arms to receive her. Alessandra embraced him, and instantly he sensed the warmth of her face, the scent of jasmine. He closed his eyes and hugged her, and felt against the palms of his hands the roughness of her smock, and her firm but delicate frame beneath—the realness of her. God, how wonderfully frightening! Then those despicable tears began to rise. But as always, he willed himself, he commanded himself not to cry. And with the anger overtaking him, his tears retreated, leaving only an empty sadness. Then a shot of fear. He was certain that this emotional bomb would destroy his dream. They usually did. He even wondered if Janey was already in the living room, tugging on his shirt, trying to wake him. But like his sadness, the dream stubbornly persisted.

Alessandra rocked him in her embrace. "Cristofori," she said with despair, "what's wrong? Caterina, what happened?"

"We don't know," Caterina said. "We were skating…and now he doesn't know where he is."

"He doesn't what?" Alessandra said.

"Memory thing," Matteo said, as if it were no big deal.

"I don't understand," Alessandra said. "Did he fall? Did he hurt himself?"

"We don't know," Caterina said.

Alessandra grabbed Chris by the shoulders and tried to push him away. "Cristofori…Cristofori, look at me—*look at me!*"

Chris reluctantly released his hold on her and gazed into her troubled hazel eyes.

"Do you know where you are?"

Chris' eyes were like saucers again, and he stared at her, still amazed at the sights and sounds. Then his sadness brought him down, and he bowed his head and nodded.

"Do you know everybody here?"

He nodded again.

"He thinks this is all a dream," Matteo said.

"A dream?" Alessandra said.

"That's what he told us," Lorenzo said.

Alessandra's eyes darted back and forth as she gripped his arms. She was searching…for something. "Cristofori, what did we talk about at dinner?"

Chris took a deep breath and looked blankly at her. He didn't know how to respond, not that it mattered.

"Don't you remember?" she said.

"I'm sorry," he said. "I don't seem to have much control over this." He wanted to touch her face, just to feel it again, but he resisted out of the persistent fear.

"We talked about your sister," Alessandra said.

"Giovanna? She's here, too?" Why did she bring this up?

Alessandra glanced nervously at the others. "Caterina, is your father home?"

"I'm sure he's still there—yes."

"Would you please ask him to come here as soon as possible, if he isn't too busy?"

"Yes, ma'am. I'll make sure he will."

"We'll go with you," Matteo said to Caterina.

"No, you boys stay, please," Alessandra said. "I need to ask you a few more questions."

Caterina turned and ran from the garden, and Chris felt his heart sink. How long could this dream possibly last?

Alessandra slipped her arm around his shoulders. "Come, Cristofori. Let's get out of the cold."

Alessandra led them into the lamplit Studio. They sat around a square wooden table with simple wooden chairs. Alessandra poured him a glass of water from a crystal pitcher and sat next to him. Chris sipped the cool drink, tasting its spring-like freshness, and gazed with curiosity past his mother at those framed paintings on the long back wall, none of which were loyal to the image back home. Instead of bold landscapes and dreamy villages that could build or alter worlds, Alessandra had been painting bowls of fruit, flower vases, forks and knives—all sorts of common household items fitting for a common homemaker. No doubt, she was hardly a sorceress (but that change he had written). Despite the mundane subjects and her lack of magical power, the paintings had a style and depth she had not displayed before. He was amazed at the detail—how real they looked, and three-dimensional, with perfect shading, color, and texture, as if he could reach in and grab each object. Talents had evolved in this dream as well.

"What's troubling you, Cristofori?" Alessandra said. "Don't they look familiar? Tell me what's on your mind. Please."

The concern she and the others expressed had not subsided. He knew they were waiting for him to say or do something outrageous. He understood their apprehension. But how was it possible to convince those in a dream that they weren't real and that they could dissolve at any moment? Even worse, what if the dream suddenly went sour and took a strange turn? What if Alessandra transformed into someone else, or some element of violence or disaster descended upon them? And now the doctor would soon be on his way. What would a heaping dose of that booming entity do to this scene? Or the probing psychological examination he would conduct? There was no way he wanted to go through that. The sudden urge to run, even in dreams, felt real and necessary. He had seen what he wanted to see, heard what he wanted to hear, and felt what he wanted to feel. And that's how he wanted it to end: with her, here and warm and alive. He needed to do what he could to end the dream, turn tail, and awaken, or else risk losing all the wonder he had experienced. But there were a few important things he wanted to say.

"I'm sorry I'm upsetting you," he said to Alessandra. "I told you, I don't have much control over all this. But I think I can tell you why I'm here. I've gotten real good at figuring out these kinda things. Christmas is coming, and we've decorated the house just like you used to—"

Alessandra looked terrified. "Cristofori?"

"—and I'm having a hard time forgiving you, for what you did."

Oddly, her expression softened. She seemed willing to accept the charge, as if she really knew how he felt.

"But now that I'm here, finally getting that chance to talk with you..."

"Yes?" she said.

He hesitated. "I just want you to know that we miss you very much, and that we think of you all the time. And I hope that you really, really are in a place like this where you are happy and surrounded by your paintings. But I don't think I should stay here any longer. I'm afraid time will just ruin everything."

"Cristofori, why are you saying such things?" Alessandra said. "Of course you should stay here. This is your home."

"Come on, Cristofori," Matteo said. "Don't you see what you're doing?"

"I know, I know. I don't expect you to understand."

"Dr. Samuele will be here soon," Alessandra said. "I'm certain that he'll be able to help."

"Yeah, well, good ol' Dr. Samuele..." Chris nodded and smiled at Alessandra, making sure he remembered every detail of her distraught face. But his encounter with the doctor would never come. He bolted from his chair and dashed through the open Studio doorway.

"Cristofori, no," Alessandra cried. "No more running!"

Chris streaked through the garden entryway and ran toward the front of the Cottage. He truly felt bigger but more powerful and faster than he ever did back home. And he was thoroughly shocked and a little disappointed that he had not awakened. Often such a jolt caused his dreams to evaporate. But this one was still holding together, its details unchanged. So he kept on running.

After he passed the illuminated dwarf evergreen, Chris stopped and whirled around. Matteo and Lorenzo were in pursuit, just now making their way from the garden. He had just enough time to take a mental picture of the scene. Yes, that was it—just like the painting. And though it was only a dream, he took the opportunity to say it: "Goodbye, Alessandra." Then he darted off along the dark and winding path.

Chris truly expected the dream to vanish with each swift step. His desire for the end should have been more than enough to burst it. But the dream stubbornly persisted—insisting that he descend the bluff, traverse the Bridge, and retrace his steps through the meadow and poinsettias. A final look at the Dream Village, another snapshot, and he ran for the white-hot glow at the base of the Great Tree.

Chris had, of course, no specific knowledge that returning to the all-encompassing glow would end the dream. But something in his mind told him so. He sprinted into the blinding radiance. The ringing and the pounding in his ears returned, softly at first, then intensified as the light consumed him.

Suddenly, Chris was on his back again—this time, staring up at the artificial tree and the white popcorn ceiling of his living room, his wet clothes clinging to his hot skin, his mouth open and an annoying but common trickle of drool on the right side of his face, as if he had been sleeping on his back for hours. The loud hammering noises began to subside. Chris sat up, wiped the drool, and reached to the back of his throbbing head where he felt a stinging knot. Then he struggled to his feet and stared at the kugels, which were no longer radiant. Confusion swept over him. Had he fainted? What was he doing here? He reached out to one of the orbs—then he remembered.

"The painting," he said.

Chris rushed to the dining room and flicked on the lights. Then he stood in front of *The Dream Village* and stared in awe at the detail before he touched the dried blobs of paint. He felt as if he were still there. He grinned. The dream would not escape him—not now, not in the morning, not ever.

But then the reality of his world took hold, and the glee dissolved into gloom. The anger in his father's voice, the rage in his eyes, the smashing of the tree, and Janey. He recalled those sounds and images, too. He was back in the real world, without her, where she no longer moved around, and lived. He turned around and looked at the den door. It was shut. No music, no sound, and no light.

Chris ran up the stairs and peered through the narrow opening into Janey's room. She was sleeping peacefully on her side with the lamp on. Thankful, Chris rush to the medicine chest and popped open the aspirin bottle before chasing four pills with a cup of water, confident the drug would do the trick. Then he staggered into his room. A beam of moonlight streaked through the window and onto his bed, revealing the wrinkles where his body lay before he saw the flames. No singeing, no soot. Just the wrinkles, and his Book of Everything. He sat on the bed and remove his square-toed boots, which he dropped to the floor. Then he gripped the Book with both hands and stared at the shadows of those stamped letters in the ghostly light. How was it possible...with all those changes? The evidence overruled his fears. He jammed the Book under his mattress, and flopped back onto his bed.

Chris tried to close his eyes, but they grew misty and burning as the dream played over and over again in his mind. He sat up, head down, feet on the floor, and fought the rising emotion.

Sandra was gone again. Not happy and healthy and in another world where she could thrive the way he really wanted her to. Just dead. There was a steep price to pay for resurrecting them fully, where one could feel the warmth of their rejuvenated skin and hear the sound of their new and vibrant voice. Now, he had to bury her one more time before he could try to sleep.

And then, all at once, the tears dried up when Chris looked at his glaring clock radio. It read: 12:13.

Chapter Sixteen

At the Vanity

"I saw Mom last night," Chris said after carefully weighing his thoughts.

They were in the spare bedroom that Sandra had used as a studio and library. It was flooded with sunlight, a Sunday light, once so special and powerful in a religious way, God's line of sight, the hints of that old power, and her, still felt, especially after last night. The room was lined with assemble-yourself melamine wood shelves (that Sandra assembled herself) crammed with his fantasy novels, his childhood picture books about dinosaurs, and his mom's trashy romance novels (that Victor sometimes threatened to toss into the trash with the paintings) that even Janey was caught reading from time to time. Janey, still in her "jammies," sat on a padded bench at the old white vanity and stared blankly at her reflection in the trifold mirror as "Marilyn" looked on from the right side of the tabletop. (Marilyn—a name he had to research—was the polystyrene head on which Sandra's wig sat. Janey refused to pack it away. The wig was a gift from Dr. Samuel, the color requested. It was, as Sandra put it, her one chance "to be a blonde.")

Chris stood behind Janey and combed her wet hair. Janey had just taken a warm bath. She wanted to go to school. Chris wanted her to stay home and rest. It was a quick debate. But she still might miss the bus. Even on a healthy day like today, Janey often had trouble deciding which pleated blue skirt and ruffled white blouse to wear, and she would stand in her ballerina pose in front of her closet—hands on hips, left foot forward and pointing to the left—as she pondered her choices. The ironing board and iron were at the ready, next to the closet, as always. Sometimes she would remove a few outfits to try them on before her mirror, only to return them to the rack. On those days, she had to be driven to school. That option was not available this morning, with Victor already gone somewhere.

"Did you hear me?" Chris stated. "I said I saw Mom last night." He noticed Janey's glassy eyes in the mirror.

"Hair today, gone tomorrow," she said innocently, with a hint of sorrow, as she repeated Sandra's lament. Then those glassy eyes shattered, and with a hard look of skepticism, she locked onto Chris. "You're not saying that because I'm sick, are you?"

"No, no, I'm serious." This was going to be a tough sell, coming from him. Chris checked the room as if it were full of spies and he were about to utter state secrets. "I even spoke with her."

"You did not. I know when you're lying."

"Well, you're wrong again, Sister Mary Janey," he said. He withdrew the comb from her hair. "She was in her Studio...at the Cottage. The one you loaned me. Just like in our Story."

"You were there," she said flatly.

"Yep."

Janey cocked her head. "How? Our Story? You don't believe in anything anymore."

"Not the Story, just something like it. A kugel brought me there."

"A kugel," she said before laughing. "That's silly."

"You're sillier."

"You're silliest."

"It's the truth," Chris said. "Happened right after you went to bed. The thing was glowing like a star. So I walked over and touched it, just to see what was happening. And then—bam!—I was there."

"At the Studio."

"You got it." He decided to retell the part of his dream that would interest her the most. "Do you know that she's painting things like flowers and fruit bowls?"

"How could I?"

Chris resumed the combing, determined to gain her trust. "She seemed very happy. It was very beautiful—better than I ever thought. But it was strange, too. I mean, think about it. How many times have you looked at that painting and wondered what it would be like to be in it?"

"What do you mean? We used to do that all the time."

"Yeah, well, never thought that I'd actually be there with her—not really. You were there, too. At least, that's what they told me. I never did see you. You know how dreams are."

"So it was a dream."

Chris shrugged. "Well, yeah, I guess. I mean, what else could it be, right?"

Janey nodded slowly. She seemed disappointed. "Who's 'they'?"

"They? Oh, Matteo and Lorenzo—I mean Matt and Larry."

"They were there?"

"Sure, why not?"

"They weren't in our Story."

"So? This a dream we're talking about, Doctor Janey."

"Sounds kinda weird to me. Mom, with those two ding-dongs?"

"They're not ding-dongs, and they weren't with her. They brought me to her. They were at the Village pond, skating. Even your geese were there."

Janey smiled. "Were they looking for me? Did you feed them?"

"You'll have to excuse me, but somehow, I forgot to dream up a sack of stale bread. Besides, I was too busy talking with Katie."

"She was there, huh?"

"Yep."

"So it was just a dream."

"I guess." It hurt a little, getting some confirmation—especially from his sister.

"I bet you liked that."

"You bet correctly."

"Yeah," she said softly, the way she always teased him—relentlessly!—about his love for Katie.

"Yeah," Chris said. Young boy falls for babysitter. It was a classic coming-of-age thing. But he never felt embarrassed about it—not even with Janey's constant ribbing. There had been other "first loves," of course, throughout grade school. How could there not, attending classes with the same girls year after year, watching them slowly approach their teens, noting the agreeable changes—and them, already fully aware of the spell they cast over him just by their mere presence? Spitballs became an early form of love letters, and—even stranger—name-calling, just to gain attention. Then the real letters came, and Valentine's cards, with astounding thoughts and words, slipped from time to time through the air slots on his locker door—words that became powerful reminders of the arrangement. He always knew who was interested. The bright smiles and the dreamy stares gave them away. But neither their advances, nor his, ever amounted to much, not with his mother's arm-crossed image always standing over him. One girl boldly sat next to him on a nearly empty school bus just starting to make the rounds. Another, sitting in the desk in front of him and leaning over her textbook, put her left hand in the small of her back so he could reach out to her. Then there was the one who lured him behind a great tree at recess and encouraged a peck on the cheek. None of these "loves" compared to Katie. During those dark days of Sandra's demise, Katie was there—constantly. She was someone near his own age who listened with keen interest to all his fears, shared those fears, and beliefs, as they discussed the hereafter with intelligence and sincerity, making it appear truthful—often in the church vestibule, where they could stare at the paintings. Katie confirmed his intelligence, that he wasn't just a little fool who didn't matter, and provided the comfort and the steady voice of maturity he so desperately needed, making him feel real and important and loved, and helped propel him in her own special way toward manhood. He couldn't help but feel love and appreciation for her. And so it was since the first day she had come to their house to watch over them, when he first saw that face, and heard her voice, and felt her touch—and his world changed forever, even as he had to concede the tornado's vital role in their meeting. She was what he wanted, not some girl. And he shuddered to think who or what he would have become by now if it weren't for the genuine love this angel from Heaven had given. If only he had been encouraged to kiss her…

"And Doctor Sam?" Janey said, suddenly bringing him back.

"Well…yeah, as a matter of fact. But I didn't see him, either. They sent for him, but the dream ended before he showed up."

"Was Mom living with him?"

Chris shook his head. "Sorry. We talked about this before."

"It's okay. What about Victor? Was he there?"

"I said it was a dream, not a nightmare."

Janey giggled as she watched Chris comb her hair. "I think that must be what it's like for her in Heaven, even if it was just a dream."

"I hope so, too."

Now she smiled. "See, more progress."

Chris shot her a perturbed look and placed the comb on the table. Then he grabbed the blow dryer. "I see you're feeling better."

"Uh-huh!" she said.

Chris squeezed the trigger on the dryer and gave her face a short blast of hot air. "Just a little present from my master—*blaaah!*" He stuck out his tongue and shook his head wildly. It was so easy to be this way, with her.

Janey pushed the dryer away. "You're sad," she said. She faced the mirror. "Let's keep going, please. I don't want to miss the bus."

Chris grabbed the roller brush with his free hand. "Yes, sir."

"Yes, ma'am," Janey said.

"Yes, ma'am, sir," Chris said. He rolled some wet hair on the right side of her head, turned on the blow dryer, and held it close to the brush. Their gazes met, and once again she offered a bright smile. But Chris wondered what Janey was really feeling. She had put on her brave face years ago when Sandra first sat on this bench, allowing her children to coif her hair while she recovered from the initial rounds of chemo. But being the patient was far different from sitting on the sidelines as a spectator. Janey was the one on the clock now. And the clock was ticking.

Chris noticed that Janey stared at the reflection of the many paintings hanging on the wall behind them. After a minute, she was still staring. Chris turned off the blow dryer and walked to the painting of the towering Christmas tree surrounded by a field of red poinsettias. "This was in my dream," he said, pointing with the roller brush. "But it was gigantic—five hundred feet tall, I swear. You should have seen it. It was amazing."

"You must have been thinking of our Story before you went to bed. Were you reading it or something?"

"No."

Janey stared at the reflected image. "I hope I get to see her there."

"Maybe someday you will."

"Someday soon, you mean."

"No, I didn't mean that."

"It's all right. I want to talk about it."

"No," Chris said. He returned to the table and picked up the dryer. "You're gonna get better, and that's all we need to say."

"But what if I don't?"

Chris squeezed the trigger and the dryer whirled to life.

Janey grabbed his hand pulled his finger from the trigger. Then she gazed at him. She didn't look scared, just resigned.

"This isn't right," Chris said. "I'll take back all those wisecracks about your headstone. You're not supposed to go before me."

"Who says?"

"Those are the rules. I was born first. I should die first."

"What if I do?"

"That's not going to happen."

"But what if I do?"

"Then I'm gonna come get you and bring you back. I can do that now, you know."

"Her, too?"

Chris grimaced. "She won't like that, will she?"

"So you can stay with us."

"Not a bad idea. Come and go as I please. When Victor gets nasty, I'll just zap myself outta here. And when you guys start getting on my nerves—"

"Bam—back to Victor!"

Chris sighed. "All right, so the plan needs work." He thought of Sandra sitting on the vanity bench, looking at him, telling him in that look what was coming. "You're not going to give up, are you, Janey?"

"Of course not. But if I die—"

Chris clenched his teeth. "Don't say that!"

"If I die," she said, "I'll still be watching over you."

"C'mon, Janey, you're sounding like Mom again."

"Well?" Her voice wavered. "Well?"

"Okay...okay, sure. I know." His lame-o time-tested reply, when it got difficult, and the words didn't come. He fought back his emotions, sighed, then brought his fist to his mouth and tapped his lips, giving both of them a chance to recover. It was one thing to banter about heavenly fantasies while whistling merrily through a seemingly endless childhood. But now she was stepping toward the pearly gates, or more recently, the *White Rose*. This topic was deadly serious, and needed a definitive answer. That was the big problem. No one teaching them was clear or convincing about how the hereafter worked. And that led to a lot of uncertainty. Religion class had many opinions that burst with color, creating big, fluffy, utopian paintings that hung on church walls, the ultimate happy ending. But these pictures did not include motion or time. What happened after we all rode into the sunset? Did we still have bodies? Did we need bodies? Did we have hands to grasp and manipulate things? Legs to move us about? Binocular vision? Mouths with which to speak and eat, and blood to create heat? Did we have a nose through which to breathe? And a brain to control it all? Was there an atmosphere to breathe? Did we even have to breathe? If we died old, would we suddenly become young again? If so, how young? And if we died young, would we stay young, or grow old? Was there an Earth on which to stand? Did it have the same mass, liquid core, and magnetic field? Did it have the same tilt, same rate of rotation? Did the same comets and asteroids once bombard it? In the same order? And did it go through the same deep freeze cycles? Was there a Moon and a Sun? Were they same size and distance from the Earth? Did this Sun have the same intensity? Was it part of the same kind of solar system? Was it in the same part of the same kind of galaxy? Did this galaxy belong to a cluster? Was the cluster in the same part of the same universe? Was it flying apart from all the others at the same speed? And was it all—the whole thing—just as old as the one we were in? If it wasn't, if one particle were off just slightly, or missing, then everything would fall apart. But if it were all the same, what would we do with all that eternity? As for his science deity, few of the living ones dared utter any sort of speculation about the hereafter for fear of being cast from their herd, even though the multiverse of signs seemed to be pointing in one direction.

(*If you want to make a human, you gotta have a big bang. Har har har!*)

Chris allowed her a moment to compose herself. "What do you think it's like, Janey?"

"You mean in Janeyland?"

Though he was embarrassed that she had discovered his dig against her beliefs, Chris glared at Janey, as she finally confirmed something that he had suspected since he first wrote in the thing.

"Oopsie," she said in a small voice. But then she popped up in her chair and smiled in the fullest way possible, showing all her teeth, looking like a mini-Sandra in her happiest moments.

And all he could do was grumble. "But I don't want to hear about the big white clouds or any textbook junk they've been cramming into us. I want to know what you really think—in one sentence." That would get her to think hard and rational about it.

Janey's smile fell, and Chris was certain that the tip of her tongue was about to pop out. But Janey didn't hesitate as her eyes found the painting of the girl feeding the geese at the Village Bridge.

"It's a place where I'll never be afraid," she said, deadly serious, "of anything."

The doorbell rang, and Chris looked quizzically at Janey, who shrugged. Then Chris thought of the last time someone came unexpectedly to their front door, and he rushed to the foyer. Chris hadn't seen Katie since Saturday when all Hell broke loose. He was delighted that she had finally returned. Had she brought the gifts?

Breathless, Chris opened the door. Dr. Samuel filled the doorway in his three-button, gray cashmere overcoat—tall, dark, and angular, like Abe Lincoln.

"Good morning, Chris," he said with his typical, unnerving boom, as if he were the dream version, finally arriving to quash Alessandra's fears. "May I come in?"

Chris stepped back, and recalled the fear he felt in that dream, anticipating the doctor's arrival. "Yes, sir." His heart settled. He felt a little deflated, too.

Dr. Samuel entered the house and closed the door. The scent of his manly cologne followed. "How's our little Janey doing this morning?"

"She seems fine, sir. She's upstairs, getting ready for school."

"School? Indeed." The news seemed to delight and horrify him at the same time.

"Yes, sir. I told her to stay home, but she won't listen."

"No, I suppose not. How's she going to get there?"

"The bus. Is that okay?"

The doctor sighed. "She's just like your mother, Chris—awfully determined, and she hides things well. You keep an eye on her."

"I do. I always do."

Dr. Samuel nodded, but his concern lingered. Then his eyes narrowed as he spotted something disturbing in the living room. "What happened in there?"

Chris looked at the floor and noticed that some of the broken glass remained scattered about like sparkling gems in the morning light. He felt mortified for not having sufficiently scoured the hardwood for the humiliating evidence, even though the doctor was more than sympathetic to their plight. Damn vacuum cleaner. Who knew he'd come over today? And how come adults always found things that teens didn't want them to see? "The tree fell," Chris said finally as his mind worked furiously to concoct a believable story.

"It fell? When? How?"

"Last night." But already he sensed failure. This was Doctor Samuel he was trying to fool, not Victor. But he had started it, and needed to finish. Then, feeling that strange reluctance and the need to defend, he said: "Victor knocked it down—by accident."

"Accident, huh? Was he drunk?"

"Yes, sir."

"Is he here?"

"No, sir." Victor had emerged this morning from his den earlier than expected, and intercepted Chris when he was brushing his teeth in the second floor bathroom. Victor showed no remorse for last night. Chris wasn't sure his father even remembered—until Victor insisted that Chris apologize for disobeying him, and making him "look bad" in front of Matt and Larry. Chris refused this demand with his silence.

"Naturally," the doctor said. Then his eyes narrowed as he stared at Chris' face. "What happened to your mouth?"

Chris ran his tongue across the swollen part of his upper lip. He had forgotten about the little souvenir, too. "The tree hit me."

Dr. Samuel bent down to examine him. "The tree did, or Victor?"

"The tree...by accident."

"Another accident?"

"He was drunk and fell into it. Then it hit me."

The doctor stood upright. "Chris, we've been through this before. As a doctor, I'm obliged legally to notify the county. If I can file an emergency report—"

"I remember."

Dr. Samuel nodded. "Then you also remember that I can't help you much if you won't cooperate with me—or them. They won't be willing to take action without definitive proof of abuse."

But back then, that was part of the problem—and it still was. The week after Sandra's death, the letter came, then the social worker—both of which pleased the Hell out of Victor, which made Chris and Janey all the more fearful of cooperating. Besides, they had just lost their mother. They didn't want to lose their house, too—or each other. And Victor could turn on the charm with the flick of a switch. After all, he had just lost his wife. Poor Victor. That was the other part of the Pact, never spoken, but understood. Splitting up the family, possibly to different foster homes and foster parents, and cast into the unknown, was something Chris couldn't allow. And Dr. Samuel had the terrible power to do it. "I know," Chris said.

The doctor sighed deeply after a few moments of silence. "Did he hurt Janey?"

"I'd never let him do that. She was in her bedroom...sleeping."

"But he could. He's tried."

Chris did not fall for the doctor's ploy. "No—never."

Dr. Samuel shook his head. Then he spotted the mound of roller chain on the small table. "What's that?"

Chris couldn't keep his eyes from betraying him. How could he have forgotten about that thing? More burning humiliation, and diversion. "Junk he sells."

"What's it doing there?"

Chris did not have an answer—he did not want to answer—and his silence drew way more attention and suspicion to something that should have remained innocuous and unconnected to the crime. The longer Chris kept silent, the more suspicious the doctor became. When Chris realized, despite his prodigious power to conceal things, that the horrible truth now seemed emblazoned on his forehead, Dr. Samuel's eyes brightened.

"My word, Chris, did he—"

"He's never hit me with it—no."

Dr. Samuel stepped to the table and eyed the chain more closely. "But there's blood on it!"

"It's not mine, it's his."

"How did that happen?"

"Some of the edges are sharp."

"Did he threaten you with it?"

"No."

"Then what's it doing here?"

"I don't know. They're all over the house."

"Chris, don't you realize what that thing could have done to you? Why didn't you call the police? Why didn't you call me?"

"What for?" Calling anyone from the house in secrecy—especially the police—was difficult, given that the only landline phone outside Victor's den and bedroom was on the kitchen wall. Then he'd really hurt them. He couldn't let that happen, either. He just couldn't.

Dr. Samuel let out another long sigh. He gazed about the foyer as if he were lost. "Very well, I've seen enough. And this time, I'm going to own it. It's obvious I need to be involved every step of the way." Dr. Samuel slipped his hand beneath the wide lapel and into the coat's inner breast pocket and withdrew a white monogrammed handkerchief. Draping it over the balled chain, he closed his long fingers around the evidence and carefully removed it from the table. Then he lifted the flap of his coat's right side-pocket and stuffed the chain inside. "I want you to write all this down—everything that happened last night, including what he did with the chain."

"I will. I always do."

"Do it soon. Do it today. I'm going to need a detailed account. And don't let him see it."

"He won't."

"And be honest."

"I will."

Dr. Samuel sighed a final time. The frustration he had displayed disappeared. He removed his overcoat and hung it on the coat tree. "You know, you and I should sit down and talk soon—man to man."

"Man to man? About what?"

"Things that are bothering you. After all you've been through, and going through now? I don't know how you do it. Strike that. I know. You may not believe this, but I'm a pretty good observer...and listener."

That was another problem with Doctor Sam. "Yeah, sure." What else could he say?

"Okay, then. Let's go see Janey."

Chris led the doctor to the spare bedroom. Janey remained seated at the vanity, waiting patiently for Chris' return. Her face lit up when they walked into the room.

Dr. Samuel crouched next to her. "How's my young lady doing this morning?"

"Real good, sir," Janey said, with Sandra's insisted formality.

"That's what I want to hear. No nausea, no dizziness?"

"No, sir."

"How about your strength?"

"Never better."

"Any shortness of breath?"

"I'm breathing okay."

"What about the pain in your joints and bones? Better? Worse?"

Janey shrugged. "It's nothing."

The doctor opened his hand and gently pressed his fingertips along the bottom of her jaw, then down the sides of her neck, all the while maintaining a sober expression. He examined her arms, looking for imperfections on her skin, then a quick inspection of the gums, for color. Finally, he placed the back of his hand across her forehead. "You feel normal. Are you sure you're strong enough to go to school? You don't have to, you understand."

"Yes, sir, I do."

Dr. Samuel touched her on the shoulder. "That's my girl. If you start feeling out of sorts later, you call me and I'll come get you." He slipped his hand into the breast pocket of his white linen shirt. "Let me give you my card."

"I know the number," she said.

He froze for a moment, then blushed. "Oh. Yes. Very well."

Dr. Samuel stood up. Janey's adoring gaze locked onto his face.

"I need to make sure there's no confusion about the cause of Janey's condition, so I wanted to clear the air as best as I can and give you a bit more details. I'm afraid I didn't do a very good job of this last time, within that whirlwind of emotion. So if I may…" He looked down momentarily and rubbed his hands. "Where to begin—where to begin?" He looked genuinely befuddled and worried, his cheeks deepening their crimson. Then: "Ah!," with index finger pointed skyward. The redness in his face drained away as he looked intently at Janey. "There are building blocks in us all—structures that make up everything in our bodies. They're called cells. Cells are made from chromosomes. Chromosomes are made of these thread-like structures called genes. The genes, mind you, are the key to this whole story. Genes hold all the information needed to build our cells. We get our genes from our parents. Sometimes, they give us genes that are…defective. They're made of the wrong information. These defective genes can cause tumors to form. And sometimes they form in our bone marrow." He stared at Janey. "You know why bone marrow is important?"

"It makes blood," she said. She popped up with a smile. Apparently undisturbed by his slightly condescending tone. What did the doctor know about talking to a precocious ten-year-old? He lived with a goddess.

"Yes, that's right," the doctor said. "Now, if you have tumors in your marrow, it interferes with normal blood production. Without good blood, we lose the ability to fight diseases and keep our organs working properly. That's the kind of problem we're dealing with. You can't catch your disorder from the air, like a germ. You can't get it from eating the wrong things. And nobody—other than your mother or father—can give you this disorder. You were born with it, Janey. That is, you were born with the information that produces the tumors in your marrow. And now…now we're going to fight back and try to get rid of those tumors. That's what all this medicine does. If we get rid of the tumors, your marrow can make good blood to keep you healthy."

"What makes the genes?" Chris said, almost compulsively. He didn't dare ask him to repeat the prognosis—not in front of his sister. It was stated only once, officially, with Sandra's "condition." After that, they battled each day as if victory were in sight. Even when her hair was gone. Even when she could barely speak. Even when Dr. Samuel came to her side for the final time, just before Father O'Hara arrived.

The doctor looked at Chris quizzically, as if he had come out of a trance. "I'm sorry, what?"

"The genes. What are they made of?"

"DNA," Dr. Samuel said quickly. His gaze returned to Janey.

"Is the DNA defective, too?" Chris said.

"Yes, Chris, that's what's really defective. The DNA."

"And what's that made of?"

The doctor just stared at him. And just stared at him. "Nu-cle-o-tides," he said finally.

"Are they broken?"

"Yes, yes. When you get down to it, that's the core of the problem—erroneous chemical structure in a four-base fragment of DNA." He paused, as if to catch his breath, and mend his nerves. "Chris?"

"Yes, sir?"

"Where are you taking us?"

"Well, it seems to me that if you can fix that structure, she wouldn't have this problem anymore."

The doctor nodded, but Chris couldn't tell if he was agreeing, or becoming more annoyed. Dr. Samuel's blank expression reminded Chris of his teachers at St. Boniface, during the days of the Grand Experiment.

"There are about a thousand nucleotides in the average gene," Dr. Samuel said. "Regarding probable inherited disorders like your sister's, only a few of these nucleotides may be in error. Sometimes they're...they're misspelled, sometimes they're missing. So ideally, if we could do the repair within the chromosome and not have to replace the entire gene, yes, fixing those defective structures would be the ultimate solution. But we can't play God, medically speaking. We don't have the ability. And even if we did, there's just too much entanglement to unravel. I'm only trying to explain to your sister that there's a complex, internal cause for her illness. I'm sure you can appreciate this. There's information and diagrams everywhere about DNA structure and nucleotides. If you want to know more about them, what they...'look like,' I suggest you do some research."

"He'll do that, you know," Janey said, breaking her uncharacteristic silence.

Blood rushed to Chris' head. "Janey—"

"I'm sorry?" Dr. Samuel said.

"He's always looking things up. Wants to know how everything works. So he takes pictures."

"Pictures?"

"With his brain."

"Janey—" Chris said.

"Really?" the doctor said. He stared for a moment at Chris with genuine admiration. "You can do that?"

Chris sighed. "I guess."

Dr. Samuel raised one bushy eyebrow. "Impressive. I do remember Sandra mentioning it a few times—how you recall details. The mind of the artist. Not that it's all that remarkable, really. We all have tremendous memory capabilities. It's the accessing part that is sometimes difficult." He paused. "Do you recall the color of my overcoat?"

A fire lit in Chris' brain, shorting it out, and he panicked. These embarrassing, memory-loss episodes were happening more and more, now that the depression—and the anger—had settled in. And now he had to perform. "Black," he said.

The doctor nodded. "Anything unusual about it? It's a little outdated."

Chris shrugged, but the panic did not fade. He kept silent.

"What about the lapels? Wide or narrow?"

"Wide."

"And the side pockets? They had another old feature."

When the doctor refused to offer more clues, Chris said: "That I don't remember."

The doctor smiled. "Interesting."

"He gets nervous when you're around," Janey said.

"I understand."

But Chris, though he knew he had failed, could tell the doctor was skeptical, and that irked him. It was one of two talents that he was proud of.

"Well," Dr. Samuel said, "if there are no more questions, I have one for the both of you." And then he hesitated, as if he were carefully selecting his next words. "Do you remember what your aunt died from?"

"My aunt?" Chris said.

"Yes, your mother's sister. What was her name again?"

"Monika." Chris glanced at Janey, who shrugged. He recalled that his aunt, a once-frequent guest at their holiday dinners, was a bit portly, and painfully withdrawn. She always appeared sick to him, but he never really knew if she was (yet another unpleasant subject that was rarely discussed). The news of her sudden death had been an emotionless nonevent to him (but he did recall stealing sugar cubes from the funeral home's coffee lounge the night of her wake). Even Sandra had done well to hide her tears. "I don't remember that, sir. I was kinda young."

The doctor nodded. "Did she have any children?"

"I doubt it."

"She wasn't married," Dr. Samuel said, apparently for his own benefit.

"They talked about that a lot, but no one ever called."

"Unfortunate," Dr. Samuel said. His eyes shifted side to side as he drew toward some conclusion. "And she was your mother's only sibling."

"Uh-huh."

"I don't suppose their parents are available."

"Sir?"

The doctor cleared his throat. "This Friday, when you come to the hospital with Janey, I want to take a blood sample from you."

"Really?"

"It's just routine. It'll help me understand Janey's condition better. And we may need a marrow donor someday. But it's far too soon for that full discussion. Perhaps we can even get Victor to cooperate."

"Sure. Okay."

"Very well, man of the house. You call me the first sign of trouble—no matter what or who it is. You know what I expect you to do. You owe your sister that."

"Yes, sir," Chris said, though he still didn't know if he could.

"All right, then." He gazed at Janey. "You seem unusually quiet. Are you sure you're okay?"

Janey nodded as she grinned, but she said nothing.

"She gets like that when you're around, sir," Chris said. "You should stop by more often."

"Very funny," Janey said.

Now it was Dr. Samuel's turn to blush again. "Oh...well, yes...I'll...I'll see you both on Friday." He turned and disappeared down the hall.

"Merry Christmas, Doctor Sam," Janey called out.

The doctor returned to the doorway. "Yes...Merry Christmas, Janey. And it will be, you'll see."

It better be, Chris thought. He hadn't forgotten about either of his Christmas pledges.

Chris followed a perplexed Dr. Samuel, who insisted the escort wasn't necessary, to the foyer and watched the doctor put on his overcoat. Chris' mind was clear now, and the panic was gone. And he saw the details of the coat that he forgot. Time for a little redemption. It wasn't impressive, the last little detail he recalled. Anyone could do it. Probably would. But that wasn't the point.

"Remember what I said about calling," the doctor said. He still looked uncomfortable.

Chris just stood there.

"Yes...well...and don't forget the account I need. Perhaps then we can have that talk."

"Yes, sir."

Dr. Samuel nodded forcefully, then turned to grab the door handle.

"Sir?" Chris said.

Dr. Samuel opened the door and looked back. "Yes, Chris?"

"Do you think the blood got on your handkerchief?"

He frowned. "I doubt it. It appeared dry. Why the query?"

Chris shrugged. "Be a shame if it was ruined—you know, since it's got your fancy blue initials on it."

Dr. Samuel grinned. "I see Janey's not the only one who's like Sandra." He turned completely to face Chris. "Give me your hand." He took it gently and turned it palm up as if he were about to read it. But all the while he stared at Chris. "You are part of Victor, without question. He's in there, part of every clinging molecule. But so is she, and she'll be there, always, wherever you go. If you want to see her, just look at your hand. If you want to touch her, just rub your fingers together. She's there, alive and well in you. There, and—" The doctor release his grip and tapped Chris on the forehead with the tip of a forefinger, "—in there. And no one—not even Victor—can ever take her away from you." He nodded, stepped out, and closed the door behind him.

Chris stared at his palm, the five main lines, the tiny furrowed lines, the polyhedral cells that lost their edges and transformed into orbs, red and blue and inexplicably white, all connected. Feeling vindicated, relieved, and complimented, Chris ran up the stairs to attend to his sister.

∞

Janey selected a blue skirt and white blouse with un-Janey-like speed and got dressed. Chris made one of her favorite breakfasts: hot "diggity" dogs with scrambled eggs and a side of "bananers"—all drizzled with ketchup (Sandra's waffles were a close second, but Chris never had much success making them, so they kept them as a fond memory). Then he slipped her books in her pink-and-green butterfly backpack, bundled her warmly in her pink down coat and mittens, and took her to the nearby corner to await the bus, as Sandra often did. Though there was time, Chris wasn't going to school today. He had cleared things with a call to Mr. Maloney's office, conveniently forgetting the part about Janey going back to school. The usually suspicious sergeant-at-arms caved when he heard the word "chemo."

Upon the bus' arrival, Chris offered to help Janey board. (She said "no.") Chris waited alongside the bus until he saw her face in one of the windows. They smiled and waved to each other, and the bus drove on. Then he stood there for a moment, lost in sadness, wondering how many mornings like this remained.

When he arrived home, Chris went to his room to retrieve his diary, then returned to the living room where he sprawled out on the floor beneath the unlit Christmas tree to write. He hadn't forgotten any of the dream's amazing details. But it was only a dream, and nothing more. His awakening last night confirmed this. And there was no sense in dwelling on it further, other than to transcribe what had occurred. Still, as he stared at one of dormant kugels that hung in the muted daylight, he had to wonder: what hellish visions or heavenly dreams, if any, would this night bring?

Chapter Seventeen

A Dream Come True

That night, while perusing the encyclopedias in his bedroom, Chris, after much procrastination, conducted an exhausting research of heredity disorders. Upon discovering more disturbing facts about the deck stacked against Janey, he committed to memory, as the doctor suggested, diagrams of DNA chemical structure. Then, still dressed, he set the alarm for midnight. But he knew it wasn't necessary. From the time he stretched out onto the bed in jeans and a sweatshirt, all the while denying his suspicions, Chris watched the green numbers of his clock radio change by the minute as the grandfather clock bonged each passing half hour. Sleep, he now realized, wouldn't be possible until he proved to himself that last night was merely a combination of worry, exhaustion, and a freakish, flaring temperature, and nothing to do with the stupid book. A myriad of thoughts crossed his throbbing mind: school, Victor, and Janey. She had an uneventful day at school and was tolerating the chemo well so far—no nausea. She managed to eat some tomato soup and crackers for dinner, but she was quiet and went to bed early with much on her mind. And she struggled to climb the stairs. Victor was on his best behavior, for Victor. Home early from "work"...a semi-convincing display of concern for "the poor kid"...no alcohol, or opera—and no apology from Chris. As for school, wouldn't that be fun tomorrow? He was a day behind in his studies. Extra homework, and difficult questions, awaited him. And he'd probably run into Larry. How was he going to handle that embarrassing meeting? Even worse, he wondered what Matt thought of last night's humiliation, and if he'd see him again. The telescope was ruined. It needed a new lens. Where would he get the money for that repair? And how could he explain to Katie, if the privilege were ever restored, why he was staring at the stars with a telescope that had no glass?

The midnight hour drew close. Chris grew more anxious, and he began to pace his room. *This is stupid. You're wasting time. The book is dead. Get some sleep, or you'll pay for it in the morning.* But he couldn't stop pacing, or wondering. When the final minute mercifully approached, he switched off the light and sat on the edge of his bed, and waited for things to happen. The clock flashed midnight, the radio came on. Then, as Chris silenced the alarm, he heard the grandfather clock tolling. He glanced around the room. No flames, no demons, no looming apparitions. Still, he wasn't satisfied. He had to see if the drama were playing out of sight, in the living room. After all, that was the launching pad.

Chris made his way down the stairs and into the living room. The tree looked shimmering, full, and proud, as always. But nothing about it seemed extraordinary. Janey's music box was closed, and silent. Then he looked at the kugels. Though gleaming, they were not white-hot—just beautiful ornaments hanging from an artificial tree. It amused him to think how powerful and mysterious they appeared last night. As a final reality check, Chris raised his hand to touch, with his index finger, the very same orb that sparked last night's journey—but at the last second, he hesitated. At last, he made contact. No spark, no flash, no dream within a dream. Sanity had prevailed—though he had to admit, he was slightly disappointed. Now, at last, he would sleep.

All during the night, Chris awakened long enough to hear the grandfather clock call out the remaining hours until daylight. One bong—had it only been an hour? He drifted back to sleep. Then later, two bongs—already? What exactly had he been dreaming? He tried to resume the dream, but, instead, began a new one. Later yet, three bongs—no, four...five...six. He sat up in bed—his flaming bed—as the grandfather clock continued to call out the hour. Seven...eight...nine. The wild tug of war resumed in the darkness. The Old Ghost was there, too, enjoying the show. Chris swiped angrily at the demons. They snarled as they scattered momentarily, like tenacious vultures from a kill, only to resume the struggle once his arm had passed.

Ten...eleven...twelve. The demons fell away while the cupids ascended. And the gleaming-gowned maiden appeared in the doorway.

"Who are you?" Chris said. "What do you want?" He knew the answer to both those questions, but wanted to force it from her, so she would say it.

The Temptress disappeared into the hall.

Chris tossed aside the covers and chased after her down the stairs. She vanished into the brilliant haze of the tree. Standing before it, Chris saw the kugels glowing furiously. Undaunted, he reached up and touched one—and in a flash, found himself running fully clothed in his old-fashioned garb through the field of giant poinsettias toward the lamplit Village. But there was no elation in his quick strides, no stares of wonder. He was finally going to get to the bottom of all this insanity.

Chris reached the pond and saw Matteo and Lorenzo rushing toward him from the Bridge. Chris met them head on, as if on the football field, and he seized Matteo by the shoulders, nearly knocking him backwards. "When's the last time you saw me?" Chris said.

"Cosa?" Matteo said with fear in his eyes.

"When's the last time you saw me?"

"What? We just caught up with you!"

Chris tossed Matteo aside and sprinted for the Bridge.

"Oh no, not again!" Lorenzo cried as he stepped out of the way.

Once atop the bluff, Chris zigzagged his way through the boulders and skirted the Cottage. Suddenly, he stood in the garden before Alessandra. She reached out to him as she always had done when he came to her for comfort. But he saw that his wild behavior had filled her with apprehension. He brought her outstretched hand to his face and felt once again the warmth of her skin. Now apprehension filled him—too afraid to admit what he knew was the truth.

"Cristofori, what's wrong?" she said sadly. "Why are you acting like this?"

"You're...you're really alive."'

"But of course I am," she said, on the verge of tears.

Chris fell to his knees, trembling. He brought his hands to the side of his exploding mind as Alessandra held him close. Dreams didn't connect to each other one night after the next like consecutive chapters of a book. Recur, yes—but continue? From the exact point where they ended? He looked up and saw Matteo and Lorenzo running toward the garden. They weren't part of a dream. Neither was the Studio, the Village, the Great Tree—none of it! Everything he saw, everything he heard, everything he smelled and tasted and touched...had become real, just for him.

He was in his Other World.

Chapter Eighteen

The Manor

"Very well," Dr. Samuele said as he paced before them in the center of the five-sided atrium, "who—*without any more hysteria!*—wants to tell me what actually happened tonight?"

Sitting in the center of a marble bench, his linen shirt soaked with perspiration, Chris stared down at the leather suspenders of his cuffed wool pants, not daring to look up at the doctor. Alessandra, still in her smock, sat to Chris' left, hands folded reverently on her lap, while Caterina, her black knee-length skirt and white blouse now revealed, sat to his right, legs crossed, booted right foot moving subtly up and down. Matteo and Lorenzo, each in the same sporting garb as Chris, remained standing on either side of them like altar boys. Suddenly, no one wanted to talk, now that the doctor's displeasure with their unexpected appearance was so visually and audibly evident. After Chris had returned to the Artisit's Studio, Alessandra insisted that they all go to the Manor immediately to seek out the doctor's help instead of waiting for him to arrive. During their frantic trudge through the snow, Chris had time to reflect more on his amazing predicament as each step he took in this New World reinforced its reality. By the time they arrived at the Manor, no doubt remained. Upon that arrival, Chris was surprised to see that the Manor, though faithful in form to Sandra's vision, was immersed in this World, like many things, in a strange new way. Even at this late hour, the Manor, often depicted as a fortress of solitude, was humming with activity. Draft beasts pulled tarp-covered wagons and carts through the service gates as labor-hardened craftsmen pounded and sawed on an ambitious "expansion project" somewhere behind the Manor. Dr. Samuele had been in the observatory with orders not to be disturbed. But Caterina had barged in on him anyway, and pried him from his "obsession with that star," as she explained it. After silencing them all, the doctor performed on Chris a cursory check for signs of trauma. Then he swept them from his small, book-crammed study to the more accommodating atrium—it, too, strangely lit with the glowing dwarf evergreens—to conduct an inquiry into the nature of this emergency visit.

True to the rules of this World, this Other World, Dr. Samuele—in dark pleated pants and matching but unbuttoned waistcoat, the sleeves of his white linene-collared shirt rolled up—looked and acted like the doctor of the real world, only slightly different. A little more handsome, a bit more authoritative, and working harder than ever. Having a large statue of an angel—the centerpiece of the atrium—with its eight-foot wingspan looming over him fed his intimidating yet compassionate aura. The "old-fashioned" clothing thing, which Sandra had insisted upon in all her paintings ("to hide the animal in us all"), was, like the odd language, fast becoming the norm to Chris. Though some Victorian elements were retained, clothing remained true to his mother's wishes, including knee-length hems for women, who were not subjected to bulky hoop skirts or "those awful confinement contraptions" once imposed on them by men in that time to accentuate femininity and restrain movement. This was her World, really. She made the rules. Despite the oddities, and his incredible appearance in this World, Chris felt amazingly comfortable with them all, as if he had truly lived here his entire life, and remembered. But the fact that his friends were here—particularly Caterina—troubled him, for a very great reason. He wonder if that part had evolved on its own, too, and in what direction.

"I'm sorry, Doctor," Alessandra said, her bonnet removed, "maybe I should have exercised better judgment before I brought him here. It's just that—"

"No, no," Dr. Samuele said as he stopped and held up a hand, "for you, Alessandra, anything—you know this. After all, my daughter's the one who convinced me of the urgency regarding your son. What was that you said, Caterina?" he said with a hint of derision, though they all had repeatedly addressed the claim. "Memory loss?"

"I haven't lost anything, sir," Chris said.

"That's not true," Lorenzo said. "He thinks he's from another world."

"Lorenzo, please!" Caterina said.

"Well, that's what he said," Lorenzo shouted.

"Indeed," Dr. Samuele said. He crouched in front of Chris and clasped his large hands together. "What's this all about, Cristofori? Another ploy?"

"Ploy? No, sir. What he says is true."

The doctor raised his bushy brow. "You think you're from another world."

"No, sir, I know I am."

Dr. Samuele nodded, trying not to show his emotions. "And this has nothing to do, somehow, with Caterina, or any other thing that you may know or feel?"

"I'm not sure what you mean, sir. I can give you my whole life's story, if you want...where I was born, where I go to school—"

"You were born here, in this World, Cristofori—I assure you," the doctor said. "I was the one who delivered you. And I, too, can reconstruct your life's history, if you wish."

Chris bowed his head briefly. "Yeah, well, I can't explain how this is all happening, not logically."

"This is important to you? The logic, that is."

"Yes, sir. More than ever."

The doctor nodded. "Continue."

"As I was saying, I thought it was a dream, but now that I've come back—"

"You've come back?"

"Yeah—I mean yes, sir. After I left her Studio, Alessandra's Studio, I went back home—where I really live. I was there for a day, with my sister. She's getting treatment for cancer."

"Your sister," the doctor said, glancing at stoic Alessandra.

"Yes. She's very ill."

Dr. Samuele looked at Matteo, as if for clarification.

"He ran away from us at the Studio," Matteo said coolly. "We finally caught up with him by the pond."

"You didn't catch me," Chris said. "I told you, I came back to get this all figured out."

"Did you witness him...disappear?" the doctor said to Matteo, sounding amused.

"Well, he did get real close to the Tree, so it was hard to tell."

Dr. Samuele's dark brown eyes flared with annoyance.

"Pardon me, Doctor," Matteo said, and he looked down.

Dr. Samuele regrouped and fixed a calm gaze on Chris. "No ploy, Cristofori?"

"No, sir. You see, as far as I can tell, when you look at me, you may see a person you think you know. But that person doesn't exist anymore. I've replaced him, in a way—at least, while I'm here. I don't know how or why, but I'm going to find out."

Dr. Samuele rose, folded his arms, then tapped an index finger perpendicularly across his lips. "I'm interested in this other world from which you claim to be."

"Father—stop," Caterina said.

"More directly," Dr. Samuele said, raising his voice to quell Caterina's objection, "how you managed to travel from that world to this."

Chris knew the doctor did not believe him—he didn't expect anyone to—but he sensed that a small part of this intimidating man was honestly intrigued by the science involved with the outlandish topic, and not merely toying with him.

"He says he has a Tree like ours in his living room," Lorenzo said before giggling.

"He did not," Caterina said. "You're twisting his words."

"Please," Dr. Samuele said, his eyes locked onto Chris, "let the young man respond in his own defense."

"This isn't a trial," Caterina said.

"I already told everyone, it's a lot smaller," Chris said, once again realizing how wild his account sounded. "You see, my sister and I made up this story, and wrote it down in a book—"

The doctor resumed his pacing. "And just how did this tree of yours facilitate your travel across, or perhaps more accurately, through space-time? Care to venture a guess?"

Dr. Samuele's choice of terms surprised Chris. "I think it was the light."

"The light."

"Yes, from one of the ornaments. Like the ones you have on your Tree."

"The light orbs?"

"Yes, sir."

Dr. Samuele stopped in front of Chris and leaned forward, hands on knees. "Indeed. How so?"

"Well, by touching it."

"Just like that," the doctor said, snapping his fingers. "Are you suggesting magic brought you here?"

"I don't know what it is, sir. I used to believe in it, but not anymore."

"Poor choice of words?"

"Yes, maybe."

"What word would you choose?"

Caterina grew visibly disturbed. "Father, I never discussed—"

The doctor silenced her with a quick glare.

"Well, again, sir," Chris said, "I'm not sure how to explain it. You probably could. I know you could."

Dr. Samuele kept his fierce gaze on Chris as all kept silent, then he stood upright and directed his attention to Alessandra, her face now racked with worry. "I don't care to make hasty diagnoses, Alessandra. Nevertheless, considering the heightened emotions surrounding the sudden turn of events, and in the absence of any apparent external injury, it may be safe to say that Cristofori is not suffering from any post-traumatic amnesia."

"Yes, thank you," she said. "And thank God for that."

"However, as you and Caterina have pointed out, and as Cristofori has plainly vocalized, there may be a serious psychological component at work here—assuming, of course, that he is being forthright with us. Given my personal experience with your son, you'll forgive me if I remain skeptical of his claims."

"Well-deserved, I'm afraid," Alessandra said.

Chris grew embarrassed, though he couldn't possibly know what his counterpart had done to deserve such a reputation.

"There is a host of other possibilities, as we have touched upon, that may need exploring," Dr. Samuele said, "but this is not the place nor the hour. It's already late and I have much more work to do. Alessandra, if you will, please return Cristofori here tomorrow by nine a.m. I don't know why this has happened either," he said, pausing to stare suspiciously at Chris, "but I, too, intend to find out."

"Doctor, if I may," Alessandra said, "I know little about these things, but are we facing a temporary condition?"

"We may be—or a more long-term problem. I'm sorry, Alessandra, I wish I could calm your fears, but I simply cannot rule out any possibility—not now."

Chris felt Caterina squeeze his hand, which was still cold from their hasty jaunt to the Manor.

"But he'll be all right, won't he, Doctor? Whatever the problem may be. Please tell me he will."

"As you well know, I always hope for the best," he said. "I'll certainly know more by tomorrow."

"Should I watch him tonight? Make certain that he's all right?"

"Oh, I think that would be very wise on any occasion."

"Father, you're being very heartless and unfair," Caterina said. "Cristofori is not lying, and he's not up to something—you know that."

"Know what, my dear?" he replied with a haughty tone.

Caterina glanced at Chris and struggled to smile, but she said nothing more.

"I'm sorry," Chris said, touching Alessandra on the arm. "I know I'm making you sad. That's not what I want to do. But I need to tell the truth."

"I still think a good night's rest will help him so—yes, I'm sure of it," Caterina said glumly. She slipped her arm around his. "Come, Cristofori, I'll walk you to the door. I'll have the coachman take you all home."

Chris did not like the pitiful manner in which they were treating him, but he understood. After all, considering his outlandish claims, what choice did they have? And as he walked with the others toward the white marble entrance hall with its over-sized wreaths and garland swags, Chris quickly realized a profound consequence of his improbable situation. If he truly understood the coming and going part correctly, it was possible for him to stay in this Other World indefinitely—for the rest of his life, if he chose, thus keeping the real world and all its problems frozen somewhere in time. It would mean that Janey's cancer would not advance, that her death could be avoided. But it also meant that her life—and his relationship with her in that world—would be suspended for eternity. And that seemed just as horrible as watching her die. But what of this mysterious new Janey, now called Giovanna, and Victor's counterpart?

They entered the hall where white-gloved servants stood by the main entrance, clutching coats, scarves, and hats. "Please forgive him," Caterina said to Chris. "He's been working very hard lately. There is much on his mind—too much, I'm afraid, for even him to cope with. His suspicions and his anger are not directed at you. He does admire you, I know he does. And he knows you would never do anything to hurt me."

"Hurt you?" Chris said.

"Cristofori," Dr. Samuele called out from the atrium.

"Yes, sir?" Chris said as he spun around.

"Just one final question before you go."

"Yes, sir."

"Do you remember what happened to your sister?"

Dr. Samuele's timing was impeccable as Chris and the others had been anticipating this inquiry from him, but Chris could not hide his concern about the dark insinuations regarding Giovanna. He surveyed the gloomy faces staring at him, and understood the doctor's intent. "No, sir—not the one who lives here."

Dr. Samuele stood motionless against a backdrop of the glowing trees and seemed to absorb every nuance of Chris' nervous motion, expression, and tone. "Then you don't remember the Storm."

"The Storm?" Chris paused uneasily. The powerful word released tough memories from another existence. But then his mind cleared as he once again accepted his role in the new reality that surrounded him, and he grew angry at this game. "What happened to my sister?"

Dr. Samuele continued staring for a few tense moments, as if he were taking mental notes and pictures. "I'll see you in the morning, Cristofori."

Chapter Nineteen

The Sleigh Ride

"What happened to Giovanna?" Chris said to Alessandra as they rode in the back of the jingling sleigh through the snow-packed woods that surrounded the Manor. "What's the big secret?"

Alessandra adjusted her scarf, then pulled the edges of her fur bonnet over her exposed earlobes void of jewelry. "I don't know if we should be talking about that now, Cristofori," she said. She slipped her gloved hands under the fleece blanket draped across their laps and looked at the trees, the shadows of their naked trunks and branches casting a wild crosshatch pattern on the snow.

"I don't understand," he said, the cold breeze tightening his face. "Don't I have a right to know?"

"But you do know," Lorenzo said from the center seat. Matteo elbowed him.

"I think you and Dr. Samuele should discuss that in the morning," Alessandra said.

"I'd rather hear it from you," Chris said.

Alessandra looked at him grimly. "Just tell me one thing."

"What's that?"

"That you are being forthright, as the doctor said."

"She's dead, isn't she?" Chris said with dejection.

All he heard was the jingling sleigh bells as Alessandra bowed her head.

"I don't get it," he said, angered by the cruel irony of regaining his mother in exchange for his sister. "I'm here, you're here, my friends are here...why wouldn't she be here? That's not consistent with the new rules."

"Rules?" Alessandra said, looking indignant. "What rules? Rules have nothing to do with this. This is punishment...for sins committed."

"So she is dead," Chris said, intent on forcing—just for once—the truth from her lips. "Was it the cancer? Tell me it was."

"Cancer?" Lorenzo said. Matteo elbowed him again—this time, even harder.

Alessandra looked away and retreated into a mournful silence. Those same characteristics that kept Sandra, as well as Chris and Janey, from discussing unpleasant truths had followed them to this World.

The sleigh broke free from the woods. The driver, in his bowler, boots, and greatcoat, gripped the reins ever tighter with his black leather gloves and guided the powerful horses over the arched bridge by the pond. Then he reduced the trot to a slow walk as he steered the sleigh down the empty, lamplit thoroughfare that took them past the darkened cottages and shuttered shops smothered in the snow.

Instinctively, Chris glanced up, his gaze momentarily fixed on the brilliant, pointy star that dominated the night sky. "What about this Storm the doctor mentioned?" he said finally. "Is that what did it? Matteo? Is that it?"

"What, me?" Matteo said. He turned to face Alessandra.

She nodded reluctantly.

"Yeah," Matteo said, sounding relieved.

That event wasn't consistent with the new rules either, Chris thought. Why hadn't it changed? Some parts of the Story, it seemed, did remain true, parts he wanted nothing to do with. He was heartbroken and devastated, now realizing he would never get the chance to cast his gaze upon Janey's human counterpart, let alone get to know her. But he found some solace knowing the real Janey waited for him back in the real world, if he could indeed return. So what was Giovanna now? And where? And did he really want to know? "How did it happen?" Chris said.

"I wasn't there, you know—well, maybe you don't know, not now, anyway," Matteo said. He was nervous, and kept his eyes on Alessandra. "But from what I understand, the roof collapsed."

More changes. Chris, too, kept his eyes on the sullen Alessandra, looking for signs of hurt or displeasure. "When did this happen?"

"Two years ago...two days from now...on Christmas."

"Years," Chris said. He still found it difficult to accept that, despite being frozen and deflated in time, this World remained attached to its own time and deep history that made the three-dimensional present real. But a tornado? In the dead of winter? And on Christmas? There was an obvious explanation. He insisted on keeping an open mind, and a fleeting hope, in case the new rules wrote a different Story. "Was I there?"

"Yeah," Matteo said, as if it were a foolish question.

"And what about Vittorio?"

"Vittorio?"

The name—just now mentioned for the first time since Chris had "arrived"—made them all uncomfortable, and Chris saw the panic in

Matteo's eyes. "Yes, my father. I do have a father, don't I? Or is that whole process different here?"

"Yes, but—"

"But what?" Chris did not understand Matteo's uncharacteristic perplexity.

"Well, I didn't realize that you had, you know, forgotten things about him—or wanted to speak about them."

"Uh-oh," Lorenzo said softly.

"Is that a problem?" Chris said.

"Well, yeah, it could be," Matteo said, now agitated.

"Your father left us," Alessandra said in a strained tone.

It was a pleasant-sounding response, to him, even with the unpleasant connotations attached. Victor? Gone? "When?" Chris said.

"Before Giovanna died."

"That's not a bad thing, is it?" Chris said, hoping for the best. "I mean, if he was anything like the man I know, we should be glad, right?"

With sad eyes, Alessandra forced a smile, but then it retreated. There was no joy in any of them about Vittorio's absence.

"Where is he now?" Chris said.

"Out there," Lorenzo said. He motioned vaguely with his head toward the woods.

"Out there?" Chris stared at the phantom trees moving past them, illuminated by the dim but ever-present light of the Great Tree, now out of view. No one volunteered elaboration. "Do you ever see him?"

"No," Alessandra said. "He's...he's not allowed here, Cristofori."

Not allowed. He knew where that law came from. "Well, that's good, too." Even his tone was unconvincing.

"Yes," Alessandra said. "Yes, it is." But again, no joy.

The driver halted the sleigh before a small, two-story cottage recessed between a bakery and a hat shop. Amber lights shown from lamps in the frosted windows, and icicles hung from its steep gable roof. "Home sweet home," Lorenzo said. He hopped out, and his heavy boots thudded into the snow. "It's been a real interesting night, folks. I sure hope you're feeling better tomorrow, Cristofori. I don't know if I can take much more of this."

"Just ignore him, like you always do," Matteo said. Then he looked at the driver. "I'll walk the rest of the way." The driver tipped his bowler as Matteo jumped from the sleigh.

"Matteo, wait," Chris said. "Will you be around tomorrow?"

Matteo gripped the black iron edge of the sleigh with his exposed hand. "Yeah, sure, of course. Why?"

"I want you to take me to the old cottage."

"The what?"

169

"Where Giovanna died."

Matteo looked with apprehension at Alessandra, who was visibly displeased. "I...I don't think I can do that."

"Why not? You know where it is, don't you?"

"Yeah."

"No, Cristofori," Alessandra said.

"Is it still there?" he said, keeping his eyes on Matteo.

"I guess so."

"Then why can't you?"

"Because he's a coward," Lorenzo said.

"Coward?" Matteo said. "I'm not the one who keeps a lantern on my bedroom sill all night." He pointed to the gable window where the lantern shined dimly through the small icy panes. "Want to tell them why you do that, tough guy?"

"No, Cristofori," Alessandra said with more force, "I don't want you wandering off. It's too far and it's too dangerous, especially this time of year. We've had enough excitement for a while. I would like to enjoy this holiday in peace. Besides, you'll be busy with Dr. Samuele tomorrow. We need to work on your health, not tear open old wounds—certainly not without the proper medical supervision. No good will come from that. None."

"I'm sorry, but I'm here now. If you want me to stay, I have to see the old cottage."

"Cristofori, please, just listen to yourself," Alessandra said. "You're not going anywhere. This is your home, this is where you live. There are no other worlds. Do you have to torment me further and fight with me? It's been a terrible night. Do as I ask, will you? For me? There'll be a more appropriate time for this discussion, if we must."

That old line. Chris hesitated, and glanced at Matteo, who winked. Then a knowing grin spread across Matteo's face. A deep connection, a signal. Just like old times, in another world. Chris' spirits rose, and he felt as if he were home. "Of course," he said finally. But now, with Matteo's encouragement and help, he did not intend to keep his promise.

Chapter Twenty

To Dream within a Dream

After Chris and Alessandra returned to the Cottage via the doctor's sleigh, they stepped into an entryway painted in a somber gray, lit by sconces, and where the brass-dialed grandfather clock from their old world house stood solemnly, ticking methodically, as its long gold pendulum swung side to side. Immediately, he was overcome by the pine and spice and sweet scents wafting separately with the cold from the outside air, aromas born from the festoons of wild flowers, berries, and fresh greenery draped on the stair rails and over the doorways, and from colorful glass bowls of perfectly ripened fruit garnished with sprigs of cloves, all resting on handcrafted tables gleaming with polish.

With white gloves already off, Alessandra closed the heavy door and stilled the air. The entry warmed again, and Chris' eyesight drifted into the dank parlor wallpapered in floral patterns, upholstered and draped in dusty velvet, and trimmed with gold tassels and white lace. Swags and knitted stockings hung from the rough, stout mantel of the dormant fireplace on which sat, in the center, just before a glowing painting of this very Cottage, a large clear vase of blue sunflowers. Warmth—without a visible means of heat. And freshness—in the dead of winter. He could not hide his astonishment. This was never in the Story. But he was home—his new home, where he had lived in quiet sadness with her for years, unaware of the other world or its related dramas.

Alessandra removed her bonnet, brushed away the melting snowflakes, which fell to the floral hand-hooked rug, then she fixed her tousled hair. She smiled back, but she still looked worried, no doubt disheartened by his reaction. They said nothing as she removed her scarf and hung it and her bonnet on a mahogany coat tree. Then he followed her up the creaking stairway to the second floor where she showed him to his bedroom. There Alessandra calmly pointed out all details of comfort and necessity—the stand-alone wardrobe, his single pole-bed with patchwork quilt, the tiny adjoining bathroom, tiled in black and white, with white ceramic sink, silver faucets, a flush toilet and claw-foot tub—*thank God...plumbing!*—trying to nudge him back into that sad but peaceful life he had lived here. And it was peaceful. No sounds from a modern world, nor this one, could penetrate the thick stucco-and-timber walls. It was just them, the Cottage, the woods, the mountains, the Moon...and the ever-watchful Star. The silence felt heavy, but comforting, like a soft blanket. Not wishing to torment her any longer, Chris played the game with her, nodding and smiling as if he vaguely recalled those days. Of course, she desperately wanted her son as he had been. And he tried his best to accommodate her. But Chris could not completely suppress his other-world wonder at being inside one of her cherished paintings, viewing more details of the Cottage that were true to her old-fashioned desires, yet ones that he had never fully imagined.

They said goodnight, and he prepared to close his room's paneled door. Chris saw on Alessandra's solemn face that her fears about his health remained. She reached forward, cradled his head in her hands, and kissed him warmly on the forehead, just like she used to do. Then she pulled away, but the warmth of that kiss lingered. It delighted and amazed him once more. Chris grabbed her slim wrists and gently squeezed them, and they exchanged faint but loving smiles. He still could not believe she was real, that he was with her.

Alessandra said good night and left the room, shutting the door behind her. Chris turned and pressed his back to the door, closed his eyes, and sighed, feeling a strange sense of guilt for not being home with Janey, as if she were sitting up in bed with the light on, wondering with tearful sadness why he had abandoned her in her greatest hour of need. But he was confident that was not the case, that the rules of passage were holding firm, and that when he returned (whenever that was) and lifted himself from the living room floor, drool and all, the ornate minute-hand of the grandfather clock would rest somewhere just past midnight, and Janey would be sleeping comfortably without the slightest suspicion of his prolonged absence.

But what of this existence? Chris was familiar with the many-worlds premise, and others, that could help explain everything. He came upon these wild concepts often in his extracurricular readings. But how it was indeed possible to move from one world to another and back again as he had done was well beyond his understanding. Would the door to this World—wherever it truly was—stay open? Could he come and go as he pleased, as he unwittingly discussed with Janey? Or was this opportunity only temporary? Exactly what kind of a New World was this? And should he indulge in its pleasures and pursue its mysteries when his sister lay dying in her bed back home? But that meant giving up his mother again. And what about his romantic relationship with Caterina which he had barely sampled? And Victor, who was "out there." These dilemmas had to be resolved. This much Chris knew: he had to see Giovanna's grave before he would ever consider slamming the door shut. Because if she had changed...

Chris approached the wardrobe, removed his jacket, and opened the right door. That's when he saw, for the first time, his New World image—in the spotted mirror which hung on the inside of the open door. The image startled him at first, then he smiled at its strangeness. Now mesmerized, Chris lifted his right hand to touch his newfound face—full confirmation that he was not immune to an unwritten and fundamental law of this New World: those from the other would be better. With much joy, Chris saw how much more mature and muscular he truly had become—the way he always hoped he would be. Even his hook nose fit proportionately on his taut, chiseled face. And yet, somehow, somewhere, he thought he had seen this face before...grinning back at him... The sight of the improvements created a rush of confidence and power. He smiled again with great satisfaction.

But once the rush subsided, Chris suddenly felt drained. Nothing new there. He glanced at his bed, and welcomed the odd notion of dreaming his first New World dream. It was one of those guilty pleasures for which he had just admonished himself. Would he dream of the old world? Or would he have visions of the new? Maybe visions of the new he could not recollect, but were already there. Maybe he would have to start anew. There was only one way to find out.

Chris hung his jacket in the wardrobe and closed the door. Then he sank in the squeaky bed to remove his boots. All at once, he realized something peculiar, something he hadn't noticed before, and simply took for granted: the manner of lighting.

There was no easy access to electricity or natural gas in Sandra's old-fashioned World. Signs of advanced technology were hard to find. This was all by her design, of course. No automobiles, trains, or airplanes allowed in her peaceful paradise. Gasoline-powered internal combustion engines were forbidden. And the buildings that used generators and turbines were rarely depicted. Heat came (or was supposed to come) from split hardwood that burned blue smoke in the stone fireplaces or potbelly stoves found in almost every room of every structure. Nearly every thing was handmade. Any "machines" that made the cut were constructed of hand-forged iron or of wood and ropes and pulleys, and powered mostly by steam, wind, or waterwheels. So if Chris wanted darkness in his room (and he did), he had to close his stove's metal door and extinguish the light from the table lamps and wall lanterns—the lighting methods that powered this World. There was only one problem: the lamps and the lanterns had no candles or wicks in them.

Chris examined his bedside lamp. It looked like a kerosene lamp, with a hand-painted porcelain reservoir. A small metal dial protruded on a stem just below the glass chimney. But instead of a wick, a warm white orb sat on a metal base within the chimney. When he turned the dial slightly, a metal cover within the base rolled partially over the orb, dimming the warm light. When he turned the dial to its fullest, the cover completely encased the orb and extinguished the light. Simple enough. He walked throughout the bedroom and the bath, turning the little dials until all the orbs were covered. Now the only light was a radiant one, and it came from outside, through the icy double-hung window opposite his headboard. How wonderfully strange to be standing here. He wished Janey were here to experience all the magic. He could not think of that word without attaching her name to it.

Chris returned to the bed and sat down. But before he could finish undressing, he flopped on his back and settled his head into the lumpy pillow. He stared out the frosted window a while longer, still amazed at how the night was all aglow, then laid his arm across his eyes and slowly drifted off, listening to his mind as it hummed...

Chapter Twenty-One

The Bridge

The horrible face pressed nose-to-nose with his own—so close that he couldn't breathe. All he really saw were two glaring, determined eyes filled with an evil intent. It meant to do him harm, this face—he could sense it. But there was no way he could escape it. It had seen him lying here, utterly defenseless. And it took the opportunity to pounce on him, and pull him violently upward, before he could move a muscle. All he could do was scream.

Chris felt his jaw drop. He knew his mouth was open. But instead of his own cry for help, all he heard was...*thump*.

The face dissolved, and Chris found himself staring at the hewn beams of his lofted bedroom ceiling. A second thump brought him to his senses, and he sat up in the squeaky bed, still in those old-fashioned clothes. What tiny bits of doubt he harbored about the reality of this New World were pulverized. Never, ever had he fallen asleep in a dream, dreamt in it, then reawakened still in that dream. The pages of the Book were turning in a rational and orderly manner, though altered as they had become. He was relieved he had been spared further agony from the nightmarish eyes, but now he had another terror with which to contend.

Someone was at his second-story window, a shadow figure, peering through the luminous icy glaze.

Chris sprung to his feet to investigate. He was more intrigued than fearful. How was this possible? And who would do such a thing? Chris grabbed the brass handles at the bottom of the sash and flung the window up.

"Aren't you ready?" Matteo said in a forceful whisper as he gripped the top rung of a ladder. Naturally, he was hatless, the collar of his wool coat upturned.

Frowning, Chris stuck his head out the right side of the window and peered down as the falling snowflakes melted on his warm scalp. He saw a tweed-capped Lorenzo standing in the radiant snow, a glowing lantern half-buried at his feet. Lorenzo held the base of the ladder as he looked up with an equally confused stare. Chris pulled his head in. "Ready for what?"

"What do you mean, 'for what?' The game, me boy—remember?" Then Matteo's brow furrowed. "You're not gonna try to pull that amnesia crap on me, are you? I mean, really, I'll concede. It was brilliant. 'I'm from another world'—oh brother, that was good. Maybe too brilliant. Kinda overplayed your game with the doc, you know? He seemed a bit ticked off. But now that little honey is lying in bed wide awake, worried to death about her poor Cristofori." He tried to suppress his laughter. " 'Come to me, Cristofori, let me comfort you. Lay your head against my glorious chest, Cristofori, and let me stroke your hair.' Oh, man. I didn't know what to think at first. But then I figured it out, of course."

"Of course," Chris said, quickly drawing a smile.

"If only I figured that out first, huh? But to the winner goes the spoils. She's all yours now—without question." Matteo reached in and tapped Chris lightly on the cheek. "Congratulations. You're well on your way to fulfilling your sole biological purpose. That's some arrangement, huh? We want to touch them and they want to be touched. You gotta love 'em. I mean, really, we're all just one hair away from apedom. And still, they just can't live without us. Did you write that in your Story, Cristofori? 'Cause if you did, you truly are a genius."

Can't live without her, he recalled. "No, just brought it with me."

"Brought it with you," Matteo said. He suppressed more laughter. "Enough with the jokes. I want you to tell me all the glorious details after it finally happens. You owe me a few juicy stories, come to think of it. Let me know if you need any pointers."

Chris was not completely surprised by Matteo's attitude or his revelations. "Yeah," Chris said.

"Come on, man, grab your jacket—but not the plaid one. We gotta get going."

"Right." Chris returned to the wardrobe, wondering exactly what kind of game he was preparing for, his old world experiences acting as his only guide. He had all kinds of questions, but as he had done earlier with Alessandra, he decided to keep silent and let the events play out. That way, he could dive headfirst into his role in this New World without making waves, and let things come his way.

After buttoning his peacoat, Chris returned to the window. Matteo had already descended the ladder and stood next to Lorenzo as they gripped the rails. Chris carefully twisted through the window opening and secured his footing on the rungs. He shut the window and slowly descended to the snow-covered ground.

"You doing okay?" Lorenzo said softly.

"Yeah, never better," Chris said.

"He confessed," Matteo said. He carried the ladder to the shed next to the Studio.

"So all that stuff about another world—"

"Weren't you listening?" Matteo said. He hung the ladder in the rack on the outer wall. "A masterful performance, all for the sympathies of the young lady."

Lorenzo giggled, then briefly covered his mouth. "You dog," he said. He punched Chris in the shoulder.

Matteo returned. "It's all about winning, isn't it, Cristofori? That's what counts in this World. And that's what we're going to do again tonight."

"They haven't caught him yet," Lorenzo said. He picked up the lantern.

"And they're never going to, are they, me boy?" Matteo said.

"Not a chance," Chris said.

"That's what I want to hear. Get in the wagon before Alessandra catches us."

"Wagon?" Chris said.

"Well, yeah," Matteo said. He led them behind the shed. A white mare with blinders and hitched to a wagon with a folded tarp awaited them in the falling snow. "I hope you don't mind. I took the liberty of getting her ready."

"No, it's okay," Chris said, trying not to act surprised. Always wary of white horses, he reluctantly climbed in the back with Lorenzo, who dialed down the lantern's light before lying prone with it.

"Come on," Matteo said impatiently as he unfolded the tarp, "we don't have all night."

Chris stretched himself out alongside Lorenzo, who looked at him, smiled, then puckered his lips before laughing.

"Don't worry, you not my type," Lorenzo said. Matteo threw the tarp over them.

"Glad to hear," Chris said in the sudden darkness. He heard Matteo climb aboard and snap the reins. Then the wagon began rattling slowly into the glowing night.

∽

The trio said little to each other as they headed for their unknown destination. Not long after they snuck away from the Cottage, Matteo warned them they were entering the Village, and Chris could hear the wooden wagon wheels cutting through the thin layer of snow and rumbling along the cobbled way. When the rumbling ceased, the wagon stopped, and Matteo threw back the tarp—fluffy snow flying into a cloud around them—revealing the soft glow of the New World's night sky.

"Okay, me boys, we're clear," he said. And then he urged the mare onward.

When Chris sat up, he saw that the cobbled walkway had disappeared. Now they were on a wide snow-covered path that followed the frozen stream westward through the pine forest, every tree flocked in white. He shoved his hands into his coat pockets.

"Won't be long now," Lorenzo said. He restored the glow to the lantern. "Nervous?"

"Should I be?" Chris said, though he was.

They rattled on and on until they came around a bend, and Matteo carefully guided them down a series of rocky, icy steps that had popped up long ago from the grinding Earth. Chris could feel the air gradually warming. The frozen stream, lined with boulders, followed the same stepped slope, and quickly became a series of steamy, hissing cascades. Below the whitewater, a small flagstone bridge arched over the refrozen stream as it flattened out into a foggy meadow. Just beyond the Bridge, a dwarf evergreen, covered in tiny white orbs, stood like a glowing sentinel against the thick fog bank that tried to encroach from the west.

"I know this place," Chris said as they approached the glistening bridge. It had been one of his mother's finest and most inspirational paintings—an unspoken demarcation point that welcomed all to *her* dream world. But the setting had been in the flowery spring, not the icy dead of winter.

Matteo frowned. "I should say you do."

Lorenzo held the lantern close to Chris' face as Matteo stopped the wagon before the Bridge. "Are you sure you're feeling all right?" Lorenzo said.

Chris pushed the lantern away. "Why do you keep asking me that?" Then he faced Matteo. "Would you keep going, please?"

"You heard the man," Lorenzo said.

But Matteo climbed down from the seat.

"Wait here," Matteo said. He grabbed the lantern from Lorenzo and started across the Bridge. When he reached the other side, Matteo turned around. His face and hands were aglow—not from the lantern, but on their own.

Chris tried to hide his astonishment.

"Coming?" Matteo said.

Chris followed Lorenzo across the Bridge. With the warming now completed, Lorenzo's exposed skin began to glow. But Chris' did not.

"Interesting effect, isn't it?" Matteo said. "So why don't you glow like us?"

"You know," Chris said.

"Yeah, I do. Do you?"

"Sure."

"Tell us, then."

Chris tried to make the connection between his two worlds, but his silence ultimately betrayed him. Game over.

"See, he's not right," Lorenzo said. "I told you we shouldn't have brought him here."

"And we should let you take his place?" Matteo said angrily. Then he softened his tone. "Cristofori, do you remember what you call us?"

"Call you?"

"Yeah, those of us from the Village."

"Born in the Village," Lorenzo said.

Chris took a deep breath and exhaled slowly. "Hot shots?"

Matteo laughed.

" 'Brights,' " Lorenzo said. "You call us 'brights.' Not real clever, but it's accurate."

"It's all in the genes, Cristofori," Matteo said. "So this memory thing is real, isn't it?"

"It's more than that," Chris said.

"We'd better go back," Lorenzo said. "We'll never win with him in this condition."

"Can't," Matteo said. "The others are already waiting. I'm not leaving them there, not with those goons." He looked at Chris. "Why didn't you tell me?"

"I wanted to see where this would take me."

"Well, here we are," Lorenzo said, "the land where you came from—*scemo*."

"That's enough, Lorenzo."

"Well, that's what he is."

"He's a *contadino*—from *L'entroterra*. What's in your head, huh? Show a little respect."

"Countryman," Lorenzo said. "He's a bumpkin."

"Was," Chris said.

Matteo gazed at Chris. "Look, me boy, we're about to go up against a tough cast of characters. And they really want something from us that they don't have."

"Like what?" Chris said.

"Half a brain," Lorenzo said.

Matteo glared momentarily at Lorenzo, then returned his gaze to Chris and held up the lantern. "This."

"A lamp?"

"Not just a lamp," Matteo said. He opened the lantern door and reached inside. "They want this." He displayed the glowing white orb, pinched between his thumb and forefinger.

Chris frowned. "Why?"

"Don't really know," Matteo said. "They have this little trick they use with burlap bags...to cover the lamps. Never seen it work, though. Even if it did, they still can't touch the orb."

"There's nothing they can do with it," Lorenzo said. "They can't even get close to it. Gives them rashes and hives and swells their throats shut. Too much inbreeding. But, hey, if they want to kill themselves over it, who am I to stop them? If you're stupid, you die. So much for the better. That's how it works in our World, Cristofori."

"It's a strange form of urticaria, so we've been taught," Matteo said. "Does this sound familiar?"

"No."

"It's the wavelength of the white light that triggers a reaction. That's why we glow. But there's no allergen involved. Like I said, it's all in the makeup. Here." Matteo tossed the orb at Chris.

Chris caught it in his right palm. The orb felt heavy, warm, and perfectly smooth.

"Don't worry, it won't bother you," Matteo said, "even though you're one of them."

"But I got in, didn't I?" Chris said.

"A moment of sudden recall?"

"Something like that." Chris looked around. "What's the Bridge got to do with this?"

"It marks the boundary between our two lands. Here and beyond, the light from the Tree gets weak, and its effects aren't so severe."

"And this tree?" he said, glancing at the evergreen, though he was certain he knew that, too.

Matteo shrugged. "Just an offshoot."

But it's not. "So why bring the orb here?"

"Because they have something we want, and that little beauty will help us get it."

"What? How?"

Matteo smiled. "That's what the game is all about, me boy. Are you up for the challenge?"

"I don't know. What do I have to do?"

Matteo drew close and whispered: "Run like the wind."

Chapter Twenty-Two

The Game

Back aboard the rattling wagon, the trio entered the cool fog bank, and they pushed on along the muddy path devoid of snow. Lorenzo held the lantern out in front of him. The illuminated fog seemed to disperse around them as if they were in a protective bubble. But recalling what he wrote about the fog and its given characteristics, Chris could not help feeling a bit uneasy about their trek, and, despite the lamplight, kept a wary eye out for any signs of movement in the solid gray while listening for the revealing sounds. It was too early to tell if those malicious traits had made the journey to the New World. He certainly hoped they hadn't.

They came to a fork in the path, marked by a pile of smooth wet rocks of all earthly colors that resembled a grave. But there was no headstone. A large wooden cross was mounted in the very center, from which draped a white, ragged cloth, ravaged by wind and weather. Yet another surprise.

"The mark of Christ the Savior," Matteo said, "the One who decided to die for some crime we never committed. Somehow, that foolish act was going to save us all from eternal damnation—am I getting that right?"

Lorenzo snickered, which Chris resented, even though he agreed with his friend's overall view. There was something about Lorenzo's "superior" attitude that he didn't admire here, or there.

Matteo stopped the wagon to stare at Chris. "Does it look familiar?"

"Not the rock pile."

"It's not what you think," Matteo said.

"How do you know what I'm thinking?"

They veered left of the pile. Matteo remained expressionless as they rumbled along the path in their protective bubble.

"So what was it?" Chris said. "Who put it there?"

"It's a marker—and a warning," Matteo said.

"About what?"

"Where we shouldn't go."

"And where is that?"

"The other way," he said. And then he said nothing more.

Chris looked at Lorenzo. "What does he mean?"

Lorenzo glanced at Matteo, who shook his head. "We'll tell you later, okay?"

"Why, what's the big secret?"

Lorenzo kept silent. He drew the lamp closer to his chest and gazed warily out into the fog.

The muddy path led them away from the meadow and into a forest, which reached out from the fog with long, crooked branches. Chris could hear the mutterings of voices in the large white glow just ahead of them. All at once, a crowd of young men with lanterns and radiant, familiar faces appeared from the fog. Some wore caps. Even a few top hats were visible. Most wrapped their necks with long scarves. Others went without head cover, and the steam rose from their plastered hair. They all seemed willing, but anxious, begging for the comforts of leadership. A hush fell over them as Matteo stopped the wagon and jumped out.

"Everyone here?" he said to the crowd.

"Damn freaky horse," a young man grumbled, staring at the blinders as he held the bridle. Then he looked at Matteo and raised his voice. "We are. What about them?"

"They're out there. Territory's a big deal to them. Set foot in it, and you'll get their undivided attention—isn't that right, Cristofori?"

All eyes aimed at Chris, and he felt strange, suddenly placed in a position of authority. He sensed they sought encouragement. "Yeah, sure. So now what?"

His inquiry drew some nervous laughter.

Matteo gripped the edge of the wagon and leaned toward Chris. "Do you recognize where we are?" he said softly.

"Not really."

"We're on a ridge," Matteo said. "The land slopes down into a grassy field, then back up another ridge. In all, it's a little more than a hundred yards long."

"Okay," Chris said, the key words sparking an old world image.

"After that, a grove of trees."

Chris nodded, the amusing vision now complete. But the game? "I still don't see what we're doing."

"You're not giving up tonight, are you?" someone called out.

"What gives, Cristofori?" another said.

"Just get to the grove as quickly as possible," Matteo said.

"Then what?"

"Hey," a voice said in a harsh whisper, "someone's coming!"

All heads turned toward the foggy field as footsteps dragged through the long damp grass that clung to the slope. Matteo snapped his fingers at Lorenzo, who handed him the lamp. The unseen figure drew close. Many in the group raised their lanterns in a defensive manner and stood with apprehension. A hooded figure emerged from the mist and stopped just on the edge of the collective glow. Though the young man's face was partially shrouded in shadow, Chris recognized enough details to identify him. The contempt he held for the young man never felt stronger. Chris and Lorenzo slowly rose in unison, wary eyes unblinking.

"Did you bring it?" Tomas said as he stared at Chris.

Chris was stunned that he was the object of Tomas' quest. Obviously, they had conversed before about something very important. "Bring what?" Chris said.

Matteo reached into the lamp, withdrew the white-hot orb, and held it high. He smiled derisively.

"That's not what we bargained for," Tomas said angrily—again, to Chris.

Matteo shrugged—then faked a toss at Tomas, who jerked his head to the right. The crowd laughed as the smile returned to Matteo's face. "We can leave, if you'd like?"

"Bring the Purple Orb next time," Tomas said to Chris.

"Purple—right," Matteo said. "We won't forget."

Tomas stared fiercely at Matteo, then glanced at Chris before he turned and started down the hill.

"Running away already?" Matteo said.

Tomas stopped, but did not turn around. "You can play your little game, if you want."

"We do," Matteo said. "We always do."

Tomas disappeared into the fog.

"What an *idiota*," Lorenzo said. The others laughed nervously.

Matteo returned the orb into the lamp. "Ready for some fun?" he shouted.

The crowd voiced its eagerness to participate, then dispersed to predetermined positions.

Matteo reached under the seat and withdrew an empty burlap bag. He handed it up to Chris.

"This is really pretty simple," Matteo said. "We'll head out first and scatter about the field, as a distraction. You follow behind—but don't get too close. They can't see you like they can see us. I can't give you a lamp—that's what they really want. So you'll have to kinda make your way in the dark. But use that ridiculous speed of yours and just stay the course. They won't be able to catch you even if they do see you. Remember, about a hundred yards or so straight ahead. Once you get there, you'll be safe. It's a different kind of light, but it still keeps them at bay. Grab as many orbs as you can, then head on back. There'll be some guys waiting here—you'll see them."

"So it's orbs I'm after?"

"Not just any orbs, me boy. These are a little...different. You'll see once we get back to the Village. Just be careful with them. They're kinda brittle." He paused. "Ready?"

Chris sprung from the wagon. "Sure."

"Good man." He stared at Lorenzo. "Are you just going to stand there?"

"You took my lamp."

Matteo faced the small group guarding the horse and held out his left hand. Someone handed him another lantern. Lorenzo jumped down and secured his protective light. Then Matteo turned to the young men assembled in a long line on the edge of the ridge and, with a sweeping motion of his left arm, signaled them to follow.

Chris watched the many lanterns scatter into the fog like a swarm of fireflies. Some let out whoops and hollers that echoed across the field. But he heard no sounds of the slightest conflict or fear. With heart and head now pounding with familiar anticipation, Chris glanced at the guards in their top hats. He still couldn't get used to that.

"What are you waiting for?" one of them said.

Chris faced the great foggy unknown, and threw himself with total abandon into the mysterious game.

Chapter Twenty-Three

The Grove

Chris streaked down the slope and hit the flat field in full stride. He saw the lanterns swarming about. He could still hear the bravado and laughter of their bearers as they moved in and out of breaks in the fog. But there was no sign of the enemy combatants, which bothered him. He understood the basics of the game, and where those ideas came from. But to what extent and severity they had evolved, he could only guess.

About halfway across the field, Chris heard the strange blaring of a crude horn just ahead and to his right. Suddenly, he caught a disturbing glimpse of a dark-cloaked figure running across his intended path as it chased a stocky lantern bearer. Still in full stride, Chris swerved to the right to stay clear of the chase—and plowed into another cloaked figure in hot pursuit of the light. Despite his newly realized physique, Chris was no match for the force behind the superior mass that struck him. He heard an explosion in his head as he tumbled on his back to the soggy ground. The cloaked pursuer landed on top of him, then grabbed him by the lapels and lifted him close. Chris' eyes widened. It was Dahlberg's counterpart, even more muscular and intimidating. Not even his loose-fitting robe could hide his powerful build.

"*Traditore*," he said, his rage expelled with the puff of his hot and rancid breath. He slammed Chris back to the ground. The muscular young man looked up and refocused on his target, then with his own burlap bag in hand, charged off into the fog.

Still a bit dazed, Chris lay on the damp ground a moment longer as the footsteps of many other pursuers raced past him. When the game shifted farther away, Chris sprung to his feet and dashed for what he hoped was the opposite end of the field. He hit the grassy slope and he felt a small amount of relief pass over him. But what exactly would he see when he reached the top?

Chris splayed his feet to improve his footing on the steep and slippery slope. Though gravity was working furiously to weigh him down, Chris ignored the burning in his thighs. He pumped his legs harder and harder to reach the top.

And when he finally made it, Chris stood breathless, staring in disbelief at the amazing sight before him.

It was a grove, all right—but nothing like the one back home. Instead of neat rows and uniform heights, the trees were in different stages of development, and were scattered about haphazardly, some in tight clumps, others on their own. As promised, they all sprouted small glowing orbs. But they did not show the colors found within the Village or on the Great Tree. Instead, most of the orbs were blue with some red ones mixed in, and their combined purplish glow, which hung high over the sprawling grove, pushed away the thick blanket of fog all the way back to the foothills of the shrouded Mountain, which itself was illuminated by the dominant star and the full Moon. He couldn't help thinking, just for a moment, about the horrors that hid within it.

Chris turned to face the foggy field. The swarming lamplights were still visible, and the innocent laughing and playful hollering still evident. Confident all was going according to plan, Chris scrambled down the slope and into the purple haze. He stared in wonder at the sights, as if he were strolling in a magical orchard. Maybe he was. He had to smile once again at the curious manner in which this New World had evolved from the old.

A cry of pain from the field snapped him out of his trance. Chris worked quickly to pluck some blue orbs from one tree, and red ones from another as he stuffed them into the bag.

Then Chris heard the sudden clatter of hoofs. He looked in the direction of the Mountain and saw a galloping white horse approaching through a gap in the grove. The horse seemed to be riderless, but it was too far away to tell. But there was no denying: it was charging toward him, with no intention of stopping.

Alarmed for obvious reasons, Chris turned and sprinted for the hill. But halfway up, he stopped. Two cloaked figures stood on the crest. They stared down at him from the shadows of their hoods and eye sockets. But this time, the purple glow provided a partial view of their icy faces, which sent a chill through him and reinforced his fear. The one on the left was tall and young, with wide shoulders. The other was shorter, slimmer, and much older, with a large head. He had an animal horn hanging from a leather string around his thin neck. Both had their hands on their hips.

"Leaving so soon?" Tomas said.

Chris fumbled with the burlap bag. Then he glanced behind him for signs of the charging horse. Thankfully, it was gone. Chris dipped into the bag and selected one of the red orbs, not for its color, but for its brightness. He gripped the orb tightly in his right hand and held it out in front of him. Slowly, he ascended the hill, keeping his eyes on the two the entire time. Chris had a strange feeling about them, apart from the eerie setting and the threat they represented. They hadn't merely changed costumes for their New World roles. There was a hint of it in their vapid expressions, and it tinged their ragged voices. Something wasn't right. Something had happened to them.

"First the church, and now this," the older man said to Chris. "What are you doing? You don't belong here anymore."

"Once a thief, always a thief—eh, Cristofori?" Tomas said. "Is that all you want? Don't let us stop you. Feel free to go back and get more, by all means."

Chris frowned at the strange offer, but said nothing. This game, this World, was still too new to him, and he really didn't know what to say. In fact, he did feel like a thief, and shamefully so. Chris held the orb out even closer to their drained faces. But again, they didn't budge.

"You did promise to bring the Purple Orb," Tomas said, "but I didn't want to embarrass you any more in front of your smart new friends."

"And the book?" the older man said. "For leaving, you owe us your book."

"Oh, he'll keep his word, all right," Tomas said, "the Orb, and the Book—which will come on its own—before the child comes. He can't help himself...can you, Cristofori? No choice whatsoever. I've been meaning to ask you, how's life in the Village? Peaceful? Feeling safe there? Invincible?"

Chris paused as he felt a burning anger rise. Out of habit, he said: "What are you up to now?"

"Up to?" Tomas said, genuinely indignant. "We had an agreement."

"What agreement?"

"More deception?" the older man said.

"I have no idea," Chris said. His Story was of no help.

Tomas raised his bony, pale hand and pointed a menacing finger at him. "What is this, Cristofori? You're not backing out, are you?"

"Backing out of what?"

Tomas' deep-set eyes flared. He seemed ready to lunge. "Don't play games with me, Cristofori. Save it for your friends. We want that Orb."

Chris hesitated, waiting for their advance. But they remained oddly steadfast, even tolerant, despite the angry words. Sensing an escape opportunity, and willing to try, Chris slipped cautiously past them and started down the hill, slowly at first, so not to arouse. Then, sensing victory, he scampered down the remainder of the slope and into the safety of the fog.

"The Purple Orb," Tomas shouted. "Tomorrow, or there'll be consequences."

And then the older man blew the horn, emitting a blat that Chris had grown to loath and fear.

At the base of the hill, Chris heard the obedient footsteps of those who were now part of the New World Horde. They appeared suddenly from the fog and parted around him on their way up the slope and into the grove. Chris set out across the field in a steady jog. He no longer felt any danger to himself or the others. The contest was over. But who won? This game, which at first seemed so straightforward and simple, was becoming mysterious and complex.

When Chris arrived at the outpost, the others had already gathered. Chris saw Matteo with a bloody rag balled in his hand attending to Lorenzo, who sat hatless on the back of the wagon. "What happened?" Chris said.

Matteo dabbed the cut below Lorenzo's right eye.

"The son of a bitch hit me!" Lorenzo said.

"Which one?" Chris said.

"I don't know. I've never seen him before. He was a lot bigger than me—and he had this crazy look in his eyes. I think they were eyes. Don't you people know the rules?"

"I'm sorry," Chris said, though Lorenzo couldn't possibly understand why.

"Stay away from him next time," Matteo said. He handed the rag to Lorenzo.

"Yeah, no shit," Lorenzo said. "What do you think I was trying to do?"

"He didn't get your lamp, did he?" Matteo said.

"No."

"So quit your crying." Matteo scanned the crowd. Their solemn faces showed traces of doubt and fear. "Anyone else get tagged?"

The others grumbled "no" while some shook their heads.

"Well, that was easy." He turned to Chris. "Let's see what you got."

Chris handed Matteo the bag.

"What's the matter, Cristofori?" someone shouted. "Can't you talk anymore?" Nervous laughter followed.

Matteo examined the contents. "Six blue and four red," he called out before a mixed reaction of cheers and whistling, their spirits slowly rising. "Not a bad haul. Don't you just love the holidays?"

"Get more red next time," Lorenzo said.

"Yeah," someone shouted. The rest muttered in agreement.

"Don't listen to that," Matteo said softly. "You did good."

"So now what?" Chris said.

"Now we go back to the Studio."

"The Studio?"

"You want to know what this is all about, don't you?"

"All of us? Now?"

Matteo turned to the eager crowd, their round eyes locked on him. "Anyone who wants to see the latest spoils of war, they'll be on display, as always, tomorrow, the usual place and time." Then he looked at Chris and lowered his voice. "Satisfied?"

Chris nodded, though he didn't know why.

"You want to take the reins?"

"I don't know if I remember how."

Matteo sighed. "We've got to get you right, me boy. I don't like being your servant."

Chris sat in the back of the wagon with Lorenzo. Matteo jumped into the seat and grabbed the reins. Then the wagon headed along the path. The victorious, glowing crowd followed, lanterns in hand. Everyone seemed bloated with confidence and self-satisfaction, now that they were on their way to their protected home.

But Chris did not feel any joy from their triumph. This game was a scam. "I ran into Tomas out there," he said to Matteo.

"Where?"

"By the grove."

"And?"

"Nothing. But he did mentioned the Purple Orb again."

Lorenzo dabbed his wound. "I don't know what he's talking about."

"I never talked about it?"

"No," Matteo said with annoyance, "you didn't. You think it really exists?"

"Well, Tomas knows about it, so I guess it must."

"Didn't think about it that way," Matteo said. "Wonder why he wants it?"

"Could be valuable," Chris said.

"How so?" Lorenzo said.

"Sure...like the one back home."

"Home," Matteo said.

"Where I'm from."

"Oh, come on, Cristofori," Lorenzo said.

Matteo's glare silenced Lorenzo. "Tell me about it," Matteo said.

"It's an rare ornament, kept in my sister's music box. So there's no telling what that means here."

"Well, it would help explain why that reptilian would want to get his claws on it. Though I don't think he gives a damn about gold coins."

"I'd be careful with Tomas, if I were you," Chris said. "He's not dumb—not hardly. I don't know how much you know about him, but back home, the guy was your enemy."

"As he is yours here," Matteo said. "You're the one who introduced us. Wonder if he knows about the music box."

"If it exists."

"Did you talk about that?"

"No."

Matteo nodded. "Got any idea where it might be?"

"Back home, we hid it in another box and kept it in the basement."

"Basement?" Lorenzo said.

"Cellar, then. Does our Cottage have a one?"

"It does," Matteo said.

"Could be there, I guess, but I doubt it."

"Why?" Matteo said.

"If this World works the way I think it does, the music box is with my sister."

"But she's dead," Lorenzo said.

"Maybe," Chris said.

Lorenzo shot a concerned look at Matteo.

"Yeah...right," Matteo said politely, though he seemed to be thinking of something else.

"I could ask Alessandra."

"No, not a good idea," Matteo said. "She might find out about our little enterprise."

"But what if it was at the old cottage?"

"If it was, it's not there now," Matteo said. "From what you told us, there wasn't much left."

"Have you been there?"

"You made it very clear that you never wanted us to see it."

"I did?"

Matteo nodded. "Why do you think you built that creepy rock pile?"

༄

After a few minutes of thoughtful silence, his sight affixed to the trailing army, Chris' doubts still poked at him. He found it particularly interesting that Tomas, not the older man, projected the authority over the game and the Horde. "They let you win, you know," Chris said, his face cool and wet.

Lorenzo removed the rag from his wound. "They what? Man, you are just full of it tonight, aren't you? Are you sure you're not feeling a little nostalgic for the old gang?"

"Let him talk, Lorenzo," Matteo said as he kept his eyes forward.

"You know those red orbs?" Chris said to Matteo.

"Sure. What about them?"

"I used one on Tomas when I came out of the grove."

"Yeah, so?" Lorenzo said.

"He didn't move an inch."

"How close was he to the orb?" Matteo said.

Chris flung his fist inches from Lorenzo's startled face. "This close," Chris said.

Matteo glanced at them. "Interesting."

"They could have nabbed me. Instead, they let me walk away. Got any ideas why they would do that?"

Matteo paused. "Well, sounds to me like they really want that Purple Orb, and you're the one who's gonna get it for them."

"But I don't know where it is."

"They think you do, and that's all that matters."

"They can get the white orbs without the game, you know," Chris said, "at the West Bridge. Maybe elsewhere, too."

"How're they gonna do that, bright boy?" Lorenzo said. "With all those orbs on the tree, the glow's a lot stronger than from one lamp. And science ain't their thing."

Chris shrugged. "So what's this agreement we have with them?"

"Agreement?" Matteo said. "You know—they try to get our orbs and we take theirs."

Lorenzo giggled.

"Nothing else?" Chris said.

"No," Matteo said. "Why do you ask?"

"Just curious. Can't remember—*remember?* They want another game tomorrow."

"Yeah?" Matteo said before snickering. "We'll give 'em all the games they want."

"And they want me to bring the Purple Orb."

"So? What did you tell them?"

"Nothing. What could I?"

"Then we'll just keep robbing them blind."

"I don't think Tomas will go for it much longer," Chris said. "I know he won't."

Matteo smiled. "What could possibly go wrong as long as we have the light?"

They came to the fork in the path, and Chris fixed his gaze on the shadowy cross and rock pile. Chris grabbed the lantern and held it up into the thick fog. It still appeared and sounded benign, but he had to wonder… "So that's the way to the old cottage."

"Not tonight, Cristofori," Matteo said.

"I helped you win your game, didn't I?"

"Point being?"

"I helped you, now you help me."

"We will. But not now."

"Why wait? We're here, aren't we?"

"That's a whole different kinda game you're talking about, me boy. Said so yourself. You were convincing enough. And you had the stories to back you up."

"Stories?"

"They're just rumors," Lorenzo said.

"About what?"

"Other things that are out there," Matteo said.

"I want to see it," Chris said.

Lorenzo laughed. "You'd think that, with all this traveling between two worlds, you'd be getting a little tired by now, you know?"

"Not tonight," Matteo said. "And not at night—no way, not by ourselves. Besides, we've got some treasures to behold. And I gotta get things set up at the Mill for the boys."

"I could jump off," Chris said. "You know you'd never catch me."

Matteo smiled. "You don't want to do that—trust me on this one."

There was just enough foreboding in his friend's tone, and mystery in the fog, to keep Chris parked in the wagon. He knew what could be out there, waiting for him. Maybe his friends knew this, too. Certainly nothing he wanted to see in the daylight, never mind the darkness. "Tomorrow, then."

"Sure—after you see the doc. I don't want Alessandra getting all upset. She needs to stay calm and content and...unsuspecting. After, not before."

Chris reluctantly nodded, then held the lamp up high, thinking of his Story. The cross and the rock pile disappeared into the ever-darkening mist.

Chapter Twenty-Four

The Orbs

While the fat and glowing flakes drifted down like feathers with an unnatural slowness, almost suspended, to the ever-deepening snowpack, the giant clock tower in the empty square bonged twice. Still in the rumbling wagon and the biting cold, Chris—his arms folded, his exposed hands tucked under his jacket's armpits—felt a small sense of relief now that they were back on much more tranquil and civilized ground. But the confrontation with Tomas, and his threats, dampened Chris' mood, as he obsessed over the meaning and consequences of the game, trumpeted as another victory for truth and sanity. In the icy light, the trailing foot soldiers quietly dispersed one by one through the slumbering snowbound Village.

Matteo drove the wagon up the bluff to the Cottage, where they settled behind the Studio and out of sight from Alessandra's shaded and darkened bedroom window. Chris didn't feel right about sneaking around in the dead of night, but it was humorous to note how some things between the two worlds had hardly changed.

The trio jumped from the wagon into the dense, shin-high snow, then Chris and Lorenzo waited patiently in the moonlight for Matteo as he removed the white mare from its bridle and led it to the stable. Chris and Lorenzo plowed after Matteo, burlap bag now in his hand, to a wide double door in the center of the Studio's back wall. Lorenzo held up his lantern. Matteo lifted the iron latch and pulled its ring. But the door refused to open.

"Why is this barred?" he said to Chris in a hushed tone.

"I don't know," Chris said.

"Well? Go inside and open it."

Chris rushed around the right side of the Studio and entered the well-lit courtyard, keeping a wary eye on Alessandra's window, and feeling delightfully foolish, as if reliving an old world exploit perpetrated in happier times. The Studio and its glass façade glowed intensely, like a roaring furnace, and the snowpack along its length was a mere film of gray slush atop the flagstone. When he slipped through the French door and felt his tight face loosen and tingle from the warmth within, and the scratch of his collar on his moist neck, Chris realized something he hadn't noticed before. No lanterns or lamps or chandeliers, and no source of heat existed. The warmth radiated from the wall of paintings. Even the finished image of a blue sunflower that rested on the easel was aglow. And the canvas? Not canvas at all, but glass. There was a single door on opposite ends of the long wall of paintings. So the existence of a back room was apparent. Chris chose the right door, as it was probably out of view from Alessandra's window. But that door was locked as well. He rushed to the left door and, after one last nervous glance at the Cottage, turned the brass knob. The door opened.

Chris stepped into the cold, dark room, brought his cupped hands to his mouth, and blew into them to chase away the rawness. The broad ray of light from the Studio revealed rows of simple wooden frames and their glass, stacked on edge according to size. Along the left wall sat small wooden crates filled with clear glass jars, some holding luminous white paint, others jammed with brushes, their tips sparkling like crystal. Chris skirted the frames and stepped before the double doors on the back wall, which was indeed barred by a long thick beam resting in u-shaped iron brackets. The instant he lifted the heavy beam, the left door swung open. His two friends stepped inside.

Matteo motioned with his head to the bright Studio doorway. "Close that door," he said in a muffled voice. He closed the back entrance, still clutching the burlap bag.

Chris rushed over and shut the door. Lorenzo set his lantern in the far left corner and selected a large frame from one of the rows. He leaned it against the left wall, then turned to Matteo, who stood in the shadows before the double doors, fumbling with the bag.

Chris approached Lorenzo and stood behind him as his stocky friend repositioned the framed glass. "What are you doing?" Chris said.

"Getting it ready."

"Ready? For what?"

Lorenzo turned and was about to answer when a look of panic seized his face.

"Cristofori!" Matteo called out from behind him.

Chris whirled about and saw Matteo frozen in a power-pitcher's stance, ready to deliver the blue orb that he held high behind him. Before Chris could blink, Matteo—in a furious motion—flung the orb at Chris. He dodged the orb as it whizzed past and exploded somewhere behind him.

"Whoa!" Lorenzo shouted.

Matteo smiled with great satisfaction.

"What's the matter with you?" Chris said.

"You wanted to know about the orbs, didn't you?" Matteo said. He calmly held out his right upturned hand.

Chris frowned, then turned to face the wall. Within the leaning wooden frame, a painting was slowly spreading outward from the center of the glass, like ripples on a pond. But this pond was now aglow. Chris glanced at the floor, looking for bits of the shattered orb, but none were visible.

Lorenzo stared at the painting with mouth agape. Chris and Matteo hunched behind him. The remaining image took shape, spreading out to all edges. Chris instinctively reached out to touch the paining, but Lorenzo slapped his hand away.

"Don't," he said, "she's a keeper. Let it set." Then his gaze returned to the picture, and he giggled. "Get a load of that outfit."

Chris held his intense gaze on the portrait. It was a plump young woman in traditional Alpine costume, with a lacy white blouse and green bodice trimmed with gold passementerie. But all background imagery was gone, replaced by that strange liquid light. The grim face was familiar—one of the many pictures from the family chest—but the woman's name had been long forgotten. Chris' eyes brightened. How was this possible? Yet, there it was—proof that the other world existed. But then he understood that, with her traditional garb, the woman could easily be walking around here, in *L'entroterra*, without drawing the slightest attention. Maybe she had, or she was.

"Got any ideas, Cristofori?" Matteo said.

"She was a relative...on my mom's side," Chris said, eyes locked on the image. "She lived a long time ago, in the other world."

"Really?" Matteo said without much surprise. "How did she get in the blue orb?"

Chris looked at him. It was obvious what the blue orbs represented, and he recalled writing his thoughts about them. How they now presented themselves in this World was logical, as it should have been. But he was growing tired of trying to convince them. "Didn't I already explain this to you...before I lost my memory?"

"You did."

"Nothing about the other world stuff," Lorenzo said. "You weren't loony then, I don't think."

"So why ask me now?"

Matteo shrugged. "Just to see if you remembered."

"Well, I don't. You'll have to tell me."

Matteo nodded a few times, but he seemed suspicious.
"Something impressive about salts, collodion, nitrates, and glass, how it all interacts with light, and changes from white to blue when touched for the first time—like wet plates, you told us, only...somehow...we get a picture

with all the colors. Never did explain that 'somehow.' Neither could I. Never bought that part about the orb changing color, either. I've held the white orbs in my hand. They never turned blue. Seen you do it before, too. You did it tonight, in fact, at the Bridge. No change. No captured image. You couldn't explain how the image remained intact even after we smashed the orb onto the glass. But something's holding it together." He stared at the portrait with a mixture of loathing and admiration. "Can't argue with the results."

"Can I see one?" Chris said.

Matteo reached into the canvas bag and handed over a blue orb. Chris held it close to his right ear and shook it, expecting to hear liquid sloshing about. But he heard nothing.

"It's not like water," Matteo said. "Go ahead, give it a toss."

Lorenzo jumped in front of the portrait. "No, don't. Those old hags at the store will be fighting over this thing." He turned and moved the portrait aside, then seized another framed pane of glass from the stacks and set it against the wall. "Now do it."

Matteo nodded at Chris who stepped the proper distance away from the frame so he could fire the orb at it.

"No, no," Matteo said, "that was just for drama. Just toss it."

But Chris did not see how he could generate enough force to shatter the orb against the glass.

"Go ahead," Matteo said.

Eager to prove his point, Chris, with an under-handed motion, lobbed the blue orb at the glass. When it struck the upper right corner, emitting a loud pop, the orb did not bounce off as he suspected it would. Instead, the glass absorbed it. The ripples spread outward, then revealed another old world image—this time, a close-up of a white-bearded "yodeler" in a gray felt hat with a small white feather set in a band of strings.

"Another relative?" Matteo said.

Chris nodded.

"We've got a few like him," Lorenzo said. "Erase it. "

"How do you do that?" Chris said.

"Toss another orb at him," Matteo said. "Doesn't matter which color."

Chris knew which side of the family tree would appear if a red orb were used. But the other? "What does a white one do?"

"Not a damn thing," Lorenzo said.

"It'll just turn everything white—no image," Matteo said. "I'd use the one from the lamp, but we're gonna need it. That's Alessandra's little secret she brought from The Hinterland. She uses the white ones for all her hand-rendered paintings. By the way, she doesn't know that you told us."

"What?" Chris said.

"No one knows the secret of the orbs—not outside our little group," Lorenzo said.

"Little group? No one's been bragging?"

"Then they're out," Lorenzo said, "and they don't get their share when we finally open for business."

"Tough to prove without evidence," Matteo said. "We keep a tight ship, and a heavy lock on the Old Mill door. So the colored orbs are safe." He shrugged, looking a little embarrassed. "Besides, who in their right mind is gonna throw one at a piece of framed glass?"

"It's not impossible," Chris said. "The white ones are all over the Village."

"But Alessandra's the only one with the special supplies for that particular light. Without them..." He held his upturned hands out wide, shrugged again, and smirked.

Chris glanced at the jars of luminous paint and sparkling brushes. "Where'd these things come from?"

"You never told us that. But I have a good idea, considering your roots. Something about a felled magical oak that was once worshipped." He smiled smugly as Lorenzo giggled.

Chris felt a little irked. There was nothing in his Story about a magical oak. His anger was more about their smarter-than-thou attitude, which he never liked about the Hotshits, even when he was one. Just because they were good at memorizing and recalling things they were told to memorize and recall didn't mean they really knew anything. The List proved that point. "What's to stop anyone from going to the grove on their own?"

"You were re-introduced tonight. They have a certain charm the Villagers don't find very appealing, wouldn't you agree? And even though the stories are just stories..." The grin returned.

"The doc has his own collection, you know—in the atrium."

"Yeah, well, if he uncovered the secret, we'd certainly have heard about it by now. He's not one to keep any discovery under wraps—as far as I can tell. With a big house and staff to pay for? I could be wrong. But I doubt it."

"He still might."

Matteo shook his head. "You heard Caterina. He's obsessed with that Star."

"And does she—"

Matteo laughed. "I guarantee you, me boy, she's the last one on this Earth who'd keep secrets, especially from you. You know how these young ladies in love are. They want to share everything with you—just like they insist that you share."

Chris grew flushed. "Maybe she knows and I didn't tell you."

Matteo held his smile. "Do you really think she'd let you put yourself in any kind of danger? Her wonderful Cristofori, who she can't live without?"

Chris stared at his ever-confident friend and sighed. He liked the sound of Caterina thinking of him that way. But he didn't like the idea of betraying Alessandra's trust. But that was nothing new. And what had once seemed like an innocent game among restless teens with too much confidence and idle time was fast becoming an elaborate ruse. He would have preferred restarting all the relationships with a clean white canvas, but old habits and character flaws had re-established themselves, too, and the mighty wheels of deception were already turning ever faster, and were difficult to stop. That scenario wasn't new either.

"Wonder what the purple one would look like?" Lorenzo said.

"We'd have to find it, first," Matteo said, his eyes still fixed on Chris.

"I told you," Chris said, "I'll look for it."

"Show him a red one," Lorenzo said.

Matteo seemed to sense Chris' discomfort. "Not now, Lorenzo."

"Not now?"

"You heard me."

"It's okay, Lorenzo," Chris said. "I got the idea. There's nothing in that bag I haven't seen before. And to be honest, I don't care to see them."

"Really," Lorenzo said.

"You wouldn't understand."

"*Really?*"

"Yes," Chris said with annoyance.

"More bad memories?"

"Something like that."

"No doubt," Lorenzo said.

Chris gazed at the portraits. "We're not going to keep these here, are we?"

"I'll bring them to the Mill," Matteo said. "Just wanted to arrange a little demonstration for your benefit. I'll need to borrow the wagon again, of course—with your permission. And I'll need a few more frames of glass, for the other orbs." He raised the burlap bag and shook it, flashing a sheepish grin. "It'll be back before dawn."

Chris sighed as he looked at Matteo. Not much had changed between them, good and bad. "She's gonna catch us."

"She hasn't yet," Lorenzo said.

"We'll be quiet," Matteo said.

"How long are we gonna keep this up?" Chris said.

"We just started, me boy."

"I don't like stealing from her. Don't you think she's gonna notice that her frames are disappearing?"

"It was your idea," Lorenzo said.

"Hey, every fledgling enterprise needs a loan to get things rolling," Matteo said. "Once we start selling these things, we can buy our own glass and frames. I promise we'll replace the ones we took. You know I will."

The vow contained a familiar emptiness. Chris' line of sight fell once more on the portraits. His eyes shifted to Lorenzo, then back on the frames. Extending an index finger, he touched the image of the old man, not knowing what to expect. The portrait was warm, but had "set," for when he looked at the tip of his finger, no "paint" had come off, and he did not disturb the image. Then he dragged his fingertip across the image, noting its rough surface. When he curled his finger and rapped its knuckle on the glass, it made a thud, as if he were knocking on something much more dense than glass should be, like a thick slab of ice.

"Good stuff, huh?" Matteo said. "The rest are nice and clear. Usually, they have a greenish tint."

"Where does she get them?"

"There's a shop at the south end of the Village, right on the edge of the forest where they can get their hands on a lot of wood. They blow glass there, too. Interesting little operation. They take this mixture of sand, soda, and lime, put it in a big iron pot, and shove it into a really hot oven. When it's all melted, they ladle it directly onto a casting table. Then they use rollers to flatten it. After the glass cools, it's cut for size."

"Sounds like a bakery," Lorenzo said.

"Sounds expensive," Chris said.

"They would be...if she had them polished."

"You know all about this stuff?"

"You gotta know how everything works, me boy, if you want to run a successful business." He reached out to the portrait of the young girl and placed it before the old man's image. "What do you say we break up this little gathering? You've got a big day ahead of you."

Chris nodded. His first night in the New World. And Janey, still frozen in time. "Don't forget our deal."

"Don't you forget, either," Matteo said.

"What if he's still like this in the morning?" Lorenzo said.

"That's what the doc is for."

"I mean before the doc sees him."

Matteo stared at Chris, who couldn't help displaying his own devilish grin. They just refused to believe who he truly was. So be it.

"I don't think he'll do anything stupid," Matteo said. But his tone betrayed his concern, justifiably.

Chapter Twenty-Five

The Morning Light

It sounded like the big-city zoo—inside the giant aviary where thousands of birds were kept. The cacophony of chatter and chirping and screeching was deafening. The pillow over his head did little to suppress the racket. But there was a problem: he wasn't at the zoo, he was—

Startled, Chris sat up in the bed. He looked around to get his bearings, then realized that he was still in the Cottage bedroom. He threw aside the bedding and rushed to the window to see what was causing the commotion.

Chris rested his hands on the window ledge and peered up through the wet glass into the naked forest canopy that encroached upon the eastern side of the Cottage. He saw familiar birds of all sizes and colors—blackbirds, sparrows, crows, blue jays, robins, and cardinals—some content to perch, others flapping about from branch to branch as they eagerly awaited the first rays of the Sun to strike them. So many birds were present, he could only see hints of blue sky. He grinned at his first morning in the New World.

It had been a restless night, Chris suddenly recalled. After Matteo and Lorenzo left in the wagon with the portraits, Chris returned to his bedroom via the window undetected. But as soon as his head hit the pillow, he resumed the struggle with his predicament. Yet this morning, there still wasn't any doubt about this fact: he was not going to abandon Janey for this World.

Despite the uproar outside, Chris heard the grandfather clock at the bottom of the stairs strike six a.m. He withdrew from the window, washed up, and quickly dressed. Then after glancing at Alessandra's closed bedroom door, he carefully descended those stairs. When he reached the front door, he looked into the shadows of the musty living room and down the darkened entry hall that led into the kitchen for signs of his mother. Convinced that Alessandra was still asleep in her bedroom, Chris carefully unlocked the heavy latch and pulled the door open. Crisp, fresh air washed over him as he stepped outside into the knee-high snow. But something much more spectacular was happening. The snow in the western part of the mountain meadow, struck by the yellow rays of sunlight, had vanished. Now that portion of the meadow exploded with color from the thousands of sweet-scented wild flowers that popped up before his eyes as if time had sped up abnormally fast. Balmy now commingled with the cold, and their battle stirred the air. In the shadows that still fell over the Cottage and its Studio, the thick blanket of snow struggled to keep its imposing weight over all. But the trickle of water from the long icicles that hung from the roof's edge and poked ever-widening holes in the pockets of gray slush below told another story.

    Stunned by the incredible sights, Chris pulled the door shut, high-stepped away from the Cottage, busting through the snow, then looked up at the forest canopy. From the very top, where the sunlight struck the naked branches, green leaves sprouted and poked with the same unnatural speed the jittery creatures that had gathered there to welcome the dawn. Where did this come from?

    Chris let out a cry of wonder, then ran as fast as he could, dodging the boulders and watching the path turn from snow to ice and then to mud. Descending the icy, shadowed face of the bluff, the cold saturating him once more, Chris saw in the great golden meadow before the Village a small army of workers, armed with scythes and rakes and pitchforks, slashing and harvesting the tall grains that waved in the ever-warming breeze as birds circled patiently overhead. His nostrils filled with the moist organic scent of chaff. Where the tall grains did not grow, green pastures took root, much to the comfort of the cattle, goats, and sheep that grazed there. On the sun-drenched western edge of the forest near the Manor's gate, workers standing in horse-drawn wagons picked at the trees actually bursting with all varieties of fruit. And as he neared the pond, Chris saw a few fishermen ashore with nets slung over their shoulders, readying their perfectly white wooden skiffs. They tipped their straw hats to Chris as he raced past. They, too, looked strangely familiar.

    By the time he reached Lorenzo's house, Chris had his plaid wool jacket clutched in his right arm. The warm sunlight worked its rejuvenating magic on the jumble of ivy that clung to the walls of the shops and cottages while the fresh waters of the rapidly melting snow invigorated the clear rushing stream. But now that the Sun had risen above the newly formed canopy, the chatter in the forests had stopped. Despite the sudden explosion of spring-like conditions that now rushed inexorably toward summer, the Village was tranquil as shopkeepers in clean linen aprons went about their humdrum routines, opening shuttered storefronts, sweeping the steamy wet cobbles with besoms, preparing for another perfect day in Sandra's paradise.

    Chris tried to suppress his astonishment so as not to draw attention to himself. He approached the yellow front door of Lorenzo's cottage as if he were expected. Before Chris reached the front step, Lorenzo poked his head from the gable window, like a cuckoo in a clock.

"What took you so long, Cristofori?" Lorenzo said, hands gripping the sill. He smiled wryly.

"You're awake," Chris said.

Lorenzo laughed. "Oh, and those crazy birds didn't get you out of bed? At least the snow is gone. Man, I hate shoveling."

"So you've been waiting?"

"Like you weren't dropping major hints last night."

"It was that obvious, huh?"

"I'm surprised your mom wasn't waiting up for you."

Chris held out his upturned hands and shrugged.

"So," Lorenzo said, "because you're here at the crack of dawn, and you don't remember we're on holiday, I take it that Caterina's good-night's-rest theory has failed completely."

"Well?"

Lorenzo grew stern. "What are you doing here, Cristofori? Don't you have an appointment with the doc?"

"I want to see the old cottage."

"Now?"

"Yes, now. It's daylight, right? What's the big deal?"

"What about the doc?"

"We still have time, don't we?"

Lorenzo glanced around nervously. "I don't know, Cristofori. You're really starting to scare me. Why don't you go ask Matteo to take you? He knew you were gonna try, didn't he?"

"Yeah, well, I don't know where he lives."

"I'll be glad to tell you, then go back to my soft bed."

"Somehow I don't think he'll agree."

"Oh, but I'm supposed to? You are crazy, aren't you?"

"All right, so I'm still having problems. Don't you think it'll help if I go there, just to see? Maybe it will unblock my memory."

"Yeah, and maybe it will make things worse. That's all I need."

"I'll go by myself, then," Chris said.

"No, don't do that—don't do that. You might get lost. And if you do, Matteo will have my head on a platter. Man, life was much easier when you weren't so insane."

"He won't know I stopped by."

"He'll still blame me," Lorenzo muttered, glum and distant, as if he were already experiencing his punishment. "I don't hide things very well, Cristofori."

"Then take me there, please. I have to see it. Can't you understand that?"

"I do," Lorenzo said. But he still seemed hesitant.

"Just a quick look and we'll come back. I swear."

Lorenzo looked on, unmoved.

"Look, you know if the roles were reversed, I'd do it for you. You're one of my best friends, right?"

"I am, yes."

"And we've always taken care of each other, haven't we, especially when we're in trouble?"

"I see you remember some things."

"Some things, sure. Come on, let's go. We're wasting time."

"I'd like to help you, Cristofori—I really would. But if I get caught—"

"I remember where the Purple Orb is," Chris said.

Lorenzo's eyes brightened and he stared intently at Chris. "So it is there? Really?"

"You take me there, and I'll show you."

Lorenzo laughed. "You think I'm that easy? We've gone through this many times before, Cristofori. 'Here, Lorenzo, you do this incredibly stupid thing with me and I'll throw you a bone.' Ha!"

"But we're not talking about bones, are we?"

"Yes we are, Cristofori—that's exactly what we're talking about. And we'd all be better off if you just admitted it."

"Okay, fine. Let's forget about the Orb."

"You couldn't remember where the thing was before you went bonkers, but now that you can barely remember your name, you're telling me you know where we can find it?"

Chris kept quiet as he held his grin. He saw Lorenzo squirming. But he refused to take the bait.

"Go back home and have a nice breakfast. You gotta be starving by now after all that cosmic traveling. And I hear she makes a mean waffle, so you've told me. Remember how much you like those waffles? I might even join you myself. But don't tell my parents. Could hurt their feelings." Lorenzo motioned with his head toward the next-door bakery with its scents of browning bread and golden pastries, and he smiled.

"Okay, Lorenzo, sorry for bothering you."

"Now you're being rational. That's what we're all about here, Cristofori. You want to remember that, too. Good luck with the doc." He lowered his voice. "I'll probably see you at the Mill later, huh?"

"Yeah," Chris whispered, though he could care less about the Paintings.

"That'll be a real eye opener for you."

Chris turned and started down the sidewalk, jacket flung over his shoulder. He heard Lorenzo slam the window shut. But instead of turning right for his Cottage, Chris turned left—for the other end of the Village and the path to *L'entroterra*.

Lorenzo's window slid open. "Where are you goin', crazy man?"

Chris turned to face Lorenzo, but kept walking, now backwards, toward his mysterious objective. "Nowhere," Chris said, "just to get lost. So very, very, very lost." He grinned disingenuously, spun to face forward, and quickened his pace. He liked the confident feeling in his deeper voice, in his clever words, and in the strides of his more-powerful, newfound body. He was growing accustomed to all these otherwise strange sensations.

"All right—woof, woof—you win, damn it!" Lorenzo shouted. "I'll be right down."

"What?" Chris shouted as he broke into a trot.

"Hey, Cristofori—wait up!"

Chapter Twenty-six

The Old Cottage

Chris (consumed by wonder) and Lorenzo (consumed by intrigue, and self-preservation) followed the wet, cobbled walkway in silence, listening to the ever-warming breeze rustle the Village pines as the slowly rising Sun stirred the environment to life. By the time they passed the last of the arched bridges and entered the cool and misty sun-streaked forest, the oaks and elms had already sprouted their green leaves, which were now changing to different shades of purples and blues—a wildly unique feature in many of Sandra's paintings ("Why not?" she often said in her defense, which Chris understood implicitly). Because of the dampness and the columns of cold air they encountered in the growing shadows, Chris had slipped on his plaid jacket, while Lorenzo, donning a heavy wool sweater, trudged along in his brimless leather cap with dangling earflaps.

They came around the bend and descended the cracked granite steps, now lichen-stained. The once-icy stream had become a rushing, soothing cascade. Just ahead, Chris saw the small flagstone bridge arching over the whitewater. But now, a lush blanket of fragrant lavender phlox surrounded it and the glowing evergreen. He thought of Auntie Monika's perfume.

Beyond the Bridge, however, the meadow remained shrouded in a thick fog, another Other World, with mystery and apprehension saturating the mists. There was a disturbing sound in those mists, far off, and drifting, like a chorus of angels holding a wary tone, on the verge of a scream.

"You hear that?" Lorenzo said.

Chris kept silent. It seemed as though it were coming true.

"I've never heard that before. What is it?"

"We'll be all right."

"I didn't ask that."

Glancing nervously at each other, they started across the Bridge, Chris leading. When he looked back, Lorenzo's skin began to shine.

"Last chance," Lorenzo said, as if it were a plea.

But though he now sensed that this next incursion into The Hinterland might have some dire consequences, Chris' thoughts were still on Janey. "Let's keep going." Even his own words startled him.

They followed the muddy path along the stream as it meandered through the foggy meadow, the tall brown grasses encased in the murk, their boots stamping holes in the crawling fog, kicking it up like dust. Chris kept alert but wary, ready to react to whatever was out there. Now that they had returned to *L'entroterra*, without their leader, Chris didn't feel secure anymore. And that opened the gates to his fears, which quickly rushed in. True to his Story, the fog still had a creeping feeling about it as it did last night, and repulsive, like a spider crawling on his face. But now, despite the muted light of day, because of the ever-rising Sun, there was more to the fog than just an ill feeling, and a fleeting, frightening song. Knowing what he knew, what he had written about the Kingdom of Darkness, Chris was certain that they were being watched. He felt some evil eyes staring from afar, or just behind them. It was a cold insanity swirling about them, a whole swarm of cold insane things, whispering in his ear, reading his thoughts, smelling his fear, and laughing, all the while welcoming them, and escorting them in. "Can you hear them?" Chris said, thinking aloud, not eager to look back.

"Hear who?" Lorenzo said. "It's a who? A bunch of them?"

They walked on, and Lorenzo, keeping close, dared not speak another word. But with his glow, he suddenly looked like he belonged here, with the others.

Yes, Chris could feel their chill and hear their little voices giggling. But there was that overpowering drive and need to continue, to take their chances. The reward was too great.

They came upon the fork and the cross set in the pile of glistening stones. Lorenzo stopped to stare up at it, as if he expected to see someone nailed to it, or knew that it had really happened. Apparently, it had, in this World. But somewhere, far off in a nameless land, and back in that very deep and unmentioned past. The impact was no less great. "Why'd ya choose a cross for your warning?"

Chris stared as well. "I don't know. Want me to guess?"

"Sure."

"It'll lead you to disappointment, and disaster."

"Is that why you left this land?"

"I suppose you could say that."

"There's hope for you yet." His spark of joy vanished as he gazed around at the fog—as if he, too, could read minds. "Are you sure you want to keep going?"

Chris nodded.

They veered to the right of the cross and walked cautiously along the path, one frightened blind man leading another. When he reached a sharp bend suddenly lined with reeds, Chris realized that they were standing before a pond in which the stream emptied. The rising Sun seemed to stir the fog with its ever-growing intensity. Now it was Chris' turn to stop and stare, while wishing he could run.

"What?" Lorenzo said.

"I think we're here."

"Here?" Lorenzo gazed out over the shrouded pond. "I don't see anything."

And then, as if annoyed, the fog began to whirl about, awakening—slowly at first, then faster and faster with every passing moment.

"Uh-oh," Lorenzo said in a soft tone that expressed a refusal to believe. "What's happening?"

"Quiet."

"Is this what you heard, Cristofori?"

"Stop."

"Is it?"

Two worlds, side by side.

"Her story, my Story, " Chris said, eyes shifting. He shuddered.

"What?"

"I think we're about to meet someone."

"Who?"

Chris stared at him, unable to explain. "Whatever you do, don't look at her."

"Huh?"

The smooth swirls began to form clumps.

"I said don't look at her!"

"Look at who?"

The clumps began to take other shapes—ghostly shapes...

"Look at who?"

...of children...

"Cristofori?"

...with black holes for eyes...

"Just don't!"

...and dressed in white gowns.

Chris shielded Lorenzo's eyes with his right hand. "She'll trap you and never let you go!"

Lorenzo slapped Chris' hand away. "Who are they?"

Neither of them could resist the urge to look, and they gazed out over the pond.

There was another spectral figure among the children—one Chris knew well.

Lorenzo's jaw dropped. "What the—"

It was the woman with the glowing garments and face. She seemed to be staring at them, just across the pond, and on its steamy surface. An icon of the impossible, the nonexistent—right before their eyes.

The children, all around her, saw them standing there, too. They held their tendril-like hands to the sides of their elongated faces. Then their mouths stretched open in a ghastly way as if they wanted to shriek.

Chris and Lorenzo were mesmerized. Neither could speak.

Suddenly, the children stretched and swirled into separate vortices, then they dissolved completely as the Sun intensified and burned away the mist. The woman remained for a moment, as if to be sure all the children had made their successful escape. Then she, too, disappeared in a brief but chiming sparkle, and left them to stand in shock in a warm beam of sunlight, just like when the storm had passed, in the old world.

Finally, Lorenzo swiveled his head mechanically, fighting the rust that had seized him, and stared at Chris with a sickened expression. "What did we just see?"

His mother's Christmas tale haunted Chris as if she were narrating, and he saw every word he recounted. Now that he was in the proper setting, the young woman's identity was obvious. But Chris wondered with much consternation why the woman—the protector of dead children's souls—had appeared in his bedroom.

"Damn, Cristofori, I've heard the rumors...were they real?"

"You've never seen them before?"

"You think I'd forget a thing like that?" Lorenzo glanced out over the misty pond. "Matteo's not going to believe this—he'll think I'm losing my mind. See what I mean about this land of yours? I don't know how you could have survived here."

"But we didn't," Chris said. He tapped Lorenzo on the shoulder and pointed to the new vision appearing before them. Now that the fog was lifting, Chris saw a crumbled structure just beyond the pond. It was a cottage—or what remained of one. Most of the gabled roof was gone. Only the far outer wall remained intact. The others had been partially torn down, exposing the inner plaster walls pockmarked with dried mud, lichen, and large holes that revealed the broken latticework. The wrecked cottage was overgrown with wild vines and gnarled scrubs that poked up through gaps in the floorboards. Even the scattering of mature trees around the cottage showed signs of tremendous trauma and destruction. Thick trunks were debarked and twisted into grotesque shapes and, where main branches had been ripped away, wispy shoots grew from knobby stumps. Chris recognized the scene. But it wasn't from one of his mother's paintings. No cheerfully bright colors welcomed them. These colors were muddy and dark, and brought on a numbing despair—the way he described in his diary the works of Caspar David Friedrich from the St. Boniface collection.

"Now what?" Lorenzo said. "Is that it?"

"Come on, let's go have a look."

"Have a look? What's the matter with you? We gotta get out of here before she comes back."

"No doubt," Chris said. He started for the cottage.

"Hey, where ya goin'? Hey, wait up!" Lorenzo followed like a frightened pup. He repeatedly glanced across the waters and looked for signs of the supernatural.

They came upon a massive, cleanly-cut stump lying on its side just to the right of the ruins. Its bark was gone. Only its decaying roots remained. It looked like some dead sea creature whose tentacles had been drained of all color. Inside the large hole where the roots once gripped the earth sprouted another dwarf evergreen with glowing white orbs. Chris wondered how many they had planted, how far they had gone.

"Kinda weird how you did this, don't you think?" Lorenzo said. He gazed around, ready to run.

"You mean the tree?"

"Yeah, the tree. You knew what it could do out here. Obviously, you thought you needed it." He gazed out over the pond. "Obviously, you did."

"Didn't work very well, did it?"

Lorenzo stared at the decimated cottage, then glanced back out over the pond. "You know, suddenly the Orb doesn't seem like such a big deal anymore."

Chris stepped over a pile of rubble and onto the weathered floorboards of the ruined cottage. He gazed about in despair. He saw the old bungalow back home, how it sat perfectly on this site. But it was hard for him to feel the same degree of sadness he felt for Janey's plight back in the old world.

"Anything?" Lorenzo said.

Chris kicked a loose brick across the floor. They followed it to a small corner room where they saw the remnants of a closet. Its louvered doors had been pulled from the framing and lay shattered before them. A huge hole had been punched through its back wall. But there was no debris within.

"Tiny room, too bad," Lorenzo said. "Now can we go?"

"It's a wall closet. We were hiding in there when the storm hit."

Lorenzo's eyes widened. "So you do—"

"No, Lorenzo—not this version. How does it end?"

Lorenzo's round face crinkled in bewilderment, but he recovered. "You tried to protect her. But something struck her in the neck and she died in your arms."

"Not from the collapsed roof, like Matteo said."

"No. He was just messing with you. He thought it was all a joke."
"But it's not."
"No—not now," Lorenzo said, eyes shifting, searching. "Not now."
"It was something else," Chris said. "It was a chain."
"A what?"
"Forget it."

Lorenzo shrugged. "Yeah well, bad stuff, I know, but you wanted to see this again. Time to go, Cristofori. Time to go."

Chris was suddenly bombarded by recollections of the day the storm decimated their home back in the old world. He recalled how, in an instant, the world went insane and disintegrated all around him as he looked out the living room window into the blackness of noon and watched the young maple trees in his front yard bend so severely that their tops touched the ground. He recalled the constant flashing of lightning, the continuous thunder, cars flipping and smashing and wrapping around big trees, boards cracking, eardrums popping, and debris flying so furiously, they seemed to spark. But most of all, he recalled the terrible wind finding its way in, rushing with the rain beneath the weatherstripping of the threshold, and how that rushing wind made such a loud and unearthly sound, later becoming the nightmarish Horde blowing into their foul horns, announcing their ghastly arrival, just like in the famous painting, and in his Story. Chris stared into the closet as the pressure built. Yeah, he remembered that part. But Janey had survived.

"You look ill," Lorenzo said. "Blaming yourself?"
"What?"
"For surviving. I'm no doc, but it seems pretty obvious to me—to everyone. Don't you think that's why you're having all these problems?"

Chris stared into the closet, his mind a blur. "She left me."
"You're angry at Giovanna?"
Chris turned a blank stare on Lorenzo. What?"
"You're angry. With your sister."
"No I'm not."
"But you just said it."

"I did?" Then he felt the urge to think something strange: *You still don't get who I am.* He felt compelled to think it again, to brighten his mind. But the relief was fleeting, as was the thought, or its purpose. The fog in his head returned, his thoughts became a jumble, and his breaths labored. "Besides, Giovanna had to die."

Lorenzo looked horrified. "Huh?"
"How do little girls become angels?"

But when he saw the bewilderment spreading across Lorenzo's face, Chris sighed, realizing the futility of continuing. No doubt, they had little time. "Where's her grave? Did I ever tell you?"

"Grave? Wait a minute, Cristofori. You didn't say anything about that. We gotta get back and tell everyone what we saw."

"I'm not going back until I see it."

Lorenzo grit his teeth. "I knew you were going to do this."

"Where is it, Lorenzo?"

"I don't know."

"You're a lousy liar—here and there."

"You come with me and I'll tell you," Lorenzo said.

"You tell me and I'll go back with you."

"Oh, no, not that game again. I'm not giving in."

"Yes you will."

"No I won't."

"Oh yes you will," Chris said. "Remember last night when we were talking about the music box?"

"Yeah?"

"Find the music box, find the Orb?"

"Yeah?"

"The music box...it's her telephone booth."

"Her what?"

"Her tomb."

Lorenzo frowned. "The Orb's in her tomb?"

"I'm not even going to bother."

Lorenzo shook his head. "Well, if that's the case, I doubt it's still there. That place has been picked clean. Even the doc got into the act."

"What, now Dr. Samuele's a grave robber?"

"Maybe not that, but where do you think he got the statue for his atrium?"

"Tell me."

Lorenzo sighed. "We'd have to go back to the field—you know, where we were last night. There's a wrecked church nearby. It's part of the complex were you went to school with that idiot Tomas and all those other goons."

Chris felt his jaw tighten as he gazed southward into the fog. Yes, he understood more and more how this World was put together. And those eyes were upon him again, staring. He thought he heard the little voices laughing. "I should have brought the wagon."

"Come on, Cristofori, we don't have time. Besides, this place is dangerous, just like you said. Who knows what's waiting for us at the ruins? Maybe worse than Tomas, huh? Maybe worse than her."

"You go back, then. I have to see it."

Lorenzo rolled his eyes. "I can't let you go there by yourself, Cristofori—especially now, with these things around."

"Then I guess your coming along."

Lorenzo cringed. "Come on, Cristofori, be reasonable. I don't want the whole Village on my back. You're already too much to handle."

Chris started across the floorboards when something in the corner of his eye caught his attention—something extraordinarily large that loomed in the distance. He turned to look south and saw two featureless gray spires poking through the breaks in the fog. He knew in an instant what they represented. "What's that, Lorenzo?" he said, curious to hear if Lorenzo would be truthful.

Lorenzo stared southward, squinting. But he couldn't hide his disappointment, or alarm. "I don't know."

"It's the church, isn't it."

"Could be."

"Think this path will take us there?"

"Don't know that either."

"Let's find out, okay?"

Lorenzo glanced one more time at the pond, its reed-lined shores now completely visible, its surface a shimmering liquid gold. "If we must."

"We do."

"Then I'm a dead man," Lorenzo said. "And so are you."

Chapter Twenty-Seven

At the Ruins

The path took them into a valley as hints of the decimated hillsides on either side revealed themselves through breaks in the fog. Like giant skeletal hands reaching in agony from the grave, the trees showed the same scars of violence—snapped limbs, stripped bark, twisted trunks—as they had by the cottage. The closer they came to the church, the more difficult their journey became. Huge fallen trees caked with moss blocked the path, and they had to find their way around the obstructions, or gingerly climb over them.

Finally, the base of the rocky bluff on which the church sat appeared through the mist as if something monstrous had risen suddenly from the Earth. They followed the rutted path as it angled its way upward like a slash across the promontory's shrouded, weathered face.

Once atop the bluff, which—void of trees—seemed more like a plateau, they came upon another dwarf evergreen, burning white-hot in the murk. Just beyond was the church's chillingly familiar stone façade, climbing up into the fog. The immense structure had not been spared the wrath of the Storm that had ravaged the area. Though the façade was intact, the many pinnacles of its two spires had been torn away, reduced to rubble at their feet. The glass of the ogival windows was gone. So, too, were the great doors and the steeply-pitched roof. The shattered remains of the giant rib vaults littered the nave and the adjacent graveyard that spread eastward into the mist.

And then...something in white seemed to be walking among the broken headstones. Or just a stirring breeze? Maybe both. A thing that was part of the fog itself. Or just the fog itself. Chris stood there, just to be certain.

That sudden pause alarmed Lorenzo. "Cristofori?" he said.

"When did all this happen?"

"The night Giovanna died."

"Did you hear it?"

"No. The light keeps out unwanted noises, too."

"Don't care to hear children screaming for their lives?"

"I didn't make up that rule." Lorenzo nervously scanned the graveyard.

"Is she out there?" Chris said.

"No, in the church, in a—"

"I know where to find her."

The mist in the graveyard remained still, no longer a threat, so Chris continued on. But his eyes moved nervously, his movements cautious, just like Lorenzo's.

Passing through the large entryway and shallow vestibule, they skirted the huge chunks of rubble before arriving at the polygonal chapel on the west end of the transept, which had been the base of another tower. But the tower had been sheared off just above the narrow arched windows, and on this ledge hung a thick blanket of moss—yet another painted image that had become reality. Through those windows, Chris saw through the gaps in the fog a distant, pale blue-and-orange mountain shrouded by yellow clouds that drifted over its yawning vent. He couldn't help staring at it, wondering...

"What?" Lorenzo said. "What's wrong now?"

"Nothing," Chris said. "Did I ever...?"

"Ever what? *What?*"

Chris gazed at Lorenzo. "Did I ever say anything about it?"

"The Mountain? No. We've heard those stories, too... Should you have?"

Chris' eyes fell to the stone sarcophagus in the center of the chapel, its heavy lid still in place. He let out a sigh of anguish. He had seen enough of this Dream World to know all too well how it was put together. And if he remained, Chris feared he would see many more dreadful sights.

"Fear not," a deep voice echoed through the ruins.

Chris whirled around and saw a hunched old man with a long gray beard and floppy, wide-brimmed hat with feather standing amidst the rubble not more than a few feet away. He wore a simple white robe tied at the waist with a length of hemp, and in his gnarly right hand he held a crooked walking stick. A single stitch fastened his right eyelid. Clearly, he had seen this mysterious figure before, but Chris had no idea what this World had done to him, or what to expect. Chris stepped back, full of trepidation, and bumped into the tomb. "I...I came to see my sister."

"Why do you seek the living among the dead?" the old man said. "You know she is not here."

Lorenzo looked as if he were ready to bolt. "Not here? Well, then—"

"Then where is she?" Chris said. "Do you know?"

The old man cocked his head while locking his glare upon Chris, as if he were studying Chris' thoughts.

"Please, sir," Chris said, "if you know where she is, tell me so I can bring her back to the Village with me."

"I know what you seek," the old man replied, "as do I." Then he stepped forward and held up the walking staff.

"Please, sir," Chris said, cringing, "we don't want any trouble."

But the old man kept coming. His movements were suddenly fast and forceful. He thrust the stick at Chris. Lorenzo dashed away. Chris sidestepped the jab, and the end of the stick caught the edge of the sarcophagus' stone lid. Instead of running, Chris held his ground.

The old man froze in his thrusting position, all the while keeping his one-eyed stare on Chris. Suddenly, with a short but powerful stab, the old man pushed the stone lid partially from the sarcophagus. Then he calmly stepped back and brought the staff to his side. "Behold the place where you laid her to rest."

Chris hesitated, and kept his wary gaze upon the menacing figure, fearing treachery. But his curiosity was so great, the tomb became a magnet, forcing him to glance into the opening. Even Lorenzo crept back to Chris' side to peek.

The sarcophagus was empty.

"And the object of your quest?" the old man said.

"I don't know," Chris said. "It should be here, with her."

The old man grumbled.

"It's true, sir," Lorenzo said. "He doesn't remember much of anything."

"And I should take the word of one from the Village that holds this land in such contempt?"

But Chris, fearing for their safety, had no succinct answer for him. "All we ask is that you believe what we say."

"Believe? Yes, thank you," he said. "A child is coming." And then he showed an awful grin.

Chris was stunned by the words. But he and Lorenzo did not move. The old man walked around them like a wolf circling its prey, looking for signs of weakness. He drew close to Lorenzo. "It was unwise to bring him here," he said. "But, of course, you know this, too. And still you come." The old man cautiously reached out with his crooked index finger to touch Lorenzo's shimmering face. When he did, he quickly pulled his hand away as if he had been shocked. Then he curled his fingers into a tight fist and stepped back.

At that moment, Chris heard a strange new haunting sound. It began as the solitary chime, coming somewhere from the fog that lay like a great blanket before the looming Mountain. After a long pause, another chime followed, higher in tone, and just as distant. The third chime sounded moments later, deeper than the other two. And then a fourth chime, similar to the first, drifted over the church ruins. There was a hint of a melody in the chimes, but the long delay between tones and their arrangement rendered the melody unrecognizable, as if a child were attempting to compose a song on the higher octaves of a piano.

"What is it?" Lorenzo said.

Suddenly, the tempo of the chimes increased. The tones rearranged themselves into a simple but appealing theme that repeated itself over and over, just like the tune from the music box.

The old man's wickedly satisfied gaze fell on Chris.

Don't let it get me, a voice whispered in Chris' ear. His eyes brightened.

"You shall weep for her," the old man said with evil in his narrowed eye. "Yes...you shall."

"Giovanna!" he cried out, and he bolted from the chapel.

Chris set his sights on the Mountain as he ran west through the remnant fog atop the bluff. The chiming continued unabated, calling him. And as he ran, his mind whirled with wonder and anticipation. The sign, her sign. She was here, as she was in the Story, as he had hoped all along. Was she in danger?

Out of the fog, a stone wall appeared, its capstones long since crumbled. But it was still intact and high enough to make it impossible to scale. Chris stopped for a moment and listened to the chimes. The song continued. But he detected another sound, more vibrant—like that of a rumbling waterfall, just beyond the barrier. Chris ran frantically along the wall to look for an opening.

Chris came upon a gate. It, too, was weathered and showed its age. But its thick boards held firm against the framing, and its rusted hinges remained bolted to the stone piers. Chris tried to release the latch. It was locked. He began kicking the gate.

"Cristofori, wait!" Lorenzo called out.

The boards refused to yield. "Help me with this, Lorenzo—please!"

Lorenzo grabbed Chris by the arms and pulled him away. "No, stop. We've been here long enough—too long! We've got to get back. This is a bad place to be—a very bad place!"

Chris spun around and freed himself from Lorenzo's grip. "How many times do I have to tell you—I don't care about the doc! I didn't come this far to give up. You don't understand what that song means. She's calling out to me, Lorenzo. I don't have time to explain. But we can't just leave her out there."

"Cristofori, Giovanna's dead. You can't change that."

"She's not dead. Didn't you hear the old man? Did you forget about the pond?"

"Then what is she? Another ghost?"

"I don't have time!"

Chris turned to face the gate, but stopped silent before he could raise his foot. The chiming had ceased. But now the rumbling of the waterfall had changed. It had become louder and more furious, and he could feel the thuds against his chest. The menacing sound triggered another dark memory.

Chris stepped away from the gate to gaze out over the wall. He could no longer see the Mountain. The fog had disappeared. All across the horizon, black and green clouds churned and billowed like smoke from a great fire. Then a great wind snuck up on them and began to rattle the lifeless trees. Chris had seen this image before and felt its fury. The fear it instilled was familiar, too. But it had nothing to do with paintings from another world. "Come on, Lorenzo, we gotta go."

"Yeah, good—*what?*"

"Come on, Lorenzo," Chris shouted with urgency. He turned to run as the rumbling and the roar of the wind grew louder. But then he stopped and whirled around. The sound of a horse's furious hoof beats overtook the wind. The horse was approaching fast, and Chris felt bound to await its imminent arrival.

Suddenly, the gate exploded inward. A black horse and its cloaked rider flew past them. With a black satchel at his side, the rider pulled on the reins, rearing the horse to a sudden stop. Then he turned the horse to face Chris.

"*L'tempest si avvicina!*" the rider shouted.

Chris was amazed, though he knew he shouldn't have been. It was Coach Joe, or rather, his equivalent—larger, menacing, and frighteningly moribund, as if he had just burst from the grave.

The rider pointed a black-tipped finger toward the approaching cloud. "The Storm is approaching!" he shouted once more.

But with all the noise and confusion, Chris could not understand him. "What?"

Fire grew in the rider's sunken eyes. "They fooled me—fooled us all. Run, Cristofori—run!" He then charged off into the retreating fog behind them.

Instinct overtook Chris. He sprinted after the Black Rider toward the church ruins. The threat to Chris' life—the first he had encountered in the Dream World—was very real. He suddenly understood that not only could he dream here, but he could also die here. If they wanted to survive, if he wanted to see Janey again, they had to find sanctuary quickly—somewhere underground. His mind sparked wildly to recall such a refuge among the devastation they had already encountered. He grew more fearful when no image appeared.

When he reached the ruins, Chris spun around. He was momentarily heartened to see that Lorenzo was not far behind. But whether or not his lumbering friend could outrun the Storm was in serious doubt. The leading edge of the roiling clouds had spilled over the wall and was gaining on him. "Hurry, Lorenzo—faster!" Chris shouted into the roaring wind. But Chris saw the terror on Lorenzo's face, for he too realized that he wasn't going to make it.

Chris briefly thought of hiding somewhere among the rubble—behind a fallen pillar or smashed vault. But another Storm had already tossed about the church's massive stone frame. The rubble and remaining structure, now severely weakened, would undoubtedly become the instruments of his demise, not his salvation. His only chance was to reach the West Bridge.

Chris took one last agonizing look at Lorenzo, then darted down the path. When he reached the base of the bluff, he heard Lorenzo cry out in anguish above the roar: "*Cris-tow-FOR-ee!*" His cry seemed to echo throughout the valley before the thunder of the Storm overtook it and crushed it from existence. And now, as Chris bounded over the fallen oaks, he turned his head quickly to see the boiling black clouds engulfing the church and spilling down the bluff. The obstructions across the path made it impossible for him to stay ahead of the Storm. And he realized that he, too, would become its victim.

Chris finally cleared the debris field near the bluff, and he saw the ruined cottage just ahead. But the Black Cloud was nearly at his heals, and the roar of the rushing wind was so intense, he could not hear himself gasping for air. Just as the Storm began to swallow him, Chris slid into the pit where the glowing evergreen stood. His midriff hit the trunk, and he spun around beneath the body of the tree like a tossed horseshoe striking a metal stake. The hot and twisting pain in his gut nearly made him vomit. His lungs felt collapsed, void of air, and he almost blacked out. But he had enough sense remaining to pull his legs in and wrap his arms around the trunk as the Storm roared all around him.

When his vision restored itself, all he saw was a spinning cloud of dust and dirt. The ground shook as if a million fists pounded the turf. But strangely, all was calm beneath the tree. Not a speck of debris struck his coiled body. And he did not feel the slightest breeze. The scene was so surreal, the terror he felt momentarily subsided. And he contemplated sticking a finger into the swirling dust just to see what would happen. But then he thought of Lorenzo, and the horrible weight of reality came crashing in on him. He closed his eyes in shame and clung to the tree. Slowly, the thunderous pounding dissipated into an odd tranquility.

But was the Storm finally over? There was indeed something strange about those black clouds. They didn't wrap around a vortex like they did in the real world. Instead, they rolled and bubbled forward like a pyroclastic flow. And when it had just about overtaken him, Chris was sure he had felt something—some things—trying to reach out to grab him. That a menacing storm would try to take his life was logical and well-documented. But there was another kind of storm in Sandra's story, too, and in his: a great, phantasmal entity condemned to roaming the night sky that would seek out and capture unrepentant souls. As for the old man, the Old Ghost, there was no longer any mystery to his identity, no misinterpreting his connection to the old world—not after the horror Chris had just experienced. The Old Ghost's direct ties to Sandra's story, and his—and the ghastly power that he commanded—had remained faithfully and frightfully intact. That Chris had now confronted him in the flesh, and would undoubtedly do so in the very near future, if he wanted to rescue Lorenzo—who needed to be rescued—made this revelation even more terrifying.

Growing ever more confident that the Storm had retreated, Chris summoned the courage to extract himself from the base of the small tree. But before he could make a move, he saw the hooves of a white horse strolling past, and he instinctively clung to the tree and held his breath. The horse stopped as if on command, then lingered a while. Was the horse part of the Horde? Did it have a rider? Was the rider looking for him? Perspiration beaded on his forehead and his mouth grew dry. He didn't want to know. After some tense moments, the horse walked away without hesitation to the north, and he swallowed hard.

A few minutes later, finally convinced he was safe, Chris pushed himself away from the glowing tree and struggled to his feet, still feeling the punch the tree had delivered. Gazing north, he saw no sign of the white horse. Snapping his head around to the south, Chris saw that the Storm had retreated to the bluff, where it seemed to suspend itself. The narrow path was indiscernible. A much wider swath of dirt had taken its place, one that had stripped the valley of its fallen trees and grasses. He followed the swath all the way to the cottage. The remaining walls had been reduced to rubble. And none of the scrubs survived. But all around in the dirt he saw deep prints—bird, cloven, hound—and others he did not recognize. Chris glanced one last time at the loitering Storm. Now was his chance to reach the West Bridge.

Chris bolted eastward along the path. The Storm seemed to energize, and once again began to spill over the bluff. But no obstructions impeded his fleet-footed escape, and he flew past the cross and triumphantly crossed the Bridge before the Storm could gather enough momentum to catch him.

Standing breathless among the blanket of flowers, Chris indulged himself in the glorious beams of warm light streaking from the purple and blue trees, as if he had awakened from a nightmare. The sound of the rushing waters soothed his immediate fears, and he was certain that he was safe. Then he turned to face the meadow. The roiling black clouds lost their ferociousness, mellowing into a wall of black. Then the black faded to gray, and the gray diffused into the broken mist that had earlier blanketed the meadow. In one such break, Chris saw the Old Ghost standing solemnly with walking staff in hand, the dazzling maiden at his side. Both remained motionless as they stared back at Chris. Then the woman vanished in a brief but chiming sparkle, quickly becoming part of the fog, as the old man turned to walk away into the mists, leaving Chris to wrestle with burdensome questions, his enormous guilt, and another chilling question: *How did the Black Rider know my New World name?*

Chris had vastly underestimated the danger he was facing. And he had been much too flippant and hasty with his decision to pursue Giovanna. Clearly, his Story had much more influence here than he first thought, even with all the strange alterations. And it wasn't a vision—it was real, with real horrors and consequences. There was too much at stake to be playing with people's lives. He had to make this World stop spinning. He had to go back to the old world, regroup, and assess his options. He had the means back home to accomplish this task. Then he would return to continue his quest for his sister, and to discover the fate of Lorenzo, their stories somehow intertwined.

Chris ran all the way back to the Village, which was now abuzz with delivery carts, vendors, shoppers, and musicians in the decorated square, celebrating a holiday that had lost its meaning, that they did not believe in. He felt the pangs of guilt, and found it odd that such beauty and happiness could exist so close to the ugliness and danger just beyond the West Bridge. It seemed the villagers, whose faces he seemed to recognize, did not care, that they were blissfully unaware, even as they stared at him in confusion, as if he had indeed dropped out of the sky. But now Chris finally realized how much he had to do with all that was happening in this World.

When he arrived at Lorenzo's family bakery, he contemplated approaching the older man and woman behind the counter. But he continued past without making eye contact, too afraid to admit his deadly blunder. How could he break the news to them? What could he possibly say? Sickened by his ever-growing remorse, and his utter failure, Chris didn't stop running until he passed through the ivy-covered gateway of the Manor.

Chris came upon the grassy clearing surrounding the grand home. He saw them all—Alessandra, Dr. Samuele, Matteo, and Caterina—adorned in the Victorian fineries appropriate for a warm spring day, and congregating around the immense urn of purple orchids in the center of the sunny lawn. They saw his rapid approach, but their concerned expressions did not change. And they looked as if they wanted to capture—not embrace—him.

"Cristofori," Caterina said. But that's all she said. And yet, he sensed that she had an inkling of all the terrible things that had just transpired, and the nature of the dreadful news he was about to speak.

Chris halted his advance, just out of arm's reach. "I...I lost Lorenzo. He needs your help."

"Lost?"

"You gave me your word, me boy," Matteo said, looking betrayed. "Doesn't that mean anything to you?"

"Come inside, Cristofori," Dr. Samuele said. "We need to talk."

"No—I can't. I have to go."

"Go?" Caterina said. "Go where?"

"Please, come inside," Alessandra said. "There's so much I have to tell you, so much you should know."

"No, I'm not ready. I have to go back home and figure things out."

"But Cristofori—"

"I'm sorry. Help Lorenzo—please. Please hurry." He turned and ran back toward the gate. But he did not hear anyone in pursuit. Of course, he knew it didn't do any good asking them for help. Soon, he would be back home, and their World—including what became of Lorenzo—would be locked once again in time. But he had to tell them, he had to say it. It was all he could do for the moment.

After rushing through the poinsettia field, Chris reached the base of the Tree. The white light overcame him, and soon he found himself sprawled on the living room floor, his head throbbing. All at once, he let the panic from the New World go. And he lay there for a moment in the smothering silence, rubbing the back of his head. How he wished he could perfect his return landing. He gathered enough strength to rise to his feet, wiped the drool from his mouth, then staggered into the foyer. Though he had been gone for days, the brass dial and date wheel of the grandfather clock confirmed that only a few minutes had passed since his departure.

Slowly ascending the stairs, Chris checked on Janey, happy to see his sister once again, sleeping peacefully within the glow of the lamp near her bed, the door willfully unchained. He wanted to embrace her and not let her go, but did not enter her room for fear of awakening her. He hoped her dreams were carrying her to more pleasant places where she was healthy and safe. It was so odd to feel such relief and tranquility in this household. But that was indeed what he was experiencing. In the morning, he would scour the Book for passages about the deadly menace that awaited him in the New World, and explore more fully the intriguing idea—similar to the original, but improved—concerning Janey's illness blossoming in his aching mind. But for now, more aspirin and the hope of a good night's rest, without the fear of terrible Storms, or the horrors that thundered within.

PART FOUR

Back to Reality

Chapter Twenty-Eight

Meeting of the Minds

"See? There he is," Chris said. He pointed to the sketch in the encyclopedia before him as he lay diagonally, on his stomach, across the foot of Janey's bed. "The guy we wrote about. We looked him up after she told us her story—right in here. That's the Old Ghost I saw. Makes sense, right? Of course, almost everyone there looks a little different than the way I described them."

At the head of the bed, Janey, her legs tucked beneath the pink daisy comforter, was propped up within the throne-like red paisley reading pillow Sandra had used during her battle with cancer, when, despite her unsettling frailty, they gladly waited on her hand and foot, like the queen she was. Crowded around Janey like her royal guards were the variety of stuffed animals that had, over the years, been banished one-by-one to the top shelf of her closet. But now that war had returned to the kingdom and their favor had been restored, the royal guards eagerly protected their queen who, for the moment, looked as strong and in charge as ever. Even the pink-and-white striped "Screw Cancer" knit cap, which Sandra had reluctantly worn before Marilyn entered their lives and which Janey proudly presented to her (she got the cap from one of her "naughty" classmates) appeared like a crown of defiance, and added to her royal aura. There were other protective measures: fake garland wrapped around the bed's white metal posts, and draped across the headboard and footboard. And, of course, the plastic bottle of disinfectant sitting amidst the pile of clean rags on her nightstand. Janey lowered the glossy cardboard volume she had been perusing and bent forward to get a better view of the sketch. She scrunched her face. "He looks like John the Janitor." Then her lips pouted. "Poor John the Janitor. Everybody made such fun of him. I'll bet he felt bad."

"John the Janitor? No, no, it says right here: *Wotan, the supreme god and creator, god of victory and the dead.* He even has the damn feather in his hat. C'mon, Janey—from Mom's story, our Story. The leader of the Demon Horde, the one looking for wayward souls like Victor. You know, the Wednesday guy."

Janey ignored him, though he wasn't sure why. Chris felt like Columbus, making his pitch before the skeptical Isabella, before he set off on his wild and dangerous expedition to unexpectedly find his new world. Janey turned around her book and held it out. "How about him?"

Chris stared at the full-page illustration of Thomas Nast's jolly, toy-toting Santa Claus. "I don't think he qualifies as an evil storm king,"

"Okay," Janey said, undaunted. She grabbed another open volume lying on her lap and displayed it. "What about this guy? He has a white beard. And he's German."

"Come on, Janey, quit joking around. I told you, from this Book. Look here." He flopped over the bulk of pages to reveal the first inscription. "*Wotan id est furor*," Chris said, underlining the words with his finger as he read. "See? Like it was destiny."

Janey lowered the encyclopedia. "You're saying that now you believe in that, too?"

Chris flashed a look of disgust. "His name is in the Book, so the science let him in."

"Well, how am I supposed to know? I've never read it. I don't even know where you keep it."

"Yeah, right," Chris said, his eyes glancing at the open volume. More irony. "Trust me. Freud, there, didn't make the cut."

"Maybe he should've," Janey said.

"Well, then he'd be dead. Dead here, dead there. One of the Rules. Mom's the only exception."

"There are exceptions?"

"Hey, it's my diary."

Janey sighed lightly. "I don't know why I ever let you talk me into all that Ragnar junk."

"It was a fantasy story, right? *Fantasy*?"

"So?"

"So, you have to have all that 'junk' in it. The magical Orb, the gods, the Mountain—"

"Who says?"

"They do."

"Who's they?"

"The authors who write the stuff. They all use it."

"Couldn't you have been a little more original?"

"Oh, right, you should talk. You think any of that romance garbage is original?"

"I don't read it. That's Mom's stuff."

"Yeah, sure. That's the second lie you've told me today. And his name isn't Ragnar, it's Wotan."

Janey shifted slightly among the guards, and readjusted a few that had fallen on their faces. "Tell me again why your diary's important."

Chris rolled closer to his sister so he could speak in a hushed tone, as if he were trying to keep his strange secret even from himself. "This World I've been to, this Other World, it's not just our Story come to life, though that's a big part of it. The Great Tree by the Village, Mom's Studio, the doctor's Manor, the goose pond, the scary paintings—it's much more than that. This World is based on everything in the Book. My school friends and enemies, our old house, the dumb game of tag I used to play, plus a few new twists and things... All my writings have come alive—the others, not so much, from what I can tell—and I'm walking around in it. Only it's for real, Janey." He stopped to stare at her placid face, looking for signs of doubt. At least she appeared willing, and was still listening. "I didn't want to tell you this, but I've been there lots of times, just briefly, in all kinds of unconnected scenes. But these last two times, it's been like a movie that I put on pause. Nothing changed when I went back the first time. And when I go back again, it'll still be in the same scene that I left it in. Not a dream. Curled up in its own reality, waiting for me to hit the play button again."

Janey's expression remained stoic. "Where'd she get that thing?"

"The Book? It's from the old country. One of the treasures."

"She never told me about it."

"Hey, you got your music box, I got the Book."

"The music box isn't a secret."

"Don't be mad. Maybe now you get why the Book was."

Janey cocked her head, and grinned. "So you think your diary is...magical?"

"No."

"That's what I'm hearing."

"Not magical. There's some science involved that I still can't explain. It's like the stars on the edge of the galaxy orbiting the galaxy at the same speed as the stars near the center."

"Huh?"

"All that empty space between them—but they're still connected somehow, like the galaxy is some kind of old spinning record."

"*Huh?*"

"And all the information black holes supposedly gobble up...only its not. It's spread out their surfaces. C'mon, Janey, you can't argue with the facts."

"How did all that crazy science get into the Book? They didn't know about that stuff back then."

"*Jeez*, Janey, you don't need to know science to do it."

"And maybe it's the magical pen, magical paper, and the magical ink. But see, you are starting to believe again in things you don't understand." Janey's smirk slowly dissolved, but her worried look returned.

"You think I'm crazy, don't you? You think I've lost my grip, gone bonkers, flipped *mi parrucca*."

"Your what?"

"Never mind."

Janey just sighed. "I've always prayed that you would be more believing and accepting of things you couldn't see…"

"Yeah? But?"

"But not like this."

"So you do think I'm crazy."

"I think that my illness is causing you a lot of problems."

"Now you sound like them."

"Who?"

"Everyone in the Other World thinks I'm crazy, too. Mom, the doc, Caterina…"

"Caterina?"

"Yes, Katie's there. I already told you that. Why so surprised?"

"Her name is Caterina?"

"Well…yeah."

"How did that happen?"

"Weren't you listening? It's all explained in here." He held up the Book once more.

"Sounds more like Heaven to me."

"Not Heaven, Janey. Another existence, separate from ours. Its own universe, connected to ours, where a live person can come and go."

Janey stayed skeptical.

"Look, I've been giving this a lot of thought," Chris said, "for a long time, now. That promise, right? So hear me out before you call the guys in the white coats."

Janey sat up. "Okay."

Chris cleared his throat again and looked into her eyes, which twinkled with great anticipation. "The only way I can convince you is to bring you there with me, so you can see for yourself."

Janey's eyes brightened with alarm. "You want me to go there…with you?"

"Of course. If I can do it, why can't you?"

"Well, I don't know…"

"It's beautiful there, Janey, more than you could possibly know. Mom's paintings just don't…and you get to be with her again. Once you go, you won't want to come back."

Janey's apprehensive look held fast. So Chris grabbed her hand and held it tight. "I'm not losing my mind, and I'm not trying to scare you. But think about what I just said—think really hard. Do you know what this means if we can do it, if we can really pull it off? You'll be with Mom and me. What do you think of that?"

The tip of her tongue came out, and her eyes darted about. "Well, I don't know…"

"You don't *know*? I promised you an escape plan, right?"

"I mean, yeah, it sounds wonderful, but—"

"I know, I know—more lunacy." He hesitated, wishing not to speak directly. "You're not listening to me, Janey. What does it mean if you go there with me? Think about it. You know the Rules—what and how you are in the Story."

"Well…I'm not sure."

"C'mon, Janey, you're not dressing for school." Chris could tell that she was trying to understand, but his overbearing approach was flustering her. So he drew in a deep breath to calm his tone, which gave her the precious moment she needed to comprehend this most important idea. "So?" he said finally.

"Well, I—"

"It means you won't have to worry about cancer anymore."

Janey looked stunned, real stunned. Then frightened again. Then intrigued. He understood all that.

"Yeah, that's right, little miss honor student, the light bulb finally comes on—no chemo, no cancer, no fear," Chris said. "It'll all be gone, because of who you will be. You can live a happy life again."

"But I'll be dead."

"No, you'll be alive. An angel that will become human again once the Child arrives. And we do want that, for you, Janey. We really do."

"We?"

Chris kept quiet, allowing her own word to do the work for him.

"I'll be an angel soon enough, if I stay here."

"With Victor? Without me and Mom?"

"You'd really leave me?"

Chris tried to be as blunt as he could: "We gotta get out of here, Janey."

Though Janey stared at him, she now seemed far away, as if she had been hypnotized. "And Victor?"

"He's gone, too."

"Because of the Great Tree," Janey said.

"And, oh, by the way," Chris said, "did I mention that Mom's there, safe and healthy, just like you'll be?" Chris smiled slyly, and gave her a moment to absorb that little idea again. "I know it's kinda sudden, but what do you think?"

Janey hesitated, her thoughts apparently dancing from acceptance to doubt and back again.

"Come on, Sister Mary Janey—ye of little faith. The skeptic comes out again just for me? How does that work?"

"I...I guess we can try."

"Yeah," Chris said. "We should. We can."

"But when?"

"Soon."

"Tonight, maybe?"

Chris expected her sudden eagerness to test things once she warmed to the idea, but he also had to start being honest about immediate problems she would face once she made the journey. "No, I'm sorry. You're just not going to show up in your jammies and slippers. I'm afraid it's a little more complicated than that. You're already there—you know, not as Janey. But you will be, in a way. Because of the way you're coming, you'll remember who you are here, just like I do. And you'll remember this world. But there are a few things I have to fix before I bring you there, because of where we are in the Story."

"The creepo with the beard, you mean."

Chris grabbed the open volume he had examined earlier and slid it before them. "Wotan," he said, pointing to Von Rosen's sketch.

"Are you gonna use the Magical Trees?"

Now Janey, starting to accept his story, was becoming more focused on their Story, and Chris wasn't sure that was such a good thing, not yet. "From what I can tell, they're already planted."

"All the way into the Terrible Shrieking Mountain?"

"That I don't know. I haven't been everywhere. And who said anything about a mountain?"

"You just did."

"I did not."

"Yes, you did. Besides, if Wotan's there, then the Mountain has to be. And if the Storm chased you, then we haven't made it to the Chamber of Darkness and Pandæmonium."

"I can't be sure that—"

Is it Christmas yet? Has midnight passed?"

"No."

Janey shook her head. "Those Trees have to be planted by then. We can't let Wotan or the Monster or that horrible lady get the Child. And we're gonna have to deal with Lucifer, too. Is He in the ice, or back in His palace?"

Janey made it sound like a game of tag. When Chris blinked, he saw Dore's Lucifer, King of Hell, from the vestibule's collection. Freaking giant Lucifer, the king of freaking Hell—feared by nearly anyone who had ever lived on this Earth. It couldn't get any worse than that. "Maybe."

"That means Pandæmonium."

"I know, Janey."

"Are you gonna be up for that?"

"Are you?"

Janey fell silent as her expression turned stone hard. He could tell that she was truly starting to believe, just a little, and that it was very easy—and silly—to talk boldly about seeing and fighting such terrible things while sitting in a comfy canopy bed with her stuffed minions, a world away from the great and real danger. She had no idea what it felt like to actually face these horrors. And they were real, which really bent his mind. Chris turned his attention to the Wotan illustration, regretting ever bringing it to light. Out of habit, he flipped the page—then snapped the book shut, his heart skipping a beat after catch a glimpse of Peter Nicolai Arbo's hellish masterpiece, which was part of the Wotan article he first saw just after Sandra told them her tale. Though Wotan and his traditional role was part of Sandra's story—and theirs—seeing that role expressed so clearly and imaginatively in color again was another horrid sight to behold, rivaling, as he once noted, the Martin engraving that he also feared. He did not want to remind himself further of either probability they may soon be experiencing.

"I never liked Wotan," Janey said. "He was icky."

"What's to like?" Chris tossed the closed volume onto the floor. "Kinda looks like John the Janitor, doesn't he?"

"Chris—"

"Well, you brought it up."

Janey pulled her knees to her chest and hugged her legs. "What else do we have to fix?"

Chris stared at her for a moment, not sure how to proceed. He knew he couldn't avoid this particular problem any longer. "I'm sorry, it's all my fault."

"What is?"

Chris cleared his throat. "Well, you know how I'm always joking about freezing out your kind from my world."

"Yeah?" she said uneasily.

"Well, you see, I...I kinda changed some things in our Story, and forgot to tell you."

Janey looked appalled.

"I said I was sorry."

"Chris, that was our Story. You promised me!"

"I know."

"Then why did you do it?"

"Well, like I told you, it's my diary."

"You said that wouldn't matter."

"I know, but…"

"But what?"

"C'mon, Janey, when we wrote it, I was just a dopey kid."

"Like me?"

"No."

"Yeah—be honest. Believe in God and you're a dope. That's really what you mean."

Chris fell silent, not sure how to babble his way out of this embarrassing corner.

"What did you change?" she said.

Chris sighed. "We might have a little problem getting you into the Village."

"What?"

"Well…you're the music box angel, right?"

"And?"

"You're not exactly…allowed in the Village anymore."

"And why not?"

"Well…the light from the Tree has kinda changed."

"What does that mean?"

Chris cleared his throat again. "It's not exactly a religious light anymore. More like the light of…of—"

"Of what? Science? *Logic*?"

"Something like that."

"You really wrote that?"

He cringed. "Now, now, remember what you told me about 'losing it.' "

She jammed her hands on her hips. "Chris, how could you?"

"Well, I just wanted to clarify things in my head. I still like the Story—and Christmas."

"Only it's not really Christmas anymore, is it? And the Child isn't coming anymore, is He?"

"That's not what the Old Ghost told me."

"Yeah, sure." Janey looked at him in disgust. "And Mom?"

"She's not exactly the Sorceress anymore—not while she's in the Village, anyway. But she still paints with light."

"But no magic."

Chris shrugged and grinned sheepishly. "There's magic in real life, if you just look closely."

"I can't believe you messed everything up—again!"

"Well how was I supposed to know it would matter?"

Janey folded her arms across her chest. "So if I'm not allowed in the Village, where am I?"

"I'm not really sure. I heard you calling to me once, so I know you're out there."

"Out there? You mean in the Kingdom of Darkness—with Victor the Monster who wants my Orb and the Lady with the dead kids who wants my soul and that Wotan guy with all the nasty creatures that just want to have me for lunch?"

"The Old Ghost wants the Orb."

"More changes?"

"Sorry, I don't know how that happened. At least you're still protected in the music box."

"How do you know that?"

"Well...I don't, actually. I just have a hunch."

Janey sighed, but as usual, began to look forgiving. "What about the alp?"

Now Fuseli's *The Nightmare* flickered in his mind. That image, too, came from the time he first researched Sandra's story. He had no need to or intention of revisiting it, now that its creatures had retreated with the Power into the Book. "What about it?"

"Is that thing out there with me, too?"

He recalled the white horse, but decided to keep things, like fear, subdued. "I haven't heard anyone talk about it."

"And you still expect me to go with you?"

"No, I told you—not yet. That's why I have to go back and fix some things. And I will."

"You can't do all that without me—what's the matter with you?" She thrust her hand out. "Let me see what else you changed."

But Chris clutched the Book to his chest and turned slightly to protect it against further advances. "That's all, I swear."

Janey withdrew her hand. "Then change it back."

"Change it back?" he said, as if she suggested the impossible.

"You heard me. You said you can make exceptions."

"That was before I hit the play button."

"So?"

"I'm in it now. It's just on pause. How do I tap into the Story and change things once it's started?"

"I don't know. Rewrite it, erase it, cross it out. You're the science guy."

"But I don't know the science, not all of it. This existence has its own Rules that built it, just like ours. What you want me to do...it'd be like God coming down out of the clouds and saying Victor never existed. Sounds

231

great, right? Problem solved. But what does that do to us? Poof! If I try to change things, I have to get everything just right. Every letter counts in this Book, and has its own power. If I screw up just one little thing, get one letter wrong, I might blow everything up, including the Way, and we'll never be able to go."

"He'd figure a way."

"Yeah, well, in case you haven't noticed, I'm not God."

They sat in a glum silence, and Chris could sense that she was retreating. He knew he had to keep her enthusiasm growing, but he was lost. The Book and its Rules were set in its Ways, just like him.

"Okay," Janey said, "how about this? Why not just rip the Story out?"

"Rip it out?"

"Yeah. You said the World is built on everything in the Book, not just the Story."

"So?"

"So if you take the Story out, but leave everything else in, won't that keep the Rules the same, where ever they are?"

Chris' mouth opened wide, then he scanned the room as if an audience had assembled, and was laughing at his stupidity. "Rip it out." He had to say it again so it would sink in. Her solution to such a seemingly complex problem was so simple, it was brilliant, just like the famous equation. Those two qualities were inexorably linked. But would it really work? All the people who were there that he wanted there, the Village setting, the new Rules—they were written about in separate entries as well and in the Story. But the horror was confined to the tale. Maybe the New World could stand on its own, without the Story. There was plenty of science remaining in the Power.

"And while you're at it, " Janey said, "get rid of all that Wotan junk in the front."

"All of it?" Her previous suggestion still stunned him.

"Why not?"

"Yeah, why not?" He knew that routine. Chris opened the Book and began turning the pages with frantic slaps of his right hand, watching the dates pull him back in time, searching for the extensive entry penned years ago when he was willing to believe. When he glanced up and saw that Janey was leaning forward, hoping to catch a glimpse of the sacred entries, he spun around so his legs dangled from the bed and his back partially blocked her view. "Rip it out," he said for his own benefit, nodding his head repeatedly with satisfaction as he resumed his frantic search.

"Why did she tell us that horrible story, anyway?"

"I'm sure she was trying to scare us so we'd be good—me more than you," Chris said, focused on the turning pages. "You know, 'you'd better watch out, you'd better not cry.' Only it was the German version, like her chili. I'll bet her mom told her the same story, as her mom did, and her mom... You know how parents think they need to do stuff like that. Look, as you enjoy telling me so often, little girl, she didn't mean any harm. I always thought her story was kinda cool."

"You would," Janey said. "Cool rhymes with fool, Chris. Things could have been a lot simpler if she hadn't tried so hard."

Chris found the lengthy entry and examined each page destined for expulsion, just to be certain that he didn't remove something vital to the New World's beauty or safety. When he was convinced he had all the evil pages grouped together, he gripped them tightly. "Ready?" he said to Janey.

"Rip away!"

But then Chris froze as more disturbing questions began pouring in. So ripping Wotan from the Book would eliminate the menacing Old Ghost from the New World. But what were the consequences of such a drastic move? Would Chris return to find the danger gone while everything else remained intact? Would Caterina be waiting for him at the Manor with open arms? Would Lorenzo be there, unharmed? Or would Chris plow into another story altogether, without the circumstances that he hoped would continue, or be rectified? And then there was Janey's counterpart. Would she now be alive and part of the welcoming committee congregating at the Manor? Would Janey, upon her arrival, find herself in the happy and healthy state Chris promised? Or would she appear in a completely strange and altered state, attached to another or even more horrible fate? What other unforeseen problems—or tragedies—would this desperate attempt cause? Would it even work? Maybe he was hitting the reset button. Maybe he would indeed destroy that New World altogether—or at the very least, break the inexplicable link with the old. That thought terrified him most of all.

Chris looked at Janey again. She sensed the dilemmas that were paralyzing him—he saw that.

"Here's the deal," Janey said. "I'm not going with you if you don't do it."

With his heart racing, Chris suddenly tore the pages from the Book. He looked at them in amazement, as if the dramatic act had been involuntary—as if he had ripped his own heart out. But then he quickly regrouped and held the pages up like a trophy, realizing that he could not show any trace of fear lest he destroy what little confidence or belief Janey had in his plan. "No more Wotan," he said earnestly. But he decided at that moment not to dispose of the torn entry, just in case he needed to put it back somehow.

Janey grinned. "No more alp—and no more scary horses!"

Then the smile drained from Chris' face as he gazed at Janey. But he said nothing. He still had to remove the rewritten version, and any ancient pages referring to the Legends.

"You're going back tonight, aren't you?" she said.

"I don't know," he said, upset that she was so intuitive, and that he was so transparent. "I mean, I have to find out if this worked before you get there, right? Because if it has, I am coming back to get you. And then you will go there with me. Think about that, Janey—think about that. I'll say it again if it hasn't sunk in—no more cancer!"

Suddenly—strangely—all the joy left Janey's face.

Chris frowned. "I'm not scaring you again, am I? You believe in me, don't you?" Of all the damn ironies. He was beginning to hate that word, too. Maybe add it to the List. And just like his mom, he needed to hear it even if it weren't true, so he would think it was, so he could rest.

Janey stared at him with a deep concern. "What if your plan doesn't work?"

Chapter Twenty-nine

Waiting

That night, Chris lay in bed and anxiously waited for the stroke of midnight, which was nearly upon him. Having removed all the Book's "evil" pages, he had come to realize that confirmation of his fears could arrive quickly in a variety of ways, well before he attempted the return to the New World. The usual parade of phantoms—and associated drama—could reappear, signaling total failure of his drastic and impetuous action. The angels and demons could return, but not the Old Ghost, signaling a partial success. Or, of course, nothing would happen, meaning that the portal had been destroyed, and he would have to explain to Janey why he could not make good on the fantastic and life-transforming promise he had made earlier in the day. That was a troubling thought. In his haste to remove all the evil, it did not occur to him till now that it was evil that had originally opened the Way.

Other New World mysteries dogged him. He did not understand how he could have been part of the overwhelming force that had destroyed the church. And while he was on that subject, what strange new power did the Purple Orb hold that made it so desirable to those who knew of its existence? Where was it? With Giovanna, as it was supposed to be? And what did the Old Ghost mean when he said: "A child is coming"? Did he already know of his plans for Janey? Or was the child *the Child*? It had been fun to write about, when it was just a fanciful Christmas story. But now that it wasn't, was He really? Really? Just like in their Story, in the story? The (former) Son of God, parading with the Blessed Virgin and Joseph into the Village of science, truth, and logic on the back of a donkey, with that Star shining directly overhead. An amazing sight to behold, no doubt. But He was already dead, right? Dead here, dead there. He wondered what would really happen.

That thought steered him to the most important mystery of all: where was Giovanna? Had she become the entity of their Story, as the Old Ghost had alluded to? Had she tried to call out to him for help, as she was supposed to do, as he suspected? Where exactly was the music box in which she slept? Was she now imprisoned within it? Though the Old Ghost apparently didn't know, Chris harbored an overwhelming feeling that Giovanna, like Janey, was in peril.

None of these concerns mattered, of course, if his drastic measures with his diary proved to be effective. But what if things in the New World hadn't changed? He had to make contact with Giovanna, to determine the exact nature of her existence and make the necessary corrections before he would subject Janey to her new fate. He had to, or it wouldn't be Heaven—not according to her definition. To accomplish this sacred task, he had to return to the church ruins and seek out the Black Rider—the one apparent link to the chimes, whose role it was to warn of the coming Storm.

If Chris still could.

Midnight came and went quietly, without a hint of supernatural drama. Hours slipped past without miraculously reversing themselves or speeding up, even as he drifted in and out of new dreams. When dawn came, he found himself following more mundane routines like showering, dressing for school, and sitting at the dining table with Janey and Victor as they ate their breakfast in silence. At one moment, Janey looked at him with eagerness for news of his latest trip to the New World. But all he could do was slowly shake his head. He could sense her disappointment, but he also sensed that she hadn't given up, knowing the difficulty of his task.

Once at school and sucked into the whirlpool of lectures, note-taking, and fuzzy interactions with teachers and classmates, Chris realized just how far away the New World seemed—and almost nonexistent, as if it were a dream. But the wreaths and garland and colored ornaments in the halls and classrooms acted as powerful and constant reminders of his travels.

For his own selfish reasons, Chris sought out Larry in the cafeteria, and felt a soul-saving relief to see him standing, as usual, alone at one of the large windows, eating his sack lunch, which he had placed on the large marble sill. Fitzgerald and his Horde were in the cafeteria as well, sitting around their favorite table closest to the stainless steel food counter where everyone had to pass by. By now, having long since been dispatched to anonymity, Chris had become a nonentity to them as they conspired to defeat others who dared challenge their authority in the current sports arena, which was now basketball. Only when Chris made eye contact with Fitz or the others did they acknowledge his existence—that often coming as a sneer or snicker, reminding him of their great victory over him. If they only knew of the battle he was now engaged with them.

In gym class, Woz was his usual stoic self, but they hardly ever conversed, only at roll call. Coach Joe had ended his playful banter with Chris, no longer speaking his mangled Italian. Occasionally, he saw the coach staring at him from across the gym floor, slowly shaking his head. But it didn't bother him—none of it did. He had but one mission on his mind: saving Janey.

※

Another night came and went, then another. Still no sign of the phantoms needed to usher him into the New World. Chris was beginning to panic, especially since Friday—and the second round of Janey's chemo—was upon them. But later, as she sat in the reclining chair with that grunting machine attached to her, they still talked of their great escape as if it were going to happen, and he saw in her eyes that she still believed, which comforted him. But he was now becoming increasingly convinced that by ripping the pages from his diary, he had destroyed the link between the two worlds. After Dr. Samuel took a sample of Chris' blood, he gave them a ride home. Chris took the opportunity to give the doctor the requested written (but watered-down) account of Victor's attack with the roller chain, and kept all the damning details hidden in his diary. But the trip was alarmingly silent—no canned speeches filled with optimism. And there was much worry in Dr. Samuel's eyes. Chris knew from Sandra's bloody ordeal that the results of Janey's first chemo session were already in. That the doctor never discussed them with him told Chris that the chemo wasn't working. And he revived the possibility of a bone marrow transplant from either Chris or Victor, dependent on a "match." After arriving at the house, Chris put his exhausted sister to bed, then went to his bedroom where he withdrew the diary along with all the removed pages, which he then returned loosely to their proper place. It wasn't exact science—no science involved at all. But at least it was worth the chance. Returning to the New World to its former troubling state was better than no return at all. He closed the Book and stuffed it beneath his mattress, then stared out the window at the doctor's home. He missed seeing Caterina—at least she had been accessible, and there for him. Katie had not been by since she took Janey's wish list. (He was often tempted to ask the doctor directly about her, but he knew Dr. Samuel would see right through his inquiry, which would cause him great pain and embarrassment. He would have none of that. So he decided to keep his secret a secret.) Chris had hoped that since Janey was going through so much agony, Katie would have become more of a supporting fixture in their lives. That she wasn't only disturbed him. That a young beauty would want to enjoy the best years of her life with young men instead of immersing herself in the gloom that permeated this household was yet another stark reminder of the cruel reality of this world. He remained hopeful that he would see her sometime before Christmas, as she had promised. But she had yet to deliver Janey's gift.

※

The next morning, Chris woke to the striking reality that, once again, midnight had come and gone uneventfully. He remembered falling asleep well before that hour, only to be awakened shortly after by the sound of Victor's noisy return from bowling. What made that normally routine event more memorable was the sound of a woman's voice—and her high heels accompanying his heavy footsteps as they across the foyer floor. It wasn't the first time after Sandra's death that Victor had brought one of his unwitting companions back to his lair. But those home-based rendezvous were uncommon. Chris suspected that Victor feared Janey's wrath, which if true was a wise assumption on his father's part. Janey had never stated to either of them what she would do if Victor ever brought another woman to the house. But it wasn't difficult to guess how she would respond. Since Victor had attempted the dalliance this night, with Janey struggling with her treatment, the callous act showed how optimistic Victor felt about those rules changing. Still, Chris recalled that, after only an hour or so of opera, giggling, and then silence, Victor and the woman had departed. Apparently, Victor didn't dare parade her past Janey's door. But the cigarette smoke and sickening perfume lingered long after they had driven off.

Chris got up from his bed and stood in Janey's doorway. She was already awake and hunched over on the edge of her mattress, legs dangling to the floor and feet in fuzzy pink slippers amid the ever-growing carnage of fallen guardians. When she realized that Chris was looking at her, she sat up and smiled. But she was ashen, and her smile quickly fell away.

Another dreadful image of his mother flashed in his brain. "Janey?"

Janey bolted from the bed and ran into the bathroom where she threw up in the toilet. Chris followed her inside and stood behind her, holding her damp hair from her face as she vomited a few times more. When he withdrew his hand, a clump of her long hair came with it. He tried to hide it behind his back, but she had already turned her white face to see the deception. She ran her left hand through her hair, then held out another clump. She looked at him and tried to be brave. But her eyes grew round and flooded with fear, and she broke down as the grandfather clock sounded the nine a.m. hour.

"Take me with you," she whimpered. "Please hurry."

And then he hugged her.

Chapter Thirty

The Letters

"Chris—get in here!" Victor shouted from the dining room.

It was the weekend before Christmas. Two long and agonizing weeks had passed since Chris had been to the New World. During that time, he had done his best to find a way back, resorting to all kinds of strange rituals from his past—including prayer. But his hopes had long since diminished. Janey had endured two more rounds of chemotherapy. All of her hair had fallen out. She no longer went to school, was woefully and perpetually tired, and inevitably, after some pitiful attempts to resume her cherished duties as housecleaner, she spent more and more time resting—well on her way to becoming bedridden. As they had done with Sandra, they silently kept track of the "good days" and the "bad days," hoping to slow down time. The bad were piling up.

Despite Janey's increasingly alarming and precipitously dropping blood counts, Dr. Samuel began the prerequisite campaign of optimistic speeches regarding her chances. But the term "refractory" finally made its dreaded appearance. And there was more talk about treatment options, the new miracle cures, including a stem cell transplant. They would need to find a suitable donor. Already aware that a sibling was the best hope, Chris immediately volunteered. Victor knew he was obligated to listen to it all. But he never responded, even when Dr. Samuel pressed him repeatedly, reminding him of moral and parental duty, and special funding. And then the doctor did something that Chris cheered inside: he gave Victor a deadline—coincidentally, January 6. Still, they had been down this path before. Janey's uncharacteristic sullenness told them all they needed about her state of mind and hopes for the future. No more Janeyisms, no more hard thinking, no more deep-throated laughs. He knew what she was really thinking. Chris no longer talked with her about the plan for her salvation. He could barely make eye contact with her. Not only did the plan seem like just a dream, it sounded crazy. (He questioned his sanity increasingly each day.) Even worse, he was supremely mortified and ridden with guilt for ever suggesting such a foolish thing. All he had done was give her a false and final hope, only to have reality smash it utterly. Now all they could do was wait for the end, which, as experience told him, could be mere months, even weeks away, depending on her ability to withstand the chemo, hold down food, fight infections, and get Victor to cooperate. So far, Janey managed. But she was noticeably gaunt, which frightened him, and her.

So as Chris left the living room where he had just placed the wrapped gifts beneath the tree, he did not feel much alarm over Victor's angry tone. Nothing his father would do or say this cold but sunny afternoon could be worse than the mind-numbing depression Chris now carried. Still, it was odd to see Victor in such an agitated state without having ingested the necessary fuel for the fire.

When Chris entered the dining room, he saw Victor sitting at the end of the table, the stack of mail before him, and a letter in his right hand. Victor was flushed, his jaw set, his eyes glaring. He looked like he was ready to pounce. Chris stopped at the opposite end, but did not take a seat.

"Do you know anything about this?" Victor said as he held the letter out.

"About what?"

Victor pulled the letter close as he put on his reading glasses. "This is from the Department of Social Services."

Chris was stunned, but in a good way, like hearing deep, rich, upbeat music from teeny-tiny speakers. "Yeah?"

"Yeah? Well, it's a little different tone this time. And it's not just about you. Now they're including Janey. You want to hear it?"

Chris remained silent, but he had an idea what was coming—something about making good on a solemn promise to become directly involved.

"Dear Mr. Russo," Victor said. "Dear—can you imagine? Like they're asking me out on a damn date. This is an official notice regarding the concerns in the attached report and subsequent investigation used in our Family Assessment on the above referenced children. Regarding whether your family could benefit—*benefit!*—from our agency's services, we have determined that—can we have a frickin' drumroll, please—your family is in need of those services, and that the County Department of Social Services will provide those services to address concerns we will discuss during the upcoming Family Assessment. Another freaking dyke social worker will meet with you and your family within five days—just in time for Christmas!—to plan actions that will address those concerns. We appreciate your cooperation throughout the Family Assessment process. If the County Department of Social Services decides not to provide services and you determine later that you need assistance, please do not hesitate to contact our office. Oh, yeah, I'll get right on that, you miserable whore. We will be happy to discuss with you the available services you may need.

"Please note—aren't they polite?—that the information you provide during the Family Assessment is considered by law to be private. You are not required to answer any questions asked. But we cannot help you—*help me!*—or investigate the matter if you do not provide information. Please also note that his information may be shared with other members in the statewide welfare system. All information will be used to offer the service you request—*request?*—or to investigate the situation as reported. Oh, yeah, I'll admit to all the bullshit you throw at me.

"If you have any questions, please contact me. Sincerely—your Fat Freaking Lesbian Valentine—Child Protective Services." He slammed the paper down on the table. "What kind of a control freak would write something like this—and who in Hell do these people think they are?"

"I don't know," Chris said.

"Oh, the Hell you don't know," Victor said as he flipped the first page over to the second. "At least this time it isn't some anonymous coward making a false frickin' complaint. The guy finally got the balls to put his name on this piece of shit report. But the real kicker is that he let them send a copy to me. You get it? He wants me to know it was him. They're supposed to keep this part confidential—unless he gives his consent." Victor chuckled. "Never knew he had it in him. It could be a mistake. You know how incompetent these government leeches can be. But I'm willing to bet the son of a bitch did it on purpose. It's starting to fit the new pattern. He's getting aggressive. I like it. But that's my territory, not his. Wanna make a guess who's behind this, just for the record?"

"No."

Victor stared at the letter. "Then I'll say it: it's your buddy, Dr. Samuel. Yeah, and get this. It isn't about me screaming and yelling and letting off a little steam. Oh, no, he's going for the gold this time—and I do mean gold. Ready for this one? Dear Doctor Scam, thank you for your report of suspected child abuse regarding the above-named family. These allegations meet the statutory definitions of neglect and, therefore, this case has been approved for a Family Assessment. If your allegations are proven and meet the definition of abuse according to state statutes, then we will conduct an Investigative Assessment, and Law Enforcement will be notified for possible Criminal Prosecution of the accused to be settled in a Court of Law." Victor paused as his jaw clenched, and Chris watched his father's jaw muscles flex independently of each other, the vein in his neck bulging, looking more like a tube. "Did you hear that? Criminal prosecution...in a Court of Law, with goddamn lawyers. Bad enough the son of a bitch tried to take my wife. Now he's after my kids."

"What are you talking about?" Chris said.

"Don't bother," Victor said. "I've always known. That beanpole always had the hots for your mother. I caught him more than once sniffing around here. Too bad he couldn't save her, huh? Yeah, that's what he gets for living in that big ol' lonely house, and working is ass off. Well, his plan isn't going to work. I already fired his ass—"

"You can't do that!"

"Like Hell I can't!"

"They'll throw you in jail."

"For what?"

"You're going to kill her!"

"*I'm* going to kill her? Haven't you seen her lately, dipshit? She's already starting to look like a corpse."

"Let me give her my stem cells."

"I can't afford it. And you don't even know if you're a match."

"You're not paying for it."

"It's my decision, not yours."

"He can make you do it. He will make you do it!"

"He's bluffing. He can't pin anything on me. It's experimental—too iffy. It's my call. End of story."

In a rare moment when he disregarded his own safety, Chris skirted the table and, with fists clenched, streaked toward Victor. His father was disrespecting Janey in the biggest way—and openly threatening her—and Chris would have none of it. But Victor was already on the offensive, glasses thrown aside, and they met halfway. Chris tried to strike Victor's angry face, but Victor caught Chris' right forearm in a vice-like grip, nearly crunching the bone. Then he slammed Chris against the painting on the wall as his head exploded with stars. His father's immense strength always astonished Chris, even though he had felt it many times before.

"I keep telling you—and him," Victor said in a low, reeking growl as he pressed his face close to Chris, "this is my house, my family. I'm not gonna give her up just before she dies. Not now. Not now. So if you see your beanpole doctor ever again—and I seriously doubt you will—you remind him to stay away. Or this criminal investigation is going to include him—*capisca*?"

Chris was too dizzy and out of breath to answer him.

"I said, 'Do you understand?' "

"Yes," he said with a strained voice.

"One more thing. And I want you to listen to this very carefully. If you think for a moment that I'm going to let you open your mouth about how big, bad Victor is abusing you, you're fooling yourself."

He dragged Chris to the kitchen entrance and, with his free hand, lifted the receiver from the wall phone. Then he put the earpiece to Chris' ear.

"Hear anything? Huh?"

Victor slammed the dead receiver onto the hook. Then, with both hands gripping Chris' shirt just beneath the collar, he jammed Chris against the wall once more. He could feel his stomach churning as his mouth grew dry, and his heart was thumping furiously, stealing his breath. Worst of all, he saw the raging blood vessels in the bright whites of Victor's hooded eyes.

"Tomorrow morning, you and I are going to sit down and map out a strategy for this...this goddamn Family Assessment so we can get these people off my ass once and for all. I'm warning you, Chris, you'd better play ball. Or there's gonna be Hell to pay. They've backed me into a corner, and I only have one way out. I'll rip right through the two of you—and him—if I have to. Now go to your room and stay there. And don't even think of running to him. I gotta figure out what to do." His eyes rose to the painting, and his rage intensified. "And take this goddamn thing with you before I put my fist through it. I'm sick to death of looking at it."

Victor tossed him aside like an empty fast-food cup. Chris brought a hand to his raw neck as he tried to catch his breath. Seeing that Victor was still glaring at him, Chris turned and removed the painting from the wall, then ran as fast as he could all the way to the second-floor bathroom where he slammed the door before setting the painting against it. He held his feverish head over the toilet and felt that sickening knot in his stomach tightening ever more as his ears began to ring and his mouth salivate, but nothing happened. When the knot loosened and the sweat cooled, Chris closed the lid and sat on it. Now doubled up, he felt the welt on his scalp. The nausea was subsiding, but his head still throbbed, and in the midst of all the anger, fear, and frustration, he wondered what he was going to do. He had been wrong to keep Victor's dangerous outbursts a secret. That was painfully obvious. He had to get them out of here. But how? Victor made it clear what Chris had feared all along. But calling anyone was now impossible. The only way he could contact Dr. Samuel is if he ran to his house. But Victor would be watching. Always watching with those all-seeing eyes. Even if Chris were successful, he would put Janey's safety in doubt. That thought, as always, he could not tolerate, and once again kept him from taking immediate action. For now, he would have to do it Victor's way and "play ball," wait and listen for his father to lower his guard, and fall into old habits. Eventually—tonight, no doubt—that time would come. Then the long-overdue rebellion could finally commence. A son should never have cause to feel this way about his own father, but he most certainly did. *He should have never let me go.* He grit his teeth in defiance.

Rising to his feet, Chris grabbed a wash cloth, soaked it in cold water, then snapped up the painting before entering his bedroom, closing the door, and chaining it. Leaning the painting against the wall, Chris sat on his bed and wrapped the cool cloth around his head. Then he lay on his side, head on the pillow, and stared at the painting while biding his time, listening for sounds of Victor while his temples throbbed like a drum. The rage cycled down, diffusing into utter exhaustion, then apathy, and his mind began to clear of all troubled thought. Soon he was lying on his back, drifting in and out of sleep, until the transition was complete.

PART FIVE

The Quest

Chapter Thirty-One

The Escape

When Chris woke, the grandfather clock was bonging wildly, and the demon flames leaped all around him. But this time, Chris remained calm. And then he did something he found even stranger: he smiled. Never had he been so happy to see such terror. The Old Ghost was there, too, in his usual and now comforting position by the door. Chris had to resist the urge to wave to him. Chris reached up and grasped with joy the tiny outstretched hand of a cupid, which helped him from the bed. Now he stood with tremendous relief, facing the glowing Temptress. "I've been waiting a very long time," he said. Despite knowing, without a doubt, what her role was, Chris was delighted to feel the warm reassurance from his own words he once feared he would never speak. But he did not expect any reaction from the shining specter. "Can we go?"

She turned and left the room. Chris followed her into the hall. And as he approached Janey's room, its door wide open, there was no hesitation in his thinking. The time for clever calculation and surgical manipulation had long since passed. Fate be damned, she was coming with him.

Chris approached her bed. With her wool cap atop her bald head, Janey slept in her usual position: on her side with her back to him. He reached out and gently shook her arm. "Janey? Janey, wake up. It's time to go."

Janey rolled onto her back. "What?"

"Time to go, Janey. The ghost lady is here."

Janey did not smile, though Chris sensed that she wanted to. She was still half-asleep, and he doubted she had enough strength this critical moment to get out of bed. But she also looked willing to give his promise one last try.

Using his foot, Chris shoved the pile of fallen stuffed animals under her bed. Then he helped Janey to her feet and into her slippers. "Can you walk?" he said.

Janey nodded, but as he let go, she began to wobble. He grabbed her by the arm to steady her, and she looked up and smiled.

"I'll be okay," she said. Those words seemed to strengthen her.

"I know," Chris said. "Think of me as your bodyguard."

Janey nodded as she swallowed hard.

"Ready?" Chris said.

She nodded again, and did her best to show some determination.

Slowly, step by step, Chris walked her into the darkened hall. He looked to the stairway and saw the vision waiting for them on the landing. "Do you see her?" Chris said enthusiastically to his sister.

Janey looked at him in confusion with sunken eyes.

"She's by the stairs—look!"

Janey turned her head mechanically to gaze down the hall. But that gaze remained empty.

"C'mon," he said. He led her arm-in-arm onward.

They took each step one at a time. When they reached the living room, the specter had already departed. But the tree was glowing like the Sun. Salvation was at hand.

"Promise me you'll be brave," Chris said as they drew ever closer to the tree. "I haven't had the chance to fix the things I wanted to, but at least you'll be there, in her World. You won't see me when you come out of the glow. You'll probably be in a dark place all by yourself—that's my best guess. But don't worry, you'll still be in safe hands. He won't harm you. If you get the chance to escape, if you see an opening, take it. Then look for the Great Tree. When you see it, go to it, run to it—fly to it! Do whatever you can. I'll meet you just outside the Village—at the goose pond by the Village Bridge. And if you can't get there, if the light from the Tree won't let you in, then just keep yourself safe in the box. But always remember this: I'll be coming for you."

Janey nodded, but she looked dazed, as if she didn't care what trouble this role of the dice would bring.

Chris patted her on the hand, hoping to instill some comfort in her. Then he looked at the tree, took a deep breath, and clutched his sister's arm tightly as they stepped into the blinding light.

When the ringing and hammering in his ears dissipated, Chris, back in the manger, felt a powerful hand grabbing him by the back of his collar. It pulled him violently from the radiance, and he fell on his back in the field of poinsettias.

"You've got to stop doing this—I mean it," Matteo said as he towered over Chris. "You're gonna burn your eyeballs out."

Chris reached up to shade his eyes. Matteo snatched Chris' hand and pulled him to his feet. Then he dragged him farther from the Tree until the intensity of the light had faded.

"All right, already," Chris said. He freed himself from Matteo's grip. The pullover white shirt with rounded collar, the light-brown breeches, and the high brown boots Matteo wore gave him a sudden and dramatic look of power and authority. For a moment, Chris—back in suspended trousers, plaid jacket, and grimy linen shirt—felt as if he were some common thief seized by the local constable. Chris looked around at the empty manger scene, the blue and purple forests, the stone-arch bridge, and the Village, not sure what to expect next. But he felt Janey's presence, and that brought on an exceptional relief. He could only hope she had taken his advice to heart, where ever she was. "Where's Lorenzo?" Chris said. "Is he at the ruins? Did the Storm get him?"

"That's what you just told us!" Matteo roared.

Chris felt a satisfying grin spreading on his face, but it was short-lived. The New World seemed to be intact just as he left it. For that, he was grateful. But if that were true, nothing had changed, including the mysteries surrounding Lorenzo's and Giovanna's fates. What was his sister now experiencing? "We have to go back there. I have to find the Black Rider."

"Oh, no," Matteo said, seizing Chris once again before he could walk away. "You're not going anywhere. You and I have an agreement."

Chris slapped Matteo's arm away with an intensity he had never displayed. Then he pointed an angry finger at his friend, who raised his hands as if Chris held a weapon. "Now you listen to me. Everything has changed—everything! My sister is here. There's a good chance she's in danger—and I put her there. I'm not going to waste my time in some stupid therapy session with someone who doesn't have a clue about what's going on."

"Alessandra does," Matteo said.

The comment temporarily disarmed him. "What do you mean?"

"Before you ran off like a lunatic, she told us something interesting. Don't you remember?"

"Yeah?"

Matteo looked at him with a hint of smugness, another I-know-something-you-don't moment. "She says she has a story to tell."

Chris' silence seemed to pique Matteo's curiosity.

"Yeah, a story," Matteo said, lowering his arms. "Another spark of recollection, me boy? She didn't tell us any details, but we got the feeling that she wanted to confess something and that we needed to hear it—kinda like what you're feeling right now."

Chris fought back his own curiosity and silenced all his questions. He felt the heat rising. "I—don't—have—time," he said. He quickly removed his jacket and clutched it with anger in his arm.

Matteo's mood appeared to turn black. "I told you not to go there. You told me not to go there. But you did anyway. And now Lorenzo's missing."

Chris was stunned to hear Matteo play the guilt card. "You don't know what's going on out there, either."

"No I don't. And who's to blame? You've been keeping way too many secrets from me, Cristofori. Time to make your own confession."

"I don't remember what I did or didn't tell you."

"I don't want to hear that anymore!"

"Besides," Chris said, feeling humbled, "even if I did tell you the truth, you wouldn't have believed me. You're one of them."

Matteo laughed. "Oh, now I'm the enemy? I thought you were one of us?"

"It's a different world, with different rules."

"I know. I've seen what the red orbs hold."

Chris nodded, though he wasn't sure what Matteo meant. "So now you know why I have to go back to the ruins."

Matteo snatched Chris by the arm before he could break away. "Who's the Black Rider, Cristofori?"

"He may have the music box."

"What is Tomas—and this infamous Storm?"

Chris saw in Matteo's wild eyes that his friend was beginning to understand. "Come with me and find out."

Keeping his firm grip on Chris' arm, Matteo led him through the poinsettia field to the stream. Chris' thoughts immediately turned to Janey, as he felt relieved that they were about to start their search. But instead of following the stream to the Village, Matteo dragged Chris in the opposite direction.

"Where are we going?" Chris said.

"Where do you think?"

Chris stopped suddenly and yanked his arm free. "I'm not interested in staring at paintings of dead people."

But Matteo looked on sternly and with determination. "I used the red orbs you plucked last night. You'll see the results when we get to the Mill. You're gonna give me a little tour of your world—in pictures—and explain to me what roles that cast of delightful characters play in that world. And then we're gonna go back to the Manor and listen to every word of your mother's story before you try to get us all killed with your wild expeditions into *L'entroterra*. She's an emotional wreck, Cristofori. And all this running around is making her crazier. We're not girls. We have to be methodical, not emotional. And you need to give control to those of us with a solid memory of this place—and patiently follow our lead."

"But my sister—"

Matteo slapped Chris' face—hard. The sting spread like a fire. "You're not listening!"

Wide-eyed, Chris became paralyzed. Never had his friend struck him, not even during their heated argument about the plot to steal the church paintings. Chris didn't know how to respond, and old habits kept him at bay.

"From now on," Matteo said, "I'm running this investigation, until you can prove that you're well. I got a lot of time and money invested in this venture, and I'm not going to let you mess it up. Understand?"

Chris nodded repeatedly, understanding the wisdom, and the anger, in that request while appreciating his honesty. For a moment, he felt as if they were back at St. Boniface.

This time, Matteo tapped Chris' face lightly. "Good man. I didn't hurt ya, did I?"

Chris shook his head, though he could still feel the sting.

"Come on," Matteo said, "we gotta hurry. They're waiting for us at the Manor. And I don't want to get the doc more involved than he already is."

Chris followed his lead as they headed along the stream toward the Old Mill. But not before he made one final glance toward the Village Bridge.

Chapter Thirty-Two

The Old Mill

"What do you know about my father?" Chris said, jacket slung over his shoulder.

Moving in and out of the wedge-shaped shafts of light that penetrated the lofty blue canopy of leaves, Chris and Matteo walked along the narrow dirt path that cut through a blanket of lush wet ferns and followed the rushing stream as it meandered through the old-growth forest of giant elms east of the Village. The pure warmth from the Sun combined at shoulder height with the cool fustiness drifting up from the forest floor. The towering mushroom-shaped trees and their massive trunks distorted with moss created a cathedral-like ambience, making him feel small and powerless, and the uniquely-colored leaves reinforced the strangeness of this land and his predicament. Chris was puzzled as to why the humbling scene had turned his thoughts to the mysterious Vittorio, who had yet to be confronted. Maybe it was all the talk of portraits and relatives and what secrets Alessandra would reveal in the tale she anxiously waited to tell, or his anxiety over Janey's arrival, and what she may be encountering this very moment. He did not regret his hasty decision to thrust her into this wild World of his own making. Given the dire situations back home with her failing health and the cornered Victor, Chris was convinced that he had made the right move. But not having any control of her here only brought on a new anxiety. That Matteo had asserted his dominance over him was not a surprise. The old feeling relieved him in a way, but also bothered him. Chris did not like the way he so easily acquiesced, and followed, despite the logic and necessity to do so.

"I never met the guy," Matteo said finally. "How could I have? All I know is what you told me, and I've always taken that with a shot of skepticism. So if you want me to repeat your own words...he was a performer, a singer. Went around to all the villages, looking for work. Except here, of course. Sang in taverns, church choirs, at festivals—wherever. From what I could tell, he was kind of a jovial guy. Liked to joke a lot. But you always seemed uncomfortable talking about him. We all kinda figured out what was going on. Nothing new. Tough world you lived in. Hard to scratch out a living, you know? Strange, too, around this time of year."

"So what happened to him?"

Matteo shrugged. "Came under a 'spell'—your word, by the way. I took that in a lot of ways. But considering that he was gone a lot and what he did for a living... You know how those entertainers are. Where he ended up, I don't know. You need to talk with Alessandra about this stuff. I've only known you a little while."

"When did we meet?"

"After you came to the Village. Right after your sister died."

"In the Storm."

"Yeah, sure—that was part of the Story, too."

"You make it sound like a lie."

"To be honest, I don't know what to think half the time," Matteo said. "I've always felt that you haven't been totally straight with me about your family and what went on before you came here. And you know how much I hate when people lie to me. Caterina certainly doesn't help."

"Caterina?"

"Well, yeah. She came with you and Alessandra. Actually, you and your mom came with her, in her wagon—the one we appropriated last night." He still seemed proud of that act.

"That was Caterina's?"

"Yeah. Had all of your mom's paintings with you, too."

"Why was Caterina with us?"

Matteo grinned. "She was your mother's attendant, me boy. She helped with the chores when your father was gone. You never told me much about that, either. But I figured it out."

"She was our attendant?"

"That's what you told me. Are you gonna change your story again?"

This New World development of an old world relationship intrigued Chris. That wasn't part of the Story. "Why would she leave the Village just to work for us? Anything to do with the art?"

"Well, yeah, but you're not getting what I'm saying. Caterina is from *L'entroterra*."

"*L'entroterra*? Caterina?"

"That's what she told me. Should I be a little leery of her, too?"

Chris saw that they were approaching a bend at the edge of the old-growth forest that led to a clearing ablaze with yellow sunshine. He could hear a loud hissing of water, as if from a stretch of shallow rapids. He slid his jacket from his shoulder and clutched it under high right arm.

"Tell you what," Matteo said. "There seems to be some kind of recollection thing going on in that messed up brain of yours. I'll give you her side of the story and you let me know if your memory comes back. She was your attendant, that we've established. She also claims she taught your mom how to paint. That was part of the deal they worked out. Her parents died in the Storm, too, so she had no place to go. And since you lost your home, she came with you to the Village. How you all got in..." He shrugged. "She never could explain that part. But I never really thought she could, or would."

Chris continued to nod, making the connections, as Matteo watched him carefully while speaking.

"She was pretty messed up too, you know? Bad experience. Had a hard time adjusting. So did you, by the way. I remember seeing you at school for the first time. Suddenly, you were there, like you had fallen out of the sky. You were kinda quiet, seemed a little angry at the world. But then we heard the story about your house and your sister, so it all made sense. You eventually came out of your shell. Didn't take crap from anyone, especially the teachers. I liked that. And, hey, you were famous—the *contadino* who defied the laws and got in."

"Yeah," Chris said, recalling those days.

"Yeah," Matteo said. "But, anyway, things just worked themselves out. Alessandra brought Caterina to see the doc, and they decided it was best for her to stay with him—you know, as a foster child—not only because of her mental state, but because of you."

"Me?"

"Think about it for a second, Cristofori. It was the right decision, the only decision—especially for you. After all, how could you be chasing after your own sister, if you know what I mean. That was another reason you were so popular. You had her, the older woman. Impressive. I mean, really, it's hard enough to get the ones our age interested in us, with all the riches and worldly experience we have to offer." Matteo laughed. "I tried my best to wrestle her away, but it was like trying to pry apart atoms, she was that tight with you."

"Yeah," Chris said. That part, of course, was never connected to reality, making the idea of his permanent stay in this World all the more desirable. But he didn't recall that Katie was an orphan or a foster child.

"Two things have always bothered me about your arrival," Matteo said. "One is, your new home."

"The Cottage."

"And the Studio," Matteo said.

"Yeah?"

They stopped in a broad column of warm light infused with tiny flying insects that swarmed above them.

"I can't tell you how many times I had been to that bluff before you first rumbled into the Village," Matteo said. "Great view of the mountains and the valleys and the Star, you know? The kind that makes a painter want to paint, or make a young lady's heart sing. I don't remember ever seeing a dwelling there, let alone an Artisit's Studio. But after you arrived, there it was, all choked with vines and trees and gardens, as if it had been there for a hundred years, waiting for you. Talk about dropping from the sky."

No surprise there, not for him. "And the other problem?"

Matteo grumbled. "How you got in."

"I've already told you how both things happened. I've told everybody. But no one wants to listen. No one gets it."

"That book again. The book of rules."

"Yeah."

"Can I see it?"

"No...you can't. I can't bring it with me. It's not here. Do you want me to say it any other way?"

Matteo turned and started along the path through the wet ferns. "So everything in this World has been written about in that book, correct?"

"You are," Chris said as he followed.

"That means a counterpart, an alternate, a parallel, based on that book. Am I getting it now?"

"You are."

Matteo whirled around. "Then why is the book immune to this almighty law? Huh? Or maybe, just maybe, everything in this World exists because its always been here, and you've got a book, or had a book—also here, somewhere—where you've written all your hopes and dreams and those very bad memories you're trying really hard to forget."

Chris tried to hide his astonishment, embarrassed that he hadn't thought of the possibility of an alternate book. It did seem plausible. The older man at the grove mentioned it. Now, suddenly, it seemed the laws demanded it. Certainly would explain how the Story had evolved. But if this book existed, was it in control of this World's makeup and the rules that governed it? And if that were true... "I don't know where it could be." But then, he did.

"Yeah, well, like a lot of things, Cristofori. That's why we're making this little detour. You think about it, all right? Let me know if you get an inspiration."

When they reached the bright clearing, Chris saw the Old Mill just ahead. True to Sandra's painting, it was a towering structure made of the large, smooth and pastel-colored stones yanked from the stream bed. It sat on a stone dam that helped form the millpond in the foreground. The mossy gable roof showed signs of rot, and some of its planks had large holes. But the wooden waterwheel was still functioning. And as it turned in the fast-flowing millrace, water tumbled and hissed from its dark blades. Just on the other side of the race, a dwarf evergreen with glowing white orbs sprouted unnaturally from atop the dam, its dark roots snaking through gaps in the mortar.

They followed the path to a frame-filled door, which had long blackstrap hinges attached to its varnished matchboards, and the brass keyhole of a lever lock set in the far right side of its wide middle rail.

Matteo glanced over his shoulder. "This way."

Chris followed Matteo around the left corner and along the stone wall, which was in the cool shadows and out of sight from the path. When they reached the far corner, Matteo squatted and began counting with his index finger the round corner stones from the ground up.

"Twelve," Matteo said, looking up at Chris. He kept his finger pointed at the stone, and waited.

"What?" Chris said.

"Twelve."

"I heard you."

"Mean anything?"

His eyes darting side to side, Chris searched his mind for a connection. "December?"

Matteo scowled. "The Twelfth Night."

Chris frowned, then his eyes slowly brightened.

"Well, well," Matteo said, "more progress. What's *La Dodicesima Notte*, Cristofori? Come on, it's there—I can see it."

Chris was stunned that Matteo was leading him on this path. But he went along anyway, confused but intrigued. "The last of the Twelve Days. The Twelve Days of Christmas."

Matteo chuckled as he slowly shook his head. "You're fighting me. We're not talking about some ancient religious holiday about gift-giving kings and a guiding star that nobody with any real intelligence gives a hoot about. What happened that night?"

In his mind, they approached another sturdy door, but it, too, seemed locked. "I don't remember."

"Too late, Cristofori. I don't believe you anymore." Matteo withdrew his finger from the stone and rose to his feet. "We're not moving until you tell me what happened."

Chris could feel the sweat in his clenched fists, which surprised and alarmed him. Back in his mind, he gripped the door handle, turned it, and pushed. The door creaked opened, but only slightly. He peered into the darkness. But then...a flickering. "It was...her night."

Matteo's eyes narrowed and his head reeled, as if dodging a swipe. "It was the night you left *L'entroterra*—the night you all got in." He paused. "Who's 'her'? Giovanna?"

"Caterina."

"I don't understand."

Neither did Chris. But his mother's ragged, whispering voice behind that door, inside that dark room, told Chris that he needed to hear it, so he told Matteo.

"Hear what?"

Suddenly, the door slammed shut, and Chris felt a strange relief. He unclenched his fists. "I can't see. I don't remember."

"Come on, Cristofori, you were almost there. Give it another try."

Taking a deep breath, Chris closed his eyes and jammed his shoulder against the imaginary door, but it wouldn't budge. He tried it again. Nothing. Now he stared at Matteo. "I'm sorry, I can't."

Matteo nodded. Sympathy and understanding shone on his face. But Chris saw that his friend still wanted clarification, as did Chris. As Chris kept silent, Matteo turned his attention to the corner of the building.

"And when is the Twelfth Night?" he said, his index finger pointing once more to the twelfth stone.

"It's not when everyone thinks," Chris said, grateful they were moving on. "You don't count the day Epiphany is celebrated, or that night."

"That's right, Cristofori. Not the night of Epiphany, the night before. But then again...this is the tricky part. Give me the time that night you got in—'her night,' if it makes you happy."

Now Chris was peeking into the darkened room, through a closed and greasy window. "Just after midnight."

"Which makes it what date?"

"January six."

Matteo smiled. "Right again, Cristofori. Epiphany, after all. See? You're coming around." He concentrated on the stones. "January." He moved his finger one stone to the right. "Six." Crouching again, Matteo moved his finger six stones down. He gripped the selected stone, twisted it a few times to loosen it from the crumbling mortar, then removed it, revealing a dark hole. He reached in and withdrew a large brass key. He held it up triumphantly by its oval bow. "And that's how you made me aware of the Twelve Days of Christmas, and Epiphany."

Chris felt a chill crawling up his spine. He put on his jacket.

After replacing the stone, Matteo, without saying another word, led Chris back to the entrance. He fitted the key into the hole and turned it, throwing aside the bolt. Chris heard some birds flapping away from somewhere above. Matteo pushed open the creaky door, and Chris followed

Matteo into a large, dank room that smelled like an old cask. Sunlight streaked through the small square window openings, void of glass, on the far wall, and the sound of the hissing water and the turning wheel filtered in. The grinding mechanism had been removed, clearing the floor for the prized cache of paintings that would one day be put on display. For now, the room was nearly empty, except for the Paintings leaning against the right wall and draped in the required canvas. In the center of the room was a long wooden table on which crates sat, containing the colored orbs. Dark fibrous beams stretched across the planked ceiling, which hung low, suggesting more floors above. To their left, wooden stairs without a rail or risers hugged the wall. Out of curiosity, Chris looked up the stairwell and saw, at the top, another frame-filled door with a keyhole.

"I wouldn't if I were you," Matteo said. "Those stairs are dangerous. We need to do some repairs." Then he held his right hand out to the collection of covered paintings. "Well, there they are, as promised."

Chris looked at the moldy canvas, feeling anxious. "Show me what I need to see."

They started across the spongy, slimy floorboards.

"The boys will be coming at noon," Matteo said, "but I doubt I'll get back in time. I set these aside last night. You might call them the greatest of the great. I call them problematic. Whatever the name, I gotta know what these things are. Sorry for springing this on you so suddenly, but I don't know any other way to do it." He bent down to grip a corner of the canvas lying on the floor. "Ready?"

"Go ahead."

Matteo rose up and threw back the moldy cover like a magician performing a trick, exposing the far right painting. The room suddenly filled with white light. "Look familiar?"

His eyes adjusted, and Chris gazed in amazement at the painting. It was familiar—that of a ghostly white horse head. Its long, curly mane trailed behind it as if the beast were caught in a tempest. It stared back at him with solid white eyes as round as orbs, and smiled as a human would who had done something horribly wrong and had gotten away with it.

"Well?" Matteo said.

"It's from another painting, called *The Nightmare*," Chris said.

"Yeah, Night-mare," Matteo said, looking at the painting in disgust, "the horse with no pupils or irises. Nothing like an artist with a warped sense of humor. One of your mom's creations?"

"No, it's not from here."

"Not from here, huh? Did you write about it?"

"It was part of her story."

"The one she told you there—and is about to tell us here."

"I guess."

"So if it's part of Alessandra's story, and the orbs hold images from your land, then this thing is alive."

"I'm afraid that might be true."

"Perfect." Matteo paused to stare at the painting, all the while flexing his jaw muscles. Then his gaze returned to Chris. "What is it? What did it do in this...Story?"

"It brought the thing that gave you nightmares."

"What thing?" Matteo said. "This?" He pulled the canvas just enough to reveal the next painting.

Chris gazed at the strange creature on the bright canvas. It had a pudgy, furry face, a hook nose, and cat-like ears. Thick, dark fur covered its stout body, and in some places, like the wrists and ankles, the fur was unnaturally long. Since there was no background other than glowing white to add a reference point, it was impossible for any naïve onlooker to judge the size of the beast. But Chris knew it was small but deadly powerful, which helped served its devilish purpose. "That's the alp," he said.

"What's an alp?"

"The thing that gives you nightmares...and makes you crazy, and hard to breathe."

"Also written about."

Chris nodded. "If you didn't behave."

"Terrific," Matteo said. "And this?" He pulled the cover along the row.

Chris recoiled instinctively as he stared at the image of the multi-horned mask. So this idea, too, had made its way through the portal. "All right—enough," he said, holding up his hand to block the view.

"What is it?"

"Vittorio."

"Your father?" Matteo laughed nervously. "Sorry, Cristofori, but I don't see the resemblance."

"It's not what he was, just what he's become."

"Become?"

"Yeah...the Monster of the Demon Horde."

"This thing is here, too," Matteo said, as if he needed convincing.

Chris nodded. "He has the chain."

"The chain?"

"To ensnare their victims. That's his role. Ask Lorenzo."

"I'd like to. Will I ever get the chance?"

Chris lowered his head and stared at the tips of his boots.

"More good news." Matteo returned his gaze to the painting. "So you described your father this way?"

"He did it to himself, really, and let the alp in. She always warned us this would happen to him. Warned us both."

A curious look remained on Matteo's face. Chris could sense he wanted to ask a lot of prying questions about Cristofori's family life, which of course Chris could not answer, but undoubtedly paralleled his life back home.

"That quiet anger," Matteo said, studying Chris intensely through narrow eyes. "What kind of a world are you from, Cristofori?"

"A scary one, I guess."

Matteo nodded a few times, then wiped his brow with his shirtsleeve as he looked at the Paintings. "We need to talk with your mom, and calm her nerves. And you're gonna sit there and listen to what she has to say—all of it—and you're not going to run away."

"That's our pact. I'm good at those."

"Good man."

"And after that?"

"Tomas is expecting us tonight. We'll go back then—with the boys." He stared at the Paintings. "We're gonna need them, and a few others. In the meantime, you can look for your book."

"And you say all these images are from the red orbs?"

"They are. By the way...did you pick them from a single tree?"

Chris frowned momentarily. "I did." These two facts caught him by surprise. He had thought, and had written, that blue was Friedrich, and red was Russo. But red here was so much more. Did each tree organize them somehow? "What's the last one?"

Still gripping the canvas, Matteo creased his forehead. "These things, as weird as they are, have some sort of logic to them. But this—"

Matteo tugged on the cover once more, revealing the final image. Chris was stunned to see what looked like a mangled automobile wrapped around a tree, its steel body mixed in with chrome, crimson, vinyl, and rubber, as if the entire thing had been caught in a giant, whirling blender that roared like the wind. More proof of the old world, following him, and stored for some unknown purpose. His heart thumped hard in his chest, up into his throat, making it hard to breathe, as old memories and emotions flooded in. He could feel the anger in that roaring wind, and in the rumbling thunder.

"Some other kind of beast we should know of?" Matteo said.

Chris took a slow, deep breath to calm himself. "No, nothing you'll ever see in this World. Just the Storm."

"I never thought the rest of these things could exist. How can you be so sure this one doesn't?"

"The technology hasn't developed. It isn't allowed."

"Not allowed, huh? Why is the rest of this insanity?"

"Coexistence, side by side."

"Is that in your book, too?"

But Chris didn't answer.

"I really would like to see that book someday."

"But you are."

Matteo pulled the canvas over all the images, returning the murkiness to the room. Then they headed for the open door.

"Can I ask you something?" Chris said.

"Go ahead."

"You've seen other images from the red orbs, right? We've collected them may times before."

"We have."

"And they look just as scary?"

Matteo stopped. "Worse."

"What did I tell you about them?"

Matteo put his hands on his hips and leaned closer. "That they weren't real."

Chris frowned. "Why would I say that?"

"Good question. I was hoping you were telling the truth. Maybe not, huh?"

"Yeah. Pretty strange, don't you think?"

"You've always been that way, Cristofori. Always."

When they reached the doorway, Chris looked up the stairs. "Is that where we keep the others?"

Matteo looked surprised, and a little embarrassed.

"And you really think someone wants to hang one of those things over their mantel?" Chris said.

"The 'things' aren't for sale, me boy," Matteo said, his confidence restored. "I'm gonna charge admission."

Of course. "No more stealing. We buy our own."

"You're the boss."

They stepped into the fresh, bright morning, filled with its natural beauty, warmth, and joy. Chris' jacket came off once more while Matteo closed the door to the gloom and the horror that would wait patiently for another day. Returning the key to its hiding place, they headed back toward the Manor to start their journey into the New World's version of *Forever Christmas*.

Chapter Thirty-Three

Natale per Sempre

 Chris and Matteo entered the hot, sunlit meadow and passed the Great Tree on their way to the Manor. With the harvest completed, the meadow looked bare, the chaff scattered everywhere, the livestock gone, replaced by jittery deer and elk and flocks of crows and blackbirds feeding off the scraps. When they reached the pond, the white skiffs were empty and back ashore, and Chris focused on the geese that drifted across the glittering surface, looking for signs, supernatural or otherwise, of Janey, more certain than ever that the rules his book had imposed over this World prevented her from obtaining the safe haven he had promised her. True to those rules, she was not at the Bridge. He thought briefly about bolting for the Village and *L'entroterra* to search for the Black Rider, but decided against it. The disaster at the church ruins had taught him a painful lesson, and without memory of this World, he agreed it was best to toss his guilt and worry aside and leave the next course of action in the hands of those like Matteo who were in a much more rational position to devise it. Seeing the image of the terrible mask helped persuade him. It meant his scathing writings about Victor also had successfully transported themselves through the mysterious portal. Now he needed to hear from Alessandra how exactly these writings had combined with Sandra's Christmas story, and in what horrific manner they had manifested in this New World.

 Avoiding the heavy wagon rumbling through the Manor's service entrance, Chris and Matteo entered the ivy-shrouded main gate and surrounding forest. Suddenly, in the clearing, with detail he had not noticed during his frantic retreat from this World, the Manor exploded into view with uncommon color from the variety of flowers contained in numerous terracotta pots and bronze urns and growing naturally on the shrubs, trees, and vines that crowded and clung to the stone façade. On the small stone patio trimmed by a low stone wall and just outside the stained glass doors of his private office, Doctor Samuele and Alessandra sat in wrought-iron chairs around an oval iron table, on which sat a notebook and a wooden dip pen in a glass inkwell. That image pulled him back for a moment. As if to show how serious they were about this session, Alessandra and the doctor were dressed for their parts. Now fully prepared to pour her heart out, Alessandra wore a sheer, patterned tea gown, a silk sash tied at her slim waist. Her dark hair was carefully gathered and pinned beneath a wide-brimmed hat trimmed with fresh flowers, and gave her the elegance and beauty she once dreamed of in another far less-glamorous existence. Dr. Samuele sported a dark suit with a white waistcoat. The white-dotted black tie polished off his scholarly, in-charge appearance.

When Alessandra saw them approaching, she rose up with exuberance and surprise, as if she had feared they would never return. She took a step toward them, but Dr. Samuele, a stern expression solidly in place, motioned with his hand, urging restraint. She remained standing as they arrived on the patio.

"Well, here he is...as promised," Matteo said.

"I'm so glad you came back," Alessandra said, sounding tired. She gazed at Chris with weary eyes. "Please don't run anymore."

"No more running, I swear," Chris said. He smiled, but it didn't seem to affect her. Nor did his empty promise. And then he looked at Dr. Samuele, who stared back with eyes that seemed more suited for the Horde. No doubt, he was ready to do battle.

"You were gone long," the doctor said to Matteo. "We almost gave up hope."

"I'm sorry, Doctor," Matteo said. "He's very fast."

Dr. Samuele nodded, but Chris could sense that details of the chase were not important to him. "May we finally begin?"

"Do you want me to leave?" Alessandra said.

"Leave?" the doctor said. "My dear woman, after your stunning admission? Before I speak with Cristofori, we need to hear the tale you've promised to tell."

"What about me?" Matteo said. "I could go help Caterina, if you want."

"Where is she?" Chris said.

"The ruins," Alessandra said.

"She went to *L'entroterra*?" Chris said. "By herself?"

Matteo glared at him. "She went to get help—in the Village."

Chris fell silent, but he was not happy that Matteo had failed to inform him of this unsettling fact.

"I have little doubt about my daughter's qualifications to deal with this latest crisis," the doctor said, sneaking an annoyed glance at Chris, "despite its terribly awkward and difficult nature. You need to stay and hear this too, Matteo, with Alessandra's consent, of course."

"Yes...I have no objections," Alessandra said. "As I stated earlier, I've kept the truth from you—all of you—much too long, and I now see the harm that I have caused."

Chris hung his jacket on the back of his chair. He and Matteo sat on either side of Alessandra, who struggled to begin her story.

"You must understand," she said, "this is no tale in the usual sense, even though I wish it were. How some of the things I'm about to tell you were possible, I can't fully explain. But there is no denying—or escaping—the past, though I had hoped to do so by coming to this village."

"The celebrated arrival—seeking new shelter, after the Storm," Dr. Samuele said. He scribbled some notes.

"It was much more than that—more about protection and safety."

"From Vittorio."

"Yes. But not just from him."

"There were other dangers stalking you."

"Not me, Doctor—Cristofori."

Dr. Samuele's head did not move, but his gaze met hers, and the whites of his eyes seemed to shine. "You're certain of this."

"After what became of Vittorio, and of Giovanna—yes, I am certain."

Now they all looked at Chris, as if for a reaction. He felt intimidated by their stares. But as the Paintings at the Old Mill had shown, there were dangerous things stalking him.

"Vittorio's fate has always been a mystery to me, Alessandra," the doctor said. "Out of courtesy to you, I have never pried deeply into this matter, though I have sensed all along that you were keeping the truth from me—that he wasn't merely 'lost,' or 'drifting' as you have previously described."

"I'm sorry, Doctor. I never wanted to deceive you. But I know how you feel about such things."

" 'Things,' Alessandra?"

"Yes, my faith."

"What does your faith have to do with Vittorio?"

She hesitated as she stared at him.

"Tell me what it is you want to say, and ignore—with my sincere apologies, of course—any unfortunate or insensitive opinions I may have expressed in the past."

Alessandra took a deep breath and slowly exhaled. "I do believe he was overcome...that he has bargained with the Devil."

Matteo looked at Chris with a knowing expression.

Dr. Samuele calmly dipped his pen in the well. "The Devil. In the religion that once pervaded your land, He is a powerful and supernatural entity immune to the proven laws of science—an angel who, with His followers, rebelled against God, and was subsequently expelled from Heaven for the fiery and subterranean chamber in this Earth called Hell. In essence, He is the embodiment of all thoughts and actions that humans have deemed as evil. And it is His desire to steal all souls and bring them to His hellish kingdom where they will spend an eternity of suffering and punishment, necessitating the birth of Christ the Savior, celebrated tomorrow, on Christmas. Do I have a clear understanding of this word?"

"You do, Doctor."

"And even though you say you agree with my assessment, you still insist that this...Devil had a hand in your husband's demise?"

"I do. Evil was its intent. Evil was the result."

"Interesting," the doctor said, followed by more scribbling. "So this is what happened to your husband—he was lured away from you by an evil entity."

" 'Poisoned' is more accurate, and in an insidious way."

More note-taking. "Did you see this Devil?"

"He did not come to us in His traditional form. That sight, I doubt, I could ever endure."

"A frightful creature, indeed," Dr. Samuel said, though he sounded amused. "I have viewed the paintings from the churches of your land. But surely you're not suggesting that a terrifying being such as this actually appeared—"

"I know what I saw."

"And what was that?"

"A reincarnation."

"Now it was a reincarnation? Forgive me, Alessandra, that opens the door to interpretation, speculation—any ordinary thing that may suddenly become 'supernatural.' "

"This creature was nothing I had ever seen before."

"A foreign species, perhaps? Or just foreign to you?"

Chris was becoming annoyed.

So, too, was Alessandra. "It was a small, hairy being—"

"Like a raccoon?"

"Not a raccoon, Doctor."

"You lived by a pond. What about a species of otter, beaver, or a muskrat?"

"No, Doctor."

Now he was belittling her, intentional or not. Chris couldn't contain his anger. "It was an alp."

They all looked at Chris with different degrees of amazement.

"Indeed," the doctor said with one raised brow. "You remember? You can confirm this, this...alp?"

Chris glanced at Matteo, who also seemed alarmed, and fearful of closely-guarded secrets being revealed.

Alessandra, however, appeared confused by Chris' interjection, but she took control of the conversation, sparing him the need for further explanation. "We all saw it—many times—but only in the holy month of December, when the fog came and strangled the Sun. We all feared it. Not even the holly, the mistletoe, the garland, or the horseshoes could keep it away."

Dr. Samuele appeared respectful, but he could not contain his doubt. He shifted nervously in his chair and refused to make eye contact. "I have heard many stories, studied the myths and legends of beings and creatures that purportedly haunt *L'entroterra* this time of year, but I must admit, I am not familiar with this entity. So you must forgive me if I seem a little...ambivalent. Alessandra, tell me about the first time you saw this alp."

Alessandra looked at Chris warily. He sensed that she, too, had never heard the actual name of the creature. But she also seemed unwilling to contradict him openly, now that he had already defended her. So she faced the doctor bravely. "It was before Cristofori was born, shortly after Vittorio and I were married. It was a bittersweet time for us. He had just finished building the cottage by the pond. But it had taken much longer than he had expected—well into the fall. And all that time, he had to juggle that enormous task while providing for us through his performances, for the sunlight is not so generous in our land, and the seasons do not come and go in a day. So that enormous task proved to be overwhelming in many ways we hadn't expected, and it strained our finances. Vittorio may have looked like a confident, carefree, and spirited man to all who had heard him sing—as I, too, in my wide-eyed youth first viewed him—but I regret to say, in hindsight, that he was not. He was fearful of the future, and incessantly worried about money and responsibilities with which he could not cope. And though the cottage was now complete, I began to see in his vacant eyes and persistently somber face that he was already harboring doubt about the burdens our union had suddenly brought upon him.

"The first month at the cottage was difficult—especially at night. Vittorio was restless. He had trouble sleeping. And often he would rise from bed well past midnight and wander off. Sometimes, he would lie on the parlor sofa before the fireplace. Other times, he would leave the cottage altogether. Where he would go, I did not know—only that he would be back at my side before sunrise. When he did sleep, he often suffered terrible nightmares that would cause him to whimper and moan like a frightened and helpless child—certainly a way that no young bride with hopes for the future ever wanted to hear. I would wake him, of course, partly out of fear and partly out of curiosity. After all, I wanted to know what kind of visions could cause him so much torment. He never confided in me, but I often wondered how much my mere presence had contributed to his nightly suffering.

"And then, one night, something strange happened. One of our horses—a white mare, the one given as a wedding present from his father—was taken from the shed."

Matteo punch Chris on the thigh. Though the act was below table level, the doctor ceased his note-taking to turned his annoyed gaze on them. Matteo smiled sheepishly and seemed to shrink in his chair. "Continue, Alessandra," the doctor said.

She, too, looked at them with puzzlement before she returned her solemn expression to the doctor. "We both heard the mare squeal and whinny and thrash about its stall. Vittorio sprung from the bed to investigate, but by then the horse and the thief had already galloped off. Vittorio dressed as quickly as he could and took up the pursuit on the stallion. But after an hour or so, he came back defeated. Our mare was gone."

"And why was that so strange?" Dr. Samuele. "Is horse thievery so uncommon?"

"No, I suppose not," Alessandra said.

"So I'll ask again—"

"Come morning, the mare was back in its stall."

The doctor raised an eyebrow. "A remorseful thief, perhaps?"

"Not a thief," Alessandra said. "Thievery had nothing to do with it."

"What was the intent, then?"

"Initially? Mischief—and, as it turned out, a test of will."

"On whose part?"

"We didn't know at the time."

"But you do now," Dr. Samuele said, even though everyone knew the answer.

Alessandra nodded. "You wanted my first recollection of the creature, didn't you?"

"But you still had yet to see it."

"Yes. That didn't come until weeks later."

"Go on," the doctor said.

Alessandra shifted in her chair. "Despite taking necessary security precautions and assuming a heightened vigilance, the thievery continued. Not every night, but increasingly more and more. It was as if it knew when Vittorio and I could no longer keep our eyes open, or where we kept the keys to the heavy padlock. Each time, the mare was returned. But each time, it looked a little different—worn and haggard, if such words are proper to describe a beast. We knew that if we didn't stop these annoying pranks, the horse would not survive. But neither one of us knew exactly what should or could be done. Eventually, the mare did not return. But by then, it was nearly dead. Worse yet, we still didn't know who was behind it or why it was being done. And this only caused Vittorio more distress. He was well-liked throughout the land. He wasn't aware that he had any enemies, that someone would think so poorly of him as to pull such a persistent and heartless stunt. I can only speculate as to the nature of our actions had the truth been discovered. Little did I know that these pranks were only a mild precursor to that great evil which would eventually descend upon the land."

"But you did discover the truth, " Doctor Samuele said.

Alessandra nodded. "One night, when Vittorio was sleeping upon the sofa, I happened to awake from the moaning and the crying in the parlor. He was calling out his father's name as if pleading for some unseen torment to end, and it puzzled me as to why this would be. He rarely spoke of him. But when he did, it was with fondness and nostalgia."

"When I peered around the corner into the parlor, I saw it—a small, white butterfly that glowed like an orb. A beautiful and graceful creature, really. It fluttered about his head, leaving a glittering trail of crystalline mist. But something about it made me shiver. Its long, forked tails appeared more like the deadly mandibles of some giant beetle. Vittorio was lying almost lifeless on his back, one arm draped across his forehead, the other dangling to the floor. His mouth was open, and he took long and difficult breaths, as if he had an obstruction in his throat. The butterfly spiraled closer and closer to his face—and then it turned completely into a wisp of that trailing glittering mist. When Vittorio drew in another breath, the mist entered through his mouth and nostrils with a violent and hateful force that absolutely jarred him. I cannot express how utterly terrified I felt as I watched this unholy event unfold before me.

"Even though he was asleep, Vittorio seemed to know something strange was happening. His eyes brightened and his breathing ceased. But his mouth remained open, and he did not move or look about. It was as if he were waiting and hoping for the mist—or whatever it was—to depart as quickly as it had entered. And when it emerged, and the wisp transformed back into the butterfly, Vittorio groaned as he exhaled. And now deflated, he remained on his back, his head turned toward me. His mouth was still open, but his eyes were shut tight. I stepped into the parlor and stared at the appalling thing. It fluttered high overhead, defiantly, as if to get a closer look at me, then it streaked for the gap beneath the front door. By now, my fear had turned to anger, and I chased after it. You see, not once during this ordeal, not once during any of the terrible encounters with the thing did I ever really think it wanted to seek me out and attack me, only my husband, and my children. I can't explain this rationale. It just appeared. So when I opened the door, all I saw and heard was the white mare galloping off into the darkness."

"And what happened to Vittorio?" the doctor said, unfazed.

"I woke him and told him what I saw."

"And what did he say?"

"He said he saw such things, too, but that they were all in his dreams."

"Did he believe you?"

"He insisted that we were both dreaming."

"A very rational assessment, wouldn't you agree?"

Alessandra did not hesitate. "It was no dream."

Dr. Samuele ran his hand through his dark hair as Matteo looked on, befuddled, and a little frightened. The alp had made a successful transition to the New World, unscathed.

"So your alp is a glowing butterfly," the doctor said with a hint of scorn.

"That's not its normal state of being," Alessandra said.

"Normal? What state would that be, madam?"

"I saw it sitting on Vittorio's chest only a few nights later. It was the small and hairy creature I mentioned—and it had the ears of a cat. It looked at me with a sinister grin that only a fiend could muster. It knew I was powerless to stop it. The mare had returned as well. It had poked its head through the doorway. Saw those eyes, those horrible round white eyes. These creatures returned many times after that, even after the children were born, and always in the holy month of December."

Matteo shot more nervous glances Chris' way.

"And was the result the same each time?" Dr. Samuele said.

"Yes—they continued to slowly poison him, making him more and more angry, and withdrawn. By then, I had sought help at the church. I needed an explanation, of course."

"Did they provide you with one?"

"You must understand, it was a terrible time in our land. Great and destructive forces were gathering. They knew it. It was just another sign."

"Are you speaking of the Storm, Alessandra?"

"That was no ordinary storm, Doctor."

"No," Chris said, unable to contain himself.

Dr. Samuele's eyes flared at Chris' reaction, then he nodded once again as he jotted more notes. But he appeared unwilling to accept their response as the truth, for now. "What did the church do for you—anything?"

"They gave me crosses."

"Oh yes, the symbol of the Savior. And did they help?"

"I am here, and with my only son."

"But not with your husband or daughter."

Alessandra bowed her head.

"What really happened to them, Alessandra?" the doctor said. "Can you tell us?"

She looked up at him forlornly, and seemed willing to accept his skeptical, judgmental tone. Then she nodded—but not before she stared at Chris, as if she wondered what the truth would do to his sanity.

∽

They remained in session at the sunlit patio table, a gentle breeze tousling a few loose strands of Alessandra's long hair. But her expression remained hard, the look in her eyes still distant. She kept them in the pall of her story. "Throughout those years, Vittorio endured many December nightmares," she said. "And I eventually came to dread a month I once had, during my youth, looked forward to with great anticipation and wonder as we celebrated the Savior's birth, and for the magical gifts from St. Nicholas. When the nightmares stopped after that first December, and the accumulating months slowly pushed us farther and farther away from those terrifying encounters with the creature, my sense of hope grew almost to the point where it all seemed, as Vittorio kept insisting, to be just a bad dream. But then the next December came upon us, then the next. And so, too—despite the added measures—did the white butterfly and the white-eyed mare.

"I watched helplessly as Vittorio's health slowly deteriorated until it greatly affected his singing. Engagements became harder and harder to come by until the church choir remained his only venue, and this, of course, only made our finances worse. To supplement our income, he tried his hand at odd jobs, doing just about any kind of handiwork he could. But he lacked the skills and the energy to be successful. This brought on more depression and anger and worry, and the cycle continued unbroken, constantly feeding upon itself. I sustained my efforts to seek help at the church, but more and more Vittorio resisted their attempts at intervention.

"This was a time where I began to doubt my own love for Vittorio. The cottage by the pond, even on the brightest and warmest spring days, was quickly becoming an ugly and oppressive trap. Had I been too impetuous, too overcome by the glitter that he was and the gaiety that he delivered in his songs to concern myself with the substance and character that made a marriage work and kept one's soul from inviting evil? Or was I still just a frightened little girl? These questions popped into my head often, but I knew I would never take the kind of action required to extricate myself from our unhappy marriage. I was committed to this man. I had sworn to my God in His House that I would love him no matter what came our way till the day I died. To break that oath and eventually face the consequences would be more unbearable than the gloom and the trouble that had already descended upon us. But still, in many silent moments when that doubt appeared, I yearned for a way to alter the ugliness, which now surrounded me. But with each day filled with household chores, the harvesting, the winnowing, the spinning, and the weaving, I could not see a means of escape.

"Desperate for any manner of that elusive intervention I felt could save our relationship, I came to hope and pray, like most innocent fools, that the birth of our first child would lift him from his melancholy, restore his faith, and give him the strength and desire to fight that which he had invited to steal his soul. But the night of Cristofori's arrival—as I know you recall, Doctor—only deepened his moodiness, and added to the almost unbearable weight of responsibility he felt for our well-being.

"But Cristofori turned out to be such a blessing for me. And I hadn't considered just how far my own spirits had declined until he came into our lives. He was such a happy and healthy child despite all the sadness and sinister machinations that surrounded him. And when I saw him each morning, it only strengthened my resolve to give him the kind of fulfilling life I once hoped for. Later on in his life, he did well with his lessons, he established friendships with his classmates and participated in their boyish games, and he embraced the church's teachings. And the jubilation he expressed each December—particularly on Christmas morning, when he discovered the gold coins left in his boot—helped to offset the dread we had to endure throughout that holy month.

"But because of Vittorio's struggles and the uncertainty we all faced, and despite the joy Cristofori's arrival brought to me, I remained wary about bring another life into our World. Vittorio's desire for me, though it never completely disappeared, was seldom expressed. So I was quite surprised when I found myself expecting again. Even more surprising, Giovanna—my miraculous Christmas gift!—proved to be a happier child than Cristofori. I think the aura associated with the day of her arrival—fortuitous or not—made Giovanna such a powerful presence in my son's life that she helped keep Vittorio's influence at bay...for a while, at least. Though Cristofori eventually became more active with the church and his classmates, he and Giovanna were nearly inseparable, constantly looking out for each other. Something about a pact. Having witnessed the nightmare firsthand no doubt contributed to that. I tried so hard to protect her from the ghastly spectacle—Cristofori, too, even when he was much younger and only suspected that something terrible was occurring—but it was impossible to keep them from witnessing the truth. As I have recounted to you, the assault each year-end was too persistent, and far too intrusive. But somehow, we endured. And often when I thought that I was about to lose Vittorio to the menace that plagued him, he would recover.

"When Cristofori began transforming into a young man, long after Giovanna started attending school, Caterina came unexpectedly into our lives one unusually warm fall afternoon. Yes, Doctor, as you are well aware, that too was a delightful time. I still recall hearing her rumbling wagon approach the cottage for the very first time. When I went outside to investigate, I saw this beautiful vision of a young lady at the reins. She wasn't much older than my son. But even at her young age, she was forced to look for work, and she professed talents at weaving and spinning, animal care, and child-minding. Though she claimed to live with her parents nearby, I had never seen her before. But as you know, Doctor, it was not a huge concern. Most cottages were isolated, scattered throughout the vast fields and forests, not concentrated like in the Village. So it was not uncommon to stumble across an unfamiliar face that had every right to be considered a neighbor in need of work. It was tempting to entertain her offer, now that I had two young people who were growing like weeds and ate as voraciously as our livestock. Even with Cristofori's able help, I struggled to keep up with all the tasks at hand. Still, I was in no position to hire her, given the troubles—financial and otherwise—we were experiencing. I expressed my regret, but she was persistent—now offering to work for the exquisite flax that grew naturally in the meadow, something she claimed was difficult to find. It was hard to counter her offer, so I immediately fretted about Vittorio's reaction once he learned she would be drawing upon our limited resources. But she promised that her requirements would be negligible.

"I must be honest, I was a little suspicious of her—yes, your endearing young daughter. How could I possibly harbor such shameful thoughts? But the fine bright linen she wore, the vigorous steed and its fancy trappings all suggested to me that this was not a person in dire need of bartering for material essential to make the clothing with her own hands that would protect her from the elements. But as she reminded me, it was her ability to barter and to spin and weave that won her such an overstated and contrary appearance.

"Her intelligence, her persistence, her confidence and her talent for persuasiveness—all bundled in a delightfully warm and endearing form— were astounding. And yet, I had one last concern. And this one was dire. During our ever-growing discourse, I had discovered that she was not a believer. And not only wasn't she a believer, she had been born into a household where our faith was never taught. She was, upon her own admission, *pagano*. I had, of course, encountered many of her kind across the land. And though I never wished upon them any ill will, I silently held an unflattering bias against them. If she were to become an influence in my children's lives, which—because of her charm and beauty—I knew she would, I had to be reassured that she would not discuss her background with them. Sadly, I did not know how—even with her great gift of persuasion—

she could overcome this last but most disconcerting objection. But much to my amazement, she did.

"'I need to believe, to get in—to be saved,' she said to me. 'God has a wondrous plan for me—I can sense it. Will you teach me while I work?'

"I was stunned, of course. But I detected the kind of intense desire needed for such a holy endeavor. I told her that I was not qualified to handle such a request, that others atop the bluff could help her much more than I ever could. But then she reminded me that with the work she would be providing, she would have little time for anything else, much less her salvation. I took her reply as a polite restatement of our soon-to-be-accepted bartering agreement where I would owe her a coveted commodity—that being my instruction.

"I took a moment to consider her request. Then my eyes spotted something in her wagon that intrigued me, something apart from the trunks and crates filled with personal items. They were the tools of an artist—brushes, an easel, and framed but blank white canvas that seemed so magical, it glowed. I had to ask: was she an accomplished painter as well?

"'Only when I can't find work,' she said. Then I inquired rather impertinently as to why she painted, probing for some insight about her that I had failed to see.

"'Sometimes when life gets really difficult and I'm rushing about to make a living, I struggle to see the beauty that surrounds me,' she said. 'Painting is just a way to recapture what I've grown blind to—and sometimes, create what I hope to one day see.'

Her words tugged at my heart. That was when I added another stipulation to our agreement: in exchange for my instruction, she would instruct me. Finally, I would have my means of escape. But I reminded her that—beginning on Advent, through December and the Twelfth Night—it was a holy time that we celebrated in private, and that I, regretfully, would not require her help again until the sixth of January.

She agreed.

⁂

"Caterina proved to be an able worker and patient instructor," Alessandra said. "With her assistance, life became more bearable—and actually improved, as she spun and wove some of the finest linen I had ever touched. Even Vittorio—who by now had become more withdrawn and restless than ever as he wandered for days on end—noticed the improvements in his garb and bed linen. She was good with the animals—especially the waterfowl—and her gentle but vigilant ways kept them healthy and content.

"When it became stormy, or when on the rarest of occasions no chores needed attention, Caterina and I would retire to the shed where she taught me to sketch and paint. We began with simple shapes—a piece of fruit, a vase of wild flowers. And then, when I realized that I did have enough talent to become an artist, we took the lessons outside. There, I slowly graduated to more complicated and desirable landscape subjects like trees and streams and cottages—moving ever closer to my ultimate goal of transforming, if only in my mind, the meadow. Each time we finished a session, we hid in the shed the easel and supplies beneath an old tarp, away from Vittorio's prying eyes.

"How Caterina kept our entire arrangement a secret from Vittorio still amazes me. She always seemed to know when he would be gone, just as she anticipated correctly when to depart before his sudden return. I found it difficult to inform Vittorio of the agreement, always fearful of his overreaction. The longer I waited to tell him, the more difficult it became. And once I realized that the arrangement could be successfully hidden, I decided to keep silent. I never encouraged the children to participate in the deception, and I knew that someday I would be punished for it. But from the very first day, they knew the consequences of disclosing the truth.

"By late November, the winds grew cold and the terrible fog of December began to gather. The concerns I had about her influence over my children had, for the most part, disappeared. She gave me no cause to fear that she had broken her promise not to discuss her upbringing. And she took my instruction to heart. Neither Cristofori nor Giovanna ever questioned me about that sensitive matter when Caterina was not present, as surely they would have, given their lessons at the church and in the classroom.

"As I knew he would, Cristofori took a special liking to Caterina. Having been charmed by beauty myself, it was unfair of me to expect otherwise. I knew she was growing fond of him as well, just by the way she smiled and laughed when they conversed while working together. He had become a charming and handsome young man, which I could not deny had been Vittorio's most significantly positive contribution to his son's future. Cristofori often talked about Caterina with admiration and respect, never uttering a hint of vulgarity that young men sometimes employ when they gather, puffing themselves up about their exploits and conquests. As for Caterina, she did not use her uncommon beauty as a means of flirtation or entrapment. She remained loyal to me, and never once jeopardized the working relationship we had successfully established. But I often wondered how long they would carry on as kindred spirits.

"When Advent was upon us, we bid Caterina farewell for the month. As a final act, she helped us with the hanging of the mistletoe and the garland, never once questioning their true purpose. It was a sad time for us all. Not only had she become a loyal assistant, she was now a trusted confidant. Giovanna expressed her concern for our animals' welfare, and her regrets that Caterina would not be present to help celebrate the miracle birthday. Cristofori had his own laments, but they remained unspoken.

"I know you have your doubts, Doctor, but this regrettable break in our relationship was necessary. December is a magical time—and in one sense, a wondrous time. Without the magic that descends upon the land, the annual visit from St. Nicholas would not be possible. Nor would the spirits of the saints who make visitations, or the angels who watch over us. But December also has its malevolent side. It is a time of demons—manifestations of evil, as you call it, such as the one that tormented my husband until the time he finally left us. I did not want to subject Caterina to that evil, especially in light of her efforts to be saved. I still had not been honest with her about what really went on in our household. And I knew the children had not discussed it with her. I had inquired numerous times, and they repeatedly assured me they had not divulged any of our darkest secrets. But I'm sure Caterina sensed that something wasn't right. After all, she was from the same land, and lived under its strange rules. I did not know if she suffered similar evils in her own household—she never once said. But I could not imagine that she had been immune to the types of visions that had haunted us.

"After we said farewell, I hoped and prayed that she would survive the month, and that she would return to us when it was safe. We waited for Vittorio to come home from his latest wanderings. But after a week had passed and he had yet to appear, I began to fear that the inevitable had finally happened.

"Something was vastly different this particular December. There seemed to be much more gloom in the air. I don't know how I knew, but it also felt as if the magic had a new and more powerful intensity, and that the frequency of ghostly visitations would dramatically increase. It was the weather, of all things, that contributed to this dreadful feeling. It remained unusually warm at night, and the snows that often blanketed the meadow refused to fall, instead replaced by that thick and oppressive fog. And the church grove...with the sudden and inexplicable spread of those red orbs.

"My suspicions were confirmed one evening when I went to retrieve a shovel from the shed. There was an odd glow coming from beneath the door, and I immediately feared that the white butterfly had returned. But as I tossed my fears aside and went in to investigate, I saw that the light was coming from beneath the tarp used to cover my paintings. I threw the tarp aside and set one of the pictures—an apple—on the workbench. It looked so real—much more so than I remembered painting it. I felt an irresistible urge to reach out and touch it, which I did. Now this is something that I regret keeping from you, Doctor, for fear of your reaction. But I was able to withdraw the apple from the painting and hold it in amazement in my hand."

Alessandra stopped her discourse and stared at the doctor, as if to allow him to weigh the words of her story. Once again, Dr. Samuele seemed to struggle with his emotions. He slowly nodded his head and scrawled on the pad.

Dr. Samuele dipped the pen into the inkwell and sat back in his chair. "I've seen this painting—at your Studio, I believe."

"Yes, you have."

"Yet I don't recall that this trick has ever been performed in my presence."

"Not there, no. There, it can't be done."

"Conveniently. Where, then? At the shed? I believe it did not survive the Storm."

"It did. But the shed is not essential for such a...trick," she said respectfully. "Only that the painting is taken beyond the West Bridge."

"And into the realm of myth and magic," he said with a trace of contempt.

"That is correct, Doctor."

He frowned. "You know how I am, Alessandra. I need to see it."

"I know you do."

"With your permission, I'll send a coachman over later today to retrieve it. I promise not to keep it for very long."

"Take all the time you require, Doctor. You need to believe."

They all seemed surprised by Alessandra's confidence in her bold statement—the doctor in particular, who undoubtedly took her claim as a personal challenge to his own manner of thinking. But then he smiled. "Whether we paint pictures or write books or perform mathematics—when it comes down to it—aren't we all doing the same thing?"

Alessandra did not answer, and looked anxious to resume control of the discussion. "There was another ominous sign that this particular December would be like no other."

"Go on," Dr. Samuele said, courteously.

"It came from Cristofori."

Matteo's eyes widened as he stared at Chris.

Chris, in turn, looked wide-eyed at his mother, unable to anticipate yet eager to hear her next words.

"Yes, it came from Cristofori," Alessandra said, "and how he battled the specter on the pond."

"I had never seen this vision before," Alessandra said, "and it frightened me more than the white butterfly ever could. For this specter was not seeking the soul of my troubled husband, it wanted Cristofori's.

"In those anxious weeks before Christmas, I noticed that his mood slowly began to sour. I had never seen him in such distress before, especially this time of year. I gave him many opportunities to confide in me, but he would not divulge the source of his troubles, and remained in a sullen shell similar to the one that Vittorio himself had constructed before he vanished. Naturally, I began to fear that the white butterfly was poisoning him. But he denied repeatedly that he was experiencing any supernatural intrusions into his life. However, Cristofori was never a competent liar, as his father was. So once again, I remained vigilant at night—well after he retired to his bedroom. But to my surprise and delight, I never saw or heard the telltale signs of the glowing menace or its galloping mare.

"And then one morning, a mere week before Giovanna's birthday, I rose earlier than normal upon the rare sight of the rising Sun. When I gazed out toward the pond, I saw Cristofori standing in his bedclothes among the reeds along the shore. A rolling mist hung just above the water's warm surface. Granted, the sunrise was a pleasant sight, given the gloominess we had been experiencing. That Cristofori would have ventured all the way out to the pond and into the damp morning to witness the event was, of course, worrisome. Had he been sleepwalking, I wondered? Was he still in that state?

"I entered the parlor, unlatched the lock, and pulled open the front door. The echoing noise I created did not disturb his trance. Before I could call out his name, the rolling fog began to gather into separate and distinct shapes—mostly as child-like spirits, like the many cupids and youthful angels painted upon our church's ceiling. But there was another apparition gathering just before him, and it much larger than the rest. It took the form of a young woman with long, shimmering hair. She was clothed in a gleaming white gown, and she was staring benevolently at my son, who seemed mesmerized by her shining beauty.

"Now, you may be wondering why I would consider such a seemingly holy and miraculous vision something to be fearful of. But you see, I had heard stories from my parents of such a being that haunted the lakes and ponds of the land—stories that came from the legends I had warned Caterina not to speak of. But I never believed these creatures truly existed.

"Standing face to face with her and overcome by her radiance, as Cristofori was, one could not see her true nature. Had Cristofori looked upon her from the angle I spied on them, he would have seen the tail that curled up from under her gown. And the cupids and angels that accompanied her weren't angels at all, but the lost souls of children and young men whom she, according to legend, had ensnared. I realized at that moment how foolish I had been for not believing in the visions of the *pagano* while at the same time accepting the existence of the divine, and for not allowing Caterina to speak of her former, non-believing ways. I had only prevented him from recognizing the kind danger that was prevalent this time of year in our land—the kind of danger he was now confronting.

"When I finally called out to him, the specter and her souls vanished into the bright morning light. But Cristofori did not move. He turned and faced me with a surly, almost angry stare. So I rushed to his side and slowly led him from the pond. He did not come willingly.

" 'Did she speak to you?' I said. And he confirmed my fear with a nod. 'And what did she say?' I asked.

" 'She wants me to bring her to the church,' he replied.

" 'For what purpose?' I then inquired. But he returned to that persistent sulking mood, and did not provide an answer. But I already knew the devilish plan she was concocting. So I told him all that I knew of her being and intent, and how he had—for the sake of his own soul—to avoid her. My story only incensed him more.

" 'Why such a display of anger?' I asked him. 'Have you seen this young woman before?'

" 'I have,' he replied, 'many times.' And his response only heightened by fear, and made it unbearable. Then I begged and pleaded for him to stay away from her, reminding him again of the dire consequences.

" 'I know—I will!' he said. And I believed him. But his anger did not subside, and it puzzled me." Then Alessandra lowered her head and fell silent, as if it were too painful for her to continue.

Dr. Samuele seemed unfazed as he looked at Chris. "Do you remember any of this, Cristofori?"

Chris shook his head, though he now saw how Sandra's story had evolved. "But it doesn't mean it didn't happen."

"Indeed," the doctor said, looking on with displeasure. Then he gazed at Alessandra. "Did this temptress ever return?"

"No," Alessandra said.

"You're certain of this? You admitted yourself that he had gone to her many times without your previous knowledge."

"Because on Christmas, the Storm came," she said, "and we had to flee for our lives."

⁓

"As I stated earlier," Alessandra said, "in the past, despite the difficulties of the month, the children looked forward to Christmas, especially Giovanna, of course, with her birthday attached to that most holy day. But this year, Christmas was different, now that Vittorio had vanished. But none of us thought that we had seen the last of him, or in what manner he would return. The unhappiness and resentment and the anger I had felt from him since our marriage began had long since been imparted to the children. So his absence had brought a small measure of relief to us all. And yet, at the same time, we all felt—as Vittorio once did—a terrible uneasiness about the future, wondering if we would be forced to survive on our own, and how exactly that could be accomplished. We had enough food stored in the pantry and cellar, and a sufficient supply of wood to last us through winter. But already, the children—well, Giovanna—was pledging the gold coins she hoped to receive from St. Nicholas toward our survival. Not that Cristofori didn't want to help. Rather, he was convinced that St. Nicholas would not appear—something odd about the holy man being 'transformed.' How he knew this, why he felt this way, Cristofori did not elaborate. But I suspected that it had everything to do with his encounters with the dazzling young woman."

"For Giovanna's selfless offer, I felt a modest guilt. I had yet to show the children the 'trick' with the magical paintings. The consequences of that discovery were still a mystery, and I worried that if I revealed the secret too soon, I might place them in danger. But it was also obviously clear to me, from the moment I withdrew the apple from the glowing canvas, the power and the opportunity the paintings provided, and that they could help us—at least during December—with the immediate struggles we faced. I had already worked feverishly to take full advantage of this temporary gift, and felt confident that I had sufficiently anticipated what troubles might come our way.

"So late on the eve of Christmas, Giovanna placed one of her boots outside the front door before she went to bed. Out of habit, I remained vigilant in the parlor, not only worried about Vittorio and the white butterfly, but also the gleaming white specter that had been tempting my son. And then a peculiar thing happened. As the clock drew ever closer to midnight, I began to wonder in an embarrassingly childlike way if I would actually see St. Nicholas appear. I had never seen him with my own eyes, not even as a child. Every young person knew that such an attempt would only deter this welcome visit—and deny us the gold coins that we coveted. Even worse, no one wanted to wake the next morning to find a tree branch in their boot—a sure sign of St. Nicholas' displeasure—and having to wait an entire year to regain, through more virtuous behavior, his good graces.

"But when midnight struck, I found myself plotting like some impetuous girl to shift my vigil from the sofa to the chair by the front window where I could break with tradition and, with just an innocent glance, spy on Giovanna's boot. The window was covered by sheer linen drapes that Caterina had fashioned just a month earlier, so they would afford me some degree of concealment, yet allow me to accomplish my goal. Surely, I finally rationed, I would not be held to the same standards as the young children whose good behavior was the objective of this annual rite.

"To assure that I would not be detected, I used the poker to displace the burning logs in the fireplace just enough to extinguish most of their light, then turned down the lamp by the window and slumped in the chair. In the darkness, I glanced sheepishly to the closed bedroom doors down the interior hall, hoping my plot would not be uncovered. Then I turned and crouched behind the upholstered back and slowly raised my head so I could peer in wide-eyed wonder just over the top of the chair and through the window sheers. Without the usual blanket of snow that countered its effects, the blackness pushed hard against the cottage. But I could sense the presence of the thick fog that had persisted all December long.

"I don't remember how long I crouched in that chair. But every creak, every moving shadow or fireplace crackle triggered an alarm in my brain and heightened my senses, and convinced me that I was about to witness something I desperately hoped to see. But as the minutes slipped past the midnight hour, I began to wonder if St. Nicholas had indeed detected me, marked his book, and bypassed the cottage.

"Then I saw movement outside the window. At first, it appeared to be the fog, rolling toward the door. But then I saw someone pressing toward the cottage, an he stirred the fog. Then an old bearded man in a long white robe appeared. I briefly ducked behind the chair as my heart pounded wildly. I had heard throughout my life from many an adult and child a detailed description—imagined or not—of St. Nicholas. And I had seen many renditions of him on the walls of churches. All seemed to confirm that he was just like the old man outside my door. How thrilled I was for Giovanna that he had finally returned. But as I slowly raised my head to peer out the window, as I watched him gaze down at the boot, I frowned at the decrepit condition in which he seemed to be. St. Nicholas was supposed to be a healthy man. The long staff he reportedly carried symbolized his holy stature and power, not used, as this man did, as a walking aid. Furthermore, he wore a floppy hat with a white feather, like some common vagabond.

"But then the old man did something that tradition said he would do: he reached into a leather pouch fastened to his belt and dropped a gift into Giovanna's boot. But it wasn't the gold coins of legend. Rather, this gift was a glowing orb of an unusual color. Still hunched over, the old man turned to look behind him, then slowly stood as high as his frail body allowed. But as he did, he looked directly at me, and I let out a startled yelp as I saw the stitched lid of his missing right eye. Our gazes locked for a moment, but it seemed like forever. He showed no surprise or anger, as if he knew all along that I had been spying upon him. But I felt terrified. St. Nicholas he was not. So who was he then—another manifestation of evil? I recalled the strange Christmas tale my mother once told me, based on the myths of the *pagano*. And I remembered the one she called Wotan, leader of a devilish Horde in search of men's souls, and whose name has been immortalized within our own language. Unlike my encounter with the thing, I feared this man's presence—that he would barge through the door or crash through the window, lash out at me, and carry me away. But the old man made no such threatening moves. Instead, he calmly turned and disappeared into the gloom.

"I remained motionless, unsure what to do. But my protective nature commanded me to go outside and check for danger. I withdrew from the chair and opened the door, looking for signs of the old man. Then I stared down at the glowing orb in Giovanna's boot. No gold coins had been left there. I hesitated to touch the orb, but its intense purple hue made it irresistible. After removing the orb, I stared in wonder at its beauty. Of course, I had held orbs in my hand before. And although this one did not feel any heavier or warmer than the others did, I sensed a strange power within. The orbs had always been a mystery to us. Like a seasonal, magical fruit, they only appeared in December with all the other supernatural occurrences. Not even the priests could fully explain them, other than as a miracle to honor the Savior's birth." She stared at Dr. Samuele. "I don't believe I've ever heard you speculate about their existence, Doctor."

"Yes, madam, I will concede: seeds, as well as fruits, are seasonal," Dr. Samuele said with a mild sarcasm. "But the orbs' light emissions have never been a mystery here, I assure you, and there is no speculation involved—none whatsoever." He paused from his writing to gaze at her. "Bioluminescence is found in many living organisms—animal and plant—as is gigantism, which explains the Greatness of the Tree. But if you insist on calling the orbs 'seasonal magic'…" He returned his attention to his notes. "You were saying something about the old man and the odd-colored orb?"

Matteo snuck a knowing glance at Chris.

"Yes," Alessandra said with a respectful tone. "Tossing all wonder aside, I began to question the intent of the gift. Vittorio had already had become prey to the white butterfly. Without my intervention, Cristofori probably would not have survived his encounter with the temptress. And now this gray old man had deposited something alluring and powerful into the boot of my youngest child. It fit the sinister pattern, and I became more convinced of his identity. Now, I feared someone wanted to take Giovanna from me."

Chris glanced at Matteo, who kept his intrigued gaze on Alessandra.

"I dropped the orb back into the boot," she said. "But I had no intention of ever giving it to Giovanna. In fact, I had become outraged that, on the eve of Christmas—my own child's birthday—some wizard with evil intentions was attempting to usurp this most beloved of all our holiday traditions. But before I could gather up the boot and bar the door, I heard a rumbling in the distance, well beyond the bluff. It was thunderous but persistent, and its strange nature froze me before the doorway. I did not immediately suspect a storm—not in late December. And there was no memory of the nearby Mountain ever coming to life. I knew of its legend, how it was so revered—and feared—as it always stood shrouded in mystery. But it was just legend to us, and nothing more. So my suspicions quickly shifted in another direction.

"As I stood there, I realized that the rumbling was growing ever louder, and that—whatever it was—it was rushing toward the cottage. Much to my horror, I heard the great immovable stones of the church tumbling to the ground. And then the trees at the far end of the valley began to snap. The air around the cottage remained oddly still. But the rumbling moved ever closer.

"Now quite certain that some type of freakish storm was almost upon us, I caught some movement out of the corner of my eye. Staring into the cottage, I saw Cristofori and Giovanna standing in the hallway. Each wore the look of dread. 'Cristofori,' I cried, 'hide your sister!'

"But before Cristofori could lead her away to safety, Giovanna rushed toward me. 'My boot!' she shouted, and she was upon me. I tried to snatch the boot away from her, but her desire to attain her long-awaited gift was too great. The ground vibrated from the terrible rumbling, and the trees near the cottage began shaking and falling. We ran into the hallway, desperate for some shelter.

"I followed the children into Cristofori's bedroom. They dove into the closet. But there was no room for me. So I dove to the floor and tried to crawl beneath the bed. That's when the roof crashed in on us.

"I don't recall what happened immediately after that. Something struck my head and nearly rendered me unconscious. But I do recall the terrible power of that cold, cold air, and the sounds—especially what seemed like rattling chains and, in the immediate aftermath, the chiming of tiny bells. I will never forget those sounds. They were much too deliberate, and out of place, to be anything but supernatural. But to this day, I have not been able to solve their riddle.

"When the rumbling ceased, I finally regained my full senses. But I was not overjoyed for having survived the Storm. My only thoughts were with my children. I cried out their names many times as I struggled to extricate myself from the wreckage. But their silence only brought on more fear. I heard the clatter of hoofs, from a lone horse. Had someone come to rescue us? Or to bring more harm? Before I could decide, the horse galloped away.

"When I managed to free myself, I stood in the cold unearthly calm, trying to get my bearings. The darkness was almost suffocating. I saw no ceiling or roof, and most of the walls were gone. It seemed impossible that what had happened—happened. But then I saw Cristofori sitting beside a smashed lamp with his sister in his arms. He was crying—such a rarity for him—so I knew immediately that something terrible had occurred. Giovanna looked like a rag doll. Her blue and lifeless body dangled limply as he rocked methodically in what was once his closet."

Alessandra stopped and drew in all her strength to halt her emotions. Then she stared at Chris with sad round eyes as the doctor and Matteo looked on.

Though images of the tragic event did not appear, Chris recalled similar moments from the old world, and could feel the terrible sense of loss his mother was reliving. "I'm sorry, I don't remember," he said.

"There is some good associated with your affliction," Alessandra said. "If only I were blessed in this regard."

"Why didn't you bring her to me?" Dr. Samuele said.

"I did not know what Cristofori already knew—that such an option was even possible. That you had stumbled upon our cottage during my pregnancy was always regarded as a miracle, given Vittorio's frequent absence and state of mind."

"I was collecting samples of the colored orbs," Dr. Samuele said. "Yours was the first cottage I came upon. Seeing you alone, in your condition…"

She nodded. "Don't misunderstand me. Cristofori had often claimed of his successful incursions into your village. But you have to realize, he—and Giovanna, for that matter—had very active imaginations, and I often had trouble distinguishing fact from divine vision and—yes, I'll be honest—from wishful adolescent thinking. When they were younger, they often regaled me with stories about an old saint who helped them plant cuttings of the small *sempreverdi bianchi d'ardore* that you see scattered about our land, to chase away, in their words, 'the evil darkness,' which, as you now know, became so prophetic. They even claimed to have been in some fantastic mountain chamber. The story of the saint seemed possible, too, though I had never seen this vision. Regarding the incursions, that was another matter. He often wanted me to witness his conquering of the West Bridge, but I refused to even entertain the idea. The consequences of his unsuccessful attempt were too great and painful to consider, and I never wanted to encourage it. He tried to convince me of his success in many ways, even describing in great detail the marvelous sights of the Village, your magnificent home, and the cottage on the bluff he insisted was waiting for us. But this, too, I attributed to his talents as a storyteller, and not as the truth. So when presented with the horrors of my daughter's lifeless body, there was no thought to attempt a crossing, let alone an attempt to contact you.

"What could you have done even if we accomplished either of these impossible things? Something horrible had struck Giovanna and snapped her neck, and left terrible markings. She was already gone. We wept and suffered the whole of the night, and in the morning, amid all the destruction in the valley, we took her, in her favorite linen dress, to the church for a proper burial. But this storm had been like no other, rooted in the evil that had been gathering and conspiring to bring about the very destruction in which we stood. The signs were unmistakable, and everywhere. The entire complex was in ruins. Even the graveyard was covered in rubble. And there was no one left to attend to our tragedy. At first, we went to the carpenter's shack to find a suitable coffin. But the shack, too, had been destroyed. But amidst the rubble, we saw a gilded burial box without the slightest scratch and no doubt meant for the child of a wealthy family. We were fortunate to find such a treasure in all the destruction. But I couldn't help but think that, somehow, it had been placed there, just for us. Since the rubble in the graveyard prevented us from digging a proper grave, I had Cristofori drag the box into the remains of the nearby side chapel. Parts of its walls had crumbled. There, we came across an empty sarcophagus. I had seen the chapel many times before. It was the resting place of church architect, a place where Giovanna herself loved to pray. But the tomb's heavy lid had been thrown aside, and the remains were gone. We put the coffin within, laid her to rest, sealed the tomb, and said some prayers. Then, with all emotion spent, we withdrew to tend to our terrible grief.

"It was an unbearable night, that first night without her. And it was evermore peculiar. The warmth and the fog, you see, had persisted, even after the Storm. But on that night, when we laid her to rest, the snow returned, it soft sad flakes drifting down upon us in a fitting tribute to our lost angel. I truly believed the angels in Heaven were crying even as they welcomed her in. Arriving at our battered cottage, we discovered something even stranger. In the Storm, the mighty oak by the pond had toppled, tearing up the earth from beneath it, leaving a cavernous hole. The tree itself was gone, except for its cleanly cut stump, turned on its side. And in that cavernous hole, a tiny evergreen had sprouted, and from its branches hung its glowing white orbs. I don't know if it was a sign, if it had anything to do with the children's story, or Giovanna's death. But I took it as such—her special way of telling us that she was indeed in Heaven.

"We might have lingered at the cottage forever, consumed by our sadness, had it not been for Caterina. Strangely, and yet in strict accordance with our agreement, she returned at midnight on Epiphany. But, as you know, we were not the only ones to suffer tremendous tragedy from the

Storm. For she had to endure the loss of her parents. Rather than wallowing in our misery and placing Cristofori's life in jeopardy, I decided to give him—with Caterina's eager blessing—the chance to prove his claims about the Village. I had to—there was no choice. The evil that seduced my husband, that had taken the life of my daughter, would be back to lay its unholy claim on Cristofori. This I was certain of. It was the one place on this Earth where I knew, if we were successful, we could live without fear—forever freeing ourselves from the malevolent forces that haunted our land. How he knew we would succeed, how we did, can only be placed on divine intervention. Even you, Doctor, must agree that our arrival here is a miracle, as no one from *L'entroterra* has ever accomplished the feat. But at the same time, I must live with a terrible guilt that, had I listened to Cristofori and acted sooner, we could have avoided the terrible tragedies that occurred on this most sacred day.

"I have tried to make some sense of the dreadful irony, that my daughter should die on the eve we celebrated her birth, His birth. I can only surmise that I, having survived, am being punished for a terrible sin I have committed. Perhaps I should have been a more loving and understanding wife. Perhaps I should not have been so eager to change my life. Perhaps I should not have deceived my husband. But there is no denying that whatever sin I have committed, it must be something so unforgivable, so unspeakable, it would warrant such a horrible punishment. What other explanation could there be?"

Silence abruptly fell, pulling them violently from the gloom. Suddenly Chris became aware of the warm sunshine, the bright blue sky, and chirping of birds. It felt as if they had just awakened from a nightmare. Alessandra was staring at Dr. Samuele, her sad eyes begging for absolution. The doctor stared back at her a bit stunned, though he appeared ready to speak. But everyone knew that whatever he said, it would be terse and clinical, lacking any kind of empathy toward her feelings or beliefs. Wisely, he kept silent for a while. Yet, her gaze remained locked on his, still pleading for mercy.

"It must be said," Dr. Samuele stated at last, "that when the Village finally understood, with your unexpected arrival, the extent of devastation this powerful storm wrought upon your land between the West Bridge and the Mountain, we did everything in our power to look for survivors, to do anything we could to help."

"Yes, doctor," Alessandra said, "I am aware of the Village's generous attempt at support."

"But your description of this storm, Alessandra," Dr. Samuele said, "at least of its terrible power, proved to be more than accurate. To this day, I don't believe any body has ever been found."

She paused, still looking sorrowful. "In that regard, doctor, we are truly blessed."

Chris rested his arms on the table and hung his head in shame. "I'm sorry—this is all my fault."

"No, Cristofori, I am the one who is sorry," Alessandra said, clasping his hand. "Now you understand why you mustn't ever return to that land. But I have no regrets bringing you to the Village, even though, in some ways, without the Church, it is a stranger place than the one from which we fled. You are my one remaining chance at salvation. And I intend to protect you with every ounce of energy I have. I can do this here—I have been given that chance." Then she looked at the doctor. "The Village has, indeed, become our sanctuary, it has been a wonderful place to heal our wounds. I had hoped that we could leave the past behind us, that terrible memories would not follow. But it is painfully clear to me now that I had hoped for far too much."

Chris smiled weakly at her, and she smiled back. But she did not understand his apology. She couldn't.

Dr. Samuele took ample time to scribble more notes, allowing the words of Alessandra's amazing tale to resonate within them all. The silence returned, and it was just as unsettling. Then the doctor carefully set the pen in the inkwell. "There is no doubt that the trauma of the past—particularly Giovanna's death—has deeply affected Cristofori. Given that we are upon the anniversary of her death only reinforces that most probable cause. But whether or not these mythical beings actually played a part in that trauma is dubious at best, and I must, as a man of science, discount them as such."

"I'm telling you the truth, Doctor," Alessandra said. "I have no reason not to."

"I'm certain that you believe in your veracity, Alessandra. And I'm not accusing you of deception. But you may not be aware that, since I took Caterina into my home, I have spoken with her many times about her days in *L'entroterra*. Her account is...similar, though I must say I had for a long time suspected that she was hiding something from me. But she has not described her experiences with the supernatural terms you employ. And you do know where I stand on that contentious subject. You are aware of my many ventures into your former lands—even during this so-called holy time. I must add, besides some unexplainable but innocuous natural phenomena, I have yet to witness the kinds of beings of which you speak."

"Then how do you explain the painting?" Alessandra said.

"Luminescence occurs naturally at low temperatures in a variety of ways. That you grind the white orbs for your paint sufficiently explains the cold body radiation of your artwork."

"I don't grind them."

"How you extract their unique properties is no concern to me."

"But I withdrew the apple from the canvas."

"So you claim."

"She's not lying," Chris said. "All those creatures exist."

Wide-eyed, Matteo said nothing.

"It's what I wrote about," Chris said, his gaze returning to the doctor, "what I allowed."

"You allowed this? So, you are the Creator, then? Is that what you'll have us believe?"

"I still don't know how to explain it. But my book has made all this possible."

"Produce it, then."

"I keep telling you—everybody. It isn't here. I can't bring it with me!"

"What about the Orb?" Matteo said to Alessandra.

They all stared at him oddly for his abrupt change of subject, and Chris was particularly annoyed.

"The Orb?" she said.

"Yes, the gift from the old man."

"I don't know. It must have been swept away with everything else."

"And the music box?"

His question seemed so strange that Alessandra could not answer.

"Matteo?" Dr. Samuele said with a low growl. Then, when Matteo was sufficiently intimidated, the doctor slowly withdrew his intense gaze and focused on his notes, though he was still visibly irritated. "And Vittorio's fate, Alessandra?"

"I haven't seen him since he last departed," she said. "I have not been back to the old cottage, and he, of course, cannot come here. My best guess is that the evil that plagued our land finally consumed him. It's as if the fog has absorbed him."

"And this anger your mother spoke of, Cristofori?" the doctor said, still engrossed in his notes. "Care to shed any light on this subject?"

The question caught him off guard. "Like what, sir?"

"Like, perhaps, the source?"

"I can't speak for him, sir, only myself."

"Then, by all means, speak."

Chris felt a need to say something—the doctor would not let him avoid it. But after carefully determining his response, he struggled to say it: "*Morte.*"

"Of whom?"

Chris rolled his eyes and sighed. He knew what name they expected, they wanted him to say. Why go through all the unnecessary motions? The question was just part of the foolish game, to get him to talk, to spill his guts in an embarrassing display of weak emotion for all the World to see—to get him to admit that she was dead. Which he knew she wasn't. This was silly—a waste of time. Now he became obstinate, and felt no desire to respond.

The questioning ceased as Caterina, also dressed for her serious role, suddenly appeared on the cobble drive. Wearing a tailleur with a tall, stiff collar and thin necktie, her long hair piled atop her head, Caterina held something in her hand. Everyone rose to their feet and waited in anticipation. When she made her way to the patio, Chris saw that she carried Lorenzo's brimless hat. He looked at her anxiously, hoping for a shred of good news. But she did not appear happy.

"We couldn't find him," she said, "only this. I'm sorry. There's too much destruction."

"Then they got him," Chris said, puzzled by the lack of emotion from Caterina and her father.

"Who's 'they'?" the doctor said.

"What about his parents?" Chris said to Caterina. "Do they know? Were they with you?"

"They were," Caterina said.

"I have to see them." Chris turned to Matteo. "Now can we go?"

"I'm not finished with you, Cristofori," Dr. Samuele said, laying a strong hand on Chris' shoulder. "You and I are going inside to work the rest of this out. And this time, there'll be no interruptions or stories of Old Ghosts." With his notepad clutched against his chest, the doctor pulled Chris towards the study's entrance.

"Go to the Village Bridge and watch for Giovanna," Chris said to his startled mother. "She's alive. She may be heading there now. She may find a way in!"

"Cristofori—not another word!" Dr. Samuele said. "Matteo, you stay here until I call for you."

"But, doc, sir, I really should go have a look. I know him better than anyone. He's really good at hiding from danger."

"Hiding? Is this entire Village in denial?" He clenched his teeth and drew in a sizzling breath. "Nobody leaves until I tell them to!"

While everyone withered from the forcefulness of the doctor's words, Chris took special note of Caterina's placid stare as Dr. Samuele dragged him into his study.

Chapter Thirty-Four

The Study

"Who are you...*what* are you?" Dr. Samuele said as he leaned over his broad golden-walnut desk, his large hands planted firmly on its sage-green leather top. The elegant stained-glass desk lamps on either side of the doctor offered a dramatic contrast to his wild glare.

Chris sunk in a deep-buttoned, red velour chair opposite the doctor, and his eyes brightened. He had been stunned by the suddenness of Dr. Samuele's rage—the kind Victor had made famous. But when he had entered the richly-paneled study—a maddening blur of double-hung oil paintings, oversized bookshelves, marble busts set on ornate pedestals, and small round tables draped in heavy tasseled cloth—Chris had anticipated that the doctor's anger would have subsided by now, and that he would have conducted a calm but probing psychological examination, complete with the same indifferent head-nodding and scrupulous note-taking used during Alessandra's session. But that anger, which had been simmering ever since Cristofori arrived in this New World, had finally boiled over, and now appeared unending. This session would be anything but typical. Chris glanced outside to the distorted, sympathetic faces staring back at him through the black diamond-shaped cames of the imperfect lead-glass windows, but his allies were too far removed to offer much comfort. "I don't know what you mean, sir," Chris said.

"I am a successful doctor, a respected psychologist, I am an accomplished researcher, astronomer, mathematician. I've published papers in the most respected journals, and I've lectured some of the brightest minds around. But now I'm supposed to abandon it all and capitulate—just like that—to some, some...demented schoolboy?"

"I don't know, sir."

"But didn't you just tell me you're responsible for all this—for everything that has happened, that is happening in this World?"

"Almost everything."

"Then explain yourself!"

"But I have been!"

Suddenly, Dr. Samuele's anger retreated, and he looked as if he wanted to cry. "How can you expect me to believe these extraordinary claims? Do you realize what you are asking of me?"

"Yes, sir," he said sincerely.

Dr. Samuele flopped back in his red-leather chair as if he had been punched in the chest. He rested his head on the top edge of the chair's high back, loosened his dotted tie, and stared blankly at the coffered ceiling. He took a deep breath. "I'm a man of science, Cristofori. Do you know what that means?"

"I think so."

Dr. Samuele rose, straightened his white waistcoat, and began to pace the floral carpet. "So as a man of science," he said, suddenly inspired, right hand extended forward momentarily, index finger pointing upward, as if he were giving a lecture, "I am required to use careful study and precise experimentation to determine, without bias, the make-up and the behavior of the physical world. *Physical.* That means matter—and mass. The things and events that you and your mother have described—they aren't possible. Devils, demons, angels, ghosts, and our very own *La Cometa di Natale*—I can go on and on. But these are all things that have no matter, that have no mass. They can't be observed naturally in the physical world or measured in the scientific way. That's because they only exist in people's minds and in the stories they write and the paintings they create—to help them explain things they don't understand."

"I used to think that."

Dr. Samuele came out of his trance, stopped abruptly, and bent over him, hands on his knees. "Good—that's good! So what happened?"

"I came here."

Dr. Samuele threw his arms in the air, and then they fell to his side. He flopped back into his chair and began tapping the desktop with his forefinger, steely eyes fixed on Chris. "Based on that last statement alone," he said with a calm and willful menace, "I could easily diagnose some sort of delusional disorder—even schizophrenia—characterized by fantastical beliefs of omnipotence or, at the very least, the possession of a great power. And no one with even the slightest medical background would or could dispute this." Dr. Samuele sat up, leaned forward, and, resting on his elbows, folded his hands over the desk. "But I don't think you believe you have any godlike invincibility. Nor do you believe this great power—which has allowed you to create an entire universe, mind you—does you one bit of good here. Am I understanding you correctly?"

Chris felt a pang of satisfaction and relief. "Yes, sir. I just want to find my sister."

The doctor absorbed Chris' declaration with an eye-opened alarm, which quickly mellowed, almost to the point of amusement. Then he kept silent a little longer as if to file the statement with all of Chris' other fantastic claims. "Quite an amazing concept, actually—regardless of its obvious insanity. Often, there is a fine line between the two. We could delve into it for hours, if not days. And yet, despite this fact, I really must press on. Such a pity." He paused again, looking disappointed. "I always regarded you as a clever young man—sometimes too clever, which requires me to keep a special eye on you, if you get my meaning." Leaning forward, he folded his hands on his desk once more and hesitated, as if to form a new tack. "Tell me, what do you think when you look at Caterina?"

Instantly, alarms went off in his head, and he grew nervous. "Sir?"

"What do you think of her, Cristofori?"

"Well, she's...she's pretty, sir," he said, although he could not comprehend where the doctor was leading him—or why.

"Pretty."

"Yes, sir."

"Very well. Tell me what 'pretty' means."

Chris shrugged. "Attractive?"

"So what does 'attractive' mean? What is it about her that you find irresistible?"

"The way she looks."

"And how is that?"

"Well, you know."

"Tell me."

Chris cleared his throat. "I'm sorry, but I don't really feel comfortable talking about this with you."

"Because I'm her father—the man responsible for her well-being and proper upbringing?"

"Yes. Yes, sir."

"But I'm a man of science as well, Cristofori, remember? I hold no bias. And you—you are my patient. And as your doctor, I have a responsibility for your well-being, which I intend to uphold."

Chris nodded, knowing he could not back out of this uncomfortable, science-sexy line of questioning. "Well, I like her long hair—"

"Her long blonde hair."

"Yes."

"Her long blonde youthful hair."

"Yes."

"Youthfulness, vitality—there's some powerful words for you, I'll wager. What else do you find attractive?" He seemed proud and encouraged, as if they were making progress, and steaming towards a miraculous breakthrough.

"She has a pretty face," Chris said.

"What's pretty about it?"

"Her eyes."

"Blue eyes?"

"Yes."

"Blue—and sparkling with youth and vitality."

He nodded.

"And her lips?" the doctor said.

Chris felt himself starting to blush. "They're nice."

"And powerfully inviting, but—at the same time—in a very subtle way. And everything about that face is well-proportioned in a decidedly smaller—with respect to our own—and non-threatening female way? The angels amongst us, to help us transform our angry, violent souls—eh, Cristofori? Doing what we want them to do. Just the way we bred them to be. You, of all people, should comprehend this."

But he didn't. "I guess," he said, out of respect.

Dr. Samuele shook his head. "You don't guess, Cristofori—you know. And do you know how you know? And I'm not speaking psychologically here. Did some teacher—did I—ever give you a lengthy and difficult reading assignment that you had to commit to memory so you could one day hope to recognize what a 'pretty' female face looked like?"

"No, sir."

"No, sir—no, sir! That's because you already knew, Cristofori. It's been determined, ingrained by years and years of experimentation and observation in the scientific way—our way!—written down over and over and over again with all the other successful strategies for survival and passed along to you, prepackaged for your instantaneous use as you continue the never-ending battle for survival. Unfortunately, it has its unsavory...attachments." He gazed around his study. "Do you see all those books?" he said, pointing right to the case of leather-bound tomes. "Somewhere, in a few of those volumes, you'll find a lengthy debate on this phenomenon. In a word, it's called 'instinct,' a fixed pattern of thought or behavior. Instinct—a foolish word. After all, how can you wrap your hands around such a thing? But it's there, consistently observable, especially in young men and women."

"I have a whole list of those words—in my book," Chris said, hoping to change the subject.

"Indeed, the book, " Dr. Samuele said. "We may have to compare lists someday."

"You'll have to fight Matteo for it. He wants to see it, too."

Unaffected by the feeble attempt at levity, Dr. Samuele stared as if he were calculating his next move. "And in this book," the doctor said, "are you explicit about your likes and dislikes regarding your world—and what you know, what you think you know as the truth? Would you say these are common themes?"

Chris paused. "I...I never thought about it that way, sir."

"No need to sound embarrassed, Cristofori. After all, what is it that humans have done throughout their brief history but decide and remember what is good and what is bad for them—and what they want for the future? It is the hallmark of intelligence." He paused, not seeming to care if Chris had a response. "But in the background there are laws that have proven themselves to work...that must be obeyed, and they decide what works and what doesn't. So we combiner the two...and get a new reality. After all, where else in this universe are the particles manipulated any other way?" He leveled his gaze at Chris. "Tell me what else you find attractive about Caterina."

Now Chris was in a full-blown panic. He had hoped the discussion would continue to trail off into another direction. But it was about to resume its uncomfortable route and onto a subject he definitely did not want to discuss. And then, much to his horror, he thought of Matteo's crude comments about Caterina.

"Her bosom?" Dr. Samuele said.

Chris felt the hot blood rushing to his face, nearly bursting from his cheeks.

"What does that tell you about her?" the doctor said calmly.

"She's a woman?"

His tone suddenly grew strong, almost to an angry shout, as he rose, planted his hands on the desk, and drew close. "And what is it that you so feverishly want to do with those eyes, those lips, this amazing bundle of womanhood? And why?" He held his right hand out, upturned, fingers splayed but curled, as if he were about to pluck an imaginary apple from a tree. "Why should you care if two apocrine glands encased in fatty tissue sprout boldly from a woman's pectorals? What is this grand vision really telling you? Hurry, Cristofori—the opportunity is there, and time is a wasting!"

With his face now fully ablaze, Chris' eyes widened, his sweating hands gripping the rails, his back pressing hard against the chair, which seemed to teeter. "Sir!"

"She can have children, lots of healthy children," he said, index finger pointing briefly in the air, "so you perceive! A very important quality to consider in a mate, wouldn't you agree? After all, how could we survive as a species on this Earth and under this set of stringent rules if we couldn't make healthy copies—better copies—of ourselves? And that's what it's all for, you see—one collection of atoms combining with another collection to make a new and, with some luck, improved collection. Atoms." He paused to think and then to smile. "And on an on through the brief history of time it goes. At one point, long ago, we didn't have much of that precious time to reproduce. The act had to be almost immediate, or our entire future would be in jeopardy." He stood tall, then turned momentarily to watched Matteo drift past the window. "Some of us are still battling that urgency, not understanding or perhaps not caring in the least the magnitude or the full consequences of their carnal pursuits. 'What's the big deal—eh, Cristofori? It's just sex. As long as it gives us pleasure—that's all that matters.' But the mind is so complex, and it remembers everything."

"That's Lorenzo talking," Chris said, the flames of his embarrassment dying, reduced to an itch. "I don't think that way."

But the doctor didn't—or refused to—hear him. He sat down and reclaimed his professional decorum. "When we finally reached a point where we had mastered the ugly matters of survival, and we could indulge for many hours each day in the kind of thought that has made us distinctly human—writing and art and science, for instance—we could be more selective with our mating choices, just as you're doing with Caterina. And so now, we've taken much of the luck out of the equation, and seized control of our future."

Chris felt the dire need to defend himself. "Doctor Samuele, I swear, I have never—" But then he saw the folly of his denial and he halted his defense.

"No apology necessary, Cristofori. It's not an indictment. I know you understand the reason for the wonderful partnership that has been established. Whether you remember or not, all your other adolescent schemes aside, you have been a gentleman with Caterina."

Matteo passed the window again, and this time he waved.

"But as I stated," Dr. Samuele said, "some of us handle urges better than others. Can't they give us another moment?"

"Yes, sir. Thank you." But Chris was confused about the timing and nature of Dr. Samuele's lecture. In the midst of all this turmoil, why was he receiving "the talk?" Or was the doctor offering a not-so-subtle warning about amorous advances?

"Now don't misunderstand me, I've done the dance, chasing my perfect, ever-elusive, and—perhaps—nonexistent angel. I don't deny the human emotion that has attached itself to and developed from this reproductive process—'love,' as we like to call it. It's made things much more civilized and desirable for all involved. But that, too, we can attribute to our ability to handle the challenges of survival, its laws still firmly in place in our

World. But the way the young use the term makes it a foolish word. After all, what do you know of the complexities of a real relationship? About bringing another life into this World, and nurturing it to take full advantage of the opportunity? There's so much more to love than finding someone attractive. And it never ceases to amaze me how a young man can elevate a young woman he barely knows to such an exalted status—as one who will bring him endless bliss, one he cannot live without. I, myself, am guilty of this crime. I married a woman who fell in love with what I could buy her, not my passions. To be fair, I will acknowledge that I chose her for the pleasures her beauty could bring me, so there is fault all around. But each time I tried to share my thoughts and ideas with her, I saw her eyes glazing over, and her intolerance and contempt building until, inevitably, she left me. I think she also understood this most important fact I am trying to impart to you. You see, love is the sweet harmony of physical and, dare I say, spiritual compatibility—not only finding a person attractive, but also appreciating who that person is inside. That is the essence of true love. I have no doubt that it can be wonderful, if you're fortunate enough to find it. So it is compatibility that you should be thinking of, Cristofori. Put that word atop your list. I'm certain that you and Alessandra have discussed this subject many times, knowing what your family has endured regarding your father. She is a very wise and caring woman whose advice you should always take to heart."

"Yes, sir, I know, and I do," Chris said. "But if you don't mind, may I ask you a question?"

"Of course."

He had to ask, because it mattered. "Do you really think that Caterina and I are not compatible?"

The doctor intensified his gaze. "What do you think of her, Cristofori? That is the stuff of your troubles."

Caterina appeared with Alessandra at the window. She shielded her eyes from the sunlight, then rapped angrily on the glass.

"Not now, Caterina," Dr. Samuele called out. "I said no interruptions."

But Caterina entered the study anyway. "What are you doing to him? Is he scolding you, Cristofori? Or giving more lectures?"

"Scolding?" the doctor said. "We're men of science, talking the language of science—isn't that right, Cristofori?"

Given the nature of the just-ended discussion, Chris found it amazingly difficult to look at her in front of Dr. Samuele. He began to blush again. And the more he blushed, the more he blushed.

Caterina looked a bit alarmed, and puzzled, as she stared at Chris. But then she continued her assault on the doctor. "From what I could tell," she said to him, "you've been doing most of the talking."

Dr. Samuele looked in bewilderment at Chris. "Sometimes I feel as if I've been plucked from a rational world and inserted into one that defies all logic—isn't that what you've been trying to tell me, Cristofori?"

Chris didn't know if the doctor were joking, or if he were suddenly being understanding and sympathetic. "Yes, sir."

"But we're in agreement, as men of science," Dr. Samuele said quickly, as if to cover up his last statement, "that a person cannot travel from one world to another, even though, according to mathematical models, the two worlds may exist, and are connected."

"I don't know about that, sir," Chris said, surprised by the doctor's partial admission.

Dr. Samuele's pleasant demeanor cracked as he held his hands outward. "You do, Cristofori. Science won't allow it—I won't allow it!" His raised hands clenched into tight, shaking fists. Then he gave himself sufficient time to calm his nerves. "Forgive me, I forgot," he said as his hands fell away, "that is your province."

"Father, please," Caterina said, "I think we've all had enough for one day."

"I know you are eager to end this session, my dear, but I am determined to see this through." He gazed once again at Chris. "So tell me, Cristofori, what do you know of that star?"

The abrupt change of subject startled him. "Which star, sir?"

"Is there really any other that instantly comes to mind? The one we can see in the daylight, of course."

"To be honest, I put it there."

The statement did not phase the doctor. "You do need to see it. Through a telescope, naturally. Then you can go off searching for your little angel, or whatever foolishness you'd like to waste your precious time on. Caterina?"

"Must we?" she said to her father.

"You know we do," the doctor said. He walked out of the study through an interior doorway that led to a long, dark hall.

Chris stared at her, dumbfounded. He didn't understand the hints and coded messages flying about. But in his confusion, Chris realized that it was the first time anyone confirmed—intentionally or not—what he knew as the truth about his sister. That it came from the doctor was the most astonishing part.

"I'm sorry, Cristofori," Caterina said as she held out her hand. "He's a terribly stubborn man, at times. This won't take long, I promise. Just go along with whatever he asks or says."

"But my sister...did you hear anything while you were at the ruins?"

Caterina frowned. "What do you mean?"

He sighed, thinking of his pledge to Matteo. "I'll tell you later."

"Then come with me," she said, her hand still extended.

Chris welcomed the opportunity to touch her, to reconnect, especially in light of the doctor's advice. But the worry on her face only fueled his apprehension. Finally, he reached out to her, and felt a familiar sensation. He could not hold back his immediate thought. "You're hands are always so cold."

"I know. You've complained about that often."

"Sorry."

"You know the saying: cold hands, warm heart."

But Chris knew from his own experience why hands were cold on warm, sunny days. So he had to wonder: anxious about what? He sensed he was about to find out.

Chris struggled to smile, and he was surprised that she did the same. Then they started for the observatory, to gaze at a famous star.

Chapter Thirty-Five

The Observatory

Chris and Caterina arrived at the end of the hall and stood before a set of narrow, floor-to-ceiling bronze doors consisting of four panels, each cast with a celestial symbol. Chris didn't recall the scene. Sandra had never painted such an image. The doctor's observatory had been included in some of her many Manor paintings. But it had always been in the background, behind the main house, and left up to the viewer to conceive its interior.

When Caterina pulled open the doors, the cool air that suddenly swirled around them felt powerful, as though it were holding them, and drawing them in. A natural light streaked through a giant slit in the cavernous copper-domed ceiling. Chris was stunned by the amazing size of the refracting telescope, cast in bronze, which he guessed to be thirty or more feet in length, and mounted on a black iron tower half as tall, on top of which sat a maddening collection of large black gears set at different angles, and accessed by circular black-iron stairs that led to a platform. The telescope was already pointed high into the bright blue sky. Green chalkboards lined the observatory's perimeter, on which the doctor had scrawled, over swirled erasure marks, not the precise coordinates of celestial objects in neat columns, but rambling and indecipherable mathematical equations filled with strange symbols, numbers, and letters. They covered every square inch of the dusty green boards, sometimes scribbled perpendicularly along the right edges of their wooden frames. Beyond the tower, on the far wall, was another set of tall iron doors stamped with celestial objects. Chris could hear pounding and sawing and a crackling sound somewhere beyond.

With his waistcoat removed, shirtsleeves rolled up, vest unbuttoned, and collar opened, Dr. Samuele stood proudly on the iron platform at the lower end of the telescope—bold and secure in his element. "What do you think, Cristofori?" he said, voice echoing. "It has an eighteen-inch diameter and it took nine months to grind the lenses. Did Alessandra ever imagine such an astounding thing?"

"I'll remind you again," Caterina said softly to Chris as they approached the platform, the sound of their footsteps bouncing off the curved walls, "he hasn't been himself lately."

"Who has?" Chris said.

"I don't usually invite just anyone into my lair," the doctor said, "but I had to make an exception in your case, considering who you are and what you're about to undertake. Not the best time of day for a viewing, to be sure, but it is remarkable the kind of clarity I'm able to attain on this, my favorite heavenly object. Speaks volumes about what you're about to observe, wouldn't you agree?"

Caterina gripped her skirt as they climbed the steps, their leather soles now stamping on the perforated metal of the circular stairs. "Your sarcasm isn't helping—or appreciated," she said.

"It's not being sarcastic, my dear. I'm merely speaking the truth. After all, isn't that what each of us should be doing?"

They reached the platform. Caterina said nothing.

"I know you're both in a hurry to completely decimate your lives, so I won't keep you any longer than I have to." Dr. Samuele looked at Chris as they stood around the eyepiece. "So, Cristofori, you've made it clear that you have no special knowledge of our famous shining star."

"No, sir."

The doctor squinted into the eyepiece, turned some dials, then pulled away. "It has been a fixture in the sky 'forever,' as the villagers like to say. Indeed, the history books and the astronomical charts have confirmed its existence since recorded time, just like any other garden-variety star, even though its intensity and proximity to our Earth gave it its unique daylight characteristic. It wasn't until recently, when I first focused my newly ground lens upon it, did I discover that our daytime star was anything but ordinary." With a sweeping hand gesture, he invited Chris to peer into the telescope. "Don't be concerned. It has a very powerful filter."

Chris looked apprehensively at Caterina, who still looked displeased with her father. Then he stepped up to the telescope. When he squinted into the eyepiece, Chris immediately thought something was wrong. Expecting to see a tiny sun against a dark, hazy background, Chris saw what looked like the remnants of an exploding star—bright and twisted clouds of yellow and orange light that streamed in all directions from a small black dot. Startled, Chris jerked his head from the eyepiece and stared incredulously at the doctor.

"Problems?" Dr. Samuele said, showing a self-satisfying calm. The muffled noise from the construction project continued to seep into the observatory.

Chris squinted as he looked up through the wide slit in the domed ceiling at the gleaming star in the bright blue sky. Then he gazed once more into the eyepiece.

Dr. Samuele turned some dials. "Concentrate on its center. That's the real story."

Chris watched intently as the black dot magnified. Suddenly, he realized that there was much more detail. The dot had a thin ring of light particles around its perimeter. Within that perimeter, Chris saw scattered light particles glittering against a black backdrop, and bands of what looked to be red and orange dust that swirled out from a speck of brilliant white light at the very core. "What is it?" he said.

"Science," Dr. Samuele said forcefully.

"Answer him!" Caterina said.

"I was hoping he would tell me," the doctor said.

Chris stared at the doctor. "Me?"

"You're the Creator, aren't you?"

"Father, stop," Caterina said.

Dr. Samuele glared at Caterina. "Stop? Stop? I've been as reasonable as I can be. I have sat and listened respectfully to everyone and to everything that has been said. And even now that I have finally accepted, or at the very least, come to tolerate these views—ones that you wholly support, I'll remind you—you want me to stop? No...no! My patience has come to an end. Now I will have my say! There's no one on this planet, in this universe more important than anyone else—not in the grand scheme of things. Our young suitor is not immune to this law. If you can think, if you can dream—if you can willingly move particles around inside your head—you have the gift. Where this gift comes from...that is the question! But no one here is God."

"You're just being stubborn and cruel—and now you're lecturing again," Caterina said. "You've already told me what that star is."

"No—only what I think it is. Big difference, my dearest one. Cristofori will attest to that."

"What?" Chris said. "What is it?"

"A hole in the sky," Caterina said quickly before her father could respond.

"It appears to be a portal," the doctor said, countering her exuberance with his professional demeanor, "and it is ejecting some sort of energy into the universe."

Dr. Samuele seemed to sense the alarm in Chris.

"You don't look well," the doctor said. "Care to amend your story? Or add to it?"

"Tell him what else you know," Caterina said to Dr. Samuele.

"It's only speculative," the doctor said, looking vindicated.

"I still think he should know." Then she turned to face Chris. "That's what he's been working on. That's what all these calculations are for."

"What?" Chris said.

"The hole in the sky," she said. "It's closing."

"Closing?"

"The portal," the doctor said, "is shrinking at an ever-increasingly accelerated rate. I estimate that it will have vanish before the end of the month—perhaps even in a day or so. When that happens, of course, the flow of its mysterious energy will cease. What those consequences are—if any—I can't say with certainty. I have never encountered such a phenomenon before. That's why I must finish as quickly as possible. But you may want to seriously reconsider how you are spending your time here, if one of the more dire options proves to be fact."

Chris stared at the chalkboards, but he could not hide the growing sense of confusion and panic he was now experiencing. He had little reason not to believe the doctor's stunning claims. Not even Caterina disputed them. So what were the consequences? No more traveling from one world to the other? Maybe not such a bad thing, now that he was certain Janey had arrived. But the thought of permanently severing ties with the old world was now oddly unsettling, despite his desire for such an outcome. It meant that the decision to remain was no longer his, and that he would finally have to accept the daunting challenges that this strange but beautiful World posed for him, with no opportunity for escape.

Then an even more disturbing thought crept into his mind: what if, after the portal closed, he no longer had any memory of his life in the old world, that he—all at once—became Cristofori?

"The very large and the very small," Dr. Samuele said as he gazed around at the chalkboards. "I will say this: the more I break them apart, the more I'm amazed at how they look so much alike, each a model of the other." He paused as he looked at Chris. Then he withdrew a chalk stick from his coat pocket and held it out. "So, care to shine some light on this extraordinary problem you see before us?"

Chris was stunned, and felt threatened. "The problem?"

"Why, the very nature of this World, of course. That truly is what we're seeking."

A familiar anxiety rushed through him as Chris tried to focus his thoughts on the here and now. "I can't do that kind of math."

"Oh yes, the mind of the artist. Forgive me. But I've never met one who needed mathematics to see. You don't have to know it to do it, Cristofori. Please, if you will—indulge me."

"He said he can't," Caterina said. "Must you humiliate him?"

The pity in her tone angered him. Just as the old world doc had challenged him to recall the details of the overcoat, the doctor's New World counterpart was challenging Chris' ability to perform under pressure.

"I don't believe he can't," Dr. Samuele said to her as he continued to hold out the chalk. "Cristofori? Show us the math. Anything you can add will be helpful—if you can find some space. Certainly, there must be something on your mind."

Chris snatched the chalk and descended the stairs, then found some space on a nearby board and scrawled the one physics equation he suspected that, since it was written in the Book, not only mattered, but—as the Star just showed him—had supreme relevance here:

$$E = mc^2$$

Chris placed the chalk stick in the wooden tray at the board's base, brushed his hands, then turned to gaze at Dr. Samuele. The doctor displayed the same smugness he expressed while watching Chris approach the board. The equation, each symbol, did not seem new to him. But then those great bushy eyebrows fell into an intense stare, his expression alternating from amazement to disdain and back again. Chris had no way of knowing whether or not the famous author was here, alive or dead in this Village, or in this World—though, according to the rules, dead seemed the likely answer. The famous author really didn't have to be here. It's not as if he established the rule, or created the energy. The doctor himself may have been the first one to scrawl it, and claim it as his own.

"There, you see, my dear?" Dr. Samuele said, turning with a flourish to Caterina, arm extended toward the board, his smugness now fully restored. "Straight from the hand of the Creator. Somehow, our young suitor knows what is at stake here. How elegant, and wise, striking at the very heart of the...matter. That is what you're suggesting, isn't it, Cristofori? I've wandered down the wrong path, and should start over? Or perhaps, that is as far as we need to go."

Chris had no idea what the doctor was talking about. But he had no intention of admitting it, not with this minor victory still shining warmly in his puffed-up chest. "I'll leave that up to you...sir."

"Some important lessons have not been lost."

"No, sir. Not there."

"Or here." He stared at Chris for a few uncomfortable moments. "And yet, as succinct as your equation is, it actually points directly at the greatest conundrum of them all, doesn't it?"

"Tell him what you're really working on," Caterina said to the doctor. "Just tell him."

Dr. Samuele became visibly annoyed. "Caterina—"

"It's just beyond those doors," she said, turning quickly to face Chris.

"Caterina, that is my affair—and mine alone."

"How can you possibly say—"

"Do not betray my trust in you!" The room fell into an uneasy silence as Dr. Samuele looked at Chris and tried to restore order to the World with a smile. "You may go now, Cristofori. I believe Alessandra and Matteo are waiting for you. Later this evening, I will send a driver to the Studio to retrieve that most famous of all her paintings. I would appreciate it if you would inform your mother of my plans and express my gratitude for her full cooperation."

Chris frowned. "Do I have enough time?"

"Time?" the doctor said. "Time for what, exactly?"

Chris became indignant. "To find my sister!"

"Talk with Caterina about her. That is not my area of expertise."

"Caterina?" Chris said. He glanced repeatedly at both of them.

"That's so unfair," she said to her father. "And you accuse me of betrayal."

"Best to keep this information from him?" Dr. Samuele said. "Is that what you're suggesting?"

"You hypocrite. I asked you—pleaded with you not to do this."

"We all have our wars to wage. I suggest that you return to your philosopher's theater, get on with your little Christmas pageant or tragedy or whatever it is you call it, have at it, and not lead him on any longer."

"Caterina?" Chris said.

"I told you—it isn't the right time," Caterina said. "And I'm not ready!"

"When, then?" Dr. Samuele said, sounding unrepentant. "On Epiphany?"

"That's not for you to decide!" Caterina ran down the metal stairs and stopped briefly to look at Chris. She had a horrible guilt in her eyes, one he never expected or wanted to see.

But before Chris could ask her a question, Caterina dashed from the observatory.

Chapter Thirty-six

Assessment

Chris chased after Caterina, who had already disappeared with an alarming speed through the set of doors at the end of the hall. By the time he burst into the doctor's study, Caterina had vanished. Spotting Alessandra and Matteo loitering on the patio, Chris ran outside to confront them. "Where is she? Did you see her?"

"Caterina?" Matteo said. "I thought she was with you."

"She was, but she got upset with the doc."

"Why, what happened? Where'd you three run off to?"

"The observatory."

"Stargazing? During the day?"

Chris backed away from the Manor until he bumped against the patio wall. Then he scanned the immense, ivy-covered façade. He had no idea what room she may be in—if any. And even though he wanted to, he did not dare re-enter the home to continue his pursuit. She was hiding from him and some awful truth concerning Giovanna, and didn't want to confront probing questions. He had a lot of experience with people like that. Forcing them to speak when they weren't ready would only cause more harm, and harden their defenses. But what could she possibly know that would cause her so much pain? Since Caterina had some specific knowledge of his sister, he needed her help more than ever. "Caterina!" he called out. "Caterina, please, I need to talk with you. I need you to come with me!"

Chris could sense she was peering out from somewhere. But the Manor's windows remained lifeless, its expression unfeeling.

"I can't wait any longer," Chris said to Matteo. "I have to find that Black Rider."

"No!" Alessandra said with alarm. "Didn't you hear anything I said? You need to stay away from there."

"I'm tired of all this. You don't understand what's happened to her."

"I don't?" Alessandra said. "How many times will you make me say it? She died in the Storm, Cristofori."

"And you think that's the end of her? After what you believe? After all that you saw at the old cottage?"

"She died and went to Heaven."

"She didn't go to Heaven—she's here!"

"Why do you keep saying that?"

"Because that's what I wrote. Because that's what she wanted to be. Because she called out to me!"

"When? Where?"

"Today. At the ruins."

"And what did you hear? Not her. What?"

"The chimes—from her music box."

"Where did you get such an idea?" Alessandra said, gripped him by the arms. "She never had such a thing!"

"But she did. We buried her in it!"

Alessandra looked on, her face racked with confusion and dread. "We buried her in a tomb!"

"This is hopeless," Chris said. He struggled from her grasp. Then he looked at Matteo. "I did what you asked. Are you coming with me or not?"

"Not now, Cristofori." Matteo glanced nervously at Alessandra.

"Yes, now. You want your precious Purple Orb, don't you?"

Alessandra looked horrified. "The Orb? No...no! It was lost in the Storm, Cristofori. Leave it be!"

"She has it," Chris said. "She's guarding it. She is its keeper. That's why it was given to her. You're the one who made that rule."

"That foul thing was not given to her as a gift—but as a curse. One fact about her death gives me comfort: Giovanna was spared the same fate your father experienced. You should be grateful, as I am, that the Orb is lost. Do not try to find it. It will only harm you."

"You don't even know what it does."

"And do you?"

Chris turned from her, but she took hold of his arm again before he could walk away.

"Please don't do this—I beg you." she said. "Just come home. People will be stopping by the Studio, looking for last-minute gifts. You can assist me with the showing and the transactions."

"No."

"Then later, I'll need some help with the Christmas dinner. You always liked doing that. I'll even let you sneak a few tastes of the whipped cream."

"No," Chris said, trying to pull away, growing tired, even contemptuous, of her familiar denial routine.

But she held him fast, her unpainted nails digging in sharply. "Tomorrow, we'll open our gifts and celebrate the good memories we have of her. Then we'll go to the Village square and listen to the music and the signing before we have our dinner. They always put on such a wonderful performance. You'll be there, too, won't you, Matteo?"

"Yes, ma'am," he said. His keen eyesight shifted between them.

"There, you see? Christmas—as we always want it to be. On Epiphany, the fog will lift. Then the danger will have passed and we can get some peace in our lives again."

"And Lorenzo?" Chris said. "What do we do about him?"

Alessandra bowed her head momentarily. "You can't go there, Cristofori. Leave the search to the others."

Chris looked at her grimly. "You know what that Storm was. You know they'll never find him. You just don't want to admit anything. But you will, when I find Giovanna."

When she seemed to realize she could not change his mind, Alessandra released her grip. Chris rubbed his arm, still feeling her sting. He glanced at Matteo, then headed across the lawn and toward the gate.

"Please don't do this," Alessandra shouted. "You're all I've got!"

And so now, they had come full-circle. But his revenge brought him no joy.

Chris stopped one last time, but not because of Alessandra's pleas. Instead, he turned to see if Caterina was watching. But the Manor looked on with the same indifference as the craftsmen continued their work. Chris walked on, sad but determined.

Suddenly, he heard someone rush up to him on the cobbles.

"You're breaking her heart...you know that," Matteo said, trying to catch his breath between his proclamations.

"I'm running out of time," Chris said. He trudged on, refusing to make eye contact.

"I thought we agreed we were going back tonight, with the boys."

"That was before I had my little talk with the doc."

"Come on, Cristofori, you're reverting back to old habits."

"I'm sorry, but I have to."

"You're talking like the World is coming to an end."

Chris stopped and stared at him. But he could sense from Matteo's sly grin that he was being sarcastic, and didn't have any understanding of the truth. "Something like that."

"Yeah, right. Always gloom and doom. I see where you get it."

"What's that supposed to mean?"

"You heard her story."

"Are you saying you don't believe her?"

"No, I do, I do. But she says there's no music box. And if there's no music box..."

"It's here—she's here. I heard it."

"What if Alessandra's right, and it doesn't exist?"

"So now you don't believe me. We're back to that?"

"We'll, me boy, you still have that memory problem. You know what I really think? I think it's Christmas Eve and all these horrible memories and feelings are coming back."

"And that again."

"Yeah, that again. Why don't you think it's possible? It's certainly the simplest explanation."

"Because you won't believe who I really am." He headed for the gap in the surrounding woods that led to the gate. Matteo walked briskly with him.

"Well, at least we know the Purple Orb is real," Matteo said. "Why do you think that old guy wanted to harm your sister?"

Matteo's true concern did not surprise him, and Chris appreciated the sentiment. "So he could capture her soul," he said.

"Soul, huh?" Matteo said.

"Whether you believe it or not, that's his purpose. He's the leader. Why he had the Orb, I can't figure out. It wasn't supposed to be a bad thing, just a source of power—protective power, from the Tree. And she was supposed to guard it. Somehow, that got messed up. All I know is that right after he dropped the Orb into her boot, the Storm hit—like he was using it to choose his next victim."

"He controls the Storm?"

Chris nodded. "Only now, he doesn't have the Orb."

"How can you be so sure?"

"Tomas doesn't know where it is, right?"

"So?"

"He's part of the Old Ghost's Horde...just as I always wanted them to be. And if the Horde doesn't know... Besides, the Old Ghost told me himself."

"When?"

"Lorenzo and I saw him at the ruins. He was looking for the Orb, too. If he had captured her, he'd have the Orb. But he didn't, so he doesn't."

"Wait a minute. What's the Horde have to do with the Storm?"

Chris looked at him glumly. "They're one and the same, me boy." He walked on, leaving Matteo in stunned silence.

"We never had a storm during a game—not ever," Matteo called out from behind.

"What do you think the fog is?" Chris reached the forest and stepped into the cool shade. He saw the gate around the slight bend.

Just then, Matteo ran up, seized him by the arm, and spun him around.

"Wait a second. Are you telling me that Tomas is—"

"So are the rest of them. I told you, they could have taken you any time they wanted."

"But they didn't."

"Because they're using you like they're using me, because they want the Orb."

Matteo stared blankly at the ground. His forehead glistened with sweat.

"Let's not forget: They have Lorenzo," Chris said.

Matteo slowly raised his head and stared at him. "You really think he's still alive?"

"In some form."

"And you're gonna go there now, by yourself?"

"They won't harm me unless I bring what they want—you know that."

"Why is it so important? What does it do? And why do they think we have it?"

"I don't know."

Matteo stared at Chris. "We gotta find that thing."

"I gotta find Giovanna. She was the last one who had it."

"Was it still with her...you know, when she died?"

"It should be, but I don't know for sure. How could I?"

Matteo turned toward the Manor. Chris followed his gaze to the patio where Alessandra stood motionless in all her Victorian glory, staring anxiously back at them.

"She would," Matteo said.

Another intriguing thought Chris had never considered.

"Do you think she may be hiding one last secret from us?" Matteo said.

"If she is, she'll never tell us."

"Maybe we should ask her anyway?"

"And what good will that do?"

"It'll keep you from doing something foolish again. I'm not going back there without the boys with a hundred lanterns, and neither should you."

Chris looked up at the bright sky and squinted, trying to see the Star. Knowing what he now knew, the idyllic scene in which he stood seemed so unreal, so removed from the awful truth at which he was staring. The tension wrapped tightly around his neck, nearly strangling him. "I don't want you to go with me," he said in frustration. "I don't think they should, either. Boys with lanterns won't survive what is waiting for us out there. You'll only end up like Lorenzo."

"Playing the martyr now, are we?"

"No, just being honest with myself."

"Oh, but you'll gladly get Caterina killed."

"She knows something about Giovanna that can help. Maybe more."

"Like what?"

"She didn't say. She didn't want to say. That's why she's hiding from me."

Matteo pressed his scowling face forward. "Listen to yourself, Cristofori. You're not making any sense. We have a plan. It's a good one, a safe one...a smart one. Let's stick with it. Go back home with your mother. Help her with her customers and the Christmas dinner. That'll give you some time to clear your mind and soften her up so you can ask those important questions. By then, who knows? Maybe Caterina will come out of her shell. Besides, you still have to search for that book. Some information we need to know might be in it. The night will come fast enough. Then we'll go looking for your Black Rider."

Chris growled with frustration. "This waiting is killing me. I'm running out of time. You heard Alessandra. That thing on the mare is out there. So is my sister. And Vittorio."

"We'll go there tonight. We have to. Tomas is expecting us."

"And the Purple Orb."

"Yeah, well, he's just gonna have to wait for that a wee bit longer. As you know, not giving it to him is what's keeping us safe."

"And if he gets impatient? You saw the Paintings."

"That's all they are, me boy."

Chris shook his head, then turned his gaze to his mother. She remained frozen in place, clutching her hands to her chest, apparently hoping for a miraculous turn. Yes, the portal was closing, but he still had time, if this World were indeed following his Story. Maybe he should give some to Alessandra—and Caterina—as well. He looked at Matteo. "Caterina needs to come along, too."

Matteo frowned. "You really want that?"

"I told you why."

"But we're still conducting business."

Chris stared at him in disgust.

"All right, all right—if she's willing," Matteo said, though he seemed to hope that she wouldn't be. "I'll come up with some kind of story of my own."

"That might not be needed," Chris said.

Matteo looked unflappable. "The light is still great, me boy. Don't forget that small fact. At least we've solved the Epiphany riddle, huh? The night she came for you—'her night'—to bring you in."

Chris nodded, but Matteo did not fully understand the challenge and the danger that lay before them. Neither did he. Yes, Matteo had seen the mask. He had even seen the alp. But he had never seen such a terrible sight as Åsgårdsreien. "Don't make me wait all night."

"I'll give you the signal," Matteo said. "Just make sure you're there."

Chris looked once again to the brooding Manor, to the patio, to ever-hopeful Alessandra. He hesitated, drew in a deep breath, then took a step toward her.

That's when Alessandra plucked his jacket from the back of the chair and came running.

Chapter Thirty-Seven

In the Kitchen

Wearing a red-and-green peasant dress and white apron dusted with flour, Alessandra stood behind a large wooden table, her high lace-up black boots firmly planted on the oiled planks of the kitchen floor. She stirred with vigor a bowl of cream with two metal forks she combined as a whisk, determined to produce the delicacy she had promised Chris. The table at which she worked had stout legs fashioned to withstand heavy use, the table's worn surface scored with knife marks from years of food preparation. From Chris' perspective just across the table, Alessandra, with loose strands of her gathered hair hanging across her glistening brow, appeared more like a feudal servant as she prepared a variety of foods for tomorrow's Christmas dinner.

The table centered the post-and-beam room, lit with many hanging lanterns. It was hot and a bit smoky, but also filled with the pleasing smells of a holiday meal he had not experienced since before she died. Directly behind her was the room's gaping fireplace. Iron utensils hung on black hooks embedded in the dark timber mantel. Within the fireplace sat a large cast-iron, wood-burning stove, which, to him, looked more like the antiquated furnace from their old bungalow, its black flue pipe running up the chimney. Earlier, after the last of the lingering Village shoppers left the Studio, and the doctor's coachman arrived to pick up the painting of the apple and some art supplies, Chris had been placed in charge of fueling the stove's fire chamber. And now that it was blazing, celebrated pies baked in the warming closet while famous bread slowly browned in the oven—all supplied from the naturally-growing, beaten grains and plucked fruits courtesy of the dawn-to-dusk cycle of winter-to-summer-and-back-again. Everything in the kitchen—the copper cookware hanging from the wrought iron hanger directly above her, the spices in apothecary jars lined up in the wall rack, the insulated wooden cabinet that served as an icebox—though not entirely unknown to him, was a direct consequence for her insistence, as old world artist and creator, on the old-fashioned, now curiously defined and manifested. Even her manner of speech was not immune to this desire. She now spoke with a formality similar to the doctor's, a manner which, in her previous life—because of Victor's tough-guy vernacular—she greatly admired, and tried to instill in Janey and him, of which he often complained about in his writings. But without any knowledge of her former ways or modern conveniences, she sounded normal and looked content.

Because of the lull, because everything appeared so routine, Chris suddenly found himself contemplating it all again, how incredible it was just to be standing here with her, how strange it felt to see her alive and thoroughly engrossed in a domestic activity she cherished, as if her death had never happened, as if they hadn't a care in the World. But his sister's absence wasn't far off in his mind, or in Alessandra's. Nor was the doctor's ominous findings and their potential consequences, or the nagging anxiety over tonight's coming journey, and the dangers he undoubtedly would face. He had hoped that the discovery of his New World diary would shine a light on the unsolved mysteries, or even offer a way to alter reality itself. But if the book existed, it was not in its traditional hiding place beneath his mattress. A search of his bedroom did not produce any results. Nor was the music box in the cramped and dingy cellar. That brought his hopes back to Caterina, and whether or not she would reveal her secrets and help him find Janey. He had yet to press Alessandra further about the diary or the Orb. The longer he stood there, watching her whisk the cream, sensing her contentment, the more difficult it became.

"Cristofori," she said, focused on the bowl, "be a dear and open a window. It's becoming unbearable in here."

Chris skirted the table and approached the double-hung window to the left of the fireplace. Before he opened the fastener and slid up the sash, he stared out between the frosted blue muntins and watched the glittering snowflakes drift downward in the ghostly moonlight, its significance not lost on him. A gust of wind kicked up and caught in a furious swirl a few of the remaining brown leaves on the ground. Earlier, while assisting his mother in the Studio, he had watched in amazement as the leaves in the surrounding forest lost their color, dropped from the trees, and curled up into dust with the waning sunset. It would not be long until the nightly blanket of glowing white returned.

"I'm thinking about spicing this up with some cinnamon," Alessandra said.

Chris turned to see her holding out one of the apothecary jars. She smiled with apprehension, as if hoping for his blessing.

"I know you like it plain," she said, "but it might be really good with the pumpkin pie."

But the strange mood born from the thoughts that had haunted him moments earlier was still with him, and he knew his expression could not hide it. She held the jar out a little while longer. But then she seemed to realize that all wasn't right, that he was still not the son she knew. Her smile dissolved, and she lowered the jar to her side. Then she faced the bowl on the table. "Yes, I think I'll give it a try. I'm sure you'll enjoy it."

Chris returned to his place opposite her at the table and waited for her to look up. But she kept her gaze on the project at hand. She removed the glass lid from the jar and dipped a small spoon into it. She sprinkled the cinnamon into the bowl, then grabbed a wooden spoon from the terracotta utensil pot on the table. She folded the spice into the whipped cream before finally making eye contact. The silence felt unsettling.

Out with it, he decided. "Are you happy here?"

She struggled to look cheerful. "Of course I am. Why would you ask such a thing?"

"I don't know. It's not exactly what you expected."

Alessandra frowned, but he understood her confusion. Still, he could only ask the questions that were important to him, and as he understood the circumstances.

"If you mean because of Giovanna—"

"Yeah."

"Well, yes, I wish we could have come here with her. You know of the guilt I carry. But I can't change what has happened. And if I dwell on it any more than I already do, it will only ruin what is left of the life we have here. I know you miss her terribly, Cristofori. Having this wonderful holiday to remind us of our lost certainly makes coping with it much more difficult. But you're going to have to accept it just as I have, or I'm afraid your anger will consume you as it did to your father, and I'll lose you as well. Do you understand this? Do you realize how sincere I'm being, how serious this subject is?"

He did. "Do you miss him?"

"I miss the good days with him—yes, I'll confess that. And I wish we could all be together as a family, with him as he used to be. That was all I ever wanted. I know this is hard for you to understand. He wasn't a good father, always being away. And I know you never felt much love for him. I don't begrudge you for that. He rarely expressed any for you. But not too long ago, he was capable of such emotion."

"I know."

Alessandra hesitated, and absorbed the revelation. "Life just got too tough for him. Instead of taking responsibility, he grew angry at the World, looked for people to blame, and that sent him down a path along which he could not return. As for now, it is good that he left us, for all our sake. I should have taken that step earlier—I see that now. But again, that is the sin I must live with, not you."

Chris could tell that she was uncomfortable talking about these difficult subjects again, especially after pouring her heart out earlier in the day at the Manor. That she was willing to talk at all was appreciated, especially since he did not know what would happen to him tonight. "What if we could change things—you know, the way you just said, with all of us together again?"

Alessandra smiled, but her eyes betrayed a sadness. "How are we going to accomplish that, Cristofori? You can't change the past."

"Did you ever see me writing in a book or a journal?"

She frowned. "The one you spoke of earlier, at the Manor?"

"Yeah. It's something I would have done every day."

"If you did, that is your secret. Why this question?"

"It's not important." But he could tell she didn't believe him. Quickly, he moved to another subject that had aroused his suspicion. "Can you tell me where you got your brushes? They seem very, you know...different."

"My brushes? You mean my artist brushes? Of course I can. From Caterina. She gave them to me."

"And where did she get them?"

Alessandra looked stunned at first, then annoyed. "I don't know, Cristofori. Does that really matter?"

"From the Village?"

"The Village? No. She gave them to me in *L'entroterra*."

"And you never bought any yourself. Ever." Chris couldn't understand his mother's irritable reaction to his line of questioning.

"When are you supposed to see Dr. Samuele again?" she said.

"I don't know that, either."

"What are you saying? Didn't he make another appointment with you?"

"No."

"But I don't understand. He wouldn't just send you away like this without further treatment. Maybe you didn't hear him when he asked you to come back."

"I don't think he has time for me right now."

"Don't be silly—of course he does. I'll speak with him tomorrow, in the square. We'll get this cleared up." She bunched up the dangling end of her apron and turned to open the oven, seemingly content to check on the pumpkin pies and avoid further questions.

But Chris was not willing to let the inquiry end. Which brought him to the most contentious topic. Instead of dancing around it, phrasing his question in a subtle way, he decided to blurt it out: "Is the Orb really lost?"

Alessandra closed the oven door and slowly stood up. But she refused to face him. "Yes, Cristofori—I told you it was. Why this obsession with it?"

"It's what got her killed."

She spun around. "As it will do to you. I'll say this one more time—and never more. You need to stay away from there and forget the Orb."

"And Giovanna?"

Alessandra slammed the spoon onto the table and sighed. "If you must? On Epiphany, not before."

"But I told you, she's not in the tomb."

"Tomorrow, we'll see the doctor."

"And if I find her, will you even want to know? Will you even want to see her? Or dare to?"

"Tomorrow—though it's Christmas—we'll see him," Alessandra said.

"Why can't you just think about it for a second instead of ignoring it—just for once! Why is it so hard? Don't you see what this has done to me—what it's doing to me now?"

Alessandra removed her apron, threw it on the table, and stormed from the kitchen.

Chapter Thirty-Eight

At the Window

The rapping at the window woke him, startled him, then filled him with a strange mixture of anticipation and dread.

After retiring early to prepare himself mentally for the perilous journey that lay ahead, allowing Alessandra to resume her cooking duties in the kitchen, Chris looked forward to his return to *L'entroterra* and the distinct possibility of finally discovering his sister's whereabouts. But he also worried that Matteo would not keep his word, putting private enterprise ahead of the search. He did not want to deal with Matteo's foolish game. There was no joy in the competition. It was just the naïve recklessness of youth in action. And he didn't trust Tomas, or the Old Ghost. Should they lose patience over an inability to secure the Purple Orb, Chris and the others could very well be facing the horrors of the Storm, which would also devastate many loved ones in the Village. He could only hope that the combined power of their lamps, as Matteo confidently expressed, would keep them safe, just as the evergreen at the old cottage did for him. Chris felt guilty, of course, for deceiving Alessandra. But now, with Matteo at the window, there was no turning back.

The rapping persisted, as he knew it would, and could not be ignored, even if he wanted to. Still dressed, Chris sprung to his feet and conjured up an angry determination. He would go along to the field, but he would not let Matteo get his way. He would stand his ground and insist that they immediately take up the search for Giovanna.

The window had frosted over, but Chris saw the shape of a head just beyond the glass, illuminated by the unusually powerful moonlight. A knuckle rapped cautiously on the window once more. "All right, I'm coming," Chris said in a low tone. He feared the commotion would awaken his mother.

Chris gripped the sash and flung it upward. Two slender, luminous hands reached around his head and pulled him forward until his lips met hers, soft and wet and moving, but oddly cold. His eyes were wide and his body tense as the soft kiss persisted. And then he began to panic. Here he was, still this fourteen-year-old, now caught in a more mature teenage body—and story—and she, even more mature, and accustomed to a much more mature response from a mature young man who knew what to do. He could feel his mind shifting, rational thought fleeing, as something deep, demanding, and unyielding took control. Then all at once—my God, the doctor was right!—he suddenly did know what to do, and he instinctively reached out to cradle her cool face and he melted into the soothing light that caressed them.

What a strange and magical experience, this kissing of someone he had desired for so long, and across two worlds. Until now, he had no idea how intensely pleasurable such a tender act could be. But now that it finally happened, he did not want to release her.

But then Caterina slowly pulled away from him. "Do you remember this?" she whispered, her lips just inches from his.

Filled with a strange new energy, Chris tried to kiss her again, but she gently placed two cold fingers across his mouth and stopped his advance as if casting a powerful spell.

"Do you remember how good you are for me, how you ease my troubled thoughts?" Caterina said. "Do you remember how I come to you each night, wanting to kiss you, wanting more?"

More? The word was strangely frightening, and sent his mind into another whirl. He desperately wanted to remember, but of course he couldn't. The irony was maddening: how appropriate that, though he was finally with her the way he always wanted to be, he had no memory of their love or intimate moments. Only the old world fantasies popped in his mind. But he did not want to lie to her. Did it matter? Did she really want an answer? Before Chris could utter something completely senseless, something that would send her retreating down the ladder with fatal disappointment, Caterina pressed her cold lips against his—harder this time, and with more passion, as if she wanted to become one with him and draw every particle of his being into hers. Instantly, he became lost in her light. The thought that she wanted to do this, that kissing him was such a desirable and righteous thing to do overwhelmed him. He never really thought that she, of all people, could ever think such things about him, of all people, that he would be in such a tender moment with her, or that she would be whispering such seductive words to him. It brought on a strange feeling of relief, and vindication. What seemed to be an eternity of self-deprecating criticism and hidden fears of rejection evaporated. Now, suddenly, the gratitude he felt for all that she had done for him in the old world poured forth with every other emotion. Now all those years pining away for her in the distance, unnoticed, did not seem so foolish. He could feel confident in his love for her, and in her love for him. This only heightened the intense attraction he felt for her.

All these gifts, just from one kiss.

Again, Caterina pulled away. "Thank you, Cristofori," she said with sad eyes.

"Thank you?" he said softly. "For what?"

"For all that you've done for me, for making me feel alive. That's all I want this night, this very special night. Can we forget about everything that was or will be and just enjoy this moment?"

"Forget?" he said. "But I have."

A smile spread slowly across her shimmering face. But then her expression grew serious, and wanting. She kissed him again, long enough that he forgot the confusion her words caused him, or what he wanted to ask her. All he could think was: *I don't want this moment to end*. But then she withdrew her lips from his, and the sadness returned to her.

"Did I do something?" he said, certain of it.

"I'm sorry, I know it's difficult for you to answer, but you must be honest, for all our sakes," she said. "This is such a terrible burden on me."

"What is?"

Caterina ran her fingers through his tousled hair. And then a tear trickled down her cheek, causing an instant flashback to the old world. "Why, Cristofori, why?"

His mind was still whirling. "Why what, Caterina?"

"Why am I the way I am?"

Caterina pushed herself from the window, and a great set of feathered wings—white, yet translucent—unfurled behind her.

Chris let out a yelp and fell backwards onto the floor. But his eyes never left the astonishing sight suspended before him. Caterina, all aglow, was draped in a sheer gown. Its skirt drifted around her long exposed legs. The strands of her golden hair floated down past her shoulders, then up and away from her outstretched arms as if she were immersed in the warm waters of a light blue sea.

"Forgive me," Caterina said. "I know I must be causing you much pain. But finally, I have come to you as I truly am. It is time." She streaked away into the cold night sky.

Time? Time for what? Chris scrambled to his feet and stuck his head out the window, only to see trail of lustrous snowflakes slowly descending to the snow-covered ground like the remnants of a comet tail.

Chris spun around, dashed from his room, then flew down the stairs. Slamming against the front door, he yanked it open and rushed outside. Then he peered up into the twinkling sky. Fat glowing flakes drifted down, adding luminescence to the existing snow cover as the trail headed over the Village.

Chris took up the chase, skirting the boulders, then down the path. When he finally reached the Bridge, some of the villagers who had gathered there were singing carols. They tried to extend their greetings to the crazy young man without a coat who stared wildly up at the sparkling trail of the anticipated Christmas Comet. But Chris did not acknowledge them. He sprinted past them all on his way to the Manor's gate.

Once beneath the portico, Chris attacked the front door with both fists as if he were trying to smash it in. Unaware of the late hour, Chris did not stop his furious pounding until the door suddenly pulled away from him. Barging in, expecting to see a phalanx of wild-eyed servants armed with clubs and canes, Chris rushed past Dr. Samuele.

"Cristofori," he said calmly.

Chris charged into the marble hall and whirled around to face the doctor, who stood there in his claret-red smoking jacket, looking almost amused, if he were expecting Chris. "Where is she?" Chris said breathlessly. "Is she here?"

He didn't give Dr. Samuele a chance to answer.

Chris streaked up the great curved staircase, two steps at a time, then down the long paneled hall of closed doors. There was no hesitation in his search, no regrets for his rudeness or wild methods. He tried each door. When a one opened, he gazed inside. When he found the room vacant, he rushed to the next door. If it was locked, he pounded on it and shouted, "Caterina!" When there was no response, he rushed to the next closed door.

Chris was halfway down the hall when Caterina stepped out from the end doorway. She adjusted her thick white robe and stood there. He ran to her.

Still wild-eyed, Chris met Caterina's unflinching gaze. She didn't say a word as they began to circle each other. Chris could not believe how powerful she now appeared to be, even as she assumed the soft feminine form he always envisioned and wrote about. He looked hard for any sign of apprehension or acknowledgement from her. But all she did was coolly stare back at him. And that told him all he wanted to know.

"Who are you?" he whispered, echoing the doctor's words, nudging along their burgeoning love story.

"*Io sono tuo*," she said softly.

"What are you?"

"I am yours," she repeated.

"I don't know what that means."

"Yes, you do, Cristofori—you know everything."

Caterina continued her little circling dance of denial with him, and Chris asked no more questions of her. He finally heard the words that he had longed all his young life to hear. But now he grew fearful of those words, unsure of his ability to handle the lofty responsibilities attached to them. So much had changed between them since that first passionate kiss at the window, given the extraordinary circumstances that had, just minutes after, burst before his disbelieving eyes. The speed of that change was breathtaking and sobering, involving so much more than obtaining that kiss. Now he had confirmation of what had been implied and stated since his arrival: In this World, Caterina the Perfect and Cristofori the Insane were lovers. They had been lovers. And they would undoubtedly be lovers for a long time to come, if the Star allowed it. That sort of relationship was far more complex than anything he had ever experienced or imagined. This one had evolved spontaneously and exponentially beyond physical attraction between mere mortals. Where would this bizarre union lead? How did it even come about? There was no correlating experience from the old world that he could recall, no thoughts jotted down in the diary that could provide answers. And yet he knew that—as with everything else—he was responsible.

"What are you doing here, Cristofori?" the doctor said from somewhere nearby.

Chris whirled around to see Dr. Samuele standing before the next doorway, his velvet jacket's cuffs upturned. He still seemed unusually calm, and waited patiently for Chris to speak. "Please excuse my rudeness, sir. I...I mean no one any harm. But I just had to see your daughter."

"Now? At this hour?"

"Yes, sir."

"And for what purpose?"

Dr. Samuele was back in his analyst mode, asking questions for which he already had the answers. Chris recalled the talk they had earlier in the day. He still didn't know how much he should reveal. "She knows things that can help me."

"I think I have already made that clear. So you're on your way to *L'entroterra*—without your coat, I might add."

Chris extended his arms and examined his shirtsleeves. But he did not feel embarrassed. "Yes, sir."

"In a hurry?"

"Yes, I am, sir."

"And do you think it is wise for me to let her accompany you on such a reckless plunge into disaster?"

Chris glanced at Caterina who showed no surprise or fear. "Only if she wants to. That is—"

"And do you think she should, knowing all the incredible things that you know?"

The doctor's question puzzled him. "I...I can't answer that right now, sir. I mean, I would never put her in any... I just need to talk with her first."

Dr. Samuele nodded. "Indeed, you do." He slipped his hand into a pocket of his elegant jacket and withdrew a gold watch.

Then, all at once, Chris realized that the doctor knew—he knew!—so much more than Chris had ever imagined.

"Cristofori?" the doctor said as he popped open the watch's cover.

"Yes, sir?"

Dr. Samuele stared at the watch, then at Caterina with that pervasive sadness in his eyes. He closed the lid and slipped the watch into his pocket. Then he entered the next room and carefully closed the door.

Chris fixed his confused gaze on Caterina.

"My father is right: you can't hide from the truth—not in this World," Caterina said. Her cold hand took his. "I need to finish telling Alessandra's story. And then I need to finish telling my own."

Chapter Thirty-Nine

Caterina's Dreams

"That other world you speak of, the one you call home, I have been there—in my dreams," Caterina said. Upon her lead, they sat on the marble bench in the center of the orb-lit atrium. "I hadn't given them too much thought, even though they seemed so real and so...consistent. I have had many strange dreams before. My life has been even stranger. So they had become more of a personal amusement than anything. But then, the other night, when you came back to the pond, and you made all those incredible claims..." She paused and stared at him with a strange and tremendous fear. "It was as if we had shared the same dreams. How could you have known—how? There is only one answer, but I, like you, still don't fully understand what's happening. Not completely."

Chris clutched her cold hands in his. And as he stared at her, listening intently to every amazing word, he still could not get over the even more astonishing event he had witnessed back at the Cottage, or who it was—what she was—he was trying to comfort. Having the marble statue of the angel towering over them only heightened his sense of awe. Unlike before, when Dr. Samuele stood in the same view, Chris now knew that the heavenly creatures were real. "The world I'm from is real, Caterina. It has...it has mass, as your father likes to say. I'm glad someone is finally listening."

"Just as my dreams were real," she said. That intense but puzzling fear was still upon her, in her quivering voice. She adjusted the thick collar of her robe and clutched its plush, rounded lapels.

"Why so scared? I mean, how can you be so sure you were in my world? What did you see?"

"I saw you," she said. Her nervous laughter quickly followed. But she also seemed willing to cry. "I'm sorry, I didn't mean it that way."

Chris smiled anyway. "I could tell what you were feeling."

"Giovanna was there, too. And my father. And Vittorio."

"So you knew he was my father—you've seen him here before."

"Yes, many times."

"What about Alessandra? Was she there?"

Caterina shook her head. "No, I'm sorry."

"Why are you sorry?" Chris said, taking a cue from the doctor.

"Something happened to her there."

"Something bad?"

"Yes."

Chris saw that Caterina did not want to speak the awful truth. "Had she died?"

Caterina nodded.

"That's right—she did. She had been very sick. What else did you find out?"

"You lived in this strange house just behind ours. Even the Manor wasn't the same. And the observatory was much smaller. We even had a pond with a bridge. I don't know what village we were in. I don't recall ever seeing one—just a lot of those strange-looking homes all jumbled together and connected by black roads used by these wheeled machines...something only my father could dream up. People rode inside them, like carriages. But I thought they were horrible. They were very big and powerful and moved very fast—too fast, really. And they were everywhere. I knew I had to stay away from them. I really did come to understand that."

"Those machines are real, too, Caterina—all of what you said is real. You couldn't possibly have dreamed it up."

Caterina nodded rapidly and gripped his hands tightly. Tears filled her eyes.

"What else—you said you saw me?" he said. He hoped that a quick change of subject would keep her fear in check.

"I did."

"Where?"

"At your house. It was daytime—and the snow was still on the ground. I remember coming to your front door and pushing a button to ring the chimes. And then you answered the door and let me in. You seemed much younger, and smaller. And you weren't my boyfriend. I was with someone else—someone I don't even know—and he was driving one of those fast machines."

Chris felt that anger rising, and he couldn't hold the words. "Why did you go out with him? You knew that would hurt me."

"But I didn't know, Cristofori—not as that young woman. But I see that here, in this World. Can you see why I find all this so amusing? But of course you can."

"Why were you there?"

"I don't know," she said. The tears began to rise once more. "Yes—to pick up a wish list from Giovanna...things she wanted from...from St. Nicholas."

"Like what? Do you remember?"

"Some other strange contraption," she said, and she wiped a tear.

"Was that all?"

Caterina pulled her hand from her face. "No," she said.

The tear fell from her fingertip to the stone floor. It crystallized into a tiny but complete snowflake with a hexagonal center, but it did not evaporate.

"She wanted some important things from you. She wanted to stay with you."

Chris snapped his head up to stare at her. "How do you know that?"

"I've already made that clear."

"Do you know why she wanted that?"

Caterina nodded rapidly. "She's sick, too."

"She's dying—that's why I brought her here!"

"I know, I'm sorry. I don't like your world. It's a terrible place."

Chris briefly held his hands to the sides of his head. "This just happened."

"What?" Caterina said.

"What you just told me—it happened right before I came to your world."

"Does that matter?"

"Don't you see? What is happening to me is happening to you." Chris pulled closer. "When you dreamt all this, did you know yourself as Caterina, or by another name?"

"I was myself."

"But were you called another name?"

She nodded.

"And did you remember anything about your life there?"

"No, only what I could gather from your mind."

"You could read my mind?"

"You let me in, Cristofori, and kept me there."

"Yes...yes—see what I mean? What about now? Do you still dream about that world?"

"I haven't lately."

"But you might—you will."

"That depends."

"On what?"

"If I go to the Chamber of Light."

"The *Chamber*?"

"Yes, the one atop the Tree."

Chris' eyes brightened. "So it does exist. You've been there!"

"Don't be so surprised. It is possible, for me. As I discovered, it is a very powerful and special place. And when I enter it, it overwhelms me with its light. That's when I dream of your world."

"But why did you go—"

"To help my father with his obsession."

"The Star."

"The hole in the sky."

"The portal," Chris said. "He knows it is the opening to my world—mine."

"As it is to this one."

"And your dreams told him so!"

"He also knows that the portal is closing. And it is."

Chris saw the worry in her eyes. "I'm not going back."

Caterina momentarily bowed her head. "You will. You have to."

"No, my sister is finally here."

Caterina nodded, but she could not hide her disbelief.

"What—why that look?" Chris said.

"When the portal closes, the Light in the Chamber dies."

"And?"

"Once that happens, the protective light from the Tree is extinguished."

Chris' brow crinkled, as he could not fully comprehend all the frightening consequences. "And then?" Chris saw in Caterina's nervous eyes that her thoughts were shifting.

"I never went to the Village to get help," she said.

"The Village?"

"Today...after Lorenzo disappeared."

"But you brought back his hat."

"Yes...I did."

Chris was befuddled, and he gave her a moment so she could explain herself. But she was reluctant to speak. "What are you trying to tell me?"

"I never wanted this." Caterina's eyes glazed over. She appeared to be coming under a trance. "A ghastly Storm is brewing, and there'll be nothing to stop it. Matteo is playing with a power he does not understand, as do you, back in your world. We must go to him before we're all overwhelmed by it."

"You know about the game?"

"I do—and the Old Mill...and the church."

"He's going to The Hinterland tonight."

"And so are we." Caterina stood before him. And when he looked up at her, Chris saw the great outstretched wings of the marble statue just behind her, seemingly part of her. At that instant, the unspoken fear he had felt for her safety waned. He once again realized how feeble he was in this strange World of his own creation. And even more remarkable, he now understood, as the doctor had tried to tell him, how much he needed Caterina to accompany him, despite their obvious "compatibility" problems. How he wished he were given the chance to address that troubling issue.

"We have to stop Matteo," she said. "They're just using him. He can't be allowed to bring those orbs into the Village."

"But what about Giovanna?"

"She is safe...for now."

Chris sprung to his feet. "So you do know where she is!"

"She is waiting for you, in her place of safety."

"The Black Rider has the box, doesn't he? Doesn't he?"

Caterina nodded, but a horrible guilt spread across her face.

"Where is he?"

"Waiting for you, as well. You know his role, what your mother told you back in your world, and where you can find him."

"But how did he become—" Chris brought a fist to his lips and shook his head. Then his hand fell to his side. He recalled the hateful words he wrote, how he condemned them all. "Take me to her—please!"

"I will. I must. But after you stop Matteo. If you don't, then the entire Village will be placed in danger—including Alessandra and me. And Giovanna. You can't run from this, Cristofori. As difficult as it is, you need to see this through and face your fears. All of them."

Chris had so many more questions, but the intense worry in her eyes convinced him that this was not the time. Being privy to his darkest secrets, she knew how to stoke his guilt. "You promised that you would finish the story."

"And we will," she said, "including yours."

Chapter Forty

The Plunder

Riding in a sleigh, Chris and Caterina arrived with urgency at the West Bridge. From the eerie light cast by the glowing pine, Chris saw the fog convulsing with a new and frightful power, gathering in a variety of grotesque forms that continuously morphed into increasingly hideous and threatening shapes of demons and creatures from nightmares long past—and then absorbed back into the fog. Already, he could hear a sporadic and angry rumbling far away, warning them of the danger that was building, and would surely approach. The blanket of snow that had slicked the skids was gone, so they had to abandon the sleigh in a mud patch just before the stream, curiously marked by a series of ruts they had followed from the Village. By now, Caterina's skin had started to glow, her clothing sheer, and the ends of her long brilliant hair began to drift about in the power that permeated the air.

Caterina handed him one of the sleigh's lanterns. "We don't have much time," she said. "Get to the field as quickly as you can. If it is abandoned, as I fear it might be, go to the grove and stop them from their harvest. They mustn't bring those orbs to the Mill."

Alarm rang through him, and he headed across the Bridge. He still did not completely understand her warning about Matteo and the orbs. Then he glanced back at her. Caterina remained motionless, and wary, as if she had just made a terrible mistake, but didn't know why. He held the amber light forward. "Aren't you coming with me?"

"I'm sorry, Cristofori," she said. "If I do—"

Her eyes widened as if something terrifying beyond him were approaching.

Chris snapped his head around to the mists. A tendril of fog lashed out at her like some giant sea creature. Caterina release a quick cry as the tendril began wrapping itself around her torso. But then she became strangely calm, and resigned. She did not struggle to escape its hold. The tendril wound tighter and tighter. She began to turn transparent.

"Caterina!" Chris said. He swiped his arm at the tendril. His hand passed through, breaking it apart. But it quickly reconnected, and held her firm.

"Don't be frightened or angry," she said, trying to be brave, "no matter what you see. Everything that transpires tonight happens for a very special reason. Now go—hurry!" The tendril yanked her violently into the fog bank, and she vanished in a brilliant flash of tiny, chiming crystals that quickly dissolved before falling to the ground.

Chris stood there for a moment wide-eyed, lantern held high. And he stared in silence for a long, long time. What had happened to her? Had she escaped its clutches by transforming? Was she taken away somewhere? Or had she become part of the fog? He had no diary reference to soothe him, only Alessandra's account. And that left him with questions more disturbing than the ones he was now considering. The fog had taken on an even greater power—one that even she hadn't suspected—and became more sinister, with the ability not only to watch, but to listen, to plot, and to lash out. He had to plunge into it nonetheless.

When he heard the distant rumbling, Chris threw all caution and fear aside and ran as fast as he could along the rutted, muddy path, hoping for the best, clinging to Caterina's last words, which offered the comfort and encouragement he needed. He wanted to believe she knew the future and the rewards it held. He just didn't see how that was possible.

Chris arrived at the fork. All the ruts turned left of the stone pile. Approaching the field, he heard more rumbling. But this noise was much closer, and far less ominous. He stopped just in time to see a series of white lights approach from the fog, followed by teams of horses pulling carts and wagons. They were filled with the red and blue orbs from the grove.

"Out of the way, Cristofori," the young driver cried. The wagon roared past him.

Another orb-laden wagon charged forward. "Thanks for showing up, *scatto*," the driver said.

Chris jumped out of the way. "No, wait—stop!" Chris shouted. The wagon disappeared with the others into the fog.

"We don't need you!" someone yelled back. And then he let out a victorious whoop.

More white lights and treasure-filled wagons approached. Chris stayed as far right as he could as he ran along the path, nearly running into the trees that seemed to jump out at him. Chris checked each wagon for signs of Matteo.

Chris arrived suddenly atop the ridge overlooking the foggy field. As Caterina had suspected, there was no game in progress, no swarm of lights, no screams of triumph, pursuit, or elation. Instead, a steady stream of lanterns and wagons thundered over the far berm and down onto the field like a glowing army of ants bringing back its plunder. Chris was dumbfounded. "Matteo!" he said.

A wagon thundered past him. "He's in the grove," the driver said. "Where were you?"

Chris streaked along the wagon train and quickly ascended the ridge. Then he stood in awe at the sight before him. The grove, once aglow in purple, was nearly darkened and smothered in fog. Only a scattering of orbs near the tops of the pines remained. Just ahead, standing in a wide lane and within a circle of white lamps, Matteo, in a fur-trimmed overcoat and black gloves, was busy writing on something resembling a clipboard. He looked as efficient and organized and in-control as ever. Chris ran to his side.

Matteo glanced at Chris. "Well, well, look who finally showed up. Brought the army I promised. Impressed?" He returned his gaze to the clipboard.

"What are you doing?" Chris said, nearly out of breath.

"Totaling up the haul, me boy. Someone has to keep the numbers. What happened to you? After all that preaching about me being late? I stood on that stupid ladder way too long. Thought for sure I was gonna get caught."

"You gotta stop them," Chris said. "You gotta bring them back."

Matteo stared at him. "Back? What, are you *pazzo*? Take a look around you. We got 'em all—well, almost all. I think the boys are exhausted. We can come back another time, now that we know your brethren won't bother us anymore."

"What are you talking about?"

"See them anywhere? They got a good look at our army and turned tail. Even that idiot Tomas character—ghost or not—ran away. Talk about an epiphany. I don't know why I didn't think of this earlier. A hundred-and-one lamps, their light fused together in one mighty and impenetrable glow, as if we held the Great Tree. The power of the light was never greater. Should give you partial credit for that since you forced my hand. Of course, we may have overdone it a bit. I mean, how in the World am I gonna get enough frames for this mother lode? But we can worry about that another time—that, and the Purple Orb, eh? Can't wait to see the results. The cat's out of the bag, so to speak. Word's gonna get around, now that half the Village knows about the orbs. But that's good, right? Nothing like free, word-of-mouth promotion. The grand opening—just in time for Christmas! Should stir quite an interest, far and wide—and fetch us a handsome sum each and every day. I can see them lining up already."

The last of the wagons passed by. The young driver called out: "one hundred twenty seven!"

Matteo frowned. He scrutinized the haul, then jotted down some numbers. "We many have to reconsider that figure," he said to the driver. "I'll make a note." Then he winked at Chris. "Gotta keep these young pups honest."

Chris grabbed Matteo's arm, and nearly knocked the pen from his hand. "Don't you see what you're doing?" he said.

Matteo seemed ready to respond in kind, but then he regained control. "Sure, I'm gonna get rich and famous. You can, too, if you just go along."

"You can't bring those things to the Mill."

"Why?"

"Because—"

"Because of your mom's tall tale? Come on, me boy. Don't you think it's time you finally snapped out of it?"

"It's not a lie—you saw those things. Even Caterina warned me about them. And you have no idea what she knows."

"Yeah, so? What are they going to do, jump out at me?"

"The light from the Tree is dying."

"Listening to the doc, I see. I've heard the rumors. He has no proof."

"He has now," Chris said.

Matteo frowned. "Even if he does—and I highly doubt it—what does that have to do with my paintings?"

"The fog got her."

Matteo raised his brow. "Caterina? When?"

"Tonight, at the West Bridge—just before she sent me here to stop you."

Matteo glanced around at the churning mists. Then his expression soured. "You told her?"

"She already knew."

"How's that possible?"

"You don't understand what she is. Just like this fog—and everything else."

"I told you not to mess around out here. Why did you even bring her?"

Chris heard the distant rumbling and stared toward the hidden Mountain.

Matteo shook his head. "Storms...at night."

"Just like Alessandra said. And Caterina. It's coming. You've got to get out—now! And don't do anything with the orbs until I get back."

"Back? From what?"

Then Chris heard the music box tune wafting through the fog.

The music came from the same direction as the rumble. The timing seemed too perfect, as if planned, as if the fog knew he were here, what he was looking for, and sent the Black Rider a message. He was convinced of it. But it also meant another chance to save his sister. She was out there, waiting. At the foot of the Mountain, or just beyond. Suddenly energized, he stared at Matteo and fought the urge to charge off. "Didn't you hear me?"

Matteo hesitated. He looked with eagerness at the slow-moving wagon train. "I can't just run away like some frightened schoolboy. My fledgling enterprise is exploding right before my eyes. I have tremendous responsibilities."

Chris clenched his teeth and dashed through the fog down the wide lane in the direction of the music.

"They're still out there, you know," Matteo shouted.

"So is my sister," Chris said. And he did not look back.

Chapter Forty-One

The Storm

Chris jogged, lantern in hand, along the wide lane through the remainder of the shrouded grove. The rumbling had stopped, but the fog churned and bubbled with that same ferocity, and he still fully expected it would lash out and swallow him whole, as it had done to Caterina.

All the while, the chiming beckoned him.

Chris listened to his labored breaths and watched as best he could for signs of danger—human or other. But he could draw no nearer to the chiming's source, which seemed to be floating away on the mists, pulling him deeper into The Hinterland, away from the Village and its light, and closer to the Mountain. He had not forgotten about the white mare and its rider. Unknown to him at the time, he had encountered it twice. Then Alessandra's story chased away most of its mystery, giving its rider substance and motive. He wondered when it would reappear, if it were stalking him this very moment. Stalking Janey, too.

Chris tried to imagine what he would encounter once he reached his objective. He recalled Tomas' threat. He hoped above all to see Caterina there. But as she had revealed at the West Bridge, this World was also built on dramatic surprises that did not seem to have their roots in his diary. Would the Black Rider be waiting for him, as promised? Maybe Tomas. The Old Ghost.

And the Monster, Vittorio. He knew that moment was coming, too.

The end of the wide land, and the grove, suddenly came upon him—a grassy rise strewn with sharp boulders and jagged outcrops. His legs became heavier with every stride as he began his climb. But now, finally, the chiming was becoming louder, as if anchored on the side of the Mountain, as it should be. His confidence soared.

Chris reached the top of the hill, burst through the boiling blanket of fog—and gazed in awe into a harsh new realm. Consistent with *L'entroterra*, the terrain remained wild and forbidding. But it had indeed evolved beyond Friedrick's gloomy visions and into Martin's even more ominous and tormented world. And though he had experienced this scene many times before, this time there was no doubt: it was real. And there was no way to blink himself to safety. The Terrible Shrieking Mountain, which from a distance had always looked smooth and placid with those drifting clouds at its benign peak, truly showed its monstrous side. The full Moon was there, just above the vent, shining its harsh and glancing light on the Mountain's craggy, barren face. It cast shadows in those deadly chasms, which seemed to be bottomless. The vent was gaping wider than ever—never angrier, still frozen in its eternal roar. It's time was almost here. The flaming orange glow from deep within illuminated the scarred inner walls. But no shrieking, just the music box chimes that echoed down upon him. He wondered again about Caterina, and if she were near.

Chris held his gaze into the glaring moonlight and saw the silhouette of a stocky man on a black horse. On a ledge high above where a small glowing evergreen shined, the animal stood sad and motionless, as if it were caught in the rain. It was hard for Chris to fathom that he and his sister had once made the dangerous trek to this terrible place. But there was the shining tree, marking the proof, and, very possibly, the entrance to the suffocating tunnel that led to Pandæmonium.

The long-coat Black Rider in the saddle bowed his head. He appeared to be asleep. The music, however, seemed to be coming from him. He trusted Caterina's claim that his sister was safe from harm. But this horrible sight strained that trust.

Chris held the lamp high and scoured the Mountain's rocky face, looking desperately for some kind of path or a series of natural steps that could take him up to the ledge. He selected a smooth outcrop on which to begin, then he painstakingly made his way, step by step, higher and higher up the face, gripping the cold, sharp rocks with his free hand. As Chris zigzagged his way closer to the ledge, the man and the horse did not move.

Chris was only a few yards from the ledge when he stopped to take one more look. Now he saw the solid black eyes of the giant horse glinting in the moonlight, and the familiar but putrid face of the rider, who was hardly sleeping.

"*La tempesta sta venendo,*" the Black Rider said, deep and subdued and confident, performing his primary role as he clutched a shrunken gilded box, its lid flipped open.

Chris didn't know what to make of the overall spectacle as a thousand confusing thoughts swirled in his mind. But he was certain that the rider knew why he had made the journey. "I've come for my sister. Is she with you?"

The Black Rider coolly shifted his frightening gaze onto Chris' lamp as the horse released powerful steaming drafts from its flaring nostrils, its well-defined pectorals twitching independently as it stamped in place. "Did you bring the Orb?"

Chris held up the lantern.

The Black Rider scowled. "The color of its light has exposed your obvious deception."

"I'm not giving it to them," he said emphatically. "You know that."

"And the Book?"

"I don't have it."

"Then your capture will bring the one who does." He tipped the gilded box. It was empty.

Now Chris had his answer. He felt angry, and betrayed. "I'm not bringing her to anyone."

The Black Rider flashed a wry smile, showing blackened teeth as he closed the lid. The chimes stopped. Then he slipped the box into his saddlebag. "But you will."

"Why are you doing this?" Chris said, trying to strike a compassionate old world chord he hoped existed within this specter, certain that some of his favorable writings about the man still had some power, despite the later condemnation. "I used to know you. You were a kind man, a man with a heart. I'm sorry for what I've done to you. I was angry. I didn't know... At least I've put you in a role where you can do good as well as bad. I want to save my sister. I need to find her. Will you help me?"

The Black Rider laughed sinisterly.

"Stop it—*stop it!*" Chris shouted. "Please answer me. I need your help! You always did before. Why can't you do it now?"

The sinister laughter continued, louder and louder. It reverberated out across the foothills and down into the chasms. Suddenly, the Black Rider's face convulsed and his eyes slammed shut, as if he were racked with pain. He let out a horrid cry that exploded like thunder across the face of the Terrible Shrieking Mountain, and Chris could feel the power of that wailing beating against his chest. He recalled another power—the one this man possessed in the other world, despite his kind demeanor. And now that he had become part of this great evil, it was ever more likely that *that* power—now enhanced—would be used against Chris. He did all he could to stand firm against the fear that coursed within, and quell the frightened voices that told him to run.

When the specter's torment ended and he opened his eyes, sadness settled over him, and he resembled the man Chris had known him to be, though he was still with the dead. "*Ti avevo avvertito,*" he grumbled, reminding Chris that he had been warned. "They fooled me into joining them, to create a deception, just as have they fooled you. Why didn't you listen to me?"

"But I didn't join them," Chris said, recalling the old world battle.

"They know what you want, what you intend to do, what will become of you. You've already given them the power they need."

"What power? The Book? The Orb? I didn't do anything!"

The Black Rider hung his head in silence.

"Why do they want the Orb?" Chris said. "What does it do?"

"To make whole all that is," he said, "the way they wish it to be."

But Chris did not understand him. Nor could he understand why Caterina had led him on, why she allowed him to come here and place his life—and everything he had worked for—in peril. Out of desperation, he said to the Black Rider: "What do I do now?"

"It's too late, Cristofori," he said. "They know of *your* deception, and they have grown tired of it. Now, as they have promised, they are coming for you."

And then the Mountain shook.

A great rumble echoed down from the gaping vent. But this time, it did not cease. Instead, it grew louder and more thunderous with every passing moment, and Chris saw the dusty rocks tumbling down the slope. Suddenly, the boiling Black Cloud began spilling out of the vent. It headed straight for him at an unearthly speed.

Wide-eyed and acting on impulse, Chris dropped his lamp. Its glass shattered, and its orb clacked here and there like a cue ball down the slope. He turned his back to the horror, and contemplated his next move. But he had to resist the urge to bound across the jagged rocks, some of which cracked and crumbled from the quaking. Even worse, Chris could not remember the safe path he had slowly pieced together just minutes ago. Before he could take a step, he realized with great disbelief that he was doomed.

Chris whirled around and faced the terrible Black Cloud. Its speed was breathtaking, its depth enormous. How small and insignificant he felt against such power. This is how it would end? *Why?* In those last inconceivable moments, Chris looked at the Black Rider. The horse had come to life as it pranced on the ledge, and the rider did all he could to rein it in.

"You have never seen a storm such as this," he boasted above the roar. "It's too late to run—even for the likes of you. How are you going to survive? Throw yourself into its darkness? Let the Mountain swallow you whole?"

"I don't know," Chris cried. "Tell me!"

The Black Rider snapped the reins as he dug the heels of his boots into the ribs of the fearsome beast. The black horse leaped high from the ledge. Chris turned away and cowered as he realized that the horse was about to pounce on him. But it landed with amazing precision atop a series of boulders all about him, and now towered over him. The Black Rider seized Chris by the collar. Then as the horse sprung from the rocks, Chris was pulled violently into the air. When they landed, Chris stood on the ledge in the glow of the dwarf evergreen.

"Stand tall and be a man," the Black Rider said in a low but forceful tone. "Their treachery knows no bounds. They will try to trick you again and again to get what they want. Do not give in!" The Black Rider snapped the reins, and he and the leaping horse disappeared into a chasm.

Now alone, Chris gazed back up the quaking Mountain and did as the Black Rider commanded—not because he thought he would survive, but because in those last frightful seconds it was all he could do. The edge of the racing cloud smothered the crags and the rocks before him, and then, with a powerful rush, overtook him and the tree. The roar in his ears was deafening, and the swirling dust blinded him. But the glow of the tree diffused enough of the rage to keep him from tumbling, and after the initial blast, Chris regained his sight. Now he stood submerged to his knees in a Boiling Black Cloud tunnel lit at the far end by the glaring full Moon. The Cloud percolated all around him, and pummeled his legs. And though the tree still managed to punch a hole in that floor, the Cloud had the evergreen surrounded, mere inches away, where it remained anxious. Chris sensed that the tree's light was at its weakest, being so far from its great parent, and rooted so close to the power that wanted to snuff it out.

Then, amongst the continual roar, Chris heard the haunting blat from thousands of animal horns as the phantasmic nightmare he had dreaded since his arrival appeared before him.

It seemed to be part of the Cloud. But as it rumbled ever closer, Chris saw thousands of dark horses with black-saucer eyes, their horned and half-dead riders brandishing swords and axes—the hooded, black-robed members of the old world Horde. And the Old Ghost, now as he truly was—he, too, of pagan legend, as Chris remembered—robust, in white robes and a flowing white beard, doing what he was destined to do: lead the frenetic charge. On the fringe of the roaring army, a new terror: small bi-pedal reptilians with hooked claws, grinning and salivating with their dagger-like teeth—visions from another cherished book, no less! They strode furiously and frightfully with the winged and horned demons that had tormented him his entire life, all taking pride in their hellish escort.

And it was their service, to be in such a role. Because the worst of the vision was rapidly approaching.

In its midst of the horror, atop yet another white mare with white-saucer eyes, rode another nightmare-creature Chris had long since feared and disdained. It was the hideously smiling man-goat, Vittorio. The line-of-sight of his menacing red eyes were already fixed upon Chris like lasers.

The phantom army parted as it overtook Chris—not because of the tree, but out of obedience to the one in the Horde who wanted Chris the most. Now he was isolated in the frenetic madness. With its anger aroused to furious heights, the man-goat snapped his chain whip and headed straight for Chris, its long black tongue flapping to the side with every stride of the mare's lightning charge. There would be no angry shouts between them. All that remained now was the final act never fully realized in another place and time.

But then Chris saw something that he truly had not expected, something that in all the fury managed to still his fear and crush his heart: the brilliant maiden with the long white gown and dazzling hair. She followed the man-goat's charge in her wagon, loaded with cowering mortals, one of whom was Lorenzo. This time, every detail of her angelic yet strangely tormented face was visible. But he could not comprehend how, nor did he want to believe that she had willingly become part of this nightmare.

The man-goat was nearly upon him. It sat high and confident in the saddle and twirled the chain like a lasso, ready to strike. Now Chris knew that the evergreen's protective light could not save him.

Chris stared at the tormented maiden, still wondering how she could have betrayed him. Much to his horror, she seemed to sense his dismay—shamed by her role in the unholy attack, humiliated that he had spotted her. And yet she kept on coming.

But as the chain hurtled toward him, Chris felt an open hand strike him like a sledgehammer between his shoulder blades, knocking him to the ledge. He stared up through the rapidly-closing hole in the Cloud. Matteo stood over him, next to the tree, a lantern in hand, the long chain wrapped around his outstretched arm.

"Stay down!" he yelled above the blats of the horns and the roar of the horses.

As the mare and the man-goat thundered past, Matteo was yanked off the Mountain. Then, as the maiden flew by, Matteo fell into the wagon while the hellish army continued its charge down the boiling tunnel. Chris lowered his head and clutched the lamp with both arms, trying to hide its light. Then he rolled away from the evergreen. The hole in the tunnel floor closed, and he lay motionless, and hidden, as the boiling cloud pummeled him, then grew weaker and less frenetic as the rumbling slowly dissipated.

At last, the Cloud retreated. When he caught his breath and what remained of his heart had settled, Chris looked up into the glaring light of the Moon and saw the Black Cloud disappear with unnatural speed into the vent as if the entire nightmare was in reverse. All of his fear had evaporated, and he just lay there, feeling foolish, used, and defeated. But another nightmare had taken over. This one was calm but surreal, and he just could not deal with the consequences. In one amazing moment, he had lost his best friend and his first true love. Soft whispers had suddenly become lies, and tender kisses those of contempt and deceit. The image of the Old Ghost and the glowing maiden, standing victoriously side-by-side, flashed in his mind, and a hidden anger exploded to the surface. He cursed his mother for her story and her vision, just as he cursed Caterina for her treachery. She truly belonged with the Demon Horde.

Despite all its terror, the *Wild Hunt's* appearance had been faithful to the terrible painting, its purpose loyal to Sandra's Christmas tale, and to his. But Kate's role in it astounded him. He had purposely kept her from the written fantasy that had evolved from all the paintings and artifacts. She had to be protected, despite what she had done. But then, from the start of this adventure, she was here. As were Matt and Larry. So it became obvious that writing about them anywhere in the Book put them in this World. Fine. He had accepted that truth. He had no choice. And then she came to him at the window. That appearance had stunned him as well, but in a good way. He had always thought of her as angelic. How could he not? But he never used that word to describe her. His thoughts and his wording about her had been calculated and precise—factual—to avoid any strong emotions that could create confusion or conflict or outright lies about her or him, which he despised most of all. So how did she assume the role of the evil temptress without the help of the dip pen? And how was she able to exist in the Village? He couldn't understand how things had gone so wrong. Now, all he wanted to do was return to the old world and forget that Caterina ever existed. But even as his mood reached its lowest point, he knew he had to stay. And he only had himself and a failed plan for his sister to blame.

It was a grave mistake to bring Janey here, to get her mixed up with all this madness. This New World was not Heaven, but Hell. And he would much rather face the daunting reality of illness in the old world over the horrors of this one, which he foolishly thought he could correct. If he could find Janey before the portal closed, he would bring her back and gladly let this existence drift away. But now, he had to find her on his own. And he didn't know where to begin.

Suddenly, the sandaled feet of a white-cloaked figure with a walking stick appeared next to him on the ledge. Without taking his eyes from the Old Ghost, now back in his usual decrepit form, Chris slowly rose to his feet, no longer caring for his safety. "What do you want?" he said.

"You know what I seek."

Chris laughed in disgust. He was tired of hearing and thinking about the damn thing. "I don't have it, okay? I never did. You gave it to my sister, and then it was lost in the Storm. If you want it so badly, find it yourself."

"I cannot."

"Yeah, well, that's too bad, isn't it? Even if I knew where it is—and I don't—I'm not going to give it to you. So if you want to call that Black Cloud down from the Mountain again, have at it." Chris turned and stepped from the moonlit ledge, choosing carefully his next few steps.

"Giving up your quest?" the Old Ghost called out.

"You heard me."

"What if it will not give you up?"

"I don't care."

"And your sister who awaits a miracle?"

Chris turned with a flourish, his eyes bulging. "What did you say?"

"Return to her bedside, if you wish. But death will follow you, and you will have failed her once more."

Chris was astonished. Was this part of the promised treachery the Black Rider warned him about? "How did you know...?" Then he fell silent, recalling that, just as Caterina had successfully slipped through the portal and appeared in his bedroom, the Old Ghost somehow had accomplished the same feat.

The Old Ghost glanced up at the Star. "You don't have much time. I must possess the Orb before the light disappears."

Chris was even more surprised to hear that the Old Ghost knew of the doctor's great secret. "And if you don't?"

"Then all that you once hoped for will be lost."

"What I hoped for?" The declaration sounded like a threat, so he would panic and do something foolish and emotional, like come to the Mountain to find a music-box angel. "Kinda frustrated that your plan didn't work, aren't you? Why do you want it so badly? What's it for?"

The Old Ghost stared at him. "Everything."

Chris thought of what the Black Rider said about the Orb. Neither of their statements made any sense. "You don't know where my sister is, do you? Because if you did, you wouldn't let me walk away from here."

The Old Ghost kept silent.

"So what do we do now? Set another trap?"

The Old Ghost glanced at the smoldering vent. "She will help you find her."

Chris laughed with disdain. "You really think I'm that stupid?"

"She is not one of them—not of her own accord."

"What?"

"And you would not be standing here if you had taken her warnings to heart."

"Oh, right—now it's my fault. And you're lecturing me about doing what's right?"

"Why are you so quick to condemn?"

"What's the problem? Don't like your role in the play either? I didn't make it up. It's from legend. And it's too late to do anything about it. I tried."

"If only you would."

Chris found the Old Ghost's statement comical, all things considered. "I don't want to hear it."

"That is your choice, one you must live with."

"Yes—it is."

"But remember, by leaving this World as it is, you will lose the love and companionship that you have always desired. And she will not be there for you when you return to that world from which you came."

"Good! Who needs her—here or there? She can do what she wants. She already has."

"Your anger consumes you."

"Doesn't that make you happy?"

"It does not."

"You're very kind and understanding all of a sudden. You really want that Orb, don't you?"

The Old Ghost remained unruffled. "Stay in this World and finish your quest. Now go to her, quickly."

"What—into the Mountain?" he said with a laugh.

"Ask her for forgiveness."

"*Forgiveness*? Are you kidding me?"

"Only then will you begin to receive everything you desire."

Chris shook his head in utter disbelief. More lies and deceit, to manipulate him, to trick him, to help them get what they wanted. But it was Matteo who was drawn in, not Giovanna. "Why are you playing this game? Don't you get it? I know who you are. You're doing exactly what you're supposed to be doing. We even gave you a day...so we don't forget you."

The Old Ghost ignored him. "You can find her in the Village."

"What?"

"Much work remains for her—"

"Work?"

"—work more difficult than you can know."

"Oh, I know all about the things she can do."

"She anxiously awaits your return. It is time."

Chris was astounded. Caterina had spoken these words, too. And Janey. "What did you say?"

"It is time."

Suddenly, he saw the light, and felt renewed, *energized*. "Where did say she was going?"

Chapter Forty-Two

The Machine

At the West Bridge, Chris recovered the horse-drawn sleigh. But he sat there for a moment, reins in hand, ready to bolt, and waited, his eyes fixed on the agitated fog as it crawled and boiled ever farther past the Bridge and into a land where it once was forbidden. He recalled every horror he had just survived. His last words to sister, that solemn promise spoken back in the old world, played over and over in his mind. So did her words about "seeing the light," the promise she had attached to them, and how—with that amazing formula, which already had appeared—those written words became part of this story. At least, that was his hope. Chris suspected that she would at last be here, or pass through here, on her way to the Manor. *When it is time, I will be there for you.* But after repeatedly calling out her name, and waiting for some answer or reaction to his fading echo—all the while listening to the ever rumbling Mountain—Chris urged the mare onward, quickly regaining the driving skills he needed to return to the Manor, and confront Caterina.

Chris' meeting with Caterina would be more than just a trap for *her*. It would be for revenge, as a final and gratifying confrontation, which he had always dreamed about. To accuse her to her face, to make her hear—with all of his pent-up anger propelling those words—what he had always felt but refused to write, not as a make-up episode between two naïve lovers. Dr. Samuele understood what and whom Chris was playing with. And finally, Chris understood the doctor's warning about his "daughter." Alessandra needed to understand, too, before he and Janey left, if there was time. And admit to the reality of this overwhelming danger, like the rest of the Village needed to do, so they could deal with it without him, if need be, and rescue Matteo and Lorenzo.

Back in the Village, Chris saw that the villagers finally knew something was terribly wrong, too, with their Paradise. They stood along the cobbled way and in the square, all eyes looking westward, as they listened in silence and for the first time to that angry Mountain. It was resting, regaining is strength for one last and devastating assault on them all. The merriment the villagers had displayed earlier had vanished. And now they held concerned expressions, even fearful ones, which was something they had rarely—if ever—showed. And that made this moment all the more frightening.

Even worse, the light of the Great Tree had turned yellow.

Chris wanted to call out to them, to warn them about the evil that was conspiring against them in that fiery Mountain Chamber, but instead kept silent. Where on this new Earth could they run to? The Old Ghost's last words came crashing in on him, and so did some of Caterina's, despite all their treachery, reminding him of his duty to the Village he cherished so, and which played so prominently in the Story. Now he realized that he and Janey would this night have to return to that Mountain to finish their Story, and do what he himself had commanded years ago with his pen.

Arriving at the Manor's portico, Chris saw that the front door was ajar, as if it were purposely left that way, as a sign. He leaped from the sleigh and burst through the doorway. But he did not charge up the staircase as he had done earlier in the night. Instead, he sought them out in the study, its door left open, too. But there was no one within. Undeterred, Chris slipped through another open doorway and ran down the lamplit hall into the observatory, its bronze doors already flung open. The cavernous room was cold, lifeless, and dark, except for a glowing blank canvas resting on an easel at the base of the iron stairs. The telescope pointed up through the dome slit at the Star, its resplendent image noticeably smaller and weaker as it struggled to shine. Even more intriguing were the blackboards. All had been erased, except for one that had been dragged next to the easel. It displayed a new equation no more than a few inches in length, and wildly circled numerous times:

$$\hat{\Omega} Y = \omega Y$$

An expression of joy, or anger? Victory, or capitulation? He did not recognize the formula. Then his intrigue deepened when he saw, on the small table next to the easel, a paintbrush and pallet, a bowl of radiant orbs—white, blue, and red—and a chart of the color spectrum, with black and purple on the far left, followed by shades of blue, green, yellow, and red. The panic he felt seemed to permeate the night sky, as if the Dark Power he had just survived was now drifting high overhead and ever closer to the Great Tree. He was tempted to call out to Dr. Samuele, but then he noticed a peculiar bluish-white light emanating from beneath the tall and closed bronze doors of the newly constructed wing. When he pushed them open, Chris detected an odd, sweet-and-pungent-and-toxic smell, like that of burning wires, or burning metal. Now he stared down another lamplit hall—this one with a vaulted ceiling. Halfway down the corridor were opposing wood-paneled double doors. The doors on the right were closed. But the ones on the left were open, and through that doorway the mysterious light glowed, accompanied by a strange put powerful crackling sound, like drops of water hitting hot oil. Chris rushed to the doorway and peered inside, nearly overcome by the heat, and blinded by the fantastic scene within.

Wearing a pair of round black goggles, a crumpled white lab coat, and the heavy brown-leather gloves of a blacksmith, Dr. Samuele, noticeably flushed and sweating, stood with his back to a row of giant, cylindrical dynamos along the far wall. Each machine sat on a thick wooden tie bolted to the floor, and had its own steam turbine fed by an enormous pipe that ran along the floor and through the right wall to an unseen power source. A thick copper cable connected the dynamos, which hummed and whirled loudly. That cable traveled up across the high ceiling then down again to the impossible contraption the doctor was intently studying, seemingly unaware of Chris' presence. Besides its own tangle of cables, wires, fuses, switches, and meters, the contraption featured a set of large, opposing electrodes—one protruding down, the other up—that looked more like giant stamens of an enormous flower. Their "anthers," the very ends of which were squashed and flattened, were enclosed in a large, clear glass globe, between which, within a gap no wider than a fist, two opposing streams of bluish-white electrical charges collided with a loud and constant zap into a tiny ball as brilliant as the Sun. It was the brilliant collision that the doctor was focused upon.

"I'd take all the time necessary to explain what these machines behind me produce," the doctor shouted as he kept his eyes on the zapping charge, "but I suspect you know much about the subject. In fact, now that I think of it, you probably consider them laughable and antiquated. But the device you see before me, now that's another matter." He pulled the goggles from his face and rested them atop his head. Then he wiped his brow with his sleeve. "You'll have to accept my apologies for the lack of a doorman to greet you. I'm afraid this contraption got me in over my head. Do you know the maximum temperature of a lightning bolt, Cristofori?"

Chris frowned as he partially shielded his eyes from the intense glow. "I don't—"

"Thirty thousand degrees centigrade," the doctor said, "hot enough to fuse sand into glass. Do you think I'm making glass out of sand, Cristofori?"

"I don't know, sir."

"You don't know—you don't know. You say that a lot, young man, but I think you know so much more than you let on." Once again, as he had done since they were introduced in this World, Dr. Samuele tried to regain his composure. "Ever try to punch a hole in the universe?"

"No, sir," Chris said.

"No—no? Of course you have. Isn't that what you've been trying to tell me? I modeled this part after your Story, you see. Oh, yes, I too can be an artist—just like you and your mother. What do you think of my creation, Cristofori? Looks a little unrefined, I know. Could blow a hole in the grand home you've granted me, if I'm not careful. Never mind what it has done to my finances. But it's our only chance. A few more billion degrees and I think we'll have it. Of course, once that happens… " The sarcastic smile fell from his face, and he looked as angry and concerned as ever.

Chris hesitated to speak, even with his urgent need to do so. "Is Caterina here? Did you see my sister?"

Dr. Samuele glared at him. "I don't wish to discuss either one of them," the doctor said. "I have much more important matters to contend with." A temporary composure overtook him as he removed his gloves. But then he threw them in disgust to the floor. He rubbed his bloodshot eyes. "What do you know of the human brain?"

"But sir!" Chris was in a panic, eager to tell him the terrible news. But he saw in the doctor's angry eyes a barrier that he could not charge through. He would have to play this game for the moment, though he was uncertain what the doctor was really asking him, or how to answer. "Not much, sir."

"That old response again. Ever see a diagram, a painting of the types of connections in the brain?"

"Yes, sir."

Dr. Samuele smiled cynically once more. "Well, congratulations—there's a real connection. There are approximately one hundred billion of them in your head, Cristofori, about as many as there are stars in the galaxy, and galaxies in the universe. I'm going to give you a little lesson now, doctor to patient, so you make sure you listen. Ready?"

"But, sir—"

"Each neuron has axons, and each axon carries electrical impulses. *Impulses*. Isn't that rich? The impulses travel to the ends of the synapse where chemical neurotransmitters are sent across a narrow gap to the receptors of another neuron. Even more interesting are the electrical synapses that send ions between membranes—especially how quickly they react to stupendous trauma. So when you have all this stuff firing all over that galaxy, that universe in your head, you get consciousness. Did that word ever make it to your list?"

"Probably," Chris said.

"I'll take that as a 'yes,' " Dr. Samuele said. "What about neurotransmitters and ions?"

"No, sir."

"Well, they're on my list, Cristofori." He put on his goggles and stared at the electrical discharge. "They and the things that create them make wonderful models to help explain the unexplainable and cope with the worst of all disasters. Ever wonder what they look like, I mean up close—really, really close, as if you were standing in one? Ever wonder if they open a door to another existence, through which everything here—and I mean everything—can flow?"

The mocking and child-like manner was unbecoming of him, and made Chris obstinate. "No, sir."

"I have," he said angrily. Dr. Samuele turned and flipped a switch, and the whirling dynamos began to cycle down as the sparks of electricity vanished. The goggles came off, then he skirted the contraption and seized Chris by the arm in a painful vise-like grip. "Let's go outside," he said as he dragged him toward the doorway. "There's something else I'd like you to see."

They approached the double doors across the hall, but Dr. Samuele did not stop to open them. Instead, he kicked them open with a powerful thrust of his booted right leg, splintering the doors around the latch. Then, through the blast of cold air, they stepped onto a snowy terrace.

Dr. Samuele shoved Chris forward. "What is that?" he said, pointing to the sky.

Frazzled and a bit frightened, Chris looked up at the fading star. "The portal."

"No, no, I mean all of it—everything you see!"

"The universe?"

"The universe," Dr. Samuele grumbled. "Don't you think that is the supremely idiotic word?"

"Yes, sir, it's right up there."

"Yes, sir, you do." He nodded a few times, then took a deep breath. "A tremendous debate is occurring within academia," he said, now adopting a tone suited for a lecture. "And this may surprise you. One side contends that the universe was created on its own, without the help of a Creator, or for any specific purpose, and that life evolved from an incredibly long series of happy accidents. That was the side on which I stood—that is, until your illness came along. Illness." He paused, but showed no emotion. "Now, some on the other side—and not the episcopal jurisdiction of your mother's faith—contend that the universe was created for a purpose...so that intelligent observers, human or otherwise, can exist, and that nothing can exist without being observed by these observers. I'll say it again in case you did not hear me: nothing can truly exist unless it is observed, with the human eye affixing its gaze on it like some magical beam of light, drawing it in, realizing it is there, and assigning its location. This helps explain the peculiar nature of your mother's so-called magical paintings—how she manipulates particles of light with her brush. The whole notion of a Creator is still being debated. So when the one side looks upon the night sky, they see stars and planets and galaxies—nothing more than a collection of gas and dust and the force of gravity as this Creator. Ever look at the night sky that way, Cristofori?"

"Yes, sir."

"Indeed. But when the other side looks upon it, they see a grand...thought. Thought. Interesting word, wouldn't you agree? Ever think of what a thought looks like, Cristofori, from a very small point of view, from within?"

Chris looked up once more and scanned the sky.

"The real questions then become: what thought...whose thought...what kind of thought, and what's its purpose? The maker of heaven and earth, indeed. Is there any wonder why the flowers follow the Sun, that all things would die without it—whatever that means? There does seem to be a purpose, wouldn't you agree? After all, why go through all the trouble, creating that spark? Or maybe that spark was caused by all the...trouble?"

Chris stared at Dr. Samuele, who now looked as bewildered and lost as Chris felt.

But then the doctor's expression grew sour, and he appeared vanquished. He turned away and started pacing on the terrace. Then he glanced up at the Star. "I assume you saw the canvas in the observatory. "

"Yes, sir."

"And the equation?"

"Yes."

"That was formulated after I returned from the Bridge."

Chris frowned. "Sir?"

The doctor stared at him. "After your mother's story, I felt an urgent need to examine the painting of the apple and its component parts in the scientific way. But that proved...fruitless. True to her words, I could not reach in and withdraw the apple—not here. So I decided to take the painting to where it could be...activated."

Dr. Samuele tried to hide the turmoil he felt inside, but Chris noted the anguish in the doctor's eyes. Just then, Dr. Samuele reached into his labcoat pocket and withdrew a red apple. He repeatedly tossed it up and caught it as it fell, and he continued speaking, as if nothing spectacular or revealing had just occurred.

"The deeper I looked into that glowing canvas, the more intrigued I became. It wasn't the fixed particles of the apple, but rather the haze...the stuff of dreams...the stuff of heaven and the soul, the Holy Spirit, or perhaps 'soup' is the best word...that is, the unpainted part of the canvas, which intrigued me the most. You see, as the new equation eludes to, those light particles of her canvas—the same kind that pervade this land, and as yet unassigned and turned into matter by the tip of her brush—possessed a unique quality. Each could exist at more than one point simultaneously." Then he appeared more lucid as he held the apple. "Do you know what I did when I returned?"

"No, sir."

Dr. Samuele took a bite of the apple, chewed on it, then swallowed hard. "I erased everything. Began anew. And then I performed a test." He wiped his mouth with his sleeve, then his gaze returned to the Star. "I won't confuse you even more with those details, since you are, indeed, running out of time. But I managed to split a beam of this light into two vertical slits. The results were recorded on a freshly created...canvas. That is how I came to my astounding conclusion. And so, you see, my initial assessment of our rather unique situation was in serious error. I must admit that I have become too specialized, like one of many creatures headed toward extinction. I finally understood that my bias had led me on a path to nowhere, that I had been fretting with insane detail over nothing more than the nuances of an otherwise precise word—like trying to count the number of angels dancing on the head of a pin. And so I did return to the beginning, just as you suggested with your elegant equation, and started anew. I have amended my prediction. And I am confident that, this time, my mathematics are accurate, and that my conclusion is irrefutable—evident by its own simplicity." He sighed, but kept his gaze upon the Star. "So the hole in the sky is closing and the light is dwindling. And when it does, the light from the Tree will be extinguished and we will be cast adrift as a permanent shadow—no substance, no certainty, just unassigned particles floating everywhere—all at once—on some artist's canvas of light, or, if you prefer, on the pages of a writer's glowing book, a whisper in a false void, all happening in the blink of an eye, as if everything were simply...a dream. For that is where we all appear to be." He looked blankly at Chris, and added nothing more to his dire prediction. "We're connected to something grand, eh, Cristofori? More than to the star-stuff, but to the light itself and its birth. It may acquire stuff, it may get rearranged, but it doesn't end. Matter to light. Light to matter. You've got to get in to get out? Is this how you see life and its purpose? Are we drifting about in the mind of God? A thought of God? His dream of us? For us? So we can dream? Is that what you see when you stare at the stars? Or, perhaps, something else?" The doctor now appeared like a demoralized child who had just witnessed a cherished fantasy crumble before his disbelieving eyes. "Why did you place us in such a hopeless void? Is this my punishment for daring to dissect God's thoughts? How is this even possible? But I know that as well, don't I? Just like you, like all of us, I have trouble facing the truth, so obvious yet so impossible to see, like the power that flows everywhere." He took a moment to gaze once again at the fading star, its horizontal and vertical spires pulsing but shrinking, all encased in a globular haze. His emotions seemed to settle as another series of thoughts entered his mind. "What an immense and energetic insanity, just above the thin layer of atmosphere that surrounds the tranquil Earth. This night sky…it's the same here as it is there, am I correct? Of course I am. He's so distant…and yet, there He is, right before us, a part of us, connecting all of us…and us, a part of Him. You're still a believer…in His image and likeness—yes?"

"Me?"

"That stuff, that…that Spirit, is still all over the place. Do you think the One who came down from Heaven—and 'down' is the right word, isn't it? And by the power of that Holy Spirit was born of the Virgin and became man…begotten—yes?—not made, one in being with the Father. I'm getting those words right, aren't I? All that now makes sense and seems possible, doesn't it, considering where we are? Do you think He really knew so long ago where we are, what we are, what we can do? And if He did…His kingdom truly will have no end." He paused again to stare hard at Chris. "So easy to push His memory aside, isn't it? Surrounded by the current landscape and all our woes, forgetting that He did walk here, and die here so terribly." Then the child in the doctor seemed to vanish. "So we draw in that energy—which powers everything—and churn it in our brains, creating particles not found anywhere else in this vast universe. And then we rearrange them the way we choose, to form another. Am I getting it right? Don't you think it's interesting how we feed off each other's atoms and ideas? There is an exquisite word for that, as well. After all, what is it that we have been doing—each one of us—ever since the moment of birth? Because, apparently, in the end, it really does matter what's in your head." But when he realized that Chris had no comments about his rambling proclamations, no answers to his tortuous questions, the doctor turned away and gazed dejectedly at the snow. "And yet I must go on, regardless."

Chris stood still, afraid to break the silence, as he watched the doctor walk toward the shattered doorway. Then Dr. Samuele stopped and refused to make eye contact.

"I didn't know your father, Cristofori."

Chris frowned. "Sir?"

"I never went to his December performances at the old church—never fully understood why this Village, even I for that matter, ever half-heartedly adopted these so-called 'holiday' traditions from your land, other than for their charming novelty or out of some subconscious desire to take a breather from the discomforts of reality. But now that *that* word is in serious question... " Dr. Samuele turned to him and smiled uneasily. "Ever wonder what original sin looks like, Cristofori? That is what you call it, isn't it?"

The usage of the term stunned Chris. "Well, I—"

"I will say this: whatever has seduced him, ravaged his brain, whatever, whoever, is powering that extraordinary storm—spiritual or otherwise—you should be aware that it has its roots in some thought that is very ancient, some thought that's in us all, that we have needed and benefited from, and yet have justifiably come to fear and despise. So for what it's worth, you take great care, and beware of the unseen force that will gladly help you raise your fist in rage—whatever you call the final manifestation you are about to face."

"I don't—"

"Your mother spoke of it, when she began her story. Caterina seems to think the confrontation will take place in some fiery lair."

Chris nodded. Still, he felt disheartened, frightened, wishing it were all a dream. "It's called Pandæmonium, sir."

Dr. Samuele faced Chris. "Pandæmonium. Yes, without a doubt, a most appropriate word. Oh, and I suppose I should play my part and tell you: your mother was here, looking for you."

"My *mother*?"

The doctor's tone was void of any real fear. "Seemed terribly worried. She left with Caterina. You can find them at the Old Mill. They are on their way presently, in the...wagon." A final pause, bowing his head, showing defeat and agony.

"And my sister?" Chris said.

From the doctor, another disingenuous smile. "You'll see me around—eh, Cristofori? Yes, you'll see me around." He took another bite of the apple, chewing as he stared, then he continued through the broken doors.

Chris stood there for a moment, speechless, thoughtless, allowing impulse to seize control. He bolted from the terrace and headed through the woods for the Old Mill.

Chapter Forty-Three

The Paintings

Chris followed the fresh wagon ruts in the snow as it led him from the Manor, past the Bridge, and along the meadow stream, where they became entangled with a host of other wheel ruts and footprints, as if he had come across the disorganized tracks of a retreating army. He did not know what to expect or how he would react once he arrived at the Old Mill. His mind was crammed with too many thoughts and questions and emotions for clear thinking as he listened to his own gasps, his quick steps on the beaten path, and the rumbling Mountain. But his suspicions of Caterina's evil intentions were never stronger, now that she had ensnared Alessandra. What was the point of that abduction? Why go to the Old Mill? And what were those paintings for? Combining those growing fears with the doctor's ever-dire predictions of their demise elevated his anxiety to a level he could barely manage, and weighed him down like lead. His throat tightened and his chest felt as if it were being crushed, making it even harder to run. But run, he did.

One disturbing fact commanded his thoughts as he drew ever closer to the Mill: as had happened to the Star, the once-powerful glow from the Great Tree had dimmed significantly—a cold yellow that cast a pale light on everything. The old world fear that he associated with this occurrence and had secretly carried with him was now apparent everywhere he looked, and crippled his resolve to defeat the even greater peril that now hung over this Dream World. Though he did not fully understand all that Dr. Samuele had told him back at the Manor, priorities—and tack—had dramatically shifted. Despite the great peril, he had to first save Alessandra from imminent harm.

As Chris streaked through the old-growth forest, the Old Mill came into view. Chris shuddered at how ominous it looked at night, like an angry jack-o-lantern, its interior all aglow. There was no army of wagons outside, just the one he knew too well—and the mare with the eyes, now able to grin here, now able to laugh. Wooden crates, filled with red and blue orbs, were scattered everywhere, as if unloaded in a hurry, and abandoned. The lone evergreen atop the dam was dark, having been stripped cleanly of its white orbs. Chris' eyes narrowed, his teeth clenched, and his determination to defeat her powered his final furious strides.

When he arrived at the entrance, Chris saw that the heavy door had been blown inward by some powerful force, its remnants strewn across the floor. He stepped inside and scanned the room. With their tarps removed, few blank-white canvasses along the far wall lit the room.

Then he heard a popping sound somewhere on the upper level.

Chris' head snapped around to the left and he gazed up at the doorway atop the rickety staircase. That door, too, had been ripped from its hinges, and a frightening glow emanated from within.

Another pop—then a startled scream.

Chris dashed up the swaying steps, stumbling at first, then bounding.

When he reached the second floor, Chris saw Alessandra standing with her back to a bank of blown-out windows, her fists clutched in angst against the wide lapels of her black topcoat. She stared in horror at rows and rows of glowing paintings, each containing a strange reptilian creature more hideous and menacing than the next, all with long thick tails, hooded red eyes, black blotches on porous red skin, curled black claws, and those black dagger-like teeth. They all seemed to be blinking, salivating, eager for their chance, for which they waited so patiently, to leap in all their horror into this beautiful existence. Gripping a small crate in one hand, Caterina—her human image restored—stood in tall black boots and long white coat midway down a long a row of canvasses, half of which were blank. Complete paintings of the creatures filled the remainder of the row. She reached into the crate, withdrew a white orb, then lobbed it into the next full painting. The orb popped, Alessandra screamed, and the reptilian image hissed and screeched before it dissolved into the pure white light.

Giovanna was nowhere in sight.

"What are you doing?" Chris said to Caterina.

Caterina and Alessandra spun to look at him, each in shock. Then his mother rushed up to him and embraced him, closed her eyes, and buried her face in his chest. He slipped an arm around her and held her tight.

"Oh dear God," she said, "what is happening?"

"Are you all right?" Chris said. He kept a wary gaze on Caterina.

Alessandra pushed away and stared wildly at him. "No, I'm not all right. Why did you go there? What are these horrid things? And what have you been doing behind my back? This is not how I raised you!"

Chris felt the burning guilt rising. "Never mind that. What is *she* doing?"

"I'm putting you out of business," Caterina shouted.

Alessandra clung to him as Caterina approached with fury in her eyes. It was impossible not to fear her.

"I've used the last of the white orbs," she said. She held the empty crate out before slamming it to floor, splintering its sides. "You were supposed to stop those greedy little idiots. But you really didn't want to do that, did you? Did you see all the crates out there? Apparently, you didn't have enough monsters locked up here, so you convinced them to get more."

"Me?" Chris grew angry at her ridiculous insinuations and high-and-mighty tone. "Are you joking? After what I saw tonight? After what you did?"

Alessandra stepped back and gazed in disbelief at both of them.

"I didn't do anything," Caterina said.

"Oh sure, right."

"Only what I was supposed to do."

"Yeah—lie to me, mess with me, then swoop in for the kill. So you and that Old Ghost thought she'd come to my rescue?" He quickly turned to his mother. "You know who she is, don't you? You saw what she did to these doors. She's—"

"The woman you wanted me to be," Caterina cried.

"That's not true," he said to Alessandra. "I didn't want her this way."

"Yes, you did," Caterina said. "It is written."

"Stop saying that. I didn't write the Story this way."

"Oh, yes you did. You put me where you put everyone after they hurt you—*didn't you?*"

Chris turned to her. "That's not true, either. And how would you know? You've never seen the diary."

"That diary has nothing to do with this!"

"But you just said it did!"

Alessandra shut her eyes and held her hands to her ears. "Stop it—*stop it!* Neither one of you is making any sense!"

But Chris was determined to get the truth out. "What are you up to? What's the point of all this?" His questions were for his mother's benefit.

"To stop these creatures from attacking the Village."

"She could care less," he said to his mother. "She wants the Purple Orb—they all do."

"That's not why we came here, Alessandra. The light from the Star is dying—so is the light from the Great Tree."

"What's that got to do with the Paintings?" Chris said.

"You don't understand what these creatures will do when the force that keeps them at bay is weakened?"

"Oh, dear God," Alessandra said.

"Yes," Caterina said. "Alessandra knows—she knows well. So does the Demon Horde. It's another way to destroy the Village should you succeed in quelling their Storm."

"You would know that," Chris said. "You're the one who gave her those brushes. Wanna tell us who gave them to you?"

"Alessandra, listen to me. We're running out of time. Haven't I always been a loyal servant? Have I ever tried to deceive you?"

"You did then and you're doing that now!" Chris said.

Caterina ignored him. "This isn't about the Orb or the Old Ghost or the Paintings—not really. It's about him."

"Me?"

"Yes, you—and your rage against me."

"She's the one trying to destroy this World."

"You're doing that all by yourself!"

Chris could see in Alessandra's tired eyes that Caterina was winning the debate, now that she spoke of that anger his mom feared so. Knowing what he would be forced to do if he did run out of time, Chris decided to give her *that* explanation. "Look, you have to know something, whether she wins or not, this World is coming to an end. Dr. Samuele knows. That's what he's been working on, all that construction—a machine that can help him escape, before it happens. And if it does—"

"That's not really true, either, Alessandra. This World may be altered, yes, but it will not come to an end."

"You trust him just as much, don't you, Mom?"

Alessandra looked bewildered. "I don't know what to believe anymore."

"I love my father," Caterina said to Chris. "He has been very good to me. And he is a very intelligent man—a brilliant man. But the things he claims to invent already exist in some other form, and occur naturally. And he doesn't know everything. How little he does know. But he's too stubborn to admit it. That's why he's had those artisans and engineers working on that ridiculous machine—just to prove his point. But he knew something was wrong with his equations and his understanding of this World the night you fell on your head. And when you suggested that you were connected to the true nature of the project, which he tried so hard to keep from everyone, you shook him to the core. You gave him the explanation—the opening he was searching for. He could have stepped through it. Instead, he slammed its door shut, and kept them working."

"Nice story, very touching," Chris said. "Quit trying to change the subject. Here's something you might want to know, Mom. I saw Caterina with the Old Ghost. You were right about him. You knew all along who he is, what he does. And, yes, Caterina's part in the Demon Horde. She was there the night Giovanna died."

Caterina's eyes brightened.

"Oh, yeah, she was," Chris said to Alessandra, finally seeing the path to victory. "Remember when you said you heard the chimes, when you saw me holding Giovanna? Well, guess what, guess *who* that was you heard?" Chris fixed his angry gaze on Caterina, who kept silent. "I know your ways—all of them...even the way they sound."

Alessandra stared in disbelief at her, apparently searching for words. "Caterina?"

Caterina looked at Alessandra and opened her mouth as if to speak. But she offered no defense.

Feeling vindicated, Chris said: "Want to tell us why you were there?"

Caterina's perplexed gaze shifted to Chris. The damning silence remained.

"You know where the Orb is, don't you?" Chris said. His accusation stunned him. But suddenly, it was so obvious, now that he had gone down this path. "*You* were the one who took it."

"Caterina" Alessandra said, "what is this?"

Caterina remained silent for what seemed like an eternity as she carefully weighed her response. Finally, she said: "Yes, Alessandra, I did take the Orb."

Alessandra drew in an astonished breath and held it.

But Chris felt no joy in Caterina's confession. It only caused more confusion. The anger he had held for her so long this night suddenly began to retreat with a familiar and debilitating speed. Now he felt exhausted and numb. "I don't understand. If you already have it, why go through all this—"

"I don't have it, Cristofori," Caterina said softly, sadly. "I am not its Keeper."

Chris felt his heart flutter, and he found it increasingly difficult to breathe. And just as quickly as his mood had swung, he understood the magnitude of her words. Though he had journeyed through so much darkness and endured so much anguish to arrive at this dazzling moment, he found it difficult to ask, afraid the opportunity would be snatched away, never to return. "Can you, will you take me to her?"

"As I have promised all along. It is time."

At that instant, Caterina turned a translucent green, and her great wings spread behind her. Alessandra did not shriek but remained silently in awe of the heavenly being standing before them, stunned by the amazing revelation, and seemingly relieved.

Caterina held out her calm hand to Chris. Now trembling uncontrollably, he reached out to her. When his fingers managed to clasp hers, her cold light immediately transformed him. Now flaring from green to yellow, they took flight.

CHAPTER FORTY-FOUR

The Chamber of Light

It was a strange sensation, flying high through the snowflakes and over the meadow, holding the hand of an angel. As a child, entrenched in the teachings, he had often imagined what it was like to be one. But there was no great beating of powerful wings, no sensation of weight or substance or air rushing past his face. He felt as if he were part of the yellow light, broken into particles of light, like the tail of a comet, oddly cold, yet still connected to his sense of being, and to hers. Below, he saw the blanket of white, the jagged stream, the dark carpet of forest that encroached on either side of the meadow, and the mountainous Great Tree, it too shining yellow, dwarfing everything, the top of which they were rapidly approaching. The beam of yellow light shining from the treetop spire was much narrower and contained small gaps that traveled quickly up and down its visible length, but which ended abruptly as it punched a hole in the ice clouds. The glow from the Chamber of Light had weakened and turned as well, and Chris saw the faint images of small structures within. Somewhere in the glow, he felt his heart beating furiously. He wanted to speak, to inquire more about their apparent destination, but the cold light that enveloped them kept him in a trance-like state that only allowed him to gaze in wonder, and permitted the clutching of her saving and graceful hand of light.

The entrance to the Chamber, an ogee arch, drew ever nearer, and its size surprised him. It was more than enough to accommodate her lengthy wingspan. When they settled upon the gray slate floor, Caterina released his hand and the unnatural glow left him, and he felt whole again as he began to warm. But he saw that she was exhausted, and that her once-intense yellow light had weakened to a greenish tint.

Chris looked around in amazement at the sights before him. This was not a place he had ever written of, never part of their fantasy. But he had often cupped the round glass that contained it and shook it to activate its floating magic. The "room" in which they stood was round and cavernous. It had a dome he guessed to be thirty feet high. It culminated at a small, round opening through which that shaft of light streaked down. The room appeared to be part of a cathedral chamber, but no frescoes or paintings existed, just plain, seamless stone, as if it had been carved out of granite and polished to perfection. On the far wall, perhaps another thirty feet away, was another ogee-arched opening through which the cool wind occasionally howled.

In the center of the Chamber, the brilliant beam of yellow light enveloped what appeared to be some objects resting on a pedestal altar. When he squinted, he saw that the pedestal was the twisted end of a tree trunk, about three feet high. A mass of shoots sprung up from its tip, spread out beneath the altar top, then up around the altar edges before tangling together in the center like a pair of opposing skeletal hands. There, they cradled an open, glowing book as thick as the Bible. The pages appeared blank. There was no pen of any kind to be found. Standing over the book was a small white statue of a youthful angel. In her cupped and outstretched hands, which penetrated the beam of light, she held an orb, also chiseled perfectly smooth from the same marble. Chris stared in bewilderment at Caterina, who kept her sad gaze on the statue. Its pose was undeniable. He swallowed hard. "Is that—"

"It is," she said.

"But is that really her?"

With no change of expression, Caterina looked at him. "It is."

Frozen out. But he never really wrote that, just thought it often. Still, he shook with anger and guilt. "And the book?"

"*Il Libro di Tutto*—where all the laws of this World are kept."

The Book of Everything. His disbelieving gaze returned to the statue as his quest for his sister had finally and suddenly ended. But there was no overwhelming joy, no cries of victory, only deep and piercing pangs of sadness, as if a knife had plunged into his heart. Chris approached the statue and raised his right hand, gently running his fingertips across the smooth face, her peaceful expression betraying a slight grin, but with eyes closed. His sister, no doubt. Unable to speak, unwilling to apply any reason, Chris looked at Caterina for an explanation.

"I removed her from the gilded coffin and brought her here immediately after you placed her in that sarcophagus," Caterina said. "She was still in danger of being captured. I had to save her. That was my role."

I never wrote that either. Chris glanced at the statue. "But how did she turn—"

"It happened that same night, at the West Bridge. I didn't even know if I could cross. I had heard the stories from those who were forbidden. I was one of them—or so I thought. But I was forced to do so, as if by another unseen power. I knew what you believed, and I believed what your mother had taught me. But I also knew my unfortunate role in this World. So I got out of the wagon and took your sister in my arms. Her body was still limp and lifeless. But as I began to cross the Bridge, I noticed two very strange things happening all at once. Her body began to turn into stone, and I began to glow. Every particle of my being seemed to separate and turn to light, as you see me now, and then I felt a power and a sense of peace I had never experienced. I thought at first that this was part of the fate that the forbidden experienced once they tried to enter, that this is what it felt like to die as all humans do. But then as I reached the other side of the Bridge and your sister's transformation had finally completed, I realized that I, too, had completely transformed. But instead of a true death, I enjoyed a new life, a new purpose, and I came to this Chamber with that in mind as I placed her in the very spot you now find her. At the time, I didn't know why she was like this, or why I was given new life and not her. But then I began to dream, and dreamt of your world. And then I found my answer."

"And what are you feeling now? Anything?"

"I could dream, if you want me to."

Chris shook his head. "She shouldn't be like this. Neither should you."

"How do little girls become angels, Cristofori? What is the curse?"

As his guilt and anger intensified, Chris stepped into the beam of light to examine the book more closely. When he reached down to touch one of the blank pages, his fingertip dipped into the book, as if it were made of a golden liquid light. He withdrew his finger quickly, and as he did, sparkling letters, numbers, and symbols trailed his hand like a strand of honey before breaking up into chiming glitter and falling back into the book. Wide-eyed, Chris touched the page once more—this time, ever so lightly. He created a ripple that momentarily revealed parts of sparkling words, sentences, and formulas as it spread across the brilliant surface. He touched the page again and watched as the ripple tantalized him again. But he could not make sense of the words or formulas, which seemed to be foreign. When he turned a page, the sparkling images trailed once more before settling down again. The new pages were just as blank and glowing.

Chris reached down and tried to slide his left hand beneath the book. He wanted to see if the front cover had any title or marking. But as he did, the spindly branches curled its tips, making a crunching sound. He backed away and stared with perplexity at the book. The cool wind reinforced the strange vision as it howled in his ear. "What have I done?" he said. His gaze found the statue once more. Then he looked at Caterina as his mind started to focus. "What about the Orb?"

"As you know, I took it the night of the Storm. It was the power they wanted the most—the power that they still seek. Once their plan has been carried out and this World is the way they want it, the Orb will cast it in a permanent shadow. So I kept it hidden, but at my side at all times, in my leather pouch, until that night at the West Bridge. Only then did I give it to the one chosen as its guardian."

Chris looked at the statue's marble orb.

"Yes, she is the one," Caterina said. "I understand that now. But that night, when we reached the other side of the Bridge, only then had her size diminished and she struck her strange pose. But when I stared at her delicate hands and noticed how they were cupped just so, I knew immediately what it was that she wanted and needed to possess. When I placed the Purple Orb in her hands, it changed instantly into marble and became one with her, where it would be safe from those who would use it for evil."

Chris sighed, his frustration growing. "Why didn't you tell me? Why put me through all this?"

Caterina hung her head in shame. "I did not want to go back to that horrible world. I wanted to forget that it existed. You seemed willing to accept her fate. Everyone did. I knew where she was. I knew she was safe. But then you fell, and I knew I would have to face the truth, as we all must do."

"So I didn't know."

"No one did. The light that shined from this Chamber made it impossible to see within. No one bothered to inspect the light. Who dares to stare at the Sun? Even my father with his fancy lenses couldn't see—it was much too close for the power of his scope. I thought that maybe you suspected, that you were beginning to understand. But you never said anything to me. I know what I did was terribly selfish. The guilt I felt was unbearable. But I was going to tell the truth. Don't hate me for it. You don't know what it's like there for me. I never wanted that existence. I never asked to be part of it. I just was. When I received my chance to leave, I took it. I had to."

"I'm sorry," he said.

His words encouraged her and she smiled weakly, even though her guilt remained as obvious as his. "But, really, what does it matter? You heard your father. This World, this Dream—or whatever it is—is coming to an end."

"No...it isn't. It's just the beginning, just...what is it you call it in your world? Practice?"

"Practice? This isn't a football game we're playing." He paused to stare at her. "How do you know about that?"

"I know everything you know of that other world."

"How is that possible?"

"I told you...you let me in." She briefly broke eye contact. "Did you see the color chart in the observatory?"

"The what?"

"Did you?"

The image popped into his mind. "Yes. Why?"

"What's the color next to green? Do you recall?"

"Blue."

"No, go backwards. Regress."

"Okay...yellow, then."

"And then?"

"Red."

"Yes, red—the oldest, the farthest away, the most ancient. Each of those creatures at the Old Mill came from one of the red orbs—two for every soul in the Village. As the Star grows dimmer, so too does its light—from yellow to orange to red. When that happens... "

Chris ran his hands through his hair. "I should have never helped Matteo with his scheme."

"Matteo? You were the one who set this whole disaster up."

"Me? But he's the one who—"

"This wasn't his idea, Cristofori. It was yours. You were their leader—you're the king of this heaven. When you lost your memory, Matteo staged a subtle little coup for his own personal gain. You taught him well. He was only following your lead."

"But he came back to save me."

"He did. He is like that, too, just as you are."

Now Chris' head was spinning as he tried once again to link both worlds. "But why would I do such a thing? All this, for gold coins?"

"No, not for wealth."

"Then what? Are you saying that I—"

"Intended to destroy the Village? No, Cristofori, it wasn't intentional. You were deceived by the terrible Dark Power that still casts it spell over *L'entroterra*."

"How do you know all this? Did I tell you?"

"You did everything you could to keep it from me. And since I had not been back to The Hinterland since we arrived in the Village—"

"Then how do you know?"

"I followed you and Lorenzo to the ruins. I knew you wouldn't wait to see the tomb. You couldn't. Only then did I discover the grand plan."

"From the Old Ghost," Chris said in disgust.

Caterina bowed her head.

"But none of this makes any sense. I love this Village. My mother lives here. And I wanted to be with you."

"I know. You made that clear to me many times—long before you and Alessandra and I sought shelter here. But your anger, your rage—it weakened your resistance, and, just like your father, you fell victim to the fog. Not even the cleansing light of the Great Tree could help you shed the terrible spell. Through you, it can exist here. Through you, it can achieve its evil goals."

Chris stared at her, feeling ashamed. "All because of Giovanna's death."

Caterina shook her head. "The anger had already consumed you."

"That's what Alessandra said, in her story. But she didn't know why."

"Don't you recall, Cristofori? We talked about it at the Old Mill."

"I know we talked about it. But you know I don't remember anything that happened back then. Why ask me such a dumb question?"

Caterina stared at him for a moment, and he feared her next words. "It was because of me."

"That's dumb, too. Why would I be angry with you? I love you."

Tears began to spring in her eyes. "You knew what I was, what I am—you saw me at the old cottage pond. And that forced you to deal with the reality that we couldn't be together the way you wanted to. I think it was too much for you to cope with. I know it was."

"But we are together—here and in the Village."

Caterina reached out and took his hands in hers. Never had they felt so icy. "Cold hands, warm heart?" She grabbed his right hand and pressed his palm just below her left breast.

He felt...nothing.

"No?" she said as a tear trickled down her face. "No. You understood this soon after our arrival—when I first came to you at the window, hoping that my new existence could break the spell. But there was nothing new about me, not really. I was, as you often told me in frustration, 'still with the dead.' And this knowledge only made you angrier, only strengthened the hold of the spell. And you, the one from the other world, knows where these unjust laws come from, where they truly are written."

Chris glanced at the glowing book. When his gaze returned to her, he saw the tear falling from her face. It transformed into perfect crystal with a hexagonal center. But instead of falling to the ground and disappearing, it remained intact and drifted about them.

The doctor's strange lecture echoed in his brain, as did his own words from the Book. Chris felt his throat growing dry. "It doesn't have to be this way. We can still be together, the way we both want. Come back with me—with me and Giovanna and Alessandra. Your father, too—anyone, if they want to. Only this time, I want you to stay there, not as part of a dream, but reality. You see, you're already there. But you'll remember how we are here."

"Think about what you're saying, Cristofori. What would happen to Alessandra if she came back to the world she left in death? What would she be?"

Chris was dumbfounded. "But she can't stay here."

"You don't know what you're saying."

"But you'll come back with us."

"No. I can't."

"Yes you can. You know the way. You've already done it many times. It's still open. Tell me that wasn't you in my bedroom."

Caterina's silence told him what he wanted to know.

"Then why would you want to stay here?" he said. "Don't you want to be with me?"

Her mouth began to quiver. "Of course I do. I owe my existence to you."

"But this dream is ending."

"No. It's not. And since it isn't, I belong here."

"You belong with me!"

"I know," she cried.

"Then why are you fighting me?"

Caterina gazed at the statue. "Have you forgotten?"

Chris sighed. "After we finish what we need to do here. Then we'll talk. For now, you can bring her across the West Bridge and release her. You have to. You're the only one who can do it."

"But then you place her in peril, with no chance of escape, as she was before she died."

"But she won't be as she was before."

"The new power, the new angelic life she receives won't save her there. And if you try to bring her back across the Bridge…"

Chris stared at the statue and clenched his fists. "How do we undo this mess? I can't leave her like this!"

Caterina stared at the book. "If we could change the laws, if we could rewrite the rules—"

"I've tried doing that. It doesn't work."

Caterina looked at him. "Nothing here—nothing at all—has its origins in the diary you keep in the other world."

"Why do you keep saying that? Everything I've written has come true." Chris frowned as Caterina stepped to the west entrance to gazed out into the darkness. The snow clouds had broken apart, and he saw the full Moon over the Mountain.

"There are two evils at work here," Caterina said, "one even more insidious than the other. One seeks to consume us, the other to alter our very being." She paused to stare at him. "You don't remember what she said to you just before she died."

"What she said?"

"The plea was spoken often before—in similar situations...in the other world. And you did keep her safe each time. But not here." She stared out over the Village. "The night of the Storm...not only were they searching for the Orb, they were coming for you as well. The evil that powers the malevolent cloud is not so discerning—it will take anyone who is foolish or weak enough to let it in. What the Horde did not know was that your sister was strong and defiant, even in death, and that the greater power emanating farther than they ever could know from this Great Tree and manipulated by its Book had other designs for her, and you. Not only did they not obtain the object that they sought, but also in their haste, they caused her death that was, as you know, preordained. But her transformation, however necessary, still left her vulnerable to the other evil that wanted her for completely different reasons. You are not safe from this terror either, Cristofori. That is why you must return to the Mountain, descend into its depths, and destroy the source of the Dark Power—that is, if you want this World to be as you truly wish."

Her prophecy of the final confrontation, a battle he forged in his Story. "I know what you're saying is true. You don't know what you're really asking me to do."

"Yes...I do. *If you could just lose the anger, and the incessant anxiety that accompanied it, then you could be somebody, and do wondrous things.*"

His shock lasted just a moment. "You've been there."

Caterina turned to look at him. "I have."

Chris scanned her face for signs of fear. But she remained stoic. "Is it really like the painting?"

"The image you fear the most."

Chris shook at the thought, and could not believe that dreaded moment was nearly upon him.

"When you enter its fiery halls, you will find at its center another domed chamber where the Dark Power resides—this chamber's anti-chamber. Ascend its steps and you will encounter something not unfamiliar to you. It is within, here as it is there, that a secret place holds the key that will determine your fate and that of your sister. You will know what to do when you see it."

The visual image he received was clear, its ties to the old world and his Story undeniably similar. "Will Vittorio be there?"

"I can't be sure. It's possible."

"What happened to him? How did he—"

"The same that will happen to you if you do not break this spell."

Chris nodded, feeling foolish about his inquiry, and did not ask for elaboration. It was the old defense mechanism at work, the one that ran in his blood. But he knew what had caused his father's demise, just as he had seen a glimpse of his own future, if he fell completely.

"Understand this," Caterina said, "Vittorio is not what you think he is. He became a victim of his rage, not of the thing that Alessandra claims. Your father is only a pawn, just one in a long line who carry the banner of the true evil that is stalking you and your sister."

Chris gazed at the book as old world memories filled his mind. "There is another painting at my church. It's a sketch, of a giant creature that lives there."

"I know the one."

"Is He the one who waits for me?"

Caterina returned her gaze to the night sky. "Whatever awaits you in the domed anti-chamber of Pandæmonium must be stopped if you ever hope to save yourself and your sister. That, I'm sure you'll admit, is the reason for all you've endured."

Chris reached out as if to touch her, and felt his hand tremble. "Won't you come with me?"

"You know what happens when I return to that land. I can't change that. They will only turn me against you, and I will not be able to resist them—not while the Dark Power still flows. I have to return to the Old Mill and tell Alessandra everything. Then I need to gather enough white orbs to erase the remaining paintings before the protective light falters any more than it has."

"And the Old Ghost?"

"You have nothing to fear from him as long as the Orb remains here with her, and the light is still strong. He is forbidden to enter. Giving him what he wants will only bring about an unexpected end."

"There is *that* little problem, too." Chris said.

"I've already told you—my father doesn't know what he's saying."

Chris nodded slowly, but he, like his mother, had trouble doubting the doctor's dire prediction. "The Old Ghost once told me that a child is coming."

"A child? Yes. You know the tale."

"And if he gets the Orb?"

"The child will die."

Chris stared at the statue. "If I do what you say, will she ever be allowed into the Village?"

"If you succeed, you will receive all you wish for—her health and happiness, and my eternal love."

"And this World?"

"It is a gift, Cristofori."

Chris ran his fingers across the statue's face, and hesitated to speak his next words, hoping she would break down and convince him to stay. But she kept silent for much too long, which forced the words from him. "How can I possibly win? I've never faced such a thing before. What do I do?"

A great rumble, born in the distance, overtook the Chamber, and for a moment the beam of light disappeared, casting them into darkness.

Now with her troubling orange glow, Caterina once again stared out the arched entry. "Go to the Terrible Shrieking Mountain, enter the Chamber of Darkness, and stop the Dark Power at its source. This must be done. You of all people know this."

Chapter Forty-Five

Pandæmonium

They settled feet first to the snow-covered ground like two falling feathers before the West Bridge. Chris immediately noticed that the fog had bubbled just across the stream, and Caterina remained at a safe distance, wary and ready to take evasive action. The evergreen was partially smothered. It shined an unearthly orange light like the one that now enveloped Caterina. The full Moon to the west was merely a diffused beam of light, like one from an unseen lighthouse, as it strained to penetrate the gloom. He could no longer see the Star. In the distance, the Mountain rumbled louder than ever, echoing throughout the valley.

They stared at each other for an uneasy moment, neither saying a word. No more needed to be said. She had her one last important task to perform, and so did he. The soul of the New World depended on them. Still, the sadness in her eyes, one that she held since they arrived at the Chamber of Light, remained—and it was terribly unsettling. Was there a hint of doubt in her prediction? Was he marching off to his death, or some other type of existence he had not anticipated? Worst of all, was she actually saying goodbye? The Black Rider's warning jarred his thinking, but he refused to accept it. He was fully committed to her now, wherever she was leading him.

Caterina's cold fingertips gently touched his face, and she struggled to form a smile. Chris touched the back of her hand and held it there, as he too struggled to smile. No more questions about the future, no more prodding for glimmers of hope, no more running away. It was time.

Chris watched as Caterina's light brightened to gold, her wings unfurled, and she streaked up into the sky, leaving behind the trail of chiming, sparkling yellow crystals. He watched a moment longer as she disappeared over the treetops. Then he turned and crossed the Bridge, and headed along the muddy path. But as he did, he plucked an orange orb from the tree and held out in front of him, hoping it would matter.

After he passed through the grove, through the foothills, and, at last, poked through the boiling blanket of fog to stand once again just beneath the Mountain ledge in the glaring moonlight, Chris did his best to keep his balance as the continuous rumbling shook loose in a series of dusty, tumbling cascades the sharp broken rocks resting precariously on the steep slope. The Terrible Shrieking Mountain seemed ready to blow. And yet, it also seemed patient, as if it waited for him. The Star was a mere flicker, the orb a pale orange. Little time remained before the demon-reptiles were released and the terrible Horde launched its final assault on the Village. He thought of Caterina's cryptic utterances about the inner workings of the Mountain, about the nature of the evil he was about to face. He still could not believe it was all coming true.

Chris carefully negotiated his way up the treacherous slope until he reached the ledge, expecting to see the Old Ghost. But the slab lay barren, except for the evergreen with its faint orange orbs. The angle of light from the glaring Moon cast a dark shadow in the crag before him. But within that darkness and above the constant rumble, Chris thought he heard the booming, rhythmic echoes of something powerful, as if it were preparing to advance toward him from the unseen depths. He had heard this terrible sound before—many, many times—and he knew its portent. But instead of growing louder, the reverberations remained static, more like the thumping of a great, dark, beating heart.

Chris stepped toward the crag. Now he saw that the shadow wasn't a shadow at all, but the entrance to the cave he suspected all along. When he reached the opening and peered within, the familiar booming echoes, now unimpeded, became louder and in rhythm with his own pounding heart, and he could feel the hot breath of the panting Mountain. It appeared once again that he was staring into the boiling black tunnel of the Storm. But this time, the tunnel was made of rock, and it bore down and deep into a fiery chamber, made small by its distance, like the fire in a great furnace, but no less fearsome. He recalled the dark paintings of John Martin, and the words of the Story, and he shivered.

Chris entered the cavern and began the slow descent along the steps of the broken black rubble. He held out the orb—which now had a warm reddish tinge—not to light the way, but out of ritual, to calm his quaking nerves and fend off any unseen threat. There was just enough red glow from the orb and the flickering Chamber below to aid his descent, and the strange light stretched his shadow across the oily, black and bumpy walls, giving the unsettling impression that something sinister was creeping along behind him. The booming echoes grew louder, thumping painfully against his eardrums, and the orb became increasingly red and hot with each precarious step.

As Chris drew ever closer to the Chamber of Darkness, the orb's heat, like the stifling air and the booming in his ears, became increasingly unbearable. At last, he could not hold onto the orb any longer, and he released it with a cry of pain. The orb fell to the rubble floor, bounced once with a loud clack, then shattered on the sharp edge of a rock. A tiny winged demon sprung up from the shards, hissed through its black teeth, then flew away with a fury down into the Chamber of Darkness, as if summoned by its master. Chris paused to catch his breath, and give his racing heart and frazzled nerves a much-needed rest. He thought of Caterina, wishing she were at his side, then wondered how far she had gone in her quest to destroy the Paintings.

And then the Mountain shook as it had never done before, rocking him on his heels, cracking the walls, and showering him with bits of rubble. The great booming intensified to a near-furious pace, like war drums preceding an attack. Now in a full-blown panic, Chris slid and scurried down the broken rocks of the cave in a reckless manner, plowing through step after step as he drew ever closer to the entrance. He dreaded to think of the monstrous sight he would behold once he arrived at the complex of Pandæmonium, just ahead, how this World had mutated for the worse the ghastly painting that hung above the confessional at St. Boniface.

When he reached the entrance, Chris felt the cooler air being sucked into the hot red Chamber—so forceful, he struggled to keep his balance. But a high mound of rubble—atop of which grew an evergreen with glowing red orbs—blocked his view. Still, as he looked up, aided by the raging fires just beyond the mound, Chris saw that the Chamber of Darkness—anything but dark—was cone shaped and beyond enormous, as if the entire Mountain had been hollowed out. The strange dark smoke, lacking all acrid scent, was reminiscent of the smoke he had experienced during the demonic visitations in his bedroom, more distortional, like dark waves traveling through fluid amber. He could breathe, but it was a struggle. How in the World had he and his sister survived this trek before?

Chris scrambled up the mound, deciding on the dramatic, just to get it over with. When he triumphantly reached the top, he stood there in awe of the sights and sounds that overcame his senses.

Most of the scene was true to its horrific origin. Pandæmonium was sprawling and imposing, like some impossible neoclassical complex dreamed up by an equally impossible tyrant—then set on fire. The radiant orange-and-yellow complex sat on a vast foundation supported by stone arches, through which rivers of flaming lava flowed. Its first level was composed of a countless number of neatly-aligned columns that supported the second smaller level, also filled with rows of columns. A third columned level, smaller still, completed the massive structure.

But from there, the image transmuted into a towering, frightful machine. A broad conical tower thousands of feet high rose up from the complex into a billowing black-and-red cloud of smoke, Bruegel's *The Little Tower of Babel* morphed into a hellish Christmas pyramid. The spiraling outer shell consisted of archways through which Chris saw the rotating inner stages where the thousands of horseback-riding ghouls of the Horde prepared for their wild ride onto the defenseless Village. All about the tower swarmed the bat-faced demons that blew into long horns that emitted a loud and repulsive blat, while the booming from the rotating stages thundered inside the cavern, and blasted him continuously, thuds against his chest.

Among the flames on a rocky outcrop overlooking the hellish vision was the Old Ghost, as expected. He seemed content to just stand there and admire Martin's—and Chris'—twisted creation. The Old Ghost slowly turned and stared at Chris, and waiting patiently for his approach.

Wiping the sweat from his forehead, Chris scrambled down the rubble pile and carefully made his way across the flat stones that formed a pathway in the molten lava field to the outcrop.

"You have returned," the Old Ghost said when Chris arrived.

Chris saw that he needed to descend the rocky steps behind the Old Ghost and continue along the path—it stones now round and white—if he wanted to reach the complex. "I didn't bring the Orb."

"I never wanted you to bring it to me..."

"I know what your plan is," Chris said. "I wrote it, remember? Now I'm here to stop it."

The Old Ghost grinned as the ghastly carousel boomed and whirled in the backdrop. "Is this not what you wanted?"

Chris pushed past him and headed down the steps.

"Do you know the way?" the Old Ghost said.

Chris turned and studied the Old Ghost's mysterious expression. Based on the hints Caterina threw his way, and his own Story, Chris knew that the Power he had to destroy resided directly beneath the pyramid, in the heart of Pandæmonium. If he retraced the flow of the lava, he would find the source. What the Old Ghost was up to, now that he knew what Chris wanted to do... It didn't matter. There wasn't time for further speculation.

Chris reached the path and stepped on the first white stone. Moments later, the demons from the tower spotted him. The trumpeters sounded a frightful alarm, and a number of the winged devils swooped down and swarmed about, hissing and lunging at him.

"Do not set your gaze upon them," the Old Ghost said from behind. "Keep steady and follow the path."

But it was difficult not to flinch in the presence of such horrible sights and threatening acts. Chris increased his pace to a scamper, eager to reach the cover of the lower level and get out of harm's way. He felt as though he were on the practice field, running an agility drill. But as he continued on, swatting at the demons, Chris saw that the stones weren't stones at all, but human skulls.

"Can you see the source of the rivers?" the Old Ghost shouted above booms and echoes.

Chris stopped at a fork, wary of the Old Ghost's guidance. Many paths led to the many arched entries. He shielded his eyes with his hand and peered into the fiery scene. Through the maze of arches, piers, and pillars, he saw, as expected, the molten rivers snaking their way from the center of the complex. He selected the appropriate path and sprinted for the entrance.

Once inside the shadowy base of the complex, the demons peeled away, bolstering his hope that he would, at the very least, reach the scene of his final battle. Through the dingy archways and forest of columns, Chris saw a massive platform of white marble steps, just as she had promised, rising up into a large opening in the ceiling that blazed angrily with red.

"Do you see it, Cristofori?" the Old Ghost called out from somewhere behind him. "Yes, the end of your quest is almost upon you."

The end of your quest, Chris thought as he ran as fast as he could along the snaking path. What did that really mean in this New World? What could he now expect to find in the heart of Pandæmonium? He recalled Caterina's doom-filled prophecy. He remembered the last time he had been in the furnace room clearing a passage to the steamer chest, and the image of that hideous mask as it unexpectedly swung out at him. Would Vittorio be there, waiting for him with his terrible chain? Or was his father, as Caterina suggested, a mere pawn used to lure him to this terrible place to stared down Dore's giant Lucifer? The Devil had been pushed aside with all the other old beliefs, until the day Chris stepped into this New World.

Chris reached the end of the path, put his foot on the first step, and looked up into the blinding, fiery light. The rumble of the rotating stages high above him remained constant. But he could not see the danger that surely awaited him. Chris took another wary step, then another. He felt as if he were climbing to the gallows.

"You were stamped with the seal of perfection, of complete wisdom and perfect beauty," the Old Ghost called out from behind. "In Eden, the garden of God, you were, and every precious stone was your covering—carnelian, topaz, and beryl, chrysolite, onyx, and jasper, sapphire, garnet, and emerald. Of gold your pendants and jewels were made, on the day you were created. With the Cherub I placed you. You were on the holy mountain of God, walking among the fiery stones. Blameless you were in your conduct from the day you were created, until evil was found in you, the result of your far-flung trade. Violence was your business, and you sinned. Then I banned you from the mountain of God. The Cherub drove you from among the fiery stones. You became haughty of heart because of your beauty. For the sake of splendor, you debased your wisdom. I cast you to the earth, so great was your guilt. I made you a spectacle in the sight of kings. Because of your guilt, your sinful trade, I have profaned your sanctuaries. And I have brought out fire from your midst which will devour you. I have reduced you to dust on the earth in the sight of all who should see you. Among the peoples, all who knew you stand aghast at you, you have become a horror. You shall be no more."

Now the Old Ghost's words left little doubt in Chris' mind who awaited him.

But when they reached the top step, and Chris stared into the center of Pandæmonium's great domed anti-chamber, he saw an exact replica of the steamer trunk sitting on the stone floor. A shaft of red light streaked up from the chest. Halfway up to the hole in the dome, the light infused with the boiling black smoke.

And then he saw it.

Chris had decided, as he was climbing those steps, before the Old Ghost's cryptic speech, that his father, or the hideous embodiment of evil he had become, would be, as Caterina described, the one who "awaits you." After all, this confrontation was about controlling the New World. Who but Victor controlled the old? But as Chris continued to stare at the terrible creature before him, his mind raged with confusion. Vittorio was nowhere to be seen. Instead, the real menace sat atop the trunk, its hairy legs pulled to its chest.

When Chris took one step towards the alp, it reared its head and shrieked.

"What do you want?" Chris shouted. "What are you doing here? Go away!" Chris glanced to either side and realized that the Old Ghost was gone. Instantly, the winged demons, one by one, began invading the chamber, and circled high above him, waiting for the right moment to strike. But then, as quickly as they appeared, the demons scattered from within the dome as the Mountain roared. Thinking the alp would maintain its jealous guard of the trunk, Chris took another step toward it.

It leaped at him, powerful arms extended.

Instinctively, Chris turned away and waited for the violent collision.

It never came.

Chris heard a thump as the alp let out a cat-like screech. As Chris gazed in amazement, he saw the alp tumble across the floor as a small golden angel hovered over him. Once the alp gained its balance, it leaped for the heavenly creature, which seized the alp in her outstretched hands.

"The trunk!" she cried in a familiar voice. And then she became entangled in a furious wrestling match just above the floor as the alp shrieked with every wild turn.

Chris hesitated for a moment, fighting the urge to help Giovanna in her struggle with the mysterious creature. But when he saw that she was holding her own, Chris ran for the trunk. He unfastened the latches, and flipped the lid open. Inside were hundreds of red orbs. The secret compartment was there, too, emblazoned with the mark of the fire lizard. Before he clenched a fist to strike the image, he glanced at the struggle to his right. Giovanna threw the alp to the floor, and it landed on its back. It screeched once more, then transformed into a glittering white butterfly before fluttering madly around her head.

She turned to him with great apprehension. "Hurry, Cristofori!"

Chris slammed the side of his fist against the compartment. Immediately, it popped open, and a leather pouch fell into the trunk. Something wiggled inside it.

Chris heard the great rotating mechanism above him grind violently to a halt. The entire chamber began to shudder as cracks appeared in the dome. Chris and Giovanna exchanged victorious smiles as the white butterfly fluttered away. Then Chris looked down and opened the pouch. A small lizard crawled out onto the orbs and looked up at him before trying to scamper away. Chris caught it by its tail and held it up in amazement. Then he examined the dangling creature as it squirmed in the air. He felt the urge to crush the lizard in his hand—for all the pain and suffering it had created. But, recalling the doctor's warning, he resisted. Instead, he flung the lizard away. It tumbled on the floor, then scurried down the steps and into the lava below.

Chris turned once again to his sister. She had transformed into the similar human image he remembered, and she stood in the simple but elegant dress Alessandra spoke of, facing him with arms extended, ready for his embrace.

"We had a pact, remember?" she said before laughing.

Was it Janey speaking, or Giovanna? Was she recalling the pact from this World, or the old? It didn't matter. He didn't care. He was just elated to see her and hear her voice, to know she was safe. Chris held his arms wide and rushed towards her. But as he did, the white butterfly made its deadly move. It, too, transformed—into a tiny cloud of fine white crystalline mist. Then it stretched into a long thin line before intercepting her advance, and piercing her mouth and nostrils. That's when the true meaning of Caterina's warning struck him like a bolt of lightning. "No!" he cried as her eyes rolled up into her head. He caught her before she fell to the floor.

Chris cradled her head in his left hand as he gently laid her limp and cold body to the floor. Her eyelids fluttered and she struggled to breathe as her mouth remained open. And all he could do was panic. "Giovanna," he said, shaking her. "Giovanna!"

But the gasping and eye fluttering continued as the chamber shook and the dome cracked and crumbled.

Then suddenly, the mist withdrew from her body and reformed into a tiny white cloud just above her face. When the cloud became a glittering butterfly, Chris snatched it in anger from the air and clutched it tightly, feeling it squirm in his palm. When the squirming stopped and his anger ceased, Chris opened his hand. He stared in bewilderment at the small snowflake with its hollow, pentagonal center.

The crystal was missing one of its five branches.

Giovanna began to stir and glow a golden yellow, and immediately Chris let the snowflake drift from his hand. She let out a few groans and coughed as she rolled her head from side to side.

"Giovanna—Giovanna, can you hear me?" Chris said as he cradled her face in his left hand. "Giovanna—it's me. Are you all right? Talk to me."

Her glow grew brighter and brighter and soon became blinding as Chris heard his words echoing throughout the chamber. But then those words became hers as the image of her face began to fill his vision. When the light finally died, Chris realized that he was back home, lying on the floor. Janey was hovering over him. Her angelic face lost its glow, and her knitted cap returned to her bald head. She looked frightened, and was still pleading with him to respond.

"Chris, talk to me—talk to me, please!"

"It's all right, Janey—I'm...I'm fine," he said as he wiped the drool. He struggled to raise his throbbing head. He was relieved to see that she had returned with him, that she had escaped the strange ravages of the mysterious alp. But he felt nauseous again, his exhaustion complete.

"Fine? You fell on the floor. And then you started moving around like a wiggle-worm. Are you bleeding?"

"Bleeding? What? Didn't you go there?"

"Chris, you didn't go anywhere, and neither did I."

Lightheaded, Chris sat up and touched the warm, fleshy wet bump on the back of his skull, trying to work out what had gone so terribly wrong. He immediately thought of her statue in the Chamber of Light. Having been encased in stone, maybe Janey had no memory of her appearance in the New World. But then again, she had been released from the stone and appeared in Pandæmonium's domed anti-chamber. At least he finally had confirmation from someone who witnesses his departure and arrival that his journey to the New World was like a dream—or in this instance, from her perspective, a bad dream. But apparently, it wasn't his body. It was his consciousness, somehow pulled from him, that made the trip through the light. This fact helped explain how his memories supplanted those in Cristofori's body. That he had transported from Pandæmonium and not the

Great Tree showed how the Old Ghost and the demons first invaded his bedroom. "I know, I know. That suspended time thing—it's a little confusing, but that's how it works. I told you: it's like watching a movie and hitting the pause button. No matter how long you wait, you always come back to the point where you stopped."

Chris rested on his elbows and gazed at her. She still looked frightened. "Sorry, I didn't mean to scare you, but you're right, it was like a terrible dream. And the return part? I guess I'd better be sitting down when I leave next time, huh?" He scanned her face for the utter disappointment he was certain she felt towards him, but this time, she appeared more angry than sad. She did her best to help him to his feet. Then she reached up and touched his wound, and examined her fingers.

"You are bleeding. We have to go see Dr. Sam."

"I don't want to see him," Chris said. "We need to talk about what happened. We need to figure out what went wrong. Your life depends on it."

"You fell down and split your head open—that's what happened. And you're not right. Let's get our coats and go—before Victor hears us. I think you need stitches."

"You hate me, don't you? I know you do. I keep letting you down."

"I don't hate you, Chris. You're my brother. Now, please, let's go."

Chris glanced at the closed den door. "No, Janey," he said in a hushed tone, "it's too risky."

"Then I'll go get him—by myself." Still dressed in her pink pajamas and fuzzy slippers, Janey headed for the foyer.

"No, don't do that. Victor will kill him!" He tried to catch her by the arm, but he remained a bit groggy, and she eluded him with a quickness he did not think was possible. One of those days, maybe her last, when her energy inexplicably returned.

Janey dashed to the coat tree and reached up to grab her long down coat. But in her haste, she had trouble removing it from the hook. As Chris approached, she reached into her coat pocket and yanked something out with enough force to pull the white lining inside out. A few pennies and some gum wrappers spilled to the floor. Janey flashed another determined look, then opened the front door and rushed out into the cold and snow, slamming the door behind her.

"Damn it, Janey," he grumbled. He grabbed his coat and quickly slipped it on, then snatched hers and headed outside. But she was already gone, her wide tracks leading around the garage.

Chapter Forty-six

Epiphany

"Janey, stop!" Chris said as he struggled through the snow to catch up to his sister, who was nearing the gap in the back hedge. She did not look back at him, nor did she hesitate. Her hands were clenched and her strides were short but amazingly steadfast, her fuzzy slippers acting like snowshoes. Since the chemo had already sapped much of her strength, and some of her muscle mass, Chris did not think that it would be difficult to catch her, especially in the ankle-high snow. But the lump on the back of his head was still throbbing, and the open wound stung from the bitter cold. He still felt dizzy, nauseous, and groggy, as if he had been sleeping for days. The effects made his legs rubbery and they often buckled, and he found it hard to keep pace with her. Even worse, he was still trying desperately to re-acclimate himself to this world, as the abrupt return caught him by complete surprise. And when he glanced back at his house, its lighted windows glaring back at him, he was fully convinced that the Black Cloud would soon boil out of the patio doors, and that Victor, with mask on, accompanied by the Demon Horde, would be in full pursuit. The nightmarish visions of Pandæmonium were still crackling in his mind, and so too were the powerful emotions tied to the unresolved battle for Giovanna's life. Confident he had destroyed the source of the Dark Power, Chris was also aware that Giovanna was in danger from the anti-chamber's imminent collapse, and he was eager to return to whisk her away. But now, when Janey slipped unwaveringly through the hedge and into Dr. Samuel's backyard, all thoughts of and concerns with the New World vanished, and Chris focused completely on his belligerent sister's apprehension.

Chris made it through the hedge, but Janey was already crossing the Bridge, the distance between them rapidly growing. When his left leg faltered, Chris fell face first into the snow, and he immediately felt its grating, icy sting. With Janey's jacket still in hand, Chris struggled to his feet and wiped the melting snow from his hot face. Then he saw Janey shivering before him with her arms folded across her chest, hands tucked in her arm pits. Though shivering, she still looked angry.

"Will you please put this on?" he said. Feeling humbled, he held out her open jacket.

Janey slipped her arms into its sleeves, then zipped the front.

"Thank you," Chris said. "Now let's go home. The last thing you need is a cold."

"No, you're going to see Dr. Sam."

Chris seized her by the arm and tried to pull her back. "You don't even know if he's there."

"I'll scream 'rape.' "

"What?"

"The whole neighborhood already knows something weird's going on at our house. Every time I look out a window, some busybody's looking back at me."

"So?"

Janey tugged her arm all too easily from his grasp. "So one peep out of me and the coppers'll come running—is that what you want?"

"You're not playing fair."

"Too bad. You need help."

"Quit playing doctor, will ya? I think the bleeding's stopped."

"I'm not talking about the bleeding." Janey opened her clenched hand to display a matchbook, through which a partially smoked, lipstick-stained cigarette was threaded.

Chris was stunned. "Where did you find that?" With all the turmoil between the two worlds, he had forgotten.

"I was cleaning."

"Cleaning? When?"

"It was in one of the missing candle bags in your closet."

"Janey!"

"There was a bunch of tissue stuffed in it, too—and a plastic bag filled with stinky liquid. You got that from the storeroom, didn't you—*didn't you?*"

"Janey, I swear, I wasn't going to—"

"What is this, Chris? What? Where did you ever learn about such awful things? And what were you going to do with it? Sometimes I wonder if I know you at all. What's going on with you?"

"Don't tell the doc. Please, don't. It's all just a big mistake."

"Mistake? This isn't a spray can. How could you even think of such a thing?" Janey tossed the incendiary device into the snow.

She glared at him a few moments longer, breathing deeply. Then, in her typical fashion, Janey quickly suppressed her anger as her expression mellowed. But in his guilt, Chris wondered if this latest outrage would cause her to lose all faith, and drain the remaining strength she needed to battle on.

"Can you make it to his house?" she said.

"Can you?"

Janey stuck her hands into the pockets. Then she turned and walked with determination toward the Bridge.

Chris reluctantly followed, too weary and too ashamed to fight her and disappoint her any more. As he drew ever closer to the doctor's half-lit house, his thoughts instinctively turned to Katie and all he had been through with her counterpart in the New World. But he quickly fought the impulse. This was not the appropriate time for his fantasies—not in his exhausted and now guilt-ridden condition. Even worse, he worried that he lacked the fortitude to withstand the doctor's intense gaze or answer any of his probing questions. He just wanted to return home to rest, and to figure out what had gone terribly wrong with his master plan to save Janey. He could only hope that no one inside the doctor's house would answer their call for help.

Chris arrived at the darkened back door where Janey repeatedly rang the doorbell. It wasn't long before the coach lights came on, and Dr. Samuel stood with a stunned expression in the doorway. He looked smaller and older.

"Chris? *Janey?* What in the world—"

"Chris fell down and hit his head."

"Fell down?"

"It's nothing," Chris said.

Dr. Samuel held the screen door open. "Get in here before you freeze to death."

They stepped inside the warm, brightly lit mudroom. The doctor closed the door.

"Is this Victor again?" he said.

Chris stared at Janey. "No." He suddenly became worried that she would tell Dr. Samuel all about the plan.

"He just slipped and fell—on the ice," Janey said.

"At this hour?" The doctor drew close to Chris. "Let's have a look."

Chris stood still as the doctor used his fingers to push aside the bloody, matted hair. "Any dizziness or nausea?"

"No, sir."

"Headache?"

"No."

"Did you black out?"

Again, he stared at Janey, who gave him the look. "No, sir."

She kept silent, but unsettled.

Dr. Samuel opened one of the white metal cabinets above the washer and withdrew a packet of gauze pads. Then he grabbed a dark brown bottle of peroxide and set it on the dryer before cracking the sealed bottle top open with a twist. "And what are you doing out of bed, young lady?" he said. He held a gauze pad to the open bottle and tipped it. "Feeling better this night?"

"Yes, sir," she said. "He didn't want to come over, so I made him. I think he's afraid of the needle—and the truth."

"The needle, huh?" The doctor dabbed the wound with the soaked gauze.

Chris clenched his teeth and took a deep breath, but did not cry out in pain, although he wanted to. A burning sensation spread across his skull with every dab.

"It's a pretty nasty gash," the doctor said, "but I don't think he'll need stitches." He tossed the bloody gauze into the silver trash bin between the appliances, then soaked another pad.

"See?" Chris said to Janey.

Dr. Samuel applied pressure to the wound, and Chris cringed while Janey smiled.

"I'm glad you came, Janey, but not dressed like that. Where are your boots? Your brother should have had enough sense to come on his own. Are you two telling me the whole truth about this?"

"Yes, sir," Chris said. "I fell, just like she said. And that's really all there is to it."

"So where's Victor?"

"In his den," Chris said.

"And he didn't cause this," the doctor said to Janey. He tossed the gauze into the trash.

"No, sir," she said.

Dr. Samuel stared at her and nodded, even though he wore a look of disbelief. "You'd tell me if he did, wouldn't you?"

"You don't have to worry about that," Chris said.

Again, Dr. Samuel nodded, but he looked troubled. "As long as you two are here, I think you should know that I filed a complaint against your father. He should be getting a written notice from the county any day now."

"Yeah, it came," Chris said.

"Already?" the doctor said, wide-eyed.

"Yeah," Chris said.

Dr. Samuel grew flushed. "I don't understand. I should have received a copy. Of course, I probably did, but I've been so busy... Please accept my apology. I meant to tell you before it happened. It's just that—"

"It's okay," Janey said. "We don't mind."

The doctor nodded a few times more, but struggled to express his thoughts. "This may get ugly, so you let me know right away if Victor does anything threatening. There's a good chance they're going to act this time. I just want you to know that I've also asked for temporary custody. You're undoubtedly unaware of this, but I'm a licensed foster parent. Catherine, you see, was a foster child."

Chris glanced at Janey. "Yeah, we know." But he couldn't tell if she were more shocked over the news about Katie or the doctor's actions.

"We do?" Janey said.

"Well, yeah," Chris said feebly, now sensing their shock.

"How?" Dr. Samuel said. "Catherine implored me to keep that information confidential—until she was ready. When did she tell you?"

"She didn't," Chris said.

"How, then—"

"My friend Matt told me."

"Cavanaugh?" Janey said. "Why would she tell him and not us? She didn't even know him—did she?"

"Well, sure she does. But she didn't tell him. He just knew."

Now both of them stared at him as if he were insane. For just a moment, Chris felt as if he were back in the New World. "So we might be moving in with you?"

The doctor hesitated, his confusion still evident. "Yes...yes, of course—temporarily. But only if the county agrees. There's still quite a process we need to go through before that happens. I'm also looking into taking this whole thing a bold step forward...that is, if you're willing. You see, when it comes to adoption, biological family members are preferred. But if none are available, the next preference is the foster parent."

Janey stared at Chris in amazement, but Chris began to panic. "But what about Katie?" he said.

Dr. Samuel frowned. "What about her?"

Chris sensed that he had made a grave mistake, that he should have never asked. But now that his question had been stated and the topic became fixed in their minds, Chris felt it impossible not to continue. "Well, does she know about this? I mean, you know, we might be moving in—and joining the family. The first part is okay, I guess, but the second part? You really think that's a good idea? We should ask her how she feels about it, right? That would be the best thing to do."

The doctor remained stone-faced.

"Well?" Chris said, feeling the heat of his embarrassment.

"Chris," Janey said. Her expression soured.

Dr. Samuel cleared his throat while touched Janey on the shoulder, silencing her. "If your asking whether or not I think she would have approved of what I'm doing, I think you know that answer, given how she felt about you two and the relationship she established with you and your mother. But if you're talking in the spiritual sense, as if I were praying for her guidance and acceptance, I think you also know my firm position on that subject."

Chris wiped the sweat from his upper lip. The nausea churned his stomach, and the dizziness grew.

"Are you okay, son?" the doctor said.

"Yeah," Chris said, though he could barely stand.

"Let's get that jacket off," Dr. Samuel said as he helped Chris remove his coat. His strong hand caught Chris beneath his left armpit as Chris wavered. "I think you'd better lie down. That fall may have been worse than you told me. Where did you say it happened?"

Chris let Dr. Samuel guide him from the mudroom and into the darkened game room as he did all he could not to lose consciousness. But the loud and familiar noises in his ears were intense, mind-splitting, and his mouth had dried up. He worried that he might vomit. Only when he stretched out on one of the brown leather sofas did he start to regain control of his senses. And then he saw Katie's gold-framed photo sitting on the mantel.

"You're burning up, son," the doctor said, his cool hand on Chris' forehead. "Janey, would you mind getting your brother some water? There's a glass in the cupboard above the sink."

Janey ran into the mudroom.

"I think we may have to bring you to the hospital," Dr. Samuel said.

Chris tried to sit up. "No, I'll be all right. I just want to go home."

"Chris, you might have a concussion, or even a fracture," the doctor said as he gently pushed Chris down. "I have to take some x-rays, just to be sure."

"Victor won't go for it. He's really very mad at you."

Janey returned with the glass of water, and the doctor's eyes locked onto the angry words knitted in her cap. "Screw Victor," he said.

Only then did the doctor allow Chris to sit up and take a sip. His eyes found her photo again, and he could not stop staring at her.

Dr. Samuel glanced at the photo, then bent to one knee at Chris' side. "You were always very fond of Catherine, I know, as she was of you," he said in that probing tone. "But maybe not in the way that you hoped. Is my assumption correct?"

Now it was Chris' turn to look stunned, and the doctor took his time observing Chris' reaction.

"A beautiful young woman, without question," he said. "I know if I were a young man, I couldn't help falling a little in love with her. Such a gentle way about her, never speaking harshly of anyone, not even your father. And such a joy, such a warm light in this cold and lonely household—not unlike your sister does for you, I gather."

Chris forced down another sip and looked at him "No, sir." He saw Janey smile nervously.

"But being the young beauty," Dr. Samuel said, "she attracted a lot of young men to the house. Some were very handsome and skilled in the ways of romance. They brought her gifts and excitement that she had difficulty resisting. I was always so busy—too busy, I'm afraid, to give her the direction she needed at times when it came to making choices. And that I still regret to this day. If only I had remembered what it was like to be so reckless and impatient, to feel so indestructible. Then, perhaps, everything might have been different."

The doctor paused to study him, and Chris felt increasingly uncomfortable about the course of the story.

"It angers me, Chris, I have to admit it. It angers me to my core when I sit alone in this house and think about what happened, what was so unfairly taken away from me. In fact, it's fair to say that it consumes me sometimes—so much so that I feel like lashing out at the world, looking for someone or something to blame for my sadness. But self-pity does me no good, either. There are people who rely on me for their well-being. I took an oath, I made a commitment to them. I intend to keep those words. And so I must go on. Do you know what it's like to have people depending on your for their very lives? Well, how foolish of me—of course you do."

Chris hung his head, now burning with anger and shame and fear, and he refused to look at anyone.

"I remember the day I found out about what happened to the church," Dr. Samuel said.

Chris lifted his gaze momentarily. Then his eyes shifted to Janey. The unsettledness she had displayed earlier was gone, and now she looked as guilty as he felt.

"I'm sorry," she said.

Chris said nothing and looked down, sinking into his embarrassment.

"Don't be angry with those who love you, Chris," the doctor said. "You'll only invite more harm. She was concerned for your well-being and your future—something about a pact. Well, after she told me the whole story, I was stunned, of course. How could this be? You were always such a fine and polite boy. I had trouble understanding your complicity in that ill-conceived and irreverent game, given your education and upbringing, knowing Sandra so well—though thankfully you had been cleared of the more serious charges. Then we had a long discussion about your mother. I wasn't surprised to hear that Sandra had often blamed herself for your rebellious tendencies, much in the same manner that I had done for Catherine's terrible decision. But instead of time constraints, it was your mother's illness, of course, that kept her from providing the kind of guidance she felt you needed. But unlike Catherine who sometimes ran with the wrong crowd, it wasn't others who inevitably led you astray...was it, Chris?"

Chris kept his head bowed as the ringing and pounding in his ears slowly intensified.

"There was anger at the Church and all it stood for," Dr. Samuel said. "But Janey insisted that another was responsible, that he was the one who caused the damage—a telling, one-word accusation concerning veracity, sprayed in black paint over precious canvas. But, in truth, as the rounds of neighborhood gossip later proclaimed, the accused merely took the fall for another's action born not only out of a growing disillusionment, but the sudden loss of a secret and cherished love. And so now he faces that dreadful prospect once more, and just like then, his anger consumes him, and it is simply too much for one person to bear."

Dr. Samuel paused as the revealing power of his words settled upon them like a heavy fog, stifling all emotion. Chris could hear his aching heart pounding.

"I've kept the article, and I look at it now and then. But not that horrible photograph they printed for all the world to see. And I must confess, I'd gladly rip out that pond hedge and welcome back those infernal creatures if I knew she'd return to me. Do you miss her as much as I do, Chris? Do you remember the night of the crash? The anniversary is almost here."

The noises in his ears had nearly overtook him. Though he was tempted to retreat once again into the elaborate sanctuary of denial he had unwittingly crafted, Chris decided in one fateful second—for just a few seconds—to let the truth soar within in him, and to embrace the terrible sadness and welcome relief left in its wake. Though his heart felt as if were about to tear itself apart, Chris found the courage and the strength to look at Janey.

"Katie Cat Kate," she said, but not in her usual teasing way. She showed no judgmental expression, only a tear, which trickled down her cheek as she stared back. A bright light suddenly appeared along the periphery and quickly closed around her. Then he heard the doctor calling Chris' name while he felt his body falling. When the ringing and pounding finally stopped and the light retreated, Chris found himself in Pandæmonium's rumbling domed anti-chamber, staring down at Giovanna's glowing face. She was still crying in his arms, and the imperfect crystals from her tears rose up as chunks of stone began to dislodge from the dome ceiling. And though he knew that she was her own being, that Janey was not within her, Chris did not feel any less sympathy or concern for her.

Suddenly, among all the tumult and storm of emotion, the Boiling Black Cloud rushed up the marble stairs, and quickly overtook them.

Chapter Forty-Seven

The Old Ghost

As the boiling cloud blew past, a horse-drawn wagon suddenly appeared amidst the rubble on the chamber floor. "Jump in—quickly!" Caterina said, holding the reins.

Chris was shocked but pleased to see her alive—to see that the entire New World, with all its horrors, was still intact, now that the old world truth still hammered in his ears. But he immediately fell into his role of savior as he scooped Giovanna up and placed her into the wagon. Once Chris hopped on-board and clung to his sister, Caterina snapped the reins, and the white horse reared up and whinnied before they roared from the disintegrating chamber and out into the fiery columned halls of Pandæmonium.

There was no elation in their charge, only urgency. The columns supporting the entire complex cracked and popped and buckled. Caterina struck an aggressive posture, leaning forward as her long, glowing hair streaked back from the speed and fury of their attempted escape. Chris held Giovanna in his arms, and she did her best to look happy. But the color of her frigid glow had grown that weakened orange, and he saw that she struggled from the alp's strange and debilitating attack. He smiled back at her as he recalled Alessandra's story of how the crystalline mist had affected Vittorio's sanity. But for Giovanna, it appeared to be lethal, and he feared for her existence. Was this how angels died?

They cleared the fiery hall just as the last of the columns broke in two. Chris turned to see the complex falling into flaming ruin as the giant tower began to fragment and topple into a roaring black cloud of smoke and fire. Whether or not the Demon Horde had escaped the conflagration, he could not tell. But the Boiling Black Cloud was still billowing up through the huge vent.

They flew quickly over the rubble pile and into the tunnel, and were soon racing a ball of flame that chased them to the entrance. Just when it seemed they would be overtaken, they exploded into the cool night air, beyond the curling tendrils of fire.

As they streaked away from the Mountain atop the blanket of fog, Chris looked up and saw the leading edge of the angry Black Cloud rumbling across the sky as the very last of it dissipated from the collapsing vent. The Cloud was headed for the Village. The Star was barely flickering, and just ahead, the Great Tree shined weakly within a hazy orange glow.

"Where are Matteo and Lorenzo?" Chris shouted at Caterina.

"They're still with the Horde," she cried.

"Did you destroy the Paintings?"

"Yes—but the Storm cannot be stopped."

"Where is Alessandra?"

"She returned home and is waiting."

For what? "Was this part of your prophecy? Was this supposed to happen? You said that if I destroyed the source of the Dark Power, I would receive everything I wanted. I did what you asked. But I didn't want this."

"We have to return to the Chamber of Light."

"The Chamber? But won't she—"

"The light is much too weak now to keep her or anyone out."

Chris didn't understand how their return could possibly help. "What is happening to her? Will she survive?"

"None of us will if we don't arrive before the Storm."

Chris clutched his sister tighter as Caterina urged on the demon horse with repeated cries and snaps. Giovanna's eyes were fluttering and she struggled to stay conscious. "You're not going to give up on me, are you?" he whispered kindly to her. "You're not playing fair. You did your part. Now you're supposed to let me save you."

Chris' lighthearted words seemed to take hold as she smiled feebly.

"I don't know what's going to happen," he said, "but I still expect to see you after it's finished, okay?"

Giovanna tried to summon another smile, but her eyes began to flutter once more. Chris hugged her tightly as they rode the fog up to the Chamber of Light.

When the wagon rolled onto the stone floor of the dimly lit Chamber, Caterina yanked the reins and stopped the horse. It nervously pranced and snorted in the once-forbidden surroundings. Chris jumped out and reached up to take Giovanna from Caterina, who had scrambled back to assist him. With Giovanna securely in his arms, Chris turned into the cold and rushing wind to look out the west entrance. The Cloud was rumbling just west of the Village as it made its steady advance.

"Now what?" Chris said to Caterina.

She looked nervously at him, then turned toward the altar. With feathered hat atop his stooped head and crooked stick in his shaky right hand, the Old Ghost stepped feebly into the shaft of orange-red light. It his left hand, he held the Purple Orb.

"Caterina?" Chris shouted as he stared incredulously at her.

"I gave it to him," Caterina said with a hint of satisfaction.

"You gave it to him?"

She nodded.

The Black Rider's warning echoed in his spinning mind, and Chris could feel his anger rise. The ray of light shined a bright red. "What is this? Why is he here?"

"To help you finish your story."

"Help me? I'm trying to save this World—and my sister."

"He's the one who made the hole in the sky possible. He helped you create the Tree—all of them—through which the light passes and is responsible for all that you see. Without him, I would not be here with you. Neither would she."

"But you told me that if he got his hands on the Orb—"

"That there will be an unexpected end?"

Chris could barely contain his rage at her complicity. "Yes!"

Caterina looked sadly at him. "Not to this World, Cristofori."

Chris gazed at her, then at the Old Ghost. With his anger now muted by confusion, Chris repeatedly shook his head. "I don't believe this."

"But you still do," the Old Ghost said. "Give praise to your sister, and to her."

The rumbling from the approaching Storm drew Chris' attention to the entryway. Suddenly, Giovanna let out a soft but sickly groan, and she grew limp in his arms as all color began draining from her. "Giovanna—no!" he cried. "What is happening?"

"Your sister is dying," the Old Ghost said.

"I know she's dying!" Chris shouted as he approached the altar. "Why?"

"You know why."

"No, I don't—*I don't!* Tell me! If you're who she says you are, if you're here to help us—then help!"

"I have little power here over this matter," the Old Ghost said.

"But the trees, the portal—"

"It is written," he said.

Chris glanced at the glowing book. "Then un-write it, re-write it!"

"You are the only one who can accomplish that task."

At that instant, Giovanna let out one last groan. Then she exhaled a long breath as the last of her glow vanished, and she became an icy, ghostly white. Her eyes remained open, and her mouth agape. Chris stared in disbelief at her as he slowly set her lifeless body on the altar. "I can't believe this is happening," he said to Old Ghost. "I can't believe you let this happen. She's only eleven years old. What's the matter with you? Why do you let people die?"

But the Old Ghost kept silent.

Chris gazed at Caterina, and despite all that she represented to him, he could not beat back the bitter feelings of this last and most devastating betrayal. "It wasn't supposed to end like this. I didn't bring her all this way just so she could die. We were going to save her. Why did you bring us here? You knew that thing was waiting there for her. You knew what it would do to her. But you brought her across the Bridge anyway. Lies—always lies. Why did you do this, Caterina? Why?"

Caterina fell into a solemn silence that seemed to acknowledge her guilt.

Chris stared down at Giovanna's body. His eyes filled with horror as she began to crystallize.

It seemed as though the crystals were eating away at her body. They began at her feet, then quickly made their way up to her torso, across her shoulders, and then across her face. And as they did, a strong wind howled through the west entry. When it struck, it swept up her crystals in a violent swirl. In a panic, Chris tried to snatch the crystals in his hands. But his desperate action proved futile. Then he watched helplessly as the crystals spiraled toward the opening in the domed ceiling. "Oh, God, no...no!"

And then, as if his entire being had split open, he felt an emotion he had worked so hard to bury this past year rush to the surface, and a tear began to form in his eye.

The gust quickly died, and windblown crystals fanned out across the dome in all directions. Soon, the drifting flakes filled the entire Chamber. Chris snatched one, and upon scrutiny saw that the crystal had a hollow, pentagon center, with separate branches protruding from four of the five angles. He snatched another, then another. All were missing a branch. He looked to Caterina, to the Old Ghost for solace, for some sign of reason and hope. But their solemn faces confirmed his fears, and he finally began to sob. His tears fell to the floor, then crystallized into their own pentagon shapes. But much to his amazement, these crystals had all five branches.

And then they began to rise.

Chris wept as he watched the crystals commingle with his sister's. The sadness he had felt moments ago was beginning to dwindle, replaced by a curiosity and a growing anticipation. With each passing moment, he heard his sobs turn to laughter. But when he saw what happened as his floating crystals touched hers, his laughter ceased.

Each missing branch was restored.

Chris gazed about the Chamber in wonder, realizing that this miracle was happening to all the damaged crystals. Once the repairs were complete, the mingling crystals grew fat, and drifted about him like feathers. Some drifted up, some drifted down, some remained stationary. Most stayed within Chamber. But a few drifted up to the hole in the ceiling and quickly flew away into the beam of light. Now overcome with joy, Chris could not resist the urge to spin about and laugh with his arms extended as Janey had done the night they resurrected the tree. He felt a tingling wherever the snowflakes brushed his skin. Glancing at the Old Ghost, Chris saw him with his head tilted upward, eyelids closed, basking in the beam of light restored to its golden hue. Some of the snowflakes gravitated to the Purple Orb, and disappeared upon landing on its glowing surface.

And then, as if caught up in the rapture of the moment, the remaining snowflakes began to mimic Chris' joyful motion, slowly gathering before him before swirling about, willfully dancing with him, drawing tighter and tighter together until they once again began to touch each other at the tips of their branches. Once the branches touched, they did not separate. And soon they began to form two long strands that soon became a spiraling structure, and Chris stopped to watch in awe at the growing spectacle.

More and more snowflakes were drawn into the spiral which began to shrink into an orb. The orb replicated itself, becoming two attached orbs that slowly shrank. But as they did, they replicated themselves into four, and four became eight as more and more snowflakes gravitated toward an evolving form. Soon, just before him, there was a growing mass of countless tiny orbs in a recognizably human shape that glowed so bright, Chris could not see its face. When the light eventually subsided, Chris saw his angelic sister standing before him. Chris let out a whimper that did little to express his euphoria, and he embraced her in the warm light as he wept uncontrollably.

Caterina fought back her own special tears. "You cried for her once before, after the Storm. Yes, I was there for a reason. And I captured it...and kept it with the bad, so you would know."

And though he was sweeping, and all his emotions were still wrapped around Giovanna, the revelation tore through him like an earthquake, and he understood everything, including the gift that he had uncovered back home.

Caterina smiled and bowed her head, then she turned and walked toward the west entrance. Then she froze in panic. "The Storm—it's approaching the Manor!"

Shock replaced joy as Chris and Janey rushed to Caterina's side. Chris saw the boiling clouds smothering the woods just to the west of the Manor. Though the Light in the Chamber had turned golden, it had yet to filter down into the Great Tree, its millions of orbs still shining red.

"Is he there?" Giovanna said to Caterina. "Should we go get him?"

"There isn't time!" Caterina said.

"Such a nightmare I have never seen," the Old Ghost said with an odd amusement. "And we were making such wonderful progress. How did all this become so?" But they were probing questions like those of Dr. Samuele, meant to inspire silent but perceptive answers.

Chris stared back, his wide eyes begging for the solution Chris was now certain the Old Ghost had. The Old Ghost removed the white feather from his hat and held it out.

"What do you know, Cristofori? And what do you want?"

Chris ran to the altar, snatched the feather from the Old Ghost, and stared at it with a furrowed brow. The "feather" was, in fact, a quill, complete with a golden tip from which a tiny but brilliant light shined. He looked at the Old Ghost again, holding his quizzical expression.

"What do you want, Cristofori?"

"Cristofori—hurry!" Caterina shouted.

Chris gazed at the glowing book for just a moment, then stepped into the beam of golden light. Carefully, he set the sparkling tip on the top-left corner of the left page, producing a brilliant flash. Then he began to write. Letters and words formed, but quickly changed to equations before being absorbed into the book. He looked up at Caterina for her reaction as red light just outside flickered and altered its glow to orange, then yellow. "Anything?" he said.

Caterina stared with anxiety out into the darkness, but she didn't move. "Yes," she said, sounding relieved.

"It got pushed away from the Manor," Giovanna said.

"But now it's coming this way," Caterina said.

Encouraged, Chris returned to his writing. As he touched the pen to the page, another brilliant flash filled the Chamber. This time, the liquid light seemed to grasp the tip. And the old themes that he once held true and now dominated his thoughts—themes of restoration, peace, and forgiveness—felt as though they were flowing from his mind through the quill and into the book.

"It's almost here," Giovanna shouted.

Chris took great delight at hearing Giovanna's New World voice. As the Light in the Chamber turned ever whiter, he looked up and saw his two guardians cowering in the entryway as the rumbling Storm Cloud approached. A blast of cold air and black mist rocked the Chamber as they shielded themselves with their arms. When the mist dispersed in the eerie calm, Chris saw Matteo, Lorenzo, and Coach Joe, still in black costume, standing in stunned silence next to each other just within the Chamber entrance.

"Cristofori?" Matteo said, as if he, too, had just awoke from a terrible nightmare.

Chris smiled as he watched Lorenzo stare in disbelief—first at him, then the guardian angels.

"What happened?" Lorenzo said to Chris. "Where are we?"

"The treetop Chamber," Chris said.

"*Thee* treetop Chamber? How did that happen?"

"How do you think?" Matteo said. He lightly punched Lorenzo on the shoulder.

Lorenzo faced Matteo. "I don't remember," he said. He returned the jab—but with much more force.

Matteo lost his balance and fell to the floor.

"That's why I'm asking," Lorenzo said.

Chris looked at Coach Joe, who was still in a daze even as he stared at the two buffoons acting out before him. He looked like the old world coach again, only better, without the decrepit touches he had shown in this World. When his gaze met Chris', the coach said: "*Momma mia.*"

They were all becoming the way he wanted them to be. It was almost Christmas, after all. Time for miracles, big and small.

Giovanna suddenly pointed out to the night sky. "Look!"

Chris set the quill on the altar and ran with his friends to the entrance—just in time to see the Storm Cloud make its final transformation, according to his Grand Decree. As the boiling blackness gradually lost its fervor and the Tree's radiance turned ever whiter, the retreating Demon Horde shrank dramatically in number, diffusing into the ice clouds. The demon horses changed into small, antlered creatures that pulled, as a team of twelve, a large sleigh. Inside the sleigh stood a strong figure with a long, flowing white beard and heavy white robes, no longer the god of terrible legend, but of a saintly one. A few others, also transformed, were in the sleigh, sitting quietly—including Vittorio. Chris had other plans for them, as well. The sleigh crossed before the full Moon and headed over the twinkling Village. The full transformation had begun, and he felt confident that it would continue until all was remade according to his wishes.

Chris turned to Giovanna and Caterina. Each gazed in befuddlement at their extended arms and hands, their luminescence gone, as if they had been cured of a terrible disease. When Giovanna looked at him, she smiled. Then he laughed heartily with her, and he realized that this experience, too, was a first for him in the New World.

But when their laughter finally ended and Chris turned to face the Old Ghost, he saw that the old man was gone. In his place—dressed in white robes as bright as the light, and surrounded by drifting cupids, his face shining like the sun—stood a much younger and healthy man, an image Chris had seen at home and in countless paintings and pictures throughout his lifetime in the old world. He couldn't help but shudder, feeling humble, frightened, and in awe of this figure—the greatest of all men who had ever walked the Earth, his extraordinary legacy tied not only to a very great belief revered by billions throughout the ages, but also tied intimately, directly, to the greatest power of all. Now He was standing before Chris, just staring at him. At him, the sole object of the young Savior's vision and thoughts. Chris felt his knees weakening, and he was ready and willing out of a genuine respect and an even deeper sense of duty to fall on those knees. But Chris could not take his eyes from the young man, who showed an intense expression, as if he were about to say something profound. And in his right hand, Christ the Savior held the Purple Orb. When the golden beam of light in which the young man stood began to flicker, Chris shuddered once more. Immediately, he thought of Janey.

And then suddenly, Chris heard the bong from the Village clock tower, wafting up into the Chamber. The countdown to midnight had begun.

"The hour is at hand," the young man said with a voice that resonated with an unsettling power. "A child is coming."

Chris thought of his Story, how it was supposed to end. But considering who the young man was, Chris did not understand. He struggled to speak, his fear still crippling him. "What happens now?"

The young Savior held the Orb over the Book. "This World, as you have built it, is about to become whole, and will separate from the other and become free."

"Now? This minute?"

"When the clock strikes midnight."

The bell tolls were halfway there.

His anger flared, and so did his panic, despite the young man's great and humbling power. "But that's not fair—I wasn't told!"

"Were you not the one who shouted the ultimatum?"

"But I have to return. I have to give her the gift!"

"And so you shall."

With his panic ever rising, Chris looked with a dreadful uncertainty at Caterina as the clock tower drew within a few tolls of the hour. If he didn't leave before then and freeze this World in time, the door would be closed, preventing his return, and the gift that he had hidden would be found much too late—or never at all. He charged the altar and thrust his hands into the light. "What do I do? Send me back!"

But it was too late. The last of the toll echoed in the Chamber of Light.

"As you have witnessed all along, I still remember you," the young man said. "Welcome, Cristofori. And Merry Christmas."

Chris stared in shock as the Orb rolled off the young Savior's fingers. It fell into the book like a large stone into a pond, splashing up its letters and numbers and symbols, creating a crater-like hole in the liquid light. Chris stared into the crater and saw all the writings swirling into a brilliant round center that was once the Purple Orb. His ears began to ring.

Just then, Caterina slipped her warm hand in his, but she kept awfully silent.

Chris saw the terrible sadness in her eyes, as if she needed to say what was breaking her heart, but couldn't, and he became even more fearful. "Caterina?"

She gazed at him for a moment, and then it came: "This is the happiest day of my life, one that I have been desperately waiting for. But it is also the saddest. You've been given a wonderful gift—a second chance, to amend so much before it came true. But there is another reason for the birth of this New World. Thank you for what you have done for me. Forgive me for what I have done to you. Now it is time to let me go. I'm sorry—I told you, it must be this way. It must. Because it can't be any other."

Chris' eyes widened. "But you said we would be together."

"I will be with Cristofori—yes—but not with you."

Tears now filled those big blue eyes, and instinctively Chris tried to burn that image into his mind. The ringing in his ears intensified, and he nearly succumbed to the pain. He could barely feel her touch. And though she had finally said what he so desperately needed to hear, so his mind could be clear and bright again, he just didn't want to let her go, not after everything, not after all. "No, Caterina—please."

But Caterina did not give in as she fought back her tears, taking just a moment to look at the young Savior for some sort of direction, as if they were on a stage. His face was barely discernible, almost part of the light itself. But Chris could still see his eyes. He seemed to nod.

"There is a star in your world," Caterina said, "the bright one you once proudly showed me. It is part of that power that is unseen, yes, but maybe not as dark as you have made it out to be. When you look at that star, think of me as I stand before you now, among all who love you. Then you will be given the power you'll need to cope. Please don't forget. Promise me you won't."

Promise me. But Chris refused to hear her. He would be forever grateful for the miraculous gifts he had received. But he could not let her go and cast her adrift for all of eternity. He had to do something. But what? "Then I'll change the rules," he said defiantly to the nagging question.

Chris tugged his hand from hers and fumbled like a drunk almost blindly for the quill pen on the altar. When he found it, he gripped its end and tried to write in what was left of the rapidly disintegrating book. But when he touched the tip to the edge of a page, the light flared and overpowered him.

And then he felt that all-too-familiar sensation of falling.

PART SIX

Miracles

Chapter Forty-Eight

The Awakening

When the bright light finally faded, Chris was surprised to find himself staring up not at the doctor in his Tudor home, but at the harsh rectangular fluorescent lights of a suspended ceiling not unlike those at his high school. But he wasn't in a classroom. Instead, feeling cold, he lay beneath a scratchy sheet and a thin white blanket tucked tightly in a soft, single bed with metal rails. A tube from an IV trailed from the stinging needle taped atop his right hand and up to a bag collection, each with clear liquid, hanging from a stainless steel pole. Narrow tubes ran up each side of his head, around the top of each ear, then across his face and into his nostrils, emitting a cool stream of oxygen. To his left, a monitor showed three moving, jagged blue lines at the ends of which were large and ever-changing red numbers. Wires from the pads taped on his chest ran from the sleeve of his gown to the display. The clothes he had worn when he fell at the doctor's house were folded neatly in a plastic bin that sat next to a phone on a wheeled table to his right. To his left, atop the metal tray attached to his bed, was Janey's music box. A bandage was wrapped around his head, which stung from the incision on the back of his scalp, as if someone had stabbed him with an ice pick and left it there. When he glanced past the foot of his bed and through the opening of the curtained walls, Chris saw the familiar pentagonal station in the center of the decorated ICU where Dr. Samuel, in a white lab coat, stood in the bright light, staring at a clipboard. All was strangely quiet, except for the slow but steady beeping of his monitor, as the other rooms were dark and vacant, their curtains thrown aside. And then suddenly there was Caterina, the sadness on her glowing face overcoming him as she tried to reached out one last time across the mysterious void between their worlds, her image now quickly breaking apart into tiny scattering blue orbs until she was gone. He still could not believe what had happened to her, and that he could never see her again. His sadness lingered, a heavy weight on his heart, but his anger was gone. And he breathed clearly and effortlessly, no thing sitting on his chest. He closed his eyes, silently thanked her, and—recalling what the Old Ghost had said to him on the slope of the angry Mountain—asked her to forgive him.

When Dr. Samuel saw that Chris was alert, he set aside the clipboard and walked purposefully but without panic to Chris' bedside. "Well, I must admit, this is certainly unexpected," he said with a calm and unwavering tone. He glanced at the monitor. "How are you feeling?"

"What time is it?" Chris said, his voice crackling.

"About ten-thirty," the doctor said. He pressed a button on the control that dangled on a thick cable from the bed. The whir of an electric motor filled the room, and Chris slowly sat up with the rising end of the mattress.

Chris tried to swallow, but his throat was painfully raw. The doctor held out a plastic cup with a straw that protruded from its lid. The irony, no longer hated, did not escape him. Chris took a sip and formed his next inquiry. He didn't need to ask where he was. And he didn't dare ask what had happened. He had a pretty good idea about that, thanks to his research. "What day is it?"

"The twenty-fourth," Dr. Samuel replied. "December."

Chris' eyes brightened, and alarm replaced the sadness. Old-world problems once again rushed in. "Where's Janey?"

"Victor took her home. They were here earlier."

"Is she all right?"

The doctor kept his sober expression. "She's stable."

Chris started to roll toward the doctor. "I have to go see her."

Dr. Samuel held out his hand to stop him, pushing lightly with his fingertips. "And how do you propose to do that?"

"You have to take me."

"Don't you realize where you are?"

"Yeah."

"Don't you want to know why you are here?"

But Chris did not want to admit his suspicions, and he uttered a tried-and-true response: "I fell and hit my head."

"You had a seizure at my house," Dr. Samuel said. "It wasn't the first, was it? Do you recall?"

"Seizure?" But he knew what that meant, too.

"How's your vision? Have you been seeing bright lights or dark spots?"

"You mean auras or scotomas? Both. Mostly lights, though."

Dr. Samuel frowned. "You've researched this?"

"After you told me to look up genes."

"What else have you been seeing? And hearing?"

Chris didn't answer. Didn't have to. As always, the doctor already knew.

"Why didn't you say anything?" Dr. Samuel said.

"That's in the genes, too, I guess."

393

The doctor sighed. "They performed a craniotomy on you today—an exploratory procedure, of sorts. It also helped relieve the pressure." And then he refused to elaborate.

Chris absorbed the telling statements. "Exploratory," he said. He knew the meaning of that term as well, and saw that the doctor also struggled with the truth. "Like you did with my mom, you mean."

Dr. Samuel nodded, and seemed willing—almost relieved—to play the game he had perfected. "Yes, in a way."

"I remember. So you could get a better look inside."

"Yes, it allows that."

The next words were hard to speak. "And after you were done, you let us take her home."

Dr. Samuel nodded repeatedly, but he looked sad and said nothing.

"But you won't let me go home."

"No, indeed not."

Chris found a dim ray of hope in the doctor's answer. "More surgery?"

Dr. Samuel hesitated. "No, it's not that. I'm no longer your doctor."

"But you're here."

His comment seemed to catch Dr. Samuel off guard, for he blushed. "The attending physician would need your father's permission."

Chris stared a little longer to see if the doctor would blurt the horrible truth. "And if he gave it?"

Dr. Samuel sighed. He struggled to make eye contact. "Then you could go home, of course."

Chris turned away and stared blankly at dark, bloody patch of skin atop his hand where the taped needle intruded, his worst fears confirmed. Suddenly, with his despair at its deepest level, Caterina's last words echoed loudly in his troubled mind.

"Chris, I don't know how to say this delicately," Dr. Samuel said. "Before Victor switched doctors, I ordered some lab work. I just received the results. I'm sorry—I tried to push it through faster. But DNA testing is far more complicated than bone marrow analysis. There's just so much need, so many others..."

"It's okay," Chris said. "You did what you could."

The doctor seemed unwilling to accept the compliment. And then he sighed. "The odds of this happening to both of you—at the same time—are astronomical. I've never encountered this before."

Chris recalled all the research he did, just after Janey fell ill. "So there's nothing to worry about—so I can go home."

Dr. Samuel kept silent, but looked remorseful.

"It's okay," Chris said.

"No, it's not," Dr. Samuel said. He hesitated. "I found your aunt's doctor. Spoke with him. He told me what she died from."

Chris kept silent, imploring the doctor to finish.

"Pneumonia," Dr. Samuel said. "Apparently, she thought it was a cold, so she never did anything about it."

"That sounds like her." Chris could sense that the doctor was struggling with more troublesome thoughts as his eyes shifted about.

"Chris, do you remember when I took that roller chain? From the foyer table. After Victor knocked over the tree."

"Yeah?"

"There was blood on that chain."

"Yeah."

"Well, that's what I had tested."

"And?"

"It wasn't yours."

"No."

"It was Victor's, just as you claimed."

Chris nodded subtly.

"Chris...Victor—he's a carrier. It's not from your mother—not from Sandra."

"Yes, I know," Chris said softly.

"You know?"

"Caterina told me...and I saw it. It didn't get me there, just here. Me...and Janey."

Dr. Samuel gave him one of those piercing professional looks, as if he feared Chris was becoming unstable, or worse.

But there was no time for an explanation. Chris knew what he urgently had to do. But he couldn't be in the worst possible circumstances. "It's Christmas Eve, sir. I have to go home and be with Janey."

The doctor glanced at the slowly beeping monitor, its readings barely changing. "Chris, I can't do that. If I do, I might lose everything, and he'll win. I shouldn't even be here. Victor's trying to blame me for this. If it wasn't for Janey's testimony—"

"But I can save her."

"Chris, we're doing all we can—for both of you."

"No, you don't understand. I can fix it."

"Chris, I'm sorry, I need to be more forthright about your illness."

"No, please—there isn't time. Just take me home so I can be with her, just for a little while. That's all I ask. Then you can bring me back and tell me everything you need to say. But please, sir, not until then. It's Christmas Eve, after all."

"Chris, you're asking me to commit a crime. Victor had his interview this week. It didn't go well for him. That's good for us. If I do something foolish now—"

"Then promise I'll get another chance, after tonight."

"Chris, we don't know—"

"That's a promise?"

Dr. Samuel sighed deeply, and he glanced with wariness at the vacant station. "Let me call Victor."

"He won't answer."

"But he asked me to...in case something happened."

"He's busy. Working."

Frowning, Dr. Samuel withdrew his cell phone from his lab coat, pushed a button, then walked away as he held the phone to his ear.

Chris turned his attention to the music box and flipped open the lid. He smiled when the chiming began, the spring already wound.

Dr. Samuel returned to Chris' bedside and jammed the phone into the coat pocket. He looked perturbed. "I had to leave a message. I'm sure he saw my name."

Chris shook his head. "He doesn't know you called. He's with her."

The doctor furrowed his brow momentarily, then his eyes gleamed with outrage. "Tonight, of all nights? He's supposed to be home with Janey."

"Yeah, of all nights," Chris said. "Is it enough to get you out of trouble?"

Dr. Samuel's jaw tightened. He dipped into his coat pocket, withdrew the phone, and began the useless ritual once more, walking far enough away so that Chris could not hear the essence of the second message. But Chris detected the word *emergency*, vociferously spoken.

The petite station nurse appeared, and she seemed surprised, and slightly intimidated, by Dr. Samuel's towering presence. He muttered something in his deep tone to her as she stared intently up at him, and then she nodded as he continued to speak. When she looked at Chris, he waved to her, and this only heightened her surprise. The doctor remained calm as he pleaded some inaudible case, then he reached with his free hand over the station counter and produced the clipboard which he held up so she could read it. She continued nodding solemnly as he spoke—then her eyes brightened with alarm. The doctor's next statement seemed to console her, but when she glanced at Chris, he saw that she remained worried.

Chris quickly whipped up some emotion. "I have rights—I want to go home and see my sister!" he shouted. "What kind of a father would leave his dying son alone on Christmas?"

The horrified nurse stared at Dr. Samuel. His next words induced a forceful nod from her. She took the clipboard and scurried off.

As the chimes began to falter, Dr. Samuel returned with no signs of victory on his face.

"How did I do?" Chris said.

Dr. Samuel stared apprehensively at the music box, then at his phone as if begging Victor to call. A few agonizing moments drifted by. "She knows the entire story. She's going to call your doctor. Someone will be on call. But I still have to give Victor time. I'm sorry."

"How much do we have?"

And then the chimes ceased.

Dr. Samuel gazed at the music box, then back at Chris, as if he understood the full meaning. Finally, the doctor glanced at the unmanned station. "Damn it," he growled through gritted teeth. His expression quickly turned placid. He stuffed the phone into his pocket. "Can you stand up?"

Chris tossed aside the covers and slowly turned. He sat up and dangle his legs from the bed, and slid from the mattress until his hospital socks touched the floor. The doctor held out his hands, ready to catch Chris if he fell. But Chris summoned enough strength to steady himself. Though his legs were weak and he was light-headed, Chris did not waver, and he extended his arms out triumphantly as he tried to hold a convincing smile. But then his knees buckled. The blood drained from his face, his vision grew fuzzy, and ringing in his ears returned. He sat back on the bed, fearfully dizzy. But this time, he did not slip into unconsciousness. When the ringing stopped, he looked dejectedly at Dr. Samuel who was scowling at him.

"What are they giving me?" Chris said, to deflect the blame.

"Carbamazepine, for the seizures, and dexamethasone—to reduce the swelling. They also added oxycodone, in case the pain was too great when you woke. Feeling any?"

The stinging was barely tolerable, the ice pick still embedded. "Just a little."

Dr. Samuel narrowed his eyes. "You're in no condition to go anywhere, young man—with or without permission," he said. His assessment was confident, powerful, and, most of all, true. He turned with an abrupt finality and started out.

Chris felt his heart sink, then despair turned to panic, and panic into desperation as he tried in vain to work up a solution.

But when Dr. Samuel reached the station, he looked about the room and down the many bright, converging corridors. Then he reached over the counter and, with a pressing motion, touched something that was out of sight. Chris' monitor let out a short beep, and its displays went black. When the doctor returned, he was pushing a wheelchair.

"This will ruin everything," he said bitterly. He stopped to grab the clothes bin.

Chris smiled. "Yeah."

Dr. Samuel set the bin at the foot of the bed. He checked the station once more. Then he took Chris' right hand and began removing the IV. "If you get very sick tonight and need machines—"

"No—no machines!" Chris said, echoing his mother's words. "I remember what *do not resuscitate* means. But that's not gonna happen tonight. No way."

"There's no guarantee—"

Chris grabbed the music box with his free hand and tucked it under his arm like a football. "Take me home, please. I have to see Janey."

Chapter Forty-Nine

The Night Before Christmas

When they arrived at the house, Chris, still clutching the music box, saw the open garage door. Victor's car was gone.

Dr. Samuel parked his car in the driveway. The headlights illuminated the empty stall. "You said he wasn't going to be here but I didn't want to believe you," the doctor said, gazing with contempt at the boxes along the garage's back wall. "How could I?" He looked at Chris and softened his expression. "Perhaps they didn't make it home yet. Perhaps he took her—"

"Janey's here," Chris said. "She's here."

The doctor sighed and pushed the lighted button that killed the engine. "I shouldn't be surprised, should I, Chris?"

"No, sir," Chris said. Though Victor had yet to return Dr. Samuel's calls, and though they had not discussed him during the ride home (they hadn't discussed much of anything, other than how Chris was feeling—which was motivated), Chris knew what had happened. Victor made the same mistake he always made this night of the year. The smoking, perfumed, giggling one undoubtedly told him the importance of being with her this special night if he wanted to continue the "relationship," which to Victor meant only one intensely physical but ultimately fleeting thing. But it was—besides being another nail in his coffin—for the best, and not just for Dr. Samuel. Now that Victor was out of the way, Chris could concentrate on the vital task at hand. When he saw the tree glowing in the window, his heart jumped with excitement. He couldn't wait to get inside to see Janey, and to give her the New World gift.

Dr. Samuel unfastened his seatbelt. "Are you sure you're up for this?"

"Yes, sir."

"What about the wheelchair?"

"No, thank you. I'll walk."

Dr. Samuel nodded. He removed his gloves and stuffed them into a side pocket of his overcoat. "We'll not stay long, I'm afraid. It's almost midnight—which, for me, might be my only salvation. And remember, we have an agreement. I'll have to decide what to do about Janey before we leave."

"I understand, sir." Tucking the music box under his left arm, Chris fumbled for the door handle. But because the car's interior was strange to him, Chris grew confused. The doctor had to open the door for him—yet another little reminder of his tenuous condition. After Dr. Samuel helped him to his feet, Chris paused ever weak-kneed and light-headed to scan the sparkling moonless sky, with the billowing star-clouds of the Milky Way, stretching from the horizons. Then as he slowly moved on toward the front door with the doctor's assistance, he noticed how surreal everything felt—as if he were a ghost, ready to rise into the cold air and simply dissolve, just as Caterina's image had done earlier in the hospital. But he wasn't ready or willing to do that—no, not yet.

They pushed quietly through the unlocked front door and Chris carefully removed his coat and hung it on a hook. But he did not remove his wool cap. He glanced at the grandfather clock (11:56), then he stared up the staircase and smiled as he saw the yellow light shining from Janey's bedroom.

The doctor looked at him with a peculiar uncertainty. "You want me to—"

Chris nodded before the doctor could finish whispering his question. Dr. Samuel ascended the stairs as Chris stepped into the warm glow of the tree, his eyes immediately focusing on the lone wrapped gift beneath it. He knelt down and set the music box under the tree before opening the lid. He removed the angel and kugel from their velvet encasement and set them up appropriately. Then he wound the spring motor and released the lever. Immediately, the chiming filled the room. As he rose to his feet and turned to face the foyer, he saw Dr. Samuel carrying Janey down the stairs in her pajamas, belligerent wool cap, and pink slippers. Her stunned expression lasted even after the doctor gently set her upright on the foyer floor. She appeared rejuvenated, and elated.

"Look at you," Janey said, half-crying and laughing. "You look just like me!"

"Yeah," Chris said, unable to say anything more.

"Oh, no," she said with a giggle. She walked steadily up to him and embraced him. The doctor turned away. "I didn't think you'd really do it."

Chris hugged her tightly and closed his eyes, afraid of losing control. He could feel her bones, and was surprised by her energy. "Do what?" he whispered into her ear.

"Change places with me." And then she pulled away. "But you really didn't change, did you? Now we're both in deep do-do—me, with my blood thing, and you, with the hole in your head."

They embraced again and laughed uncontrollably through their tears, and Chris found her comment amazingly perceptive.

And she looked at him, and saw his tears. And he smiled and laughed some more and did not try to hide them. And she smiled and laughed some more with him. And all the while, Dr. Samuel looked on in bewilderment, and he started to cry, too.

And then the clock struck midnight.

Never was Chris so happy to hear that toll. He wiped his eyes and summoned the greatest smile yet. "It's Christmas, Janey," Chris said with his most enthusiastic voice, as if all were well. "The best Christmas ever."

"Yay," she said, "we made it!"

"We did," Chris said, suddenly realizing all was well. And then he slowly backed away and looked at her, glowing in all her happiness. "It's time for some Christmas magic."

Janey smiled again, but he saw that she did not fully understand what he was saying.

"The gifts?" he said, holding one hand out toward the base of the tree.

"More?" Janey glanced down as she wiped her tears from her flushed cheeks, then stared at him in horror. "But I didn't get you anything!"

"But you did," Chris said. "You gave me the greatest gift of all."

"I did?" she said, though Chris knew she did not believe him.

"Of course you did. You saved me, Janey, just like you said you would."

"I did?" she said. She looked more confused than ever. "How?"

Chris glanced at Dr. Samuel who was standing in the shadows. He stared at the floor and refused to look up. But Chris could tell that the doctor was still listening intently, recording and analyzing every word, so he drew closer to Janey, lowered his voice, and tried his best to be precise. "Do you think that one belief—one very great one—that you almost destroyed, but didn't, can help you beat death? I do. *Everyone who lives and believes in Me will never die.* I still believed it, Janey, all along. I almost lost it, but it was still there."

Janey grinned briefly. And as Chris looked at her, he saw that his question, meant to confirm his restored beliefs, only increased her anxiety. She wore the same expression of fear and confusion she had shown each time he spoke of the Dream World as if it were real. It was woefully apparent she did not realize how serious his condition was. When he glanced at Dr. Samuel, Chris saw him standing on the edge of the foyer step, gazing back with concern and ready to take appropriate professional, even fatherly, action.

"But you can't just say you believe, can you, Janey?" Chris said.

"No."

"It has to be planted and it has to grow and exist—and shine."

"Like the tree."

He smiled. "Like the tree."

"Structure," she said joyfully.

"Even miracles have them." Chris offered a hopeful grin. "Let me get one." He bent down slowly and snapped up the wrapped gift.

"No—wait," Janey said. She walked carefully to the fireplace mantel, grabbed the Nativity figurines, and placed them in their appropriate settings beneath the tree. She looked down upon the scene with a warm satisfaction, then returned to his side. "Okay," Janey said, "it's officially over. Now we're ready."

Chris extended the wrapped gift toward the doctor. "Here, sir," he said, "this is for you."

Dr. Samuel looked surprised. "Indeed. Isn't this for your sister? Perhaps you're getting a little confused."

"No, sir, no confusion. I was going to give it to her so she could give it to you. But since you're here…"

"Why would you do such a thing?"

"For all you've done for us, sir—and because this may help."

"Help? Help what?"

"Understand."

Dr. Samuel nodded in his mysterious way, reached out to take the gift, then respectfully backed away, as if in the presence of deity. "Thank you," he said.

"Aren't you going to open it?"

Dr. Samuel's nervous eyes studied both of them. "Of course." And then he tore open the wrapping. "A book? And an old one at that. Very impressive. And heavy."

"It's the family diary."

Janey looked stunned, that he would be offering up something he used daily and jealously guarded.

"He needs to read it, don't you agree?" Chris said softly to her, to ease her fears. Then he turned his attention to the doctor and raised his voice. "You will read it, won't you, sir? I've added a few things about Victor, too. You know…"

The doctor's left brow shifted upward. "Of course," he said, now enthusiastic. "Of course I will. Thank you again, Chris. A wonderful gift. Magnificent. I promise to return it as soon as I'm finished. It shouldn't take long."

"Yes, sir, thank you. And don't forget, I do write in it every day, so I will need it back." Chris smiled and nodded, then looked at Janey. She still appeared concerned. So he smiled again. "And now for yours, Janey."

Chris knelt down and grabbed the open music box, which by now had unwound its spring. Then he carefully rose to his feet before sitting next to Janey on the sofa and setting the music box in his lap. He looked at her slyly, just like in healthy times.

With her attention now successfully diverted from her worries, Janey smiled briefly. Then she frowned.

"What?" Chris said. "After all we've been through, you think I would forget yours?"

"The music box?"

"What better place to hide a gift for a woman than right under her nose?"

"You're sad," she said.

Chris removed the purple kugel from the angel's loving hands. "I believe this is yours," Chris said as he handed it to Janey.

Still looking a little confused, Janey nonetheless clutched the ornament to her chest. "Thank you, Chris. It's the best present ever."

"No, no, no," he said with a scowl, "that's not it. *Jeez*, Janey."

"Sorry."

"You're hysterical."

"You're hysterical-er."

"You're..." He paused. "You know what you are." Chris shook his head and sighed. Then he wrapped both hands around the angel and carefully removed it from the box. After Janey took the angel, Chris stuck the tip of his index finger into the hole in the velvet cover. He pulled it off and quickly closed the lid.

"Did you ruin it?" Janey said.

"No," Chris said, a little insulted. He set the cover aside.

"I didn't know it did that."

He flashed a fake smile. "I did."

"Of course."

Chris set the box in her lap and opened the lid. In a gap among the working parts sat a small square wrapped box with a smashed red bow.

"Cheater," she said.

"Could try to take it back, but it'll be tough. No receipt."

"What is it?"

Chris looked at Dr. Samuel, who kept his respectful distance. "Sir, would you come here, please? You need to see this, too."

As Dr. Samuel approached, Chris reached into the music box and carefully pinched the gift with his thumb and forefinger. He removed it, then set it in the palm of his left hand. As he held the gift out to Janey, his hand began to tremble with excitement, from exhaustion, and with joy, thinking of it all. And then he stared wide-eyed at her. "It's from the Other World."

Janey's eyes flew open as Chris nodded and smiled, then she glanced up at Dr. Samuel. They exchanged worried looks. Janey took the gift and held it in her hand. She seemed afraid to open it.

"Caterina—I mean Katie—brought it here," Chris said proudly and confidently as he gazed at the doctor. "She figured out a way to break the rules. Then she helped me find it. How she knew we would need it, I still don't know. No, that's not true, either."

"Chris—" Dr. Samuel said.

"That's because she was here. She's alive, Doctor. She's alive and well. And she's delivered a Christmas miracle. Doesn't that make you happy?"

"Chris—"

Chris turned to Janey. "Go ahead, Janey, open it. You won't believe what it is—not in a billion years. I don't think I can even explain it, or how it works. But Dr. Samuel can. All that I went through, all the horrible things I told you about...it all happened so I could be him and be healthy and make this for you—so I could give you this gift. It's what you asked me to do, Janey. And Mom, when she said to use the Book. And I did it, just for you."

Once again, Janey looked at the doctor, who reluctantly nodded. She offered Chris a cursory grin. "That's not the Book she was talking about, Chris."

Chris' eyes widened, and he let out a nervous laugh. "Oh. Well...but I guess I still did, in a way."

Janey smiled, then seemed cautious as she began to tear the box wrapping.

Chris ignored their obvious skepticism and held his excitement. He finally had his proof that what he had told Janey was the truth. Most important of all, Janey would receive the miracle Christmas gift she had hoped and prayed for. And he relished the thought of witnessing, if he were given the chance, Dr. Samuel's reaction once the test results came back.

After peeling away the wrapping, Janey removed the cover. Then she stared in disbelief at the open box.

It was empty.

Astonished, Dr. Samuel saw it too, as did Chris, who even now, with the awful truth glaring back at him, managed to keep his enthusiastic smile. But when he looked at Janey, his smile faltered, then fell from his face as a burning shame overtook him. She desperately wanted to believe in him— that he could see—but he had failed her too many times. And even though it was Christmas, and by another miracle they were together, she could not hide her disappointment in the outcome, or the sadness she held for him.

"It was real—I held it in my hand," Chris said in a feeble attempt to convince them. "I swear to God, I put it there."

All Janey could do was stare sorrowfully at him.

"Chris," Dr. Samuel said, "I let this go on much too long. We need to leave. Janey, you'd better come with us. Maybe I can turn this night to my advantage."

But Chris ignored him. "Janey? Don't you believe me?"

"I couldn't have wished for a more loyal and loving brother," she said with a smile as she closed the box. "He has always been with me, at my side, protecting me from all the world's harm. And all I've done every night since I can remember is to thank God for you. What better gift could I ever hope to receive?"

"But Janey," he said, and then he lost his train of thought. Stunned by her words, it never occurred to him that she had always viewed him so admirably, so lovingly, and he suddenly felt ashamed for being so shocked.

"Come on, Chris," Janey said as she slipped her arm in his, "we both need our rest."

Chris stared at them for a moment, still unwilling to accept this last but greatest of his failures. But deep down, he knew the box had to be empty, given what she really was. "Yeah," he said dejectedly, "rest in peace."

"No self-pity, Chris," Janey said.

"No," he said, "none." With great reluctance, suddenly feeling like an old man, his joints painful and creaking, Chris allowed his sister to help him to his feet. He scooped up the music box from the sofa, and then they walked arm-in-arm to the foyer. Dr. Samuel helped Janey into her down coat. Then he held out Chris' jacket in one hand and extended his other in a silent offer to take the music box. But Chris would have none of it, and he clung desperately to it. Dr. Samuel placed the jacket over Chris' shoulders, then opened the door.

As he and Janey stepped outside, Chris looked up at the sky. Swiftly moving ice clouds blanketed many of the stars. His mind drifted naturally to the New World, now free. *What thought, whose thought, what kind of thought?*

And then it began to snow. But Janey ignored the fluffy crystals, as big as feathers, as she and Chris slowly walked toward Dr. Samuel, who had already opened the rear passenger door.

Then Chris recalled Caterina's last request. An intriguing thought sparkled in his mind. He stopped and looked to the night sky.

"What?" Janey said. "What's the matter?"

Through the breaks in the ice clouds, Chris lowered his gaze and stared down the street, searching for Sirius along the southern horizon. And when he found it, just above the tip of a tall pine, shining so much brighter than all the stars in the Winter Circle, with spires so pronounced, her last words took shape in his mind, and he saw them all standing in the Chamber of Light, the young Savior in the beam of light, contact restored. He could feel the power of that saving light rising within him, rising throughout all existence, all worlds.

And then he realized all at once that the portal was still open—for him—and he knew what he had to do.

"Come on, Chris, not now," Janey said. She tried to pull him closer to the open car door.

But he resisted, and turned to face her. "Janey...the angels."

She frowned.

Chris wore the most sincere look he could fashion. And then he nodded with great hope as he began winding the music box.

Janey's frown became muted, and then her expression grew more and more knowing.

When Chris grinned, she smiled back—and then they began to laugh. He opened the music box and the chimes filled the cold night air. But she held her ground.

"A Christmas gift...for me?" he said to her. "You do owe me."

Janey hesitated, smiled again, then released his arm and took her place in the driveway behind the doctor's car.

"Young lady?" Dr. Samuel said. "Where do you think you're going?"

Janey giggled as she looked nervously at the doctor, and then began her joyous circling dance, slowly at first, and cautious, arms barely extended to test balance and stamina. But as the chiming music spurred her on and the fat flakes fell with increasing intensity, Janey spun faster and faster with her arms jutting fully from her side, her palms turned to the sky. God's ballerina, dancing as she was meant to do. She tilted her head back and began catching the snowflakes with her tongue. The more she caught, the louder she laughed. The louder she laughed, the faster she spun.

"Young lady!" Dr. Samuel said.

Chris looked at Sirius, allowing the snowflakes to brush off his face. The star was three times, five times, ten times as bright, and growing brighter by the second. When he caught one of the crystals, he saw that it had a hollow, pentagonal center, with five unbroken branches. Chris glanced at the doctor, who stared wildly at the crystals in his own upturned palm.

"What in the world—?" Dr. Samuel said.

Chris briefly closed his eyes and sighed deeply at the doctor's confirmation, thanking God he was still alive to witness this extraordinary moment. This was no hallucination. He had never felt such relief or joy in his life, and he was equally grateful for the sights and sounds of his sister sharing this special night with him, especially for her, which he silently vowed he would never forget, no matter where he went. Despite all the horror that had conspired against them, despite all the horror he had inflicted upon them, it was the best Christmas ever.

And still Sirius kept growing brighter, and showed no signs of stopping.

"We have a pact, you know," Chris said, his sight locked on the heavens.

"I know," she said tenderly, fully engrossed in the chimes and her dance.

"So I want you to see me at the Village Bridge...if you'll have me."

"The Bridge?"

"C'mon, now. I'll even sing for you—anything you want. Just say you will, please. Please, Janey, hurry. I need to hear it."

"Okay, I will...I will. You know I will."

And he smiled, for he believed her.

Sirius was already brighter than the Sun. Its spires of light now stretched north and south, east and west across his field of vision.

"Thank you, Janey. Forgive me. Happy birthday. I can't wait to see you again. And M-Merry...Christmas."

"Merry Christmas," she said. "It is—isn't it? Just like we knew it would."

The light surrounded him, and he fell for the last time.

CHAPTER FIFTY

Between Two Worlds

As the brilliant light faded, Chris felt himself moving forward peacefully, floating through a long and lighted tunnel, at the end of which was another brilliant light that shined like a tiny sun. The experience was not strange to him. But this time, the edges of the tunnel were circling around him, and he suddenly understood what he was passing through, and that it was made entirely of angels. Dore's angels. *Paradiso. White Rose.*

And he could hear voices. Not angelic voices. Whispering voices. Weepy voices. Angry voices. They drifted in and out of the tunnel through the gaps in the brilliant angelic walls. He could hear Victor crying, somewhere, while Dr. Samuel—yes, he was sure it was the doctor—admonished him. He could distinguish the words *diary, manic depression, hallucinations,* and *delusions of grandeur.* He discerned the strange new terms *comorbid, autosomal, occipital, glioblastoma*—and, most of all, *Li-Fraumeni.* Then he heard the words *neglect, abuse,* and *felony,* and the vow of successful prosecution. He could feel an enormous sense of relief, greater than the light itself.

Dr. Samuel's voice overtook him, and it did not falter. The doctor now sounded as if he were beside Chris, whispering in his ear. He was discussing Janey.

"Chris, I know you can hear me," he said with his usual calmness. "She's is here, with me. And she is going to stay with me, so you don't have to worry. She hasn't left your side. She understands. She wants you to be at peace. She thanks you for the story, and the reward at its very end. And she says she will indeed see you someday, when her time comes, at the Village Bridge. Can you hear her, Chris? Can you feel her squeezing your hand?" There was a pause as Chris continued to move toward the brilliant light, the tiny sun growing ever larger. "I have to know, Chris, how did you do it? How did you fix it? I know it was you—wasn't it? Can you tell me, Chris? It's very important. I know this must be difficult, but please, please try."

And then his whispers dissolved into echoes, and Chris—no longer aware of who or what he was, with no sense of time, breaking apart into new light, a nebulous cloud of blue and red particles that trailed ribbons of white and swarmed and swirled about, then collapsed in on itself, tighter and tighter, into its own entity of purple—rushed ever closer to the great blinding sun, becoming part of the sun, all color drained away, the journey at its end. The intense light suddenly dispersed as tiny particles into a great and heavy darkness, and a giant face appeared, forming a new memory and a new existence. Then he, with that new sense of self, was thrust upward, and he heard himself cry out as the stars exploded into view.

Chapter Fifty-One

Cristofori's Dream

In the snowy meadow outside the Village, Cristofori stared upon a sliver of the Moon that hung low in the sky, allowing the wondrous glowing cloud of the Milky Way to reveal itself. The night sky had gone through quite a transformation in recent years. But now, strangely, it was starting to transform itself again. He saw a new universe developing—and a new explanation.

And he saw His brilliance, felt the warmth of His presence and the unseen Power of His Thought, flowing everywhere, connecting everything.

"Is there a problem?" Caterina said with mock concern. "One of your stars is missing?"

But he didn't flinch. "You know that dream I've been having about the giant face?" he said as his gaze reluctantly fell from the sky. "I know what it is, now—whose it is. It's your father's." He paused to look at her. "I remember the night I was born."

Dressed in her shimmering white coat, fuzzy scarf, and fur hat, Caterina stared at him—then laughed.

"I know you don't believe me," he said, unashamed to share these deep thoughts with her, "but it's true. I've been thinking a lot about it. And now I know that it's true."

Caterina said nothing as she continued staring, then she laughed again—louder than before. "You and your half-baked theories. How do you know? You couldn't possibly remember such a thing."

"You really think it's impossible?"

"Yes, I do. The brain isn't developed enough at such an early stage for that kind of recall."

"Well, how surprising, coming from you. Is this your father speaking?"

"No."

"So how do you know?"

"I just do."

"Oh, that's real scientific. Should make him proud."

"You don't have any proof to back up your claim."

"I remember, don't I?"

"It's just your interpretation."

"A belief?"

She nodded. "An even better word."

"See, I think you're wrong. I think we carry memories, behaviors, impulses that are, I don't know—buried, but somehow, are still there, still affect us. They're old things, ancient things—some passed on from generation to generation, some from even from farther back." He stared at her. "Kinda like having a nose."

"A what?" she said.

"No, I'm serious. You have one—a cute little one. Not like mine, of course."

"Thanks for noticing."

"And the reason it's cute and little has everything to do with your human heritage. But the reason you have a nose at all...well, that's a much deeper part of the same story. Now there's an interesting word."

"Is that what you're writing about these days, Cristofori? The story of my nose?"

He frowned at her attempt at humor, and stayed the course. "Why should the story of the mind be any different?"

"So how far back are you suggesting?"

"You don't want to talk with me about that."

"To the monsters?"

Caterina seemed proud that she knew where he was taking the discussion—no doubt, her father's influence. That she was willing to listen to him at all was a small miracle. But that's what he loved about her. "Well, they're part of us—always will be. And we wouldn't be here without them. Just gotta know how to identify their voices when you hear them—and how to resist their calling. Some of us are pretty good at it. Others...?"

"That's why we have our faith," she said.

Cristofori glanced at the sky. "That's one reason."

His comment seemed to raise her suspicions. "And is creating Heaven another?"

Her question surprised him. "Can't have one, it seems, without the other."

" 'Belief in Heaven opens the door to Heaven, which we, ourselves, create.' The universe, Heaven—each as a 'grand thought.' You've been talking with my father."

"Sorry. He gave a lecture the other day at school. He got my attention."

Caterina crinkled her brow.

"Well, it's that time of year," he said warily. "And in his own way, he's consistent with Scripture."

"Scripture? Him?"

Cristofori was walking on treacherous ground, and he knew it. He slowly began his retreat. "At least, in that scientific mind of his, he's trying to quantify faith. You just said it. Even he admitted it might be needed to 'open the door.' "

"Belief in an afterlife, in other worlds—yes, but not necessarily in God or His Son."

" 'A sure-fire way to create Hell, not living the life He did. And the laws had to come from somewhere.' "

She stared at him. "Your words?"

"Your father told us that."

Caterina appeared surprised, then frowned. "You can live the life and not believe."

"We talked about that, too. He said: 'Living the life is the stuff of believing.' "

" 'Stuff,' huh? That's him, all right." Caterina hesitated as the surprise returned. Then she looked down and shook her head. "I don't know why he's being so stubborn. He just can't get himself to admit it. The man who must have proof... Why do you think he won't go to church with us tonight? Why do you think he's afraid to join the Procession?"

"Yeah, I know. Pretty wild."

They kept walking along the snowy path, but she was still deep in thought.

"Sounds wonderful, having that kind of power," she said, as if she were talking to her doubtful self. "But each time I inquire as to whether he's in my 'grand thought' or if I am in his, he doesn't answer me. I don't know if he wants to, or can. And even if he could, I'm not sure I want to hear it. Talk about madness..."

"If the universe is what he claims it is," Cristofori said. "But that's a pretty big 'if.' Still, when you think about it, if one day you wake up in Heaven and find yourself staring down the bridge of that cute little nose—or at a giant face—that means you brought with you all the laws and events that made each of them possible. And—"

"Cristofori—"

"I'll have to ask him more about this," he said hastily.

"You do that—only, please, not tonight, not this night. It'll ruin everything."

As they withdrew into an uneasy silence, he frantically tried to think of a more agreeable topic. But then, she asked the one question he did not want to hear, but wholly expected.

"Do you think we're in Heaven, Cristofori?"

He looked at her and, instead of panicking, quickly smiled. This kind of question, with all its hidden meaning, was a trick, a death trap that he had encountered many times—sometimes becoming ensnared. But he had already formed an answer—and the right one, too. As he held back that answer, holding his smile, she seemed to grow anxious.

Caterina stopped and slipped her mittened hands into her fur-trimmed pockets. "You're not answering."

He leaned forward as if to kiss her, and when he smelled her sweet perfume and felt the warmth of her skin, he closed his eyes momentarily, allowing himself to drift in all her magic, and he nearly lost his train of thought. But then he recovered and whispered in her ear: "From where I'm standing at this very moment, it sure seems likely."

Caterina pushed him away, cocked her head, and glared at his obvious attempt to charm her. He could tell that she did not want to surrender her hardened expression. But then the edges of her mouth quivered with the beginnings of a smile.

Cristofori chuckled, which sounded more like a cough. Suddenly, their laughter burst forward simultaneously, and echoed across the meadow. When their hysterics finally subsided, Caterina shook her head, locked his arm in hers, and they continued on the beaten path toward the Village. Cristofori sighed with relief. Caterina seemed pleased, which meant everything to him, and he was pleased that he had successfully restored the special holiday feelings they were experiencing before he turned his ponderous gaze to the night sky. But still, the intriguing thoughts and questions remained, and he couldn't help but wonder.

They came upon the small snow-matted evergreen that stood like a sentinel near the partially-frozen pond. Cristofori paused to stare at the tree as it triggered a sense of familiarity it had never generated before. He wondered why no one from the Village ever bothered to decorate it for the holiday.

"Something else on your mind?" Caterina said.

He hesitated. "Well?"

"Go on."

"The dream I had last night was even stranger—and I've had it before, too."

"Another one? I may have to charge you this time."

Caterina appeared more receptive, so he continued. "I was at this school, playing a strange game with this odd-shaped ball. My mother had died, and my father...well, speaking of monsters—"

"Yes?"

"He had turned into one—but not the kind you might think."

"Poor Alessandra. See what your theories are doing to you? And your father—how horrible for such a wonderfully talented man. That's no dream, Cristofori, that's a nightmare."

Caterina became quiet as they walked along. But once again, he suspected the silence wouldn't last.

"Did I make the extravaganza?" she said.

"You did."

"How so?"

"I don't know if I should tell you," he said, now realizing his error.

"Why not?"

"Well...you didn't fare so well, either, I'm sorry to say."

"Uh-oh. Maybe we should try to interpret those hidden meanings. Sounds like you may have some latent hostilities."

"Yes, Doctor. And maybe I should have kept my mouth shut."

"Could be more buried memories."

"And let's keep them that way."

Cristofori's eyes narrowed as they approached the lamplit Bridge. A young girl with her auburn hair in a long ponytail stood at the edge of the pond, clutching a leather satchel. She fed the few geese that had congregated in the patch of steaming water below the arch. She wore a ragged pink sweater, scuffed black boots and worn-out slacks—but no hat, coat, or mittens. "Oh, yeah," he said with a hint of disgust, "and she was in it, too. See what you started?"

Scowling, Cristofori carefully stepped down the snow-packed slope to the young girl's side. "Whatcha doin' here, little girl? Looks like you left the Cottage in a hurry."

"What's it look like I'm doin'?" she said. She tossed bits of stale bread into the water, causing a noisy scramble.

"Trying to earn some last minute credits?"

"Maybe."

Cristofori looked up at Caterina, who smiled. "Always scheming," he whispered. Then he gazed at his sister. "But your brilliant plan is a two-edged sword, my dear. Does Mom know you're here?"

"Uh-huh!" Giovanna said as she tossed more bread.

But he didn't think that was possible, having just left Alessandra at her annual Christmas showing in the Old Mill Gallery. "Why do I get the impression that you're not being completely truthful with me?"

"I don't know. Maybe you need some therapy."

His disgruntled gaze returned to Caterina as she momentarily clamped her open mouth with her mitten. Then she carefully stepped down the slope and stood at his side. But she couldn't stop smiling.

"Yeah, well, I'm not the one with the goose obsession," Cristofori said to Giovanna.

"They're starving—and it's Christmas," Giovanna said.

"Starving? You feed them any more and they're going to explode. Maybe we should bring one home for our holiday dinner."

Giovanna said nothing, though he knew she was smoldering, and already plotting her revenge. She slipped the satchel off and dumped the remaining crumbs into the pond, setting off a final splashing scramble. She turned to him and smiled—victoriously.

Cristofori just grumbled and shook his head. "You're incorrigible—and you're gonna miss the start of the concert."

"No I won't."

"You're not even dressed properly."

"It won't take me long to change."

"Since when?" Cristofori held out his hand. "Come on, Giovanna, we gotta get you ready."

"Speaking of which," Caterina said, "I'll see you in the square." She kissed him on the cheek and headed up the slope for the Manor.

"Don't you be late," Cristofori called out. He could still feel the warmth of her magical kiss.

Caterina spun around. Her eyes turned steely and she grinned with an almost wicked pleasure. "Not tonight," she said with a measured, confident tone. "Not a chance."

The entire Village, it seemed to Cristofori, felt this way. "Then we'll dance," he said.

"After, not before." The playful wickedness dissolved from Caterina's expression. She waved, smiled warmly, and continued on.

Cristofori watched Caterina walk toward the Manor's open gate, her golden hair flowing down in perfect, subtle waves from beneath her fur cap and just past her shoulders. He felt his heart leap as his thoughts once again returned to last night's strange dream—relieved that it was just a dream, and nothing more.

Giovanna took his hand. "She's an angel."

"So are you...sometimes."

"Very funny."

"You're funny-est." He pulled her up the slope and onto the icy cobbled path.

Now she looked humbled. "You're not going to tell on me, are you?"

"I should."

"But you won't—not tonight."

"Yes, yes, I've already been reminded of its importance. Why, I might have forgotten about Christmas entirely if it wasn't for you two."

Laughter from the Village caught his attention, and Cristofori turned to the festive sights and gatherings as a blanket of broken white clouds moved in swiftly from the tranquil mountains far to the west. There was excitement in the air, and great anticipation, not only for tonight's celebration in the square, but also for St. Nicholas' midnight arrival. While Giovanna would be home, trying to sleep with one eye open, Cristofori would be at the Village church with Caterina, celebrating the great birth of an even greater belief, recalling exactly how it all came to be. Then they would give thanks for all that they had, for all that they believed in, and for all the miracles that would bloom each day with the rising Sun. After, just before midnight, they would join *La Processione delle Lampade* that would take them to the West Bridge west of the Village, past their old cottage, and into the meadow, where they hoped to catch a glimpse of the young man in the dazzling white robes who appeared this night on the right hand side of the glowing dwarf evergreen atop the bluff, and who many believed, including Cristofori, was a vision of Christ the Savior. The One born from the Light, the One who returned to the Light, who with that Light cleanses the mind and opens the Way, who kept watch over the Village, and safe from all harm.

Giovanna gazed at the Village. "Do you think you'll do well?"

"No reason to think otherwise."

"But it's your first time, and everyone will be there...all those goofball friends of yours, your teachers—and Doctor Sam. You know how he can be."

"So? Even he loves Vittorio. They all do. Why wouldn't they love me?"

"Dad's very proud of you. I've never seen him so." She looked at him thoughtfully. "I think I'll be a singer when I grow up."

"I thought you wanted to be an artist?"

"Can't I do both?"

Cristofori nodded a few times, suppressing his urge to laugh. "Well, it's possible. Those are gifts for me—and you."

"Don't you just love gifts?"

"God knows I do. Couldn't live without them."

Giovanna smiled. "Yeah."

"Yeah," Cristofori said. He removed his coat and draped it over her shoulders. "Come on, birthday girl, let's go home. Christmas is almost here."

They crossed the stone-arch Bridge arm-in-arm, then headed up the lamplit path as it began to snow, with the spires of Sirius shining magnificently through the breaks.

Reviews (the good, the bad, and the indifferent) are important for and appreciated by Indie authors.

To post your review, please visit my Website for my Amazon and Goodreads pages:
Robert-Italia.com

Follow me on Twitter:
@RobertItalia

Made in the USA
Middletown, DE
06 October 2015